Cellars

John Shirley

(i)
infrapress

MANUFACTURED IN THE UNITED STATES OF AMERICA
TRADE PAPERBACK EDITION ISBN 0-9742907-8-5
HARDCOVER EDITION ISBN 0-9742907-9-3

Published by Infrapress,
a division of Writers.com Books
Akron, Ohio

www.infrapress.com
publisher@infrapress.com

www.writers.com/publishing/infrapress
publisher@writers.com

TRADE PAPERBACK EDITION LIBRARY OF CONGRESS CONTROL NUMBER:
2005927434

HARDCOVER EDITION LIBRARY OF CONGRESS CONTROL NUMBER:
2005930613

CELLARS was first published by Avon Books,
a division of the Hearst Corporation.

Book covers and interior designed by Paula Guran
Front cover photograph by Matt Dula

02100411060615

Author's Note for the 2006 Edition

I edited this edition of *Cellars* in the way I would have done if I'd had time and perspective when I wrote it in the early 1980s. Most of the editing consists of strategic cuts. I feel it's a much stronger book now.

Cellars still contains a great many scenes I'm proud to have written because they accurately depict the New York City, especially the Lower East Side, I knew in that era. I lived there and I reported on it. The novel is about the atmosphere prevailing at the time—one that seems to be coming back, now, stronger than ever—which constantly reinforced the idea that anything was permissible if it made you a success, if it made you rich, powerful, famous. Parts of New York City, in those days, were in a sad state of decay. There have been improvements, sometimes at the cost of gentrification and a loss of housing for the poor. But I described it as I saw it.

I originally had an epilogue in which we learn that things aren't quite what they'd seemed at the end of the last chapter. But either an editor or my dark mood at the time convinced me to cut the scene.

I decided to restore it from memory. So this edition has some new text—and it's text that belongs there.

John Shirley
April 2006

Introduction to the New Edition of Cellars
By Edward Lee

True story, and I hope it bids a laugh. In December, 2004, I'm at Tampa International waiting to take a flight back to Maryland to visit my mother for Christmas. I'm flying Southwest, and they don't do assigned seating. They do boarding groups, and I get Group A, the first on. The only problem is, if you want to be up front in your group, you have to stand in line well before they begin to board. In other words, you can't sit. You gotta stand. So I'm standing there in line, and I'm re-reading John Shirley's novel *Cellars*.

It's one of my hands down, all-time favorite horror novels, by the way, a book I think of as one of the most important of its kind. Originally published in 1982, it was a novel that ruptured the boundaries of what we thought of as the horror genre and macheted a by-way through the sensibilities of the readership, to give a lot of freshman writers, myself included, a hopeful new path to follow. And I was re-reading it in the airport to refresh my memory for this introduction that I am indeed very honored to write.

Anyway, I'm standing there, see? I'm in my boarding group line, reading *Cellars*. That's when I get the good old proverbial feeling that…I'm being watched. I peek over the top of the book several times and soon realize that it ain't no "feeling." Other people in the line are giving me funky looks: stern grimaces, frowns, expressions of disapproval and even disgust. I tell myself it's just my imagination and forget it. Then I get on the plane.

I'm sitting in my seat now, still reading, not making a sound, not bothering anyone. I'm simply reading a book and minding my own business.

Introduction

But people are still staring at me.

Anyone coming down the aisle shoots me a stare. The lady sitting next to me (who looks like Mrs. Howell on *Gilligan's Island*) actually seems distressed. Then the flight attendant glides by to close the overhead bins and even SHE frowns at me.

Do I have a booger hanging out of my nose? What, am I—*funny*? Do I look like an asshole? Why is everyone on this GODDAMN PLANE staring at me?

Then it occurs to me...I turn my copy of *Cellars* around and there it is on the back cover, in big red block letters, in letters bigger than any cover copy I've ever seen in my life, these words: FLESH FOR SATAN.

No wonder everyone was looking at me like I'm the Boston Strangler. In this day any age of airline paranoia, I'm surprised they didn't throw me off the plane, or check my luggage for black mass candles and baby skulls. Yessiree, that was it, all right. FLESH FOR SATAN.

Which brings me to *Cellars*.

The protagonist, writer Carl Lanyard, is quite an atypical main character; he has to be for this kind of book, and for the excursion that awaits. After trial and error, he's rejected traditionalist values: wife, kids, upper-class 9-to-5 office job, and the four-dollar cup of Starbucks every morning. Instead, life has hammered him into an edgy neo-existentialism, selfish-through-insight, keenly-perceptive-through-failure, and—by way of his utter disillusionment with the modern world and all its corporate, capitalistic, and industrial trimmings—he's seeing the way to his own actualization. Lanyard's a good guy but not necessarily a nice guy. Was Gregor in Kafka's "Metamorphosis" a nice guy? Of course not. But through his symbolic and ghastly transformation, he becomes enlightened in a world even MORE ghastly, and is able to refurbish a functional morality. All Carl Lanyard wants is enough money to sit in a room and write full time (hey, wait a minute, that sounds like me!) because in doing so he will indeed harness the meaning of his life and his place as a human unit in a very hostile Sartrean universe; hence, my existential allusions. Lanyard is a modern day Roquentin. He is Candide finding his rebirth not through the sea but through the bowels of New York City, through channels and sewer passages and catacombs, and through "interminable tunnels leading to cellars beneath cellars."

Introduction

If my analysis of Lanyard sounds stodgy, don't get me wrong. That's merely my jubilant interpretation of the character. (I LOVE this character!) *Cellars* is not a book pretending to be a literary event. It is not a morality play. It is not a covert examination of man's inhumanity to man. And it's not some arcane egg-heady symbol *about* something else. Sometimes a cigar is just a cigar! All you critics out there want to know what *Cellars* is really "about?" I'll tell you.

It's about devil worship. It's about selling your soul for power and profit. It's about sex and violence and demons and evisceration as homage to hell's hierarchs and burying puppy dogs up to their necks!

It's about FLESH FOR SATAN!

Here's why I bought this book way back in 1982. Certainly we had some very cool stuff in the genre at large, mostly "quiet" fare, sure, but fine work. However we didn't find a whole lot of books that had the balls to really live up to the potential of the genre's title (HORROR), and only a precious few broke past the borders into "hardcore." (I...ramble a lot, don't I?) \When I first saw *Cellars* I almost didn't pick it up. The original paperback cover wasn't that great; I almost walked away from it because it looked like one of those "mad dog" novels. But then I looked at the small print beneath the title, and here's what I saw:

Descend into the darkness beneath the city streets and die in hell.

Holy shit! Is that cover copy or what? (Hallmark needs to put that line inside a greeting card.) Then I turned the book over and got poked in the eye by those three magic words: FLESH FOR SATAN.

Nope, this definitely wasn't "quiet" horror. This wasn't armchair stuff. By page twelve, *Cellars* lived up to its cover-copy and then some:

...Her skirt had been hiked up around her waist. Her breasts had been symmetrically quartered, like fruit sections in a salad. Her solar plexus had been neatly opened and laid back in four sections...Intestines, gray mottled with blue-pink and glistening with drops of red, had been extracted, severed, and rearranged in a pattern that reminded Lanyard of a Chinese ideogram.

This scene was just the first drop into the very big and very demented bucket of blood that John Shirley emptied onto the heads of thousands of unsuspecting readers back in the cutesy days of E.T., *Mork & Mindy,* and Cabbage Patch dolls.

Introduction

What a wonderful outrage. What a delicious disregard to the candyass mainstream. Bear in mind, back in 1982, it was almost unheard of to find imagery this abundant and this explicit in a mass-market paperback novel sitting in every bookstore in the country right next to John Saul and Sidney Sheldon. *Cellars* thrilled me, not just because it's a thrilling story but because it gave me hope. I was just starting out as a writer myself back then, and what I foresaw was a pretty dull future as far as mass-market horror went—until I read *Cellars*. The book opened a door for me. It showed me that I could dare too.

There were a lot of more marketable things John Shirley could've chosen to write back when Reagan first came into office. But he chose to write *Cellars*. He chose the hardcore.

Cellars proved to be one of my strongest creative inspirations, ever. It seems unreal to me that I first read it nearly a quarter of a century ago. (Damn it! Where'd this gray hair come from?) Yet after all that time, it's one of the few horror novels I'm first to recall. Because it was a progenitor to a good-sized pie wedge of the horror market in 2006. Some books are timeless, immune to fading from their original creative luster, and Shirley's early masterpiece of the form is one such endeavor. I hope this new edition of *Cellars* inspires new writers today the way it inspired me so long ago.

The bottom line is this: *One of the very first hardcore horror novels truly remains one of the very best, even after two and a half decades.*

Edward Lee
St. Pete Beach, Florida
January 20, 2005

Cellars

PROLOGUE
Carl Lanyard, 1955

"Maybe he's a gypsy," said the taller of the two boys. Both boys were blond and pimply, and both were Carl's age, ten years old. But they were very much bigger than Carl. He gazed up at them, hoping he didn't seem so defiant that they would take his look as a challenge. The smaller blond boy snapped his fingers under Carl's nose, and, thinking he was about to be struck, Carl flinched back, blinking.

The boys laughed. They stepped closer, crowding him.

Carl was frightened, but he couldn't help but think: *It's funny the things you notice when you're afraid.* He'd been frightened, too, at his uncle's funeral. Frightened because he'd never seen a corpse before, and because he thought he glimpsed dark things squirming in the air over the coffin, though he knew nothing could be there. Frightened—yet he'd noticed that one of Mrs. Gilder's front teeth was yellower than the others, and the funeral chapel smelled like Bon Ami cleanser, and Mr. Bruckner kept sniffing surreptitiously at his own armpit, and, even though it was a funeral, Sandra was flirting with that guy Earl who owned the Cycle Shop, and Mr. Connely was arguing in a whisper with Mrs. Connely, who kept trying to shush him up.

Now, just after school had let out for the weekend, as the two boys were leaning over him about to pound him into the ground, Carl was aware of the Indian Summer sun warming the back of his neck and the strong scent of mown grass coming from the house across the street from the school, and that someone had mowed over a heap of dog waste because you could smell it mixed with grass cuttings; he noticed a flock of birds too distant to identify was flying south in a ragged formation; he noticed a black terrier carrying off one of the school's softballs, pausing now and then to drop it all slathery and gnaw the ball like a bone.

He noticed when he was frightened he looked at the details of everything except the thing that frightened him.

"Yeah, a gypsy or sumthin'," said the taller boy. His name was Frank Bonham, Carl remembered suddenly, and his friend was Manny Something-or-other. Manny yanked at a lock of Carl's black hair; Carl jerked his head free and tried to smile. "Actually," Carl said impulsively, "I'm part English, with some black Irish ancestry. The black Irish part is why I'm so dark. Uh—you see, the survivors of the Spanish Armada were washed up in Ireland and they married into—*ow!*"

Manny had yanked Carl's hair again. Frank, blue eyes glazing, reached out and grabbed a handful of hair on the other side of Carl's head, then jerked it hard, twice, accenting certain words with each yank: "'I'm part *English*, with black Irish *ancestry*'!"

"Black? Part nigger. That explains it," said Manny.

They were in a corner of the school grounds, shielded from the school windows by the sports field's bleachers. No one saw Carl twist free and turn to run; no one saw the two boys, yipping in imitation of TV cowboys riding herd, darting after him, tripping him so that he fell face down. They dropped onto his back, knees jabbing him in the kidneys and ribs. He didn't cry out, only because the pain was so deep and sharp that he was paralyzed with astonishment.

"You been looking at Mr. Connely's house and—"

"Never mind, Frank," the other boy cut in.

Carl tasted dirt and there was a weird ringing in his ears. He thought he would break in half from the pressure on his back.

Frank banged on the base of Carl's skull; Carl found himself worrying that they would break his teeth on a rock and he would have to come to school with gaps in his teeth and everyone would say—

He didn't complete the thought, because Frank was shouting in his ear: "Just shut up about seeing anything but the dirt under yer nose, nigger-gypsy!" Carl could feel the boy's spittle on his cheek. "You don't see nothin'! You don't hear nothin'!"

"You understand that?" Manny was twisting Carl's arms behind him; Carl could feel the wrist bones strain, near cracking. "You understand that?" Manny shouted at him.

"Yeah, yeah I do," said Carl fervently.

And then the weight was gone; the noise was gone. He was lying alone in the dirt of the sports field. He could hear the slap of their tennis shoes as they left him.

He realized, then—"*You been looking at Mr. Connely's*"—that Mr. Connely had paid them to beat him up so he wouldn't tell anybody about hearing Mrs. Connely's voice. Mrs. Connely was dead. Mr. Connely said she'd fallen off the ladder. Accidentally. Carl hadn't said anything to contradict that. Not Carl. He'd only told a few people what Mrs. Connely had told him, when he'd walked past the place where she'd died.

But he wouldn't anymore. No more hearing, no more seeing. Except the details that didn't hurt. Except the dirt under his nose. The kids had made fun of him for two years. The pain in his back told him: No more.

And after that he didn't hear the voices, didn't see the quick movements in the air; the movements he'd called "magician's hands," those flickerings like disembodied hands fluttering. No voices, no hands; nothing but the dirt: and the schools and the roads and the trees and the houses and the people on the dirt.

ONE
Carl Lanyard: 1981

Fingers trembling slightly, Lanyard punched out the number on the pay phone. Partly he was nervous because he had to report his failure to Maguss. And partly he was nervous in the way he always was when he spoke to Simon Maguss. Carl Lanyard had never met his employer. All their communication had been by phone or by mail. An unnatural way to do business, in Lanyard's view.

"May I help you?"

Lanyard gave the operator his credit card number. He glanced at his watch—it was ten AM.

As the phone at the other end rang, Lanyard glanced over his shoulder at the currents of humanity tangling through Kennedy International Airport. He frowned, thinking for a moment that he'd glimpsed Madelaine Springer at the information desk. Lanyard wasn't wearing his glasses; he wasn't sure. It was unlikely she'd be here. It would be a disturbing coincidence. Maybe he could—

"Yes?" Maguss's voice. Cranky, impatient. "Who is it? And why are you calling me at this hour?"

"Lanyard. I called to tell you I'm returning—"

"Returning where?"

"San Francisco. The editorial offices. The next issue has to be put to bed, I've got a column to write, and I don't think there's any hope that I can get—"

"I don't want you back here without that interview, Lanyard."

"She refuses to be interviewed."

"What? She's the hottest up-and-coming psychic on the East Coast. It's in her interest to be interviewed. What is she—"

5

"You don't understand, Mr. Maguss. She isn't interested in making money off her gift. She has repeatedly refused money, and lately she also refuses publicity. She further refuses to be tested. Says she gives of her gift when she feels it's right. We had a nice talk about a number of things. She's opposed to abortion. But we didn't touch on psychic phenomena. She steered around it, flatly refused to let me record her at all."

"It's probably another gimmick. Playing coy, playing hard to get, attracting publicity by avoiding it. Really, Lanyard. Get on it. Be persistent."

"No, I'm sorry. I can't. You can fire me. I respect her. I'm not sure she has a gift. I'm not sure anymore that the people we've been reporting on for ten years aren't all frauds. Or self-deluding. I'm sorry—uh..." He disliked talking to the old man. Something in Maguss's voice made him think of his childhood. Sometimes, talking to the old man, even on the phone, he thought he glimpsed things, squirming, at the corners of his eyes.

"I can hear it in your voice, Lanyard."

"What?" Lanyard was shaken. "Hear what?"

"You're amorously involved with this woman. To put it politely."

Lanyard was annoyed now. Because it was almost true. Madelaine and Lanyard at dinner had allowed their eyes to lock more than once. Madelaine and Lanyard in the cab had allowed their knees to touch, and to remain touching.

"No," he said. "You're quite wrong."

"Am I?"

"I don't intend to...to harass this woman for an interview. So fire me."

"Is that a dare?" Maguss chuckled. "You're getting restless in this job. We'll talk about it when you get back here. See if you can come up with a column. Look out the window and have a vision. Look for your childhood in the clouds. You write for *Visions* magazine. Give us a vision. Cough up the goods." The rasping chuckle again.

Lanyard disliked his boss's sense of humor.

"All right, then. Good-bye." Lanyard hung up and turned from the pay phone.

Madelaine Springer smiled as he stepped back, startled.

"How—um—how did you find me here?" he asked, after a moment.

"Hoping I'll say it was psychic?" She shook her head. "Nope. I came here looking for you and I spotted your loud red-check tie."

Lanyard laughed.

"You ready to give me the interview now?"

"No. Sorry." She held his eyes. "No interview."

Somehow, he was relieved.

"You know something, Mr. Lanyard? I read your magazine today, just a little while ago. First time. Didn't care for it. Your column was endlessly skeptical—almost snotty—about the supernatural. And the rest of the magazine was exploitatively enthusiastic. It all struck me as false."

He nodded thoughtfully. "Sure, Maguss makes good money sensationalizing hoaxes, maybes, could-bes, and probably-weren'ts. All I make is an unimpressive salary. I think he prints my stuff to give the gee-whiz stuff in the rest of the rag credibility. How do you make your living? You never told me, and more than once I—"

"I take in sewing."

"Very funny. You're not going to tell me?"

"I'm an actress. Right now I'm between engagements. I was in a Minder production, *Nero*. I get unemployment till I luck into another gig. I don't make money from 'readings,' Mr. Lanyard."

"I believe you. Look—I'd like to talk to you some more. I mean it. I'd like to talk to you about *anything*. But they're announcing my flight—"

"Write if you get work." She put two fingertips to his cheek, the lightest touch. She dropped her hand and he shook it, lingeringly.

Her skin was mildly dusky, her eyes brown-black, dark-lashed. Her nose was gracefully prominent, a counterpoint to the deep in-curve of her cheeks, her dimples; her full, expressive lips were painted dark burgundy, a complement to her wildly curly shoulder-length blue-black hair. She wore snug black Spandex pants, a tight light-green wool sweater, and jade scarab earrings. She was slightly plump.

She was Lanyard's type.

Reluctantly, Lanyard murmured, "Bye." And turned toward Gate 12.

"United 256 for Denver and San Francisco now loading at Gate 12…"

"Lanyard?"

"Yes?" He turned back to her too eagerly.

"You won't be going back to San Francisco today."

Once more the faint, electric brush against his cheek. She walked away. He watched her walk away. Grow up, he told himself.

LANYARD WAS STARING at the orange polyester back of someone's leisure suit—staring through it, really, having gone into the time-eating brown study that makes waiting in line seem shorter. He looked up, blinking. Bristle-knuckled hands had closed around his biceps. On both sides. "Whuh?" he said, dully, confused, as they pressed him from the line, to the left. One of them bent to pick up his travel bag. "You're Lanyard, right?" said one of the two men flanking him. He was a beefy man in a suit coat that needed pressing; he had steel-gray hair and a red, pitted face. The other man was tired-looking, wore a black suit and tie; his hair was thinning, he had a slight potbelly, but he was strong. Stronger than Lanyard. They directed him with their sheer bulk and firm squeezes on his arms, managing to look friendly for passersby while conveying a stern message to Lanyard.

"*Sure* it's Lanyard," the other man was saying. "I just looked at the picture. He's one of those guys with a hole in his chin. Not many of those guys around."

Lanyard winced. It's a dimple, he thought. Not a hole. Aloud he said, "You guys prepared to explain yourself?"

"Police," said the shorter man in the black suit.

"Lieutenant Gribner wantsuh seeya," said the larger man, and with his free hand he flashed a wallet badge.

"Some kind of emergency. Don't be alarmed." But his tone expressed no real concern for Lanyard's sense of well-being.

"What do you mean, 'Don't be *alarmed*'?" Lanyard said, trying to hold back against their relentless push. They simply dragged him along, and people stared. It was embarrassing. Lanyard let them lead him.

They took him straight to a patrol car parked in the taxi zone. A uniformed cop waited in the driver's seat. Lanyard got into the back seat, between the two plainclothes cops.

"You boys ever take civics in high school?" Lanyard asked, trying to keep the shrillness from his voice. "Think back now. Remember something called the Constitution? The rights of the arrested?"

The larger cop laughed at him. "You ain't arrested. Just wannuh ask you some questions. How can we ask you questions when yuh on a plane?" The man actually winked at him.

"But you can't just *drag* a man…"

"Now, wait a minute," said the other cop, in the tone of a comedian setting up a joke. "You're in the position of a man on the *Titanic* who keeps insistin' it's unsinkable as he's going under."

Lanyard was the only one in the car who didn't laugh at that.

Absently, he took his glasses from his coat pocket. He put the wire-rims on and looked out the side window, across the cop's ruddy chin, at the streets. They were driving through Queens, passing row houses, tenements, playgrounds splashed with graffiti. The graffiti was spray-painted, laid on with magic markers and felt pens, most of it in a mystifying, loosely ornate, hooked, arcane style; Lanyard sometimes thought the future of a city could be read in its graffiti the way a divination is read from tea leaves. He peered through the wet October morning, the rain falling like static, trying to read a slogan written in black spray paint. It seemed to say:

WATCH UNDERGROUND

Steam spumed from manholes, plumed from sewer grates. "Sombitch," the driver mumbled, pounding his horn as the intersection was clogged by pushy cabs.

"Hit the siren," said the red-faced man.

The cabs moved grudgingly aside for the patrol car as the siren whooped hysterically. Lanyard identified with its nervous shriek just then; some internal siren was warbling in him, and to blanket it he asked, "What's it about? What sort of questions does this lieutenant of yours want to ask? Regarding what?"

"All I know is it's regarding a homicide. And we supposed to take you the subway station. Lower East Side. Bleecker Street station onna Lexington Avenue line. I dunno what's up."

"Subway station? You mean police station?"

"No, I don't mean police station." The red-faced cop was irritated. "Did I *say* police station? I said subway station. Onna way here they called us. Said atta last moment we should take you the subway station and not the police station. They waiting in the subway."

"Christ. How long is this going to take? How far is it to this place?"

"It's just over the river. You're an out-of-towner, huh?"

"What?" The tired-eyed cop. "You didn't know he was an out-of-towner? Sure, I knew that, pal. Moment I laid eyes on him. Had his bag on the floor.

Wasn't touching him. He wasn't checking it out. Hell, if we hadn't come along he probably would've had to make a report on a stolen item."

"I dunno. Lot of guys, y'know, moved into the city, look like out-of-towners. They used to be. Not anymore. I thought maybe he was going on a business trip to San Francisco."

It annoyed Lanyard to be talked about as if he weren't there.

They drove beneath overpasses, through tunnels, over a bridge, and into a neighborhood that was alternately staid brownstones and burned-out shells of apartment buildings. A Puerto Rican hot-dog-pizza-barbecue café had an animated neon sign showing a man chasing a pig with a knife. The neon man's arm raised the knife and stabbed down with it, raised it and stabbed down...

They stopped at an intersection only because a freight truck was blocking the way. A man walking a small, fluffy white dog noticed the police car adjacent to him and made a great show of bending with a newspaper to scoop up the dog's waste. The truck passed and they drove through the red light with siren warbling. The man with the leashed dog dumped the dogshit on the street as soon as they'd passed. Lanyard watched him dwindle in the rear-view mirror.

They pulled up opposite a heavy blue-painted metal fence around the stairs leading into a subway station. Stairs leading down. He began to feel a little scared. He didn't want to go down there.

"Lanyard?"

"Yes?"

"You won't be going back to San Francisco today."

Okay, Lanyard thought, she was right. But before you get spooked, ask yourself *why* she was right. Not necessarily a psychic flash. She might have had inside information. She might know someone at the police station. This might be her clever, oblique way of making an impression on him. Maguss could be right about her.

Lanyard didn't want to believe that.

Abruptly becoming briskly official in the proximity of their superiors, the plainclothes cops hustled Lanyard from the car, across the street, and down the greasy-gray metal-edged steps of the subway, needlessly repeating, "Come this way, please."

He was escorted through darkness and into the gray light of the platform at the end of a corridor. Graffiti was everywhere. In the half-light Lanyard wondered, for a moment, if the men with him were really cops. He'd only glimpsed the badge. They might be bringing him down here to kill him. They might—

He was startled by a flash of artificial lightning. The strobing came from the flashbulbs of police photographers at the far end of the subway platform.

To one side were two vending machines, both of which had been pried open and rifled. There was a passageway chained shut, with a sign that said PASSAGEWAY ACCESS TO UPTOWN PLATFORM CLOSED BETWEEN 7 PM AND 6 AM. The bathroom had also been chained shut. Near the ceiling, the walls were threaded with cracks. Water dripped onto the ancient tracks from the tangle of pipes overhead. The usual musty laundry-room smell of subway stations was tainted with another odor.

It took Lanyard a few moments, approaching the small crowd at the other end of the platform, to recognize the smell. "Blood," he murmured.

And there was also the smell of fresh spray paint.

The men at the end of the platform, by the smudged blue-tiled wall, parted to let Lanyard and the two cops through. Lanyard found that he didn't want to look at what it was their circle enclosed. He found himself looking at the graffiti for distraction. Most of it was names. Kids, he supposed, trying to be real, trying to leave their mark in some way.

"You Lanyard?"

Lanyard could look away no longer. Nodding, he looked at the corpse on the concrete floor. It was much worse than he'd expected

He wanted to run from the sight. The roar of fear and revulsion inside him exploded around them, and the air shook with it so that Lanyard was amazed that the others didn't cover their ears. But then he realized it was a subway train roaring into the station with an incredible clamor that the others acknowledged not at all.

A woman was spread-eagled on her back. Her blouse had been torn away. The shreds of her hose remained around her ankles, along with bloodied, ripped white underwear. Her skirt had been hiked up around her waist. Her breasts had been symmetrically quartered like fruit sections in a salad. Her solar plexus had been neatly opened and laid back in four sections, exposing intestines and other organs Lanyard was unsure of. Intestines, gray mottled with blue pink and glistening with drops of red, had been extracted, severed, and rearranged in a pattern that reminded Lanyard of a Chinese ideogram.

Her sternum had been pried apart; her heart, extracted, lay, brown-crusted and barely recognizable, tucked under her right cheek, against her jaw. Her head was tilted to the right.

Conscious configuration, Lanyard thought.

A cross within a circle had been cut into the skin of her forehead. Her eyes had been closed with red wax drippings. Lanyard was grateful her eyes were closed.

The candles still remained, one at each point of the pentagram spray-painted—recently, he judged—on the concrete around her. The pentagram was rough but unbroken, within a magic circle. The pentagram was red, the circle black. Between the five points of the star were figures rather awkwardly inscribed with felt pen. Heavy blue-black felt pen. Figures in Aramaic, Greek, Hebrew, ancient Persian—an odd mix.

One of the red candles was still lit. It flickered leeringly in the wind from the subway train—the train was passing on. Faces flashed by, inspecting the scene with mild interest.

Blood filled the girl's mouth. Her hands were open, limp. One hand contained a scrap of paper on which something was written that Lanyard couldn't make out.

He felt numb. For the moment he was beyond gagging or crying out.

God, he thought, I hope she was a murderess. I hope in some way she deserved it. I hope she was a child-beating murderess. I hope she brought this on herself.

But somehow he knew she hadn't. He became aware of a small man with mismatched socks—one gray, one white—brown shoes, black trousers too short for him, a chewed downturned pipe clamped in his teeth, a fretful look about him; balding, pinched, the look of a worrier. The little man was asking him a question, over and over again.

"What?" Lanyard said. "What did you say?" Another train arriving, bringing its racket and its rocking gray bulk. It slowed as the little man pointed at the corpse with one hand—in the other was a wallet badge. He was a lieutenant. What had the other cops said their lieutenant's name was? Gribner?

"This!" He meant the corpse. "This!" he repeated, lifting his shoulders in something like a shrug that seemed to say, *Can't this guy speak English, or what?* He gestured toward the corpse again. "What do you know about this?"

Two

Everyone looked expectantly at Lanyard. The train stopped; the station was relatively quiet, for a moment. And then Lanyard became aware of the plaintive yowling of a siren, the drone of cars, the ticking of water trickling through the ceiling onto the platform.

The train's motorman said something incomprehensible through the intercom; a Hasidic Jew in a black hat rushed down the stairs and through the turnstile in time to block the train's closing doors, wedging his body between. He struggled or a moment as the motorman said, "Move back from the doors or we will not get under way." Then the Hasid, tucking his beard under his chin to see that it didn't get caught in the doors, pressed through. The train lurched, groaned, rolled, picked up speed, and moments later the platform echoed with its departure.

The man hadn't noticed the cops standing around the body of the woman laid open on the splashily painted concrete.

Lanyard turned to Gribner. "You accusing me—?" He pointed at the woman's body. He envisioned a massive misunderstanding; someone fitting his description seen earlier from the platform, knife in hand—a tragic resemblance causing Lanyard to go to the gas chamber, despairingly muttering, "But I was nowhere near there…"

He was relieved but no less dazed when Gribner said, "No, no—what? You? No. We—when we saw it was the same pattern as the other killing, the subway setting, same symbols on the floor, same kind of cutting, we figured we got a devil worshipper of the old school and you seemed just the man to advise us about that. No offense intended. We need advice on the way they think, the nature of the symbology in the circle here—to help us trace the killer. Look, my name's Cyril Gribner. I'm in charge of the case. I'm sorry about jumping out at you like that—'What do you know about this… ?'" He laughed softly. Sadly.

"I don't see anything funny," Lanyard said flatly.

"Anyway, I think she was killed this morning, maybe between four and five. Maybe as late as five-thirty. But no one found her till not much more than a hour ago because the station was closed—normally it's open all night but the token clerk had to leave about three because his wife got mugged, she was at the Bellevue emergency room. They couldn't get anybody to replace him on short notice, so they closed the station till about nine-thirty. When they opened it they found the gate broken—we think the killer stunned the girl on the street, dragged her down here, broke the gate with a tool, and laid her out on the platform—"

"Can't you for God's sake cover her up?" Lanyard's eyes kept straying to the cyanotic corpse on the dead-gray concrete floor.

"We'll see." Gribner spoke to a man in plain clothes, who nodded, and covered the body with an ambulance blanket. "They're done with the layout photos now. So: What's your theory about—"

A bubble of anger burst in Lanyard. "What the hell is the idea, dragging me down here with no explanation when my plane is about to leave? There must be lots of people able to give you the same information. The curator of the Museum of Natural History, or—"

Gribner nodded slowly, apologetically sheepish. "I suppose so, but my wife reads your magazines. She leaves them around, and I read them sometimes. I thought of the magazine and I knew you were in New York because I saw you on that talk show. I didn't know where you were, so I called the magazine's office in San Francisco and the answering service put me onto a Mr. Maguss. He told me he'd just talked to you, said you were the ideal man. Said I should get you before you leave. Told me you were at the airport, about to leave for San Francisco. Almost missed you. I got a picture of you from the magazine—sent it by computer to a patrol car—forgot to explain what the situation was. I guess they thought you were wanted—I—"

"Look, there are other people qualified to handle this—people better qualified than me. I don't like the way I've been treated. Now, if you don't mind, I'm going to return to the airport—"

"Actually," Gribner began, packing his pipe sloppily, shreds of tobacco falling on his brown shoes, "I was kind of hoping you'd maybe stay and help us out on this. This is the second killing of its type, I got reason to believe we're maybe having a small epidemic of—"

"I told you, I'm not qualified." Lanyard was angry at the way he'd been treated—but most of all he wanted to get away from the thing under the blanket on the subway platform. And he was very much afraid of having to examine another like it.

He turned and pointedly strode away from the cluster of men about the corpse, and went, almost loping, up the stairs and onto the street.

He stood on the sidewalk, leaning on a mailbox, gasping. The mailbox was blue in the few remaining spots not covered with layers of peeling posters and spray paint. Numbly, he picked at the edge of the poster, prying it up, feeling for the moment incapable of anything else. *Call a cab*, he told himself. But there was another priority. Out of the numbness came anger, like the headlights of a subway train in a tunnel, bearing down. The anger had to be discharged. He went to a corner pay phone, open to the drizzle. For the second time that day he punched Maguss's phone number. No response. He punched the Operator button repeatedly, annoyed, until he noticed that the coin box had been jimmied open. The phone was out of order.

He walked a block through the gathering grayness, stepped over an old man who was grimed the same color as the sidewalk. *He's be come one with the sidewalk*, Lanyard thought.

He found a working phone booth, tried Maguss's number again, gave the operator his credit-card information, and waited.

"Hello." Even more high-pitched with impatience than before.

"Maguss? I understand that it was at your recommendation the police kidnapped me at the airport and detained me with a defiled corpse at a subway platform…?"

Maguss laughed. "That must be Lanyard. I only recommended that you might be willing to help them look into the matter. Not only because you want to help solve a crime, like any decent man, but because there's a story in it for us."

"The hell there is. I resign. That's that."

"Fine. Don't work for the magazine anymore. Instead, work for me, privately, on this last…inquiry. I'll give you ten thousand dollars—half now, half when—"

"No…"

"Twenty-five thousand."

"No."

"Fifty."

"I don't care to be dragged about for the use of whomever—"

"One hundred and fifty."

Lanyard hesitated. "Are you offering me a hundred and fifty *thousand* dollars?"

"Yes. Fifty now, the rest when you've turned something up. All right?"

"I…" Something bitter in his mouth. It was a lot of money, and Lanyard had learned that money, when there was enough of it, could be independence. He craved independence. He didn't want to work for anyone else. This way—one job—he could invest $100,000 of the money, and live on the rest for two years, if he were careful.

At the same time, he wanted to tell Maguss to roll the cash up in a neat little spindle, and shove it.

Various sayings about missed opportunities passed before his eyes like ad copy on the Times Square electronic message board.

"Shit," he said.

"I'll take that as a *yes*. What hotel are you going to stay at?"

"The—" He changed his mind. "You paying expenses *plus* this fee, right?"

Maguss laughed in consent. Nothing jolly about that laugh.

"Okay. I'm at the Hilton. I'll let you know what room. You wire me the advance. I'll get to work. The hell with it."

"Lanyard—my advice is…tell the police only—um—what you have to tell them…about what you find out. They'll tell reporters. We want the story first."

"Yeah." Privately, Lanyard resolved to tell the police everything he thought could be useful. Delays in obtaining information could slow the police investigation.

But why was Maguss sticky about the police? The magazine was monthly. No way it could scoop anyone.

He turned thoughtfully away from the telephone—and took a startled step backward. Gribner was there, smoking, staring vaguely into space.

"How long you been standing there listening?" Lanyard asked.

"Not long. You're a touchy sort of guy."

"Maybe seeing disemboweled corpses makes me irritable. Anyway, I'll help you if you want me to. I've changed my mind. I suppose I know as much about occultism as the man at the Museum of Natural History…"

Without changing his dour expression, Gribner said, "Sounds like you're doing a sales pitch on me."

Lanyard shrugged.

"Okay, then...That writing with the body? What language is it in?"

"Some Greek, some Aramaic, but the important stuff was—I think—Ancient Farsi...Persian. I recognized the name of a deity—Ahriman. That type of mongrel mix of ancient languages is something you get with Western occultism..." Lanyard's voice trailed off. "Sorry. I'm queasy."

Gribner nodded. "Me too."

"You? You must see stuff like this all the time."

Gribner's dim gray-blue eyes became a shade more hooded. "Sure." He snorted, faintly.

Then he said, "Actually—no. Not like this."

LANYARD SAT ON the edge of his hotel bed, wishing he hadn't given up smoking. A cigarette would have been soothing. He took a slip of paper from his jacket pocket, unfolded it, and punched the phone number that was written on it in narrow, feminine handwriting. Ear to the receiver, he waited, chewing his lower lip.

"Yes?" Madelaine's voice.

"I'm glad you didn't pick it up and say, 'Hello, Mr. Lanyard.'"

"No, no, I'm not out to impress anyone." She didn't laugh. That disappointed him.

"I guess, then, you're not going to be smug about being right...about my not leaving town."

"Is it my imagination or are you a little hostile today, Mr. Lanyard?"

"Carl. I've been calling you Madelaine. Are you going to make me feel I've stepped out of line?"

"Carl."

"Yeah, I'm a little hostile. I'm sorry. I'm tired. Had a bit of a shock this afternoon. The police asked me to help them on a ritual killing—I don't mean they want me to help perform one..." She didn't laugh at that either. "I mean, they asked me to...oh...about the..."

"You're nervous. You're trying to tell me they asked you for information about the sort of ritual involved?"

"Yeah. And yes, I'm nervous. Trying to work up nerve to ask you to have dinner with me. Purely social. No attempt at interviews. I'm not working at *Visions* anymore. I never fitted in there anyway. I was always too evasive in my articles about whether I believed…and sometimes I brought my skepticism out in the open. But they didn't fire me. I quit. I'm staying at the Hilton."

"You quit? My, my."

"You don't sound surprised. But about dinner…"

"How's your appetite after what you've seen?"

"How'd you know I'd seen the actual—Never mind. My appetite is not good. I'd just like a few drinks. But if you're hungry, I—"

"I'm supposed to have dinner with some friends, at Joey Minder's club. The Valencia. He just bought it, so he's celebrating. You're welcome to come with me."

"You really don't mind?"

"I'd like the company—I don't know most of the people he'll have there." But she sounded distant, distracted. "You remember my address?"

"Sure. Etched in my mind."

"Meet me out front at nine. Okay? Bye." She hung up.

Slowly, he replaced the receiver in the cradle. He ruminated on what he knew of Joey Minder. Smears of dirty black newsprint ink on the scandal sheets. Raffish producer, plays and films; notorious for wild parties and sudden disappearances, turning up in odd spots overseas. Madelaine had had a part in *Nero*—how big a part? And how big was Minder's interest in her? And who the hell was Carl Lanyard to object?

Who the hell *was* Carl Lanyard?

Lanyard wondered about that, because he'd just passed his thirty-fifth birthday. He had reached the midpoint of his fourth decade, and he could see middle age ahead. He'd worked at *Visions* for just under a decade—now what?

He had one divorce behind him. Jill. A short and disastrous marriage to a tall and dissatisfied woman. Too tall for him, for starts.

Lanyard had wanted to live in the city, near the university where, at the time, he'd been lecturing on anthropology. Jill had wanted to live in the suburbs, had wanted to belong to women's clubs, had urged Lanyard to "join a lodge. Daddy was in the Elks and Mom said it kept him—well, he always had something to do."

"A *lodge*, for Christ's sake," Lanyard muttered.

Cellars

He went to the suite's bar, mixed himself a highball, and sipped without tasting it, eyes tracing the Manhattan skyline through the thirtieth-floor window.

In the waning light, the buildings deepened their shadows from blue-gray to indigo, the skyscrapers taking on rosy highlights as the sun expanded in the smog belt at the horizon. The light glanced brilliantly from the scaly white-metal roof of the Chrysler Building but was soaked up with hardly a glint by the polarized windows of the Citibank tower. Most of the older buildings were graduated to the top, almost like ziggurats; a few roof gardens added forlorn touches of green. So tightly packed was the island, so bristling with monolithic buildings, Lanyard felt for a moment that he was looking out at an underground cluster of crystal; the clouds were dense and oppressive—like the roof of a cavern. Lanyard sipped his drink uneasily.

There are always caverns beneath caverns, he thought, remembering the subway platform. Caverns under caverns and deeper, darker places under those.

He smirked, remembering a movie he'd seen as a boy. *Invasion of the Mole People.* Worlds within worlds.

He peered down, between buildings. The streetlights were coming on. The traffic moved with what seemed from this height to be astonishing orderliness. The appearance of order was deceptive: He had just braved a harrowing cab ride. "The bastards don't use turn signals. Drive like skateboarders on an obstacle course." But the memory made him smile. "Running red lights..." He realized he was talking to himself. Maybe he'd been a bachelor too long. He'd had a string of affairs after he'd explained to Jill that he didn't want to move out of San Francisco, didn't want to live in the suburbs, didn't want to join a lodge, didn't want to raise children and give them Christmas presents and advice and college educations, didn't want to become part of a social set. So she'd left him. Expecting him to break down and call her up and promise to reform. Instead, his attorney called her. What had alienated her most was his indifference to financial ambition. He didn't mind making money, and Simon Maguss had given him a fairly easy opportunity. But he was damned if he would pursue it like a greyhound chasing a mechanical rabbit. She'd been nagging him to go to law school; she had an uncle, a corporate lawyer, who told her more than once he'd be glad to take Carl into the firm—providing Carl went to The Right School and passed the Bar. But Carl's father had been an attorney, a "fixer" for the more successful criminals, springing men everyone knew should be jailed. In a letter to his mother, just after he'd left home, Carl had described his father as "a cold-blooded sonuvabitch." Carl did not want to emulate him.

The divorce had been the beginning of a two-year crisis for Lanyard. He'd been twenty-six, an assistant professor at the U. of C. After the divorce, he felt lost; he'd formed his life around Jill as a raindrop forms around a particle of dust. Then the raindrop hit the ground. Not that they'd had much in common. In the last eight months of their two-year marriage they had trouble even making conversation.

Two years of marriage, two years of getting over it. But it wasn't just the marriage. His mother had died. Why couldn't it have been his father? He winced, despising himself for the thought. His mother's long, elliptical letters had been one of Lanyard's greatest pleasures.

Lanyard lost his job when he told the dean to his face he was "a senile, purblind demagogue" because the old man wouldn't approve his prospectus for a course called "Delusions of the Supernatural."

Shortly before his mother's fatal stroke—which came just before Lanyard's divorce, and contributed to the tension that made the divorce necessary— Lanyard's mother had been increasingly interested in psychic phenomena. Lanyard didn't want to think of *her* as doddering—so he tried to become a little less hidebound on the subject. Like Arthur Koestler, Lanyard supposed that although nothing was definitely proved, there was too much that was difficult to disprove. And too many damned "unexplained coincidences." Largely to please his mother, Lanyard had written a paper on synchronicity, expressing both his skepticism and his fascination.

Maguss had read Lanyard's paper and offered him the chance to write a column. "I need someone coolly objective," Maguss had said. Lanyard would have a salary to sustain him while doing research, and additional money for each column. The job paid better than the assistant professorship had. Lanyard shrugged and accepted. But, he wrote to his mother, "I'm never quite at home, working for *Visions*."

Lanyard by now had begun to feel his life was aimless, pointless, hopeless. He'd lost his teaching job: then he'd lost the one relative he cared about; and then he'd lost his marriage. Life had to be more than a great obstacle course. The world seemed to be falling apart. There was a feverishly rising crime rate.

There was inflation. There was the pathetic debauchery of the bored rich. Soaring drug-addiction statistics. Neoconservative fanaticism. The government turning the country over to big business. Mounting national tensions. Pakistan and India glaring at one another and frantically building hydrogen bombs.

There had to be some hidden pattern making sense of it. Beneath it all.

He looked down at the streets. His eyes strayed to a plume of steam rising from a manhole. The steam marked some mysterious activity beneath the streets; a steam main venting pressure, perhaps. The underground of a city was orderly place. New York City had the largest, most complicated systems of water distribution, sewage disposal, and underground mass transit in the world. Its sublevels were a whole different city. So many miles of subway tunnels. So many stations.

Gribner had said both the killings happened in subway stations.

Moodily, Lanyard watched the steam rising from the manhole.

AND MOODILY, MADELAINE Springer tried to compose a letter to her brother. Her brother Leonard was six years older, and so protective she'd moved away from Seattle to escape his "guidance." She loved Leonard, but she was rarely in the mood to obey him. He was old-fashioned, like Daddy. But she'd enjoyed talking to Daddy, while he was alive.

Daddy was more difficult to talk to now.

She sat at her dressing table, writing with a Flair pen, frowning as she chewed the pen's plastic cap, glancing up occasionally at herself in the mirror, rearranging a strand of curly black hair.

Her bedroom was austere. There was a mattress on the floor covered with a light-blue sheet and there was a blue frame around the window—she'd painted it herself. The small living room wasn't much more elaborate. A white vinyl couch, hell to keep clean, and a crucifix Jesus, which she'd painted white, almost invisible against a white wall. The crucifix gave her a sense of protective harmony. Somehow, it kept her from being frightened of the Voices that called from the places inside the walls.

There were no pictures on her walls. When she looked at a painting or photo it sometimes became a kind of signal, transmitted via her Gift. Once, gazing at an Aubrey Beardsley print, she heard a woman's voice reciting:

"...*I shall never forget the sight. The vessel of crystallization was three-quarters full of muddy water...and from the sandy bottom there strove upwards a grotesque little landscape of variously colored growths: a confused vegetation of blue, green, and brown shoots...remarkable not for its appearance, strange and amazing though that was, as on account of its profoundly melancholy nature...It turned out that these growths were entirely inorganic in their origin; they existed by virtue of chemicals from the apothecary's shop...as the result of a physical process called 'osmotic pressure' there sprang the pathetic crop...pathetic imitations of life...*"

She wrote down what she could remember of it, and was told by a more scholarly friend that it was from the H.T. Lowe-Porter translation of Thomas Mann's *Doctor Faustus*...and that the most recent edition of the book bore on its cover a reproduction of the Beardsley drawing she'd admired. Someone had been reading the book, had paused to admire the cover and made the psychic connection with her.

All this was routine for Madelaine, and she screened it out, when she could, as a victim of tinnitus tries to deny the constant ringing in his ears.

Now, she bent again over the letter and, raking her hair back with her white fingers, she wrote: .

I've been thinking about Daddy, and the similarities between you two. I rarely feel him around anymore. I know he would have said the same thing about my going to Joey Minder's. You both worry too much. Joey Minder's reputation is nothing to take seriously. In New York it's kid stuff. Maybe Minder is a little dissolute. But I'm never alone with him. Within reason, I mean. I think it's important to meet people, it's good for me, good for my career. And Joey Minder knows everyone. I'm determined to follow up my career. I've got to feel like someone normal, if I'm going to keep sane. I'm still picking up more than I want to. Lately, my attitude is that any amount of psi-flash is too much. I'd like to tune it out forever.

She sighed and sat back. She couldn't concentrate on the letter. She found herself thinking of Carl Lanyard. She wasn't sure what it was about him that attracted her. Maybe it was his intelligence, combined with his vulnerability. She'd acted on impulse when she went to see him at the airport, which was completely uncharacteristic of her. Normally Madelaine didn't pursue men.

Thank God he quit his job at that awful magazine. She wondered if she'd made a mistake in inviting him to accompany her to Joey's. She had agreed to have dinner with Joey again because when she was around him, her Gift was quiet. The messages, the flashes stopped coming. She had no idea why that should be. She only knew that it was a great relief. More often than not, her Gift was a torment to her. She had taught herself to remain insulated from it in certain mental states—when she was involved in a character on the stage, it rarely troubled her. But when she was around Joey Minder…

There was not even a whisper.

The man in the apartment beside hers was playing his TV too loudly again. She plugged her ears. But still she heard:

"Police revealed that the killing was the second ritual murder on the New York subways in two weeks. Lieutenant Gribner of the Ninth Precinct…"

That's all she heard. The rest was blocked by a formless roaring, and a picture of a little boy.

The little boy stood with something unseen clasped in his hand. Something glossy on a chain.

The boy was scowling, staring through the narrow crack between the curtains separating his bedroom from his aunt and uncle's living room. The boy was visiting. He didn't like it there. He wanted to go home. But he didn't like home, either. He was a brown-eyed boy, too skinny, with a birthmark on his right cheek. He watched the old man in the living room; the old man was playing with a pair of Pekingese dogs. The boy didn't like the dogs. The Head Underneath told him he ought to kill the dogs. There might be a garbage disposal in the kitchen…

The vision faded.

The familiar throbbing behind her eyes was there. She heard herself say, "Gribner." There was another name she nearly said—but stopped herself. The name of the Head Underneath.

The Head Underneath spoke with many voices from the places inside walls.

GRIBNER SMILED WHEN Randi jumped, all four paws off the rug, trying to nab the rubber ball from his fingers. The ball was well chewed, slick with the dog's saliva. The two Pekingese dogs chased one another, snarling, in frenetic circles, as Gribner crouched over them. Gribner threw the ball to the other end of the room; it bounced and rolled to spin in place behind an old wooden rocking chair. The dogs flounced after the red ball, skidding on the hardwood floor, racing to get behind the chair. They collided with the chair, which began rocking as if someone invisible were sitting in it.

Cyril Gribner was glad his wife wasn't home. Trudy was a needless worrier, always about inconsequential things. But Gribner himself would have been disturbed if there were damage to the small ceramic knickknacks on every available surface in the living room. Every two days Trudy carefully dusted the miniature Victorian courtiers. Gribner had been mildly annoyed by them at one time. But over the years the miniatures had become emblems of domestic security.

Strangely, the dogs disturbed nothing. They wended skillfully between the low lamp tables, the coffee table, the heavily shaded, lace-edged antique lamps, too many for the room. Gribner found comfort in the durable tackiness of the furnishings. That's why it had bothered him when Everett defaced the seventy-year-old photograph of Trudy's father in Iran. The yellowing tintype showed a young man smiling foolishly in a burnoose; her grandfather had been in Iran on business. He'd bought a number of artifacts for the British Museum. She was fiercely proud of the old framed picture.

Their nephew Everett had drawn a human skull with a beard on the glass, over the old man's smiling face. In red crayon. Fortunately, Gribner had caught the boy at it while Trudy was in the kitchen, making dinner. He'd quickly scrubbed the skull face away with a bathroom washcloth. Gribner had asked Everett why he'd drawn on the tintype. "It was there back then, that time," Everett said, seeming mildly confused about his own motives.

"Who was there?" Gribner asked.

He waited in vain for a reply. The boy had seemed to be studying a framed GOD BLESS THIS HOME sampler. Gribner asked, "You mean the bearded skull was there?"

The boy nodded, vaguely. Then he shrugged and went back to his room. He hadn't apologized.

Now, watching the dogs play tug-o'-war with the ball, Gribner felt Everett watching him from the next room.

The boy was odd that way. Was it shyness? Wanting to participate but not knowing how?

Whatever the reason, Everett had a disquieting habit of watching from the next room, sometimes for hours at a time.

Two nights earlier, Trudy had sent the boy to bed. Gribner sat up watching TV, using earphones so it didn't keep anyone else awake. He'd sensed the boy watching through the curtains closing off the tiny bedroom. Gribner had assumed the boy was sneakily watching television, until he realized Everett couldn't see the screen from that angle. He was watching Gribner watch TV.

Gribner turned now and took one long step, sweeping aside the curtains over the little alcove, more than half filled by a bunk, that they called "Everett's room." Everett stood beside the bed, gazing up at him. He clutched something in his hand.

"Watcha doing, Everett?" Gribner asked, trying to smile, ashamed that he'd tried to catch the boy unawares.

"Nothing, Uncle Cyril." Mechanically delivered, predictable answer.

"Would you like to come out and play with Randi and Louie?"

"No. I think they are creepy. They look like dust mops."

What *Gribner* thought was creepy was the way Everett carefully spaced his words, as if trying each one for the first time, never using contractions. He said *they are* when anyone else would've said *they're*. But the boy was only eight, and his mother said he had a reading problem. Dyslexia, maybe. But that didn't account for the boy's perpetual sulkiness. Probably Everett's father was the cause of that. His mother—an alcoholic—had hinted that her husband sometimes caressed Everett rather too intimately. "He was bothering the hell out of the poor child," she'd said. "If you know what I mean. And Everett, he's all the time moping and muttering. Not healthy for a boy. I haven't been well…and I'm thinking: Maybe Cyril and Trudy, they'd like to take him for a while, a few weeks…?"

But Everett didn't seem much happier here. He knew few of the neighborhood children. Trudy said that most of the time he played alone.

"What you got in your hand there, Everett? You got maybe something special?" Gribner asked. The boy's knuckles were white around the thing he clutched.

The boy's face reddened, bringing the diamond-shaped birthmark on his right cheek into prominence. He shook his head, too briskly.

Gribner sighed. He was very much afraid that Everett had gotten hold of one of Trudy's miniatures. "Can I see it, please, Everett?"

Everett shook his head and took a step back.

"So—what's the big deal?" Gribner muttered. He put out his hand.

Slowly, Everett extended his hand and opened it, palm upward. Within, sticky with perspiration, was a bit of rusty necklace chain and a cracked piece of jade, no bigger than a walnut. It was shaped like a head. Looking closer, Gribner could see the head was without a nose or eyeballs. Skullish, though not quite a skull. The figure had a sort of Fu Manchu mustache and a spade beard....

"Who...where did you...uh...?"

"Father gave it to me," the boy said. He looked away, and put the thing in the pocket of his blue jeans.

Gribner was certain the boy was lying. But why would he lie about it?

The phone rang, and Gribner guessed it would be Leibowitz. He'd told Leibowitz to call when the autopsy was complete. He went to the phone.

"Hello, yes, what?" Gribner said.

Leibowitz said, "You want the thing in a nutshell?"

"Sure, so speak already."

"Two different guys did the killings."

The phone buzzed to itself in the lull. Gribner shook his head and finally said, "No, that's...they were just alike, the killings."

"So, maybe we got a cult that does them and all of them do it alike. Maybe they give out franchises. But it was two different guys. Two different cutting styles. Same type of blade, though. Surgical. Real scalpels. Did I say same type of blade? Both scalpels, yes—but not the same scalpel. One had a heavier blade than the other."

"That doesn't prove it's not the same guy."

"The cutting style proves it. It's like a signature. There was a lot of it for me to study, remember."

"You can't be sure of that. Maybe he was in a different mood, maybe he used a different hand, maybe—um..."

"Sure." Leibowitz's laugh was like the wind through a holly hush. Scrape scrape scrape.

"Hell. Hokay, operating on the assumption—" Gribner began, grudgingly admitting to himself that Leibowitz was usually right, "—that it was two different people, you get anything more on them?"

"No prints. Rubber gloves, for sure. I think we can assume that the whole cutting took nearly a half hour. You'd think someone would have come down into the subway in that half hour, late as it was. Trains run not so often that time of night...but good chance someone saw something and they're afraid to speak. Maybe a reward, a call for help...I wouldn't want to sort through all the crank calls, but—"

"You got nothing more?"

"I got carloads more, Lieutenant. But we got to collate facts. You get a positive I.D. on this girl?"

"This afternoon. She was studying to be a computer programmer. Not much in common with the other, except they were both about the same age. They didn't know one another. Her parents say she was well liked, had no enemies, no problem with current boyfriend. She probably didn't know the killer."

"How about the note in her hand?"

"Got that translated. It's Greek. I guess there was Greek, Hebrew, Persian in spray paint, but this note was—"

"But what does the note say?"

"It said, roughly, *I give to you that you will give to me.*"

Gribner was silent. "Just the beginning..." he murmured.

"What?"

"Never mind. Uh, how long dead?"

"Three hours, approximately, before the Transit cop found her. Died maybe just before five AM. Stab wounds to heart. Lot of stuff I could have learned if she'd been brought to me earlier."

"I had an expert I wanted there, I delayed the removal. Was she sexually assaulted?"

"No. But I'll tell you something: Your killer had a cup of coffee just before the killing and he ate his steak too quickly, didn't chew enough, the night before."

"Now how you know that?"

"He threw up. There were traces of it mixed with the girl's blood. So well mixed, I couldn't tell much about him—except that it was definitely a *he,* and it was *his* emesis content. I tell you, I don't think his heart was in the job. Couldn't stomach it..."

For God's sake, did Leibowitz think that was funny? "Anything more?"

"Not at the moment. More later."

Gribner hung up. He stood at the telephone, hand on the cradled receiver, thinking, staring into space. Moving mechanically, he filled his pipe from a leather pouch. He put the pipe in his mouth, wrongly tilted, and half the tobacco fell out of it. He didn't notice. He was thinking about Lanyard, wondering if it had been a mistake to bring him in on it, when he saw, from the corners of his eyes, Everett going out the front door. "Everett!" he called. "It's too late at night to—"

Everett closed the door behind him.

Trudy came into the room and crossed in front of Gribner without looking at him. She was a wiry little woman who always wore one of two flower-printed housedresses indoors; she shuffled everywhere, head down, inspecting "her things" as she went.

She went to the bedroom, to change into her "meeting dress." She was going to her spiritualism seminar. She was still trying to get in touch with her father. It was her only vice. "Your dinner's on the kitchen table," she called from the bedroom. "And we could have eaten it together if you'd come home at something like a dinner hour, Mr. Big Cop." Mr. Big Cop was the closest thing to an affectionate term she had for him.

But he was staring at the door Everett had gone through, formless unease creeping up on him. He went to the door and opened it. The elevator doors were closing.

Why's he taking the elevator? Gribner wondered. Why doesn't he take the stairs? It's only one flight down to the street.

He watched the lights on the elevator's floor enumerator. Second floor blinked out, and the first-floor light came on. But to Gribner's surprise the elevator didn't stop there. It kept going down. It passed B.

It stopped at SB.

Sub-basement.

THREE

Madelaine lived in a well-kept Italianate apartment building in the West Eighties, two blocks from Central Park. The building even had a doorman, a small Asian man of indeterminate age who clearly didn't trust Lanyard; he asked him his name and business twice. Perhaps Lanyard had dressed too casually. He usually did. Lanyard wore a rumpled blue suit jacket over an equally rumpled shirt—the shirt was a luminous lime, a shade that did not complement his coat—and gray dress slacks. The crease in the pants zigzagged. His wholly inappropriate brown oxford shoes were scuffed.

Lanyard was short, well-muscled, dark, his hair shaggy over his ears; his only vanity was a close-clipped mustache, which his ex-wife Jill, wincing, had called "early Errol Flynn."

As the doorman looked him up and down, Lanyard realized he'd clipped his mustache but had forgotten to shave his chin; his jawline was bristly.

The doorman shook his head and grudgingly called upstairs. "Gentleman says he's Mr. Lanyard, here to see you, Miss."

"I'll be right down," she said, her voice tinny through the intercom.

Lanyard turned his back on the doorman and went outside to wait.

It was a windy evening. The clouds had descended even lower, obscuring the tops of some of the skyscrapers. In the distance, the dark mass of trees in Central Park lunged in the wind; Lanyard pictured something huge and scaly shouldering through the trees.

Don't walk in Central Park at night. People in Manhattan said it a little apologetically, a little defensively. They complained about taxes and housing shortage and subway-fare hikes and cab-fare hikes, but they couldn't be shaken from their implicit conviction that it was the only city in the world where anyone could reasonably want to live.

29

He almost felt that way himself when Madelaine met him on the sidewalk. She had dressed elegantly and carefully. In his rumpled clothes, Lanyard might look silly beside her.

She wore a soft red satin evening gown; her bare shoulders were wrapped in a shawl of the same material. No longer quasi-punk chic, she looked Continental and moneyed. A common preoccupation in Manhattan, Lanyard had observed, was looking more moneyed than you were.

And renting apartments in buildings one couldn't really afford, for the sake of appearances. Madelaine clearly worried about being accepted. Perhaps her gift made her feel freakish and lonely. "You look lovely," he said. "And that inadequately describes the facts."

"You look like a writer, I'm afraid," she said. "That's fine. They'll find it touching."

"Yeah, well…I guess I should have gone to a dry cleaner's, but there wasn't time to—"

"Never mind." She kissed him on the cheek gingerly, so as not to leave lipstick. "I think that when formality is expected, one should be casual, and when casualness is expected—"

"One should be formal. Right."

When they reached Columbus Avenue, he hailed a cab. The cab swerved from the other side of the street, cut across three lanes in front of a bus and two limousines, then backed up erratically to them. Lanyard opened the door for her.

"There'll be different sorts of people there," she said, getting into the cab. "It's Joey's way, to invite an odd mix. So don't sweat it."

"Hey, I'm not sweating anything. Not where they're concerned, anyway," he said, getting into the cab beside her, aware of her nearness, her subtle perfume, and the fact that she didn't move to put more room between them on the seat.

Madelaine gave an address, and the cabdriver, a dark-eyed fellow with a big mustache, said: "I will be getting there good, sure hokay, but please giving directs, I'm in United States only two months, hokay?"

Madelaine spent the next twenty minutes struggling to make the cabbie understand her directions.

The cab pulled up in the middle of a row of nineteenth century, gray-stoned, smog-sullied buildings of varying heights but packed side by side with not an inch between them, their façades zigzagged with rusting fire escapes. They were somewhere in the East Village, near University Place. A long pink-and-white-striped awning on thin metal poles cut across the sidewalk to the curb. On the awning's face, in faded gold-paint lettering, was the single word VALENCIA. Strange spot for a nightclub.

Lanyard paid the driver, nervously overtipping him. A tall, hefty black man, in an orange-and-green flower-print polyester shirt, met them as they stepped inside the glass doors.

"Private club," he said in a monotone, "closed party tonight. Invitations?" He didn't look at them as he spoke, but stood squarely in their way, gazing past Lanyard's shoulder at the empty street.

Madelaine showed him her invitation. She didn't seem to notice the doorman's brusqueness. The man stepped aside and hooked a thumb at a wide flight of descending stairs. Madelaine took Lanyard's arm.

They descended a curving staircase covered with a synthetic pink rug. Lanyard looked twice to be sure: Yes, it was, for God's sake, pink. The stairwell's walls were artless mosaics of mirror-glass fragments. Simulated-crystal mini-chandeliers hung from the ceiling. Lanyard looked around in confusion. He had seen an article in *New York* magazine that called Minder's country home "tastefully opulent." It didn't fit with the tackiness of his private club.

The room at the bottom of the stairs was at first glance a broad jumble, difficult to assimilate. The centerpiece was a full-length swimming pool. The surface of the chlorinated pool gave off curls of mist, and its shallow end was half-hidden by an artificial waterfall spilling feebly from an arch of brass tubing. The ceiling was made up of mirror squares alternating with small rotating balls of simulated crystal that threw off pseudopsychedelic shards of colored light, stimulated by red and blue mini-spots set on swivels at regular intervals.

Blurring this contrived ambience further was a glitter-tiled disco dance floor, over which hung a huge mirror ball like a monster spider's egg sac. The man-high speakers around the dance floor were silent and the DJ's booth unoccupied. Beyond the dance floor were curved rows of couches and piles of floor pillows. The brick walls, at rear right-hand corner, split into a big fireplace; insignificant in its walk-in hearth, a small fire crackled faintly among artificial logs, giving off multicolored flames.

Madelaine confidently led Lanyard along a tiled walkway, skirting the swimming pool. Young women in string bikinis decked a long buffet table with a variety of hot foods.

A number of square metal café tables had been pushed together and covered with a gold-colored cloth; white wrought-iron patio chairs lined the table, empty. The people standing around the table, sipping cocktails from transparent plastic cups, struck Lanyard as having one characteristic in common—self-consciousness. The formally dressed were self-consciously formal and the casually dressed were self-consciously casual; it was all Statement. Minder was nowhere around.

Lanyard allowed Madelaine to tow him about the gathering; he permitted himself to be introduced to a series of set designers, actresses, art dealers, more actresses, composers, wealthy attorneys, and local politicians. Madelaine invariably introduced him: "Carl Lanyard—Carl's a *writer*." As though that explained his rumpled clothing. She held onto his arm as if to challenge anyone who wondered if he were fit company for her. And it was only then that he admitted to himself that, yes, he wanted her badly.

She seemed to come alive in the party atmosphere, as if some pressing distraction had left her. Lanyard stood near her, sipping sherry and smiling now and then, laughing when it seemed appropriate, admiring the diversity of her expressions, the internal energy revealed in her eloquent, fluttering hand gestures.

Only once did he see a shadow cross her face—when someone asked her, in a low voice, almost a shamed whisper, if she could give a "reading." The request came from a nervous young woman who'd over applied her makeup, and whose white cotton jumpsuit was ostentatiously trendy. She radiated insecurity. "I'm just so funny—well, maybe funny's not the word—but I just can't psych myself up for...I mean have this audition and Joey's supposed to talk to the casting director..." She lowered her voice, looking to see if Minder had come into the room yet. He hadn't. Lanyard wondered if Minder was always late for his own parties. "And I guess I need a reading on—uh—my career."

Madelaine was saved when Minder bulled into their conversational circle. He arrived with a suddenness that was probably calculated to be disarming. "Maddy! Centerpiece of my wet dreams!" he shouted, embracing Madelaine.

Lanyard stood by, his smile frozen.

Minder was tall, chubby, soft looking. Lanyard had the impression that Minder wanted to seem jolly, earthy, playfully sexy, like some satyr variation of Andy Devine. His voice was an adolescent cackle. But he had a genuine presence. And Lanyard suspected that Minder was trying out new material on them as he howled, "I had a wet dream about Maddy that was banned in my left lobe—" and so forth. Minder watched them carefully for their reactions. He wore black trousers, an amber silk shirt, and a black bow tie; his clothing was cut to minimize his heavy belly and the shelves of his buttocks.

Madelaine scoffed amiably at Minder's ribaldries. "Hey, c'mon, you haven't got time for fantasies about *me*, Joey. You can hire the *best* wet dreams. I might qualify as a mild sort of daydream."

"Maddy, you ever hear that song by Rob Hardin, called 'Live Your Daydreams at Night'? Now that's where it's at."

Lanyard didn't like him, but Minder's grin was infectious. Lanyard didn't trust him, but he found himself laughing at Minder's bad jokes.

"Hey I'm *hongry!*" Minder shouted, imitating a cowboy at the chuck wagon. He led Madelaine by the arm to the buffet table. The party, everyone gossiping and joking and discussing the selection of foods, queued up at the table behind Madelaine and Minder and Lanyard, taking plates and filling them. "Maddy, try some of this orange-sauce chicken…No, dear, let Elma serve you, that's what she's paid for, you just relax…Elma, see that this lady has some…Yeah."

Lanyard ate kasha and kielbasa, and he was gratified when Madelaine came to sit beside him, close on his right. Minder sat across from them, beginning to eat even before he'd pulled his chair in to the table. The room droned with conversation; periodically the guests quieted to listen and laugh ritually as Minder raised his voice so the whole room could hear. The waterfall swished into the swimming pool behind Lanyard's back. Lanyard found himself staring past Minder's shoulders at a doorway hung with a curtain of translucent pink beads; the curtain was partly tied back, and the room beyond was empty except for what looked like wrestling mats covered in pink sheets. "What's this?" he asked Madelaine. "That room…they have amateur wrestling tournaments?"

Madelaine laughed, just exactly as if Lanyard were joking.

Sometimes Minder sat quietly, listening to the chatter, his eyes panning from face to face, as if assessing some mysterious potential. Those times, Lanyard was disturbed by something predatory in Minder's sunken, bleary blue eyes. Small eyes, ringed with bluish skin. His hair was wiry black, tailing over his ears, tousled, at first glance, so as to seem youthfully carefree—when actually it was carefully arranged.

Lanyard watched Minder—as Minder watched Madelaine. Lanyard didn't like Minder's speculative expression.

Madelaine told an anecdote. Minder laughed excessively and pounded the table. Lanyard smiled and drank red wine.

An earnest young man in thick glasses and a tuxedo asked Madelaine, abruptly, "Aren't you the lady with some expertise in psychic phenomena?"

Madelaine tried to hide her discomfort with an airy wave of her hand. "Oh, no, really. I'm an actress, and not a very successful one. Nothing particularly exotic about me."

"But seriously," the young man went on, "aren't you—"

"Actually," Lanyard interrupted, attempting Madelaine's rescue, "psychic phenomena is an area in which no one can claim expertise. No one knows enough about it to be an expert in it. Too little is proven."

"If I'm not mistaken," Minder said, "our Mr. Lanyard here is the same Carl Lanyard who writes for *Visions*."

"Used to," Lanyard said. "I quit. Ceased to believe in the subject matter of the magazine. Never saw any evidence that the supernatural exists. Don't know what I'm going to do now…"

"It's my understanding you're earning a fee—" He paused, smiling nastily. "—as an investigative reporter on the subway killings." Heads turned. The steady matter-of-factness in Minder's voice was a sharp contrast to the cawing he'd indulged in before. Lanyard could feel Minder watching him.

How did Minder know about his present gig? And the fee?

"Oh—uh…" Lanyard began, wondering how to explain his position without revealing too much. Lanyard was at first inclined to deny everything, then decided to deny only part of it, the part about the fee. "It's true I'm doing a little background on the style of occultism involved."

"Just public-spirited?" asked a man to Minder's right. He was a portly little man, nearly bald, wearing a loud suit and a number of gold rings. He looked as if he'd had his face lifted; the skin was unnaturally taut, and bluish. His green eyes glittered. Lanyard had noticed him before, heard him talking to other people. He invariably brought the conversation around to money and influence. "*That's a nice tie,*" he'd say. "*How much did it cost?...What did you pay for those designer jeans?...Is that twenty-four-carat, or—? Unquestionably, gold jewelry is a good investment, though real estate...*"

Since the man was addressing him, Lanyard smiled politely and said, "I don't think we've met...?"

"This is George Tooley," Minder said. "My secretary."

"Well, George..." Lanyard noticed a small gold coke spoon on a chain around Tooley's neck. "It's not just public-mindedness. The police rather pressured me into it. They practically kidnapped me from the airport. They weren't particularly gentle about it. I'd say they stepped on my rights two or three times. The detective in charge of the case seems like a nice enough guy, though."

"Gribner?" Tooley said. His gold-and-diamond rings flashed as he put a cigarette into a holder and lit it with a personalized platinum lighter.

"I know old Gribner," said Minder loudly. "Decent guy, for a cop. Never tried to shake me down—at least not too often." Polite laughter from the guests.

"What is your opinion of the case?" Tooley asked, looking up at Lanyard. There was something oddly vibrant in his gaze.

Lanyard was uncomfortable, realizing that everyone was waiting for his answer.

Madelaine sat leaning on one elbow, half slumped, thoughtfully stirring her coffee.

"I'd say," he began, "that the people who did it are new to the sort of occultism they're dabbling in. There's an amateurishness about the way the magic circle was drawn, the way the words were written out, the quality of the foreign script." He cleared his throat. "I had the impression that it was all copied from a piece of paper."

"How do you mean?" Tooley seemed mildly startled.

"I mean...as if they copied it out of a book, from a diagram or something... without really knowing what the words meant. But it's so thorough, and the magic symbols involved aren't commonly available in Western occultist texts.

So I'd say that someone knowledgeable is directing an ignorant—uh—lackey. Points to a cult, or at least two people. Bad news. Especially considering that the words in the circle are part of a supplication for power and *material gain.* There's a recession on. People out of work are desperate for money. A lot of people could get into it, if they're dumb enough to believe it'll work. Human sacrifice to the demon Ahriman, an aspect of Ahura Mazda—the two-faced Persian god. In certain Mazdaen cults, innocents were sacrificed to Ahriman to—ah—appease him, and for material gain. He was the personification of a lust for money and power. He—" Lanyard stopped, feeling his face redder. He took a sip of wine. "It seems," he said, putting his glass down, "I've been pontificating..."

"Not at all!" shouted Minder, pounding the table. The noise startled Lanyard. "Man's got a right to pontificate about what he knows best! You should hear Jerry preach from the pulpit about stage sets!"

It was an hour later that the dinner guests began to leave. A party of three departed, and that seemed to trigger an exodus—since there was a precedent, it was suddenly all right to go.

As Lanyard helped Madelaine into her wrap—quite unnecessarily, but it was an excuse to touch her shoulders—Tooley stepped up to them and, fingering his coke spoon meaningfully, said softly, "Joey would be honored if you'd stay. The club's about to open. A lot of interesting people will be coming soon. And you're here already—you'll get in for free." He smiled. "You can meet a lot of influential people here..."

"The club's *about* to open?" Lanyard asked. "Hasn't it been open all this time?"

Madelaine looked at him incredulously. "Oh—I see! I thought you knew what the Valencia Hotel was—it's sort of famous. It's not a hotel anymore. It's a swingers' club."

Laughing in surprise, Lanyard turned to look at the room containing the wrestling mats. "And that's...?"

"An orgy room," Madelaine said, nodding.

Tooley smiled, shaking his head. "There's no pressure here for you to do anything. Some special friends, an atmosphere of intimacy. There's a heated pool, a hot tub, music, free refreshments...and entertainment." He tapped his teeth with the coke spoon.

Lanyard shrugged and looked at Madelaine. She shook her head fractionally.

Lanyard said, "No, thanks, not tonight. Sounds lovely, though. But Madelaine has to get up early. I...." He shrugged again, embarrassed.

"As you please." Tooley's smile was sardonic.

Lanyard felt Tooley's watching them as they left.

In the cab, headed uptown, Madelaine said, "You know, it's funny, but when I'm around Joey Minder...I don't get any flashes. No psychic intrusion."

"No? Why not?"

"I don't know. But the effect lasts for a few hours after I've left him, too. Like he's a drug insulating me from it. It's crazy. That's the main reason I see him, I guess It's a relief. I don't like having to sort through..." Her voice trailed off.

"The main reason? Not because he's a connection? A contact?" Lanyard immediately regretted having said it, when her eyes narrowed and she said:

"So you figure I'm just another rung-climbing stage slut?"

"No, I—I'm sorry. Didn't mean it like that. It's just that I have the feeling that what should be carved on the base of the Statue of Liberty shouldn't be 'Give me your tired, your poor...' Instead it should say, 'Use Your Contacts.' That's New York's actual slogan."

She smiled. "Okay, back out of it, then." Her eyes were large and soft in the half-light of the car's interior. "I know you don't take it seriously when I talk about 'psychic intrusion.' You think it's a crock, so my real motives must be—oh, I don't know. But since you're not writing for *Visions*, I suppose I can talk about it a little. Long as you don't write anything down."

"About your gift? Don't worry. I'm not here with you because I'm interested in that."

They pulled up in front of her apartment building. He paid the cabdriver and they got out of the cab. Then he stopped on the sidewalk, startled by a realization. "Oh...sorry. I got out with you just as if—well, I mean it's presumptuous of me—"

"Not at all, It seemed the natural thing to me too. Psychic phenomena of a different sort: two minds with but a single thought."

"My mind had nothing to do with it. Do you have any wine on hand?"

SEVERAL GLASSES OF wine apiece. Two hours of conversation. And lots of eye contact.

Then came the awkward silence. The usual obstacle.

Lanyard toyed with various possible solutions, The first step, of course, would be the kiss. They had waited the requisite decent interval.

But she was sitting on the opposite side of the kitchen table. "Hey," she said, "how about helping me pick out a record?"

He followed her to the next room.

She didn't have any records. She had old eight-tracks. She fumbled through them with her right hand, her left bringing her fourth glass of wine for another sip. It was red wine, and a few drops sloshed over the rim—she was tipsy, held the glass uncertainly. The wine ran from the corner of her mouth and down across her chin, like diluted blood. Her tongue darted to lick it clean, while her eyes focused on the tape deck. He didn't care for most of her records—shrill folk-singing. But when the music began—Joni Mitchell—he was relaxed enough to like it. And it sounded better when he slipped his arms around her. She came to him easily. Her kisses were long and slow and wet and crackling with a note of desperation. His hard-on arrived instantly, making him feel ridiculous—his anxiety melting when she snugged her hips closer to him, moving languidly against his erection, welcoming it. Two more glasses of wine. Twenty minutes of whispering and nonverbal sounds. And lots of eye contact.

Later: the bedroom curtains were closed, the only light a murky blue from a shaded floor lamp. They sat side by side. She looped a leg over one of his and they kissed. It was a good kiss: He lost track of time.

But there was another obstacle he hadn't foreseen. Suddenly and unreasonably self-conscious, he said: "Does it feel good when I…I mean, if I caress it too hard or too softly—if there's anything you'd like to tell me, to make it better for you, go ahead and tell me. It makes me feel closer to you, when I know I'm making love to you the way you like it."

He'd whispered it softly—but it didn't have the effect he'd anticipated. She froze up, and seemed to be listening, as if hearing a burglar in the next room.

"What's the matter?" he asked.

"Nothing." She relaxed a little. "I'd better tell you something. I don't know how you'll feel about it, because you're a skeptic. But I can't make love if there's talking. If either of us talk, the words trigger off the Gift, sometimes. There's so much closeness, when I make love to someone, that if they speak I begin to pick up what they're thinking. That's not always a nice experience. I get flashes about things that will happen to them. I have to go into a sort of fanatic concentration on the feeling, and nothing else, otherwise the Gift comes and distracts me." She lay back on the pillow and draped an arm over her eyes. "I don't know why they call it a Gift. I'd like to give it back to whoever gave it to me."

Lanyard was shaky inside. It wasn't, he realized, because their lovemaking had been interrupted. It was because he believed what she was saying.

"Okay," he said. And that's all he said. After that, it was all caresses, and gentle probings, and damp explorations. They made love three times that night, which was three times Lanyard's average.

But as they lay limp, exhausted, huddled together, something she said made it difficult for him to sleep.

She was drifting into sleep herself. But she spoke for the first time in hours, murmuring dreamily, "When you spoke before, I had to stop it because...I had a flash of you...saw a little kid...following you in a tunnel. This little kid...his head changed, it grew into...the head of a mummy, sort of, long mustache on it...Maybe I picked up something you dreamt...But I had a bad feeling when—oh, I don't know...But don't go on the...I don't know..." Seconds later she was asleep.

But now Lanyard was wide awake.

HE WOKE AT ten AM after about five hours' sleep. Madelaine was just coming back from the shower, wrapped in a towel. "Good morning, Old Log-Sawer," she said.

"Yeah..." He grinned weakly, sitting, aware that he probably looked all tousled and pasty-faced. His tongue was coated with a septic film. "Ugh. Can I use your phone? I'm already late on a call. Detective What's-his-name."

"Sure—then you want to go out for some breakfast?"

"Absolutely." He reached for the bedside phone, punched Information, got the number of the Ninth Precinct, and put in a call for Gribner.

"He's not here," someone said. "He said you supposed to meet him if you called before noon. You should come immediately to the...lessee...Fairbright Arms at Bleecker and Seventh Avenue. He'll be in the basement. That's all the memo says."

Shit," said Lanyard, hanging up.

"What's the matter?" She was applying eyeliner, her face comically elongated as she strained to hold her eyelids still.

"Seems I have to forgo breakfast. Got to go see Gribner."

"That's okay. Take a shower if you want."

He showered, borrowed her toothbrush, but his clothes were even more rumpled than they had been the night before.

He stood awkwardly in the doorway. He didn't want to leave her, and he didn't want to keep his appointment.

It's absurd, he thought. It's like canceling a honeymoon to take a tour through a slaughterhouse.

But he kissed her briefly, and said, "Bye," and found his way to the elevator.

DESCENDING IN AN almost identical, but more deteriorated elevator in the Fairbright Arms, Lanyard tried to analyze his growing unease. He felt fairly certain there were a number of people involved in the killings. Maybe an organization. They would want to defend themselves.

They might see Lanyard as a threat.

He was an out-of-towner, and somehow that made him feel particularly vulnerable. But then, everyone was vulnerable in the city. There were snipers. There were people who dropped cinder blocks on other people from rooftops in Times Square. And there were those who stalked.

No way to know who might be waiting around the next corner. Or outside the elevator, in the hall, when the doors slid open.

The doors slid open. Basement level.

Rigid, he stared across the hall and through the doorway into a mist-filled underground room. An unnatural fog half-shrouded four large white, hulking shapes that shivered and growled in the dim chamber.

Lanyard forced himself to take a step closer. There was a sensation in his belly that made him feel as if he'd swallowed live eels.

He looked closer—and laughed. He was looking into a laundry room. The fog was steam leaking from a dryer's out-vent, where the hose had broken. The white hulking shapes were washers and other dryers, shaking as they went through their cycles. Expecting the fear to leave him, he laughed again at his own foolishness.

But the laughter was forced and brief. The fear didn't leave him. He turned away from the laundry room, moving reluctantly down the concrete hallway toward the sounds of men's voices.

The voices were coming through an open door on the right. Lanyard stopped, just before reaching the door. He glanced over his shoulder. A tentacle of steam was curling from the laundry room, curving toward him. He felt small and lost, oppressed by the bulk of the old brick building around him. He clearly heard the rising thrum of a subway train approaching, not far on the other side of the walls, like some great animal growling as it nosed through the underworld. He took a deep breath, and moved toward the furnace room—and stopped.

Someone unseen was pushing a corpse out of the room. The corpse was on its back, strapped into place on a gurney. The sheet over its head had been insecurely fastened. The motion of the gurney made the sheet fall aside, exposing a grinning, bloodless face.

Why is he grinning?

The gurney angled into the passageway and thrust the wobbling head toward Lanyard. It bore down on him like some perverse destiny. Pushing the gurney was a young man in a white uniform. He was chewing gum. The gurney came to a sudden halt. The corpse's head was adjacent to Lanyard; he glanced down long enough to see that it was a boy about twelve years old. A boy who would never be thirteen.

The boy's face was a hideous satire of joy.

Lanyard looked away. The young attendant grinned at Lanyard, his expression uncomfortably similar to that on the corpse's face, and Lanyard felt sure he was stoned. Probably on 'ludes, judging by the idiotic laxness of his facial muscles. "Shit, goddammit, I keep forgetting I gotta pull it and not push it." He moved to the other end of the corpse and, without bothering to cover the dead boy's face, bent to pull the stretcher away down the hall.

"Lanyard!"

Lanyard turned. It was Gribner, pipe wagging in his teeth as he spoke. "Lanyard, where you been hiding, tell me that, huh? I'm calling your hotel, I'm chasing around, I'm calling your employer—sure, ignore us and—"

"Let's get this over with," Lanyard said firmly, hurrying toward the furnace room. It was easier, knowing the victim was gone.

"I tried to keep them from taking the body before you could get a look, but Forensics said they had to—"

"Don't do me any favors," Lanyard interrupted, pushing past Gribner and stepping into the furnace room. The door, opened inward, was held in place

by a black rubber chock, and was stenciled in drippy blue on white: FURNISS-
NO INTERING.

"No *intering?*" Lanyard murmured. "Someone was interred here, for a few
hours."

He was looking at the star-shaped spill of blood on the concrete floor. The
blood splash was an asymmetrical star half obscuring the symmetrical pattern
of the pentagram spray-painted just beneath the grille of the oil furnace. The
furnace was like some malformed troll of gray metal climbing from the cellar
floor, the tin pipes curving up from its torso and angling, as if they had elbows,
to grip the plaster ceiling.

The room was about thirty by thirty-five, and it was hot. It was sticky
hot: Lanyard, still gazing at the stain on the floor, the multicolored spray
paint, the overturned candles, put a shaky hand to his brow and wiped away
clammy sweat. Maybe the room wasn't hot. Maybe he was coming down with
something. He felt feverish. It had seemed a rather warm day, Indian Summer,
perhaps. Too warm to turn on a furnace.

"Sure is hot in here," said one of the two men standing with Gribner on the
far side of the pentagram.

Gribner's hangdog features creased as he bent, scowling, to peer through
the grate of the furnace. "Furnace isn't on. Maybe it was on, and heated up the
place and they turned it off."

He tapped the squat machine gingerly, then ran his fingers over it, leaving
traces in the dust. "It's cold. I lay you bets it wasn't used today."

No one said it, but everyone thought it: *So how come it's so hot in here?*

Lanyard felt odd. His skin crawled, and he felt an anomalous pressure
behind the bridge of his nose, between his eyes. His eyes stung. The scene
became unnaturally grainy, and the air seemed tinted, as if he were seeing the
room through a blue filter. He closed his eyes.

And instantly snapped them open again.

"Something the matter, Lanyard?" Gribner asked, mopping his forehead
with a white handkerchief. "Looked like you were gonna faint...Too hot in
here for you, yes?"

"No, I...Maybe I didn't get enough sleep..." He turned to look at the furnace.
It had come from that direction He'd closed his eyes, and something had seemed
to leap through the darkness—the darkness that waits behind the eyelids. It had

been something animalistic, and outlined in crackling lines of red-white, as if it were made of electrical arcs. He took a deep breath, and closed his eyes again.

He looked through the darkness behind his eyelids as if he were looking from a lighted room into a dark night. The prospect was black, smeared with retinal afterimages and restless specks of every color; it was like a rain of volcanic ash. Through the ashen landscape something came bounding, four-footed, spectacular—because it had sharp-edged form, a definite shape in a vista of shapelessness. It was a snarling thing made of crackling red lines, a neon outline, but somehow very substantial in its carnivorous presence. It moved too quickly for a clear image—he had an impression of four hugely clawed legs, gaping jaws, ratlike eyes, a body like a great hound—it bounded toward him like an aroused attack dog, jaws gaping—

"Lanyard!" Gribner was shaking him, shouting in his ears. He opened his eyes and looked around. There were only the three other men and the furnace—no red neon hounds bounding toward him. But he stood rigidly, dripping sweat.

Lanyard muttered, "Sorry…I yell, or something?"

"You were shouting and waving your hands in front of your face!" said one of the plainclothes cops loudly—accusingly. Lanyard recognized the big red-faced cop who'd accosted him at the airport.

"Yes…well…"

Gribner stood back from Lanyard, watching him warily. "I feel funny in here, too…Lanyard, where you going?"

"Hm?" Lanyard stopped. "I was going to have a look behind the furnace."

It had come from behind the furnace.

"We already looked there. Nothing there. In your opinion, was this circle," Gribner pointed at the pentagram, "made by the same person who made the other one you saw?"

Lanyard glanced down at the smeared floor. The blood puddle was beginning to dry, brown around the edges. In the middle it was dark red, so dark it was almost purple; it reflected the two caged light bulbs glowing glumly overhead. "Well," Lanyard said. "It's the same invocation, from what I can see of the lettering, the names they called. I'm no handwriting expert, though, I can't be sure it's the same person. I doubt it is. I think it's a cult. And I think…well, it could be the same cult, though a different killer."

"So tell me something new. We have forensic evidence to that effect, from the last one…" Gribner began. He fell silent as Lanyard moved toward the furnace again.

Lanyard ducked under a pipe and peered into the sprawling shadows back of the furnace. He couldn't see clearly. He forced himself to move against the current of his fear.

The concrete wall was pitted, but otherwise ran unbroken from the ceiling to a shallow recess three feet above the floor. The recess was three feet high, two feet wide, three inches deep. It struck Lanyard as the opening of a shaft, plugged by a concrete slab. The plug had a rusty iron ring set into it. Lanyard reached out and, hesitating just a moment, closed his fingers over the ring and tugged hard. The slab made a creek as it tilted outward from the recess and fell against the floor—Lanyard pulled his hand back at the last moment. The slab had broken into three parts. It was perhaps four inches thick. The shaft was open, dark, malodorous—and hot.

Lanyard banged his head on a pipe when he straightened too quickly, suddenly afraid to remain at the opening alone. Holding his head, wincing, he backed away. Gribner came to stand beside him.

"Wunnerful," Gribner muttered. "You broke a hole in the wall .

But his tone carried no real reproach. He seemed intrigued.

Lanyard blinked—but he was careful not to close his eyes for long. "Gribner, you think the killer lives in this building?"

"If he does, he's stupid. If it's a he. Most maniac killers don't shit in their own backyards. They have some cunning. The boy who was killed lives in the building. No connection with the two women killed, so far as we know. He was picking up some laundry for his mother—it was past midnight. She works late, she says. Kid stays up half the night, I guess. So he was down here picking up the stuff. The super found him this morning—there are signs of a struggle in the laundry room. The way the thing looks is someone grabbed the kid, and the kid fought with them. They knocked some steam pipes loose. The killer hit the kid, lacerating his head—there was a little blood in the laundry room—and dragged him in here, maybe so they wouldn't be interrupted. Butchered him pretty much the same as the others."

"What sort of security is there?" Lanyard's voice sounded weak and far away in his own ears. He couldn't bring himself to take his eyes off the gap in the wall.

"That's the thing: Two guys playing cards with the elevator man most of the night at the front door. They say no one came in after midnight. The roof entrance was sealed off long ago. Iron bars on all the windows, not likely he slipped in through a fire escape. Maybe he got in during the day, was waiting down here for hours…"

"Maybe he came in there," Lanyard pointed at the dark place in the wall.

The red-faced cop stood just behind Lanyard. He spoke up abruptly: "That's a service gate for a steam main. They used to pump steam around from a central plant to these buildings aroun' here. My old man used to do that shit for a living. Cleaned 'em out, patched 'em up."

"You think it connects with other utility tunnels?" Gribner asked.

"Good chance. Sometimes they do. You think maybe the guy went down in some manhole—or maybe a subway tunnel—and came up here?"

Gribner stuck out his lower lip and squinted. "I think that's a possibility, yeah, sure. That door come out pretty easily. Like it was just hanging in place, looked to me."

"Easily…" Lanyard nodded, dreamily.

"And all three killings were underground…"

"Three?" Lanyard asked.

"I told you—there was another, but we kept it quiet for a while—before the one you were brought in on. Much the same. Lanyard, this cult of yours—any reason it should be underground?"

Lanyard nodded slowly. "Ahura Mazda had two priests, one for the good side, one for the malevolent side of the deity. The priests for the malevolent side had their temples underground…"

"Closer to hell," Gribner murmured.

They stood staring at the shadow within a shadow where the shaft began, behind the furnace.

Lanyard could feel a current of thick, tepid air issuing from the horizontal shaft. He thought he glimpsed, for a moment, in that rectangular blackness, a flicker of red light.

But he knew—even as Gribner sent out for men with flashlights to probe the tunnel—that nothing would be found but pipes and rat droppings and more tunnels, interminable tunnels leading to cellars beneath cellars.

LEANING BACK ON the couch, his stockinged feet on a footstool, toying with an unlit pipe, Gribner waited for the call from Leibowitz. He had just returned from an exhausting four hours with Harold Cannaber in Research. They'd turned up a few instances of ritual murder—all but one had been solved. The one unsolved case concerned voodoo, which Lanyard assured him had no relevance to the subway killings. They'd searched back issues of newspapers. They'd spoken to various self-styled occultists, two professors of anthropology, and one associate professor of comparative religion. No one admitted having come into contact with acolytes of the religion Lanyard described; no one seemed more than mildly interested in it.

The possibilities were maddeningly numerous. There might he an unknown connection between the three victims; someone might be killing for personal reasons and leaving the ritualistic traces as a red herring.

Gribner's experience, coupled with cop's intuition, told him that the victims had been chosen more or less at random. They were all young—the boy had been only twelve years old—and all relatively innocent, though the girls had not, apparently, been virgins. What was it Lanyard had said? *All that is necessary is that the victims are young, and what the cultists would consider "infidels." Anyone not their own religion.*

That left millions of possible victims.

Something distracted Gribner from his brooding. A noise? No, the lack of a noise. Everett was supposed to be taking a bath. The kid had been in there for twenty minutes and no sound of running water yet. He'd come home all sooty again. Playing in the basement. What was it he got into down there that left him so grimy?

Gribner rose, causing the Pekingese female, Randi, to sputter sleepily as she was dislodged from his lap. He stood, stretched, and went toward the bathroom. Louie was outside the door, crouching, tail thumping slightly. He sat watching the door like a terrier watching a rat hole, making almost inaudible sounds in his throat.

A grating sound came from the bathroom; it wasn't a toilet or tub noise. It wasn't the pipes—after years in the same apartment, Gribner knew the pipes' dissonant singing by heart. It was the sound of some unguessable animal, growling.

Louie backed away from the door.

Gribner reached for the knob, hesitated as his hand grasped the cold metal.

He's not my kid, he thought. Wouldn't be right to barge in on him. He's a house guest.

He heard a squeak, the sound of bare flesh against porcelain.

And then the growling again.

But maybe it was a moan. Maybe the boy had fallen and hurt himself. Using this convenient rationale, Gribner opened the lockless bathroom door and looked in.

The grating noise had recommenced. It was like the turning of a great iron hinge, with an undertone of throaty warning.

Everett was on his hands and knees in the tub, naked, staring transfixed at the bathtub drain.

He was clearly completely unaware of Gribner. Or ignoring him utterly. His eyes didn't waver from their fix on the rust-flecked metal throat of the drain. Gribner glimpsed something red and bright glimmering there. Maybe a bug.

Everett was tense in the bone-dry bathtub; knees red, knuckles white. Everett's small circumcised penis was erect. Slowly, never removing his eyes from the drain, Everett moved his right hand back, balancing on the flat of his left. He began to massage his penis—unthinkingly, no expression of pleasure showing on his face—eyes still locked on the drain.

And then the grating growling came from the drain. It was a deep, echoey sound this time. It was answered. The answer came from Everett's slightly parted, foam-flecked lips.

Gribner was breathing shallowly. There was a band of coldness contracting around his temples. He hadn't been so afraid since he'd told Benny the Twitch to drop his gun, and Benny had raised it and fired instead. Gribner had returned fire, and his aim had been better than Benny's.

But now all he could do was quietly back away.

He was careful to make as little sound as possible as he backed out of the bathroom and closed the door. He didn't want to disturb Everett. He didn't want Everett to look at him.

But it had to stop.

He felt safer now, with the closed door between them.

He raised a fist and pounded on the door. "*Everett!* Hey, I thought I told you to take a bath!"

Another deep, grating, echoey growl began—and stopped midway.

A moment later the sound of water splashing into the bathtub made it possible for him to relax, to breathe again.

Louie was still staring at the door.

The phone rang. Moving mechanically, Gribner answered.

"You want the report now?" It was Leibowitz.

"Uh—sure."

"The boy was cut up pretty much the same as the others. Except for the chewing—"

"The what?"

"You didn't look very close, huh? Kid's genitals were chewed away. And I'm telling you *chewed*, Lieutenant…I figure this guy's got a dog. Only—it's not exactly like—bite marks."

"Chewed…If not a dog, a man?"

"Not a man. Not a dog. Some big animal. Not sure what yet."

"Hey—save the rest of the report until tomorrow."

Gribner hung up.

He wasn't sure, but he thought he heard the growling coming from the bathroom again. The growling of some big animal.

FOUR

An unseasonable heat had come to the city. The heat was sticky and it trapped the smog under a windless inversion layer. To Lanyard, out walking Thursday afternoon, the air seemed gray-blue, the color of dead skin. He could feel it palpably when he rubbed his thumb and forefinger together. It had the oiliness of insecticide.

Eyes burning in this miasma, he walked from the Hilton in midtown Manhattan, down the Avenue of the Americas to Thirtieth Street. He turned west to walk through a district of furriers—raw skins hang in windows, brushed furs as yet untanned, their rough sides like the scabrous skins of scalping victims. A taxidermist's window displayed a whole fox and a golden eagle frozen in motion, glassy-eyed.

Strong young men in tank-top shirts, new shoes, and neatly pressed jeans asked him for spare change. Sweating, he took off his sweater in the prickly heat and turned east to Third Avenue, which he followed down to the Bowery area, in search of the Ninth Precinct station. He had an appointment with Gribner at three. He regretted walking. He felt tired and confused, and began to suspect he was lost. Had Gribner said the station was at Fifth Street and Second Avenue, or second Street at Fifth Avenue? He should have written it down.

In front of the boarded-over buildings, young black men in striped hats drew small crowds for Three-Card Monte: "Say my man ten get you twenny just pickuh red card outuh th' black, wherezuh red card who wantsuh bet—I pay with a smile if you in—checkitout an' don' make me shout!" Hollow-eyed women in dirty blouses forlornly hawked books no one would want, scratched sixties records, and down-at-heel shoes, all on frayed blankets spread out in the shade.

Lanyard passed a burned-out building. He paused to peer into the gutted storefront that had once made up most of the building's first floor. The windows and doors were gone, and no one had troubled to board them over. Between two blackened window frames someone had spray-painted: DETH TO LNDLRDS!! LNDLRD TRCHED BLDG FR INSURANCE!! 3 DED IN FIRE!! The spray paint was red and gaseously air-blown at the edges, like writing in fire. Lanyard was startled to see a child moving through the black interior of the building. Two children, one white and one Puerto Rican, preschoolers in shorts and T-shirts and tennis shoes, giggling, whispering urgently to one another as they clambered through the dead-black rubble. Each carried a stick which they poked into sumps of melancholy violet water that had collected in the craters of the ashen floor. The children were anomalies of color and animation in the dead, monochromatic, almost lightless interior; the walls were black, the rubble on the floor was black; the ceiling was black and where fire had eaten holes in it black wires dangled down. It was like the lava fields he'd seen in Eastern Oregon; like one of the cooled-lava tunnels that led deep into the dead volcano. Desolate and primeval.

A cloud covered the sun. Now the cloud moved away, and from behind Lanyard light struck the second story of the burned-out building's façade; the lower half of the ruin was still in shadow, the light partly occluded by the buildings across the street. A ray of sunlight entered the lifeless window at the second story and slanted through a burn hole in the floor, striking down through the ceiling over the ground floor to splash across the face of the red-haired white boy just as he and his companion turned to squint at the street. The boy's face, shining in this momentary brilliance, showed crisscrossing red and blue lines, applied with finger paints, in an almost cubistic variation of Indian war paint. At least, Lanyard took it to be Indian war paint, then.

On the child's face was an expression Lanyard had once seen on the face of a ferret that had snarled at him from its hole in the bank of a certain pond a long time before—a pond in which he'd almost drowned, later, panicked by a ghostly face he thought he'd seen in the murky water.

The child's face began to fade into the gloom as another cloud blocked the sun. The children turned away to poke with their sticks at a puddle, just under a gutted TV set lodged crookedly in the jagged rubble at their feet. Lanyard thought he glimpsed something pale and rubbery reach up from the water to grasp the stick, to tug at it almost playfully. The children giggled and sprang back. Lanyard decided his eyes were playing tricks. He turned away.

Farther down, the street was raucous with the calls of sidewalk vendors, the constant churn of traffic, the periodic hysteria of sirens, the clatter and grind of street construction. Normally, the activity would have pleased him. Today it was an unhealthy swarming, like the scuttling of cockroaches surprised late at night in the kitchen when the light is suddenly turned on. Like something that had crawled up from underground.

To his left, a street crew worked behind wooden barriers, using picks to clear hard-packed dirt from around a tangle of rusty pipes. Beside the work crew was a shaft dropping between vertical planks into pitch darkness. The air over the shaft wavered, distorted by the release of heat. But there was no plume of steam. What was giving off the heat?

Lanyard remembered the torrid air roiling from the old utility access door behind the furnace. In the room where the boy had been disemboweled.

For a moment he stood stock still, gazing at the dark pit beside the sidewalk, thinking: This unnatural heat—this weather itself—was it created underground? Like a fever in the city's body. Some underground sickness.

He shook his head and smiled.

But the next time he approached a repair trench, he crossed the street to avoid it. And he skirted subway stations, as if afraid they might erupt some unguessable predator. He pictured the brutal head of a moray eel darting from an undersea crevice.

Blinking through perspiration, Lanyard stopped at the corner of Third Street and the Bowery. Lost in thought, he'd walked too far. Thinking sometimes made him unthinking.

Fifth Street and Second Avenue. Gribner had definitely said Fifth Street and—he froze, eyes locked on a deserted building on Third Street, diagonally across from his corner.

Something had moved—had moved strangely—behind one of the empty windows on the second floor.

It was an old building, old as a steam locomotive, and the faces of imps looked brokenly down from the square granite false front. Most of the windows had been broken out and boarded over. To the right was a vacant lot piebald with knee-deep heaps of trash, chiefly liquor bottles. Trash and garbage, some of it melded by time and weather into monochromatic brown heaps, bunched in the old building's doorways. The first-floor windows were closed off with stapled flaps of flattened cardboard boxes; the sidewalk was littered with chunks of fallen cornices. Lanyard stared in fascination at one of the lower windows, where the cardboard flaps overlapped. The flaps were moving, bending outward. A man's hand emerged, groping, from between two of the flaps. It was followed by another hand, wrists, arms, and between them, wriggling, widening the gap, was a grisly matted head. It was an old man—or a young one, prematurely aged—pressing out head first. He pulled himself out, clawing and elbowing ahead. He popped from the slats and clanked on all fours through tin and glass debris. Lanyard relaxed: The man was just another tramp. The tramp stood, shakily, and turned like a crazily bent weathervane, to shout at the window what sounded like "COMUNGORYUHFUGGINSHIDUNB ASTUD-UNSTOPYERTGUXNERDIPSLEFUGGINSHIDS!" As if in reply to this invocation, another tramp pressed lobster hands and a blocky face out the same cardboard flaps, legs popping free last. Now two tramps stood shouting at the cardboard flaps. Apparently in response, a third derelict struggled through the gap in the blinded window, upper parts out first—it was like a grotesque birth, as if the derelict building were distilling an essence of itself. A fourth wino began to emerge. He was tubbier than the others, and dirty. His potbelly stuck in the thick cardboard flaps, and the other three, laughing, staggering, tried to pull their friend free, and succeeded only in wedging him more firmly. He wriggled spasmodically, face down, yelling: "FUGGINBASSUDSSUNSUHBITC HES YUH KILLIN ME YUH KILLIN ME FUGGUN BASSUDS YUH KILL ME," so loud that heads turned two blocks away. Finally the old coot popped out, *glop*, onto the sidewalk. His friends helped him to stand and all four staggered off, howling drunk, leaning on one another, stopping to urinate every thirty feet.

Lanyard laughed, and felt lighter. Some of the unplaceable aura of the sinister seemed to have left the street. It was simply a place of neglect, classic human deterioration.

He walked back uptown, toward Fifth Street. Passing closer to the building, he glanced at it once more. Something about one of the red spray-painted scrawls of graffiti itched at the back of his memory. Hurriedly, he dismissed the scrawl from his mind. Only much later, that night, lying in bed, would he seem to see it again, superimposed over the flickering negative landscape on the back of his eyelids: a crudely spray-painted approximation of an ancient mystical sign. The sign of Ahriman.

Cellars

"Sorry the air-conditioner's broken," Gribner said, his tie fluttering in the wind from the fan on the dented file cabinet. The fan rotated jerkily, and when it faced Lanyard, seated opposite Gribner, it riffled the pen-scrawled forms in the desk's *In* basket. "This heat is funny, isn't it? I guess it happens now and then...every few years, in the fall..."

Lanyard murmured something inarticulately affirmative. He could see that Gribner wasn't thinking about the weather at all.

"You got any kids?" Gribner asked suddenly. He put his elbows on the stained blotter of the wooden desk. He wore a sweat-soiled white shirt, sleeves rolled up. His pipe lolled loosely in his shirt pocket—he hadn't cleaned it properly, and half-charred tobacco spilled from it when he moved, flecking the report spread out on the blotter.

"Kids?" Lanyard looked up dully. He felt thick-headed. "No. Oh, I've got some nephews. Used to take care of them occasionally. Why?"

Gribner's fishy blue eyes met Lanyard's. "Isn't it pretty common for kids to start acting weird like...like right before puberty? Ten or eleven or twelve, round that age?"

"I'm no expert on child psychology. I understand they can get a little odd as their chemistry starts to change. Why?"

"Taking care of a nephew of my own. He acts sort of strange. Never mind...I guess."

"You find any link between the victims yet?"

Gribner looked down at the report, shaking his head. "No, we sure haven't, and it's pretty ticklish around here, I'm telling you, pressure's building up: Find the killers. So far we're pretty sure it's more than one. And whoever they are, they're careful not to leave fingerprints, not to be seen."

Lanyard glanced up, saw one of the uniformed policemen, hatless, his jacket on the back of his swivel chair, reading a copy of the *New York Post*. The tabloid's banner headline screamed: Boy Butchered in Basement. A smaller headline for another article said: Minder Cleared In Drug Charge.

"You read the article in the *Post*—?" Lanyard began.

He was startled when Gribner interrupted him with uncharacteristic avidity: "Sure I read it, yeah! Listen, it's got me down, the way they have this tone that says the police are hardly trying—it's implicit, you know?—and they're trying to make money, selling papers by panicking everyone, implying the killers are out there waiting for just any—"

"No, no—I was going to ask you if you'd read the article about Minder. What's it all about? I had dinner with the guy the other night. Neither he nor anyone else mentioned drug charges…He did, however, mention knowing you."

"Joey Minder?" He waved his hand airily. "Oh, I guess somebody found a little light dope at his place during the raid last year. They dismissed the charges because the search warrant didn't—"

"Raid? What raid?" Lanyard felt the stirrings of alarm.

"Ah…Joey had one of his wild parties." Gribner's smile was faintly apologetic. "Some girl didn't want to play, so to speak, and I guess one of Joey's friends was a little drunk and tried to force her. She called it attempted rape—though he didn't get very far with her—and her parents are friends with the D.A. The D.A.'s kind of a prude. We had a go-round over a pornographer, when I was working in Vice. The D.A. wanted to prosecute him, and I said we have bigger fish to fry, like a certain pusher and a child pornographer. But for some reason the D.A. picked on this guy who was in my territory, and who was a friend of Joey's. Joey paid for the guy's attorneys and he got off. Anyway, the D.A. raided Joey's place because there was a rumor he'd kidnapped some girl and had her there. Turned out to be sheer bullshit. They found a little opium, some hash. Not much. No big deal."

"What about these 'wild parties'?"

"Not much relevant to what we have to talk about, Lanyard. Anyway, if I was a rich playboy I'd have wild parties, too. Me, I got a meshugge old lady who goes to spiritualists, and two dogs. Joey's got a lot more, and he plays hard. People get jealous, they make up stories about people they envy. I've seen no evidence he's raped anyone or any of this other stuff."

"I understand he's a friend to the police. That he donates to their relief funds, and special retirement funds and—"

"Hey, Boxell!" Gribner shouted, waving at someone he saw over Lanyard's right shoulder. The main room of the Ninth Precinct station was divided into sections by a wooden railing. The walls were dirty green and bare. There was an old manual typewriter on the corner of every desk. Moving down the center aisle between two railed-off sections, a heavyset uniformed cop grinned and tossed his hat at Gribner.

"Eat my hat, Gribner!"

Gribner caught the hat, a flicker of humor showing in his eyes, though his face was deadpan. "You going in the back to check your still, Boxell?"

They exchanged friendly digs for a while, and Lanyard realized that Gribner had called to Boxell as a means of evading his question.

Lanyard thought about Madelaine and wondered if she were through with her audition. Probably. Suddenly he was in a hurry to be free of Gribner.

Lanyard stood, and Gribner turned back to him, a smile fading. "Well, Lanyard, here's the report. Give us your professional opinion, if you really want to be of help." He slid the sheaf of papers across the desk. "We checked out that tunnel. Didn't find a goddamn thing."

Lanyard folded the papers in half, nodding, "Do my best." Thinking: *Send a copy of this to Maguss.* He winced at the thought. He didn't feel like communicating with Maguss.

But there was the money to consider.

"It's too hot," Buddy Rothstein complained. "It's not supposed to be this hot this time of year." He kicked at a broken squirt gun lying next to the yellow fire hydrant. He wished the squirt gun wasn't broken. He might have started a water fight.

Everett was standing behind Buddy. Everett was eight; Buddy was nine. Everett was in the shade of the alley's mouth. Buddy knew he was there, but he ignored him. Buddy was talking to his dog, Shag-Rug. It was too hot for Shag-Rug. No one was quite sure what sort of dog Shag-Rug was, but he was shaggy. The black and white fur covered him thickly from his collie's nose to his husky's tail. Buddy was talking to Shag because none of the other kids seemed to be out on the streets. They were probably all inside watching afternoon cartoons. Buddy thought cartoons were dumb.

Of course, Everett was there. But Buddy felt nervous around Everett. He didn't like to talk to him much. Everett talked funny.

But he turned around when he heard Everett say, "I don't know why you say it is supposed to be fall. It is fall. That is something anyone can see. The leaves are dead. I've seen them fall. They are dead."

"You talk like Mr. Spock," said Buddy, tugging Shag-Rug's tail just to see him snap at it.

"Who is Mr. Spock?" Everett asked.

"He's on TV. He's got pointed ears. He's on reruns. I wish my goddamn squirt gun wasn't broken. I'd get Paco. Have a squirt-gun fight." He was conscious that, he had said *I'd get Paco* and nothing about allowing Everett to play with them. He hoped the slight would make Everett go away. Everett's eyes narrowed a little. That was all. That was all you could see on the outside. But with a guy like Everett, hard to tell what he really thought. His face didn't change very much.

Everett came out of the shade, blinking, his hands tenting over his eyes to block the late-afternoon sun. Shag-Rug trotted off when Everett got near. He always did. Buddy would have followed Shag-Rug, except that Everett said:

"If you want to cool off, we could open the fire hydrant."

Buddy was intrigued. "I wish we could," he said wistfully. "But they put new caps on them and you can't open them with a wrench anymore. You have to have some special tool nobody but firemen have."

"That is for those who don't Know," said Everett.

There he goes with that stuff again, Buddy thought. "Oh, fuck off," said Buddy. He didn't know what the words *fuck off* meant, exactly, but he'd heard it said a great deal and he knew it was a powerful means of dispensing with someone. But it was lost on Everett.

"Do you want me to open it for you so you can play in the water?" Everett asked.

Buddy considered. Maybe Everett *was* like Mr. Spock, always coming up with last-minute technical answers to problems, saving the day. Everett was less likable, but he might be just as smart. No one knew much about him. He'd only come to the neighborhood two weeks ago. He was Mr. Gribner's nephew, and he was excused from school for some reason.

"How come you get out of school?" Buddy asked, enviously.

Everett ignored that, too. "Do you want the fire hydrant to work?"

Slowly, Buddy nodded. "But...I don't know if the water's any good. I don't like dirty water."

"What is wrong with the fire hydrant's water?"

"I don't know. My mom said the water's going bad some places. She's afraid to use our water. She says it tastes funny. We buy bottled water. My dad said some of the fire hydrants have something stuck in them. Some pollution stuff. I don't know. Can you get the cap off?"

"You wait up here. Do not stand close to it. I will come back."

"Okay," said Buddy, looking up and down the street for Shag-Rug. It was one of the nicer streets on the Lower East side. It was clean, all the trash in garbage cans beside the stoop and not spilled over the street. The fire hydrants and spike-topped metal fences along the stairwells were painted bright yellow, which gave the block a cheery look. Here and there, small trees protected by small round fences shed leaves into the heavy air. But it didn't feel like October. It felt like August.

He looked back at the alley. Everett had gone into the building, probably to get a tool. Shag-Rug was nowhere around. Mrs. Bassett was walking her poodle; she had a patented pooper-scooper in her hand; she waited patiently as the dog snuffled along the curb. A few taxis moved by a block down. Buddy waited, wondering if Everett were playing a joke on him. Maybe he wouldn't come back at all. After all, Everett was only eight. Little kids lied and made things up all the time. Buddy had outgrown that, his mother said. But Everett still told stories. Like that stuff about the Head Underneath.

It became darker.

Just like that it was darker. It was because—Buddy reasoned—the sun had dipped behind the skyline. He looked west; sure enough, the sky was orange and pink between the high buildings. It grew even darker as he watched, and, though the heat didn't diminish much, he felt a chill.

The chill deepened when the long, echoey, growling noise came from the fire hydrant. Buddy looked at the hydrant, and backed away. The cap on the nozzle, where the firemen attached the hose, was turning. It was turning, squeaking, all by itself. It was turning outward on its threads. Suddenly it popped off, making Buddy jump. The metal cap bounced on the pavement and rolled in a circle, heading for the gutter. Buddy followed it with his eyes, his mouth drooping in amazement. When he looked back at the fire hydrant, something was leaking out around the edges of it—something that wasn't water. It was a red foam. A thick, gooey red foam. He stared, and moved back even farther when the red foam burst out, spattering the sidewalk in a way he didn't like. It was followed almost immediately by a surge of clear water, scattering the red foam and jetting over the sidewalk and curb, causing heads to turn on stoops down the street. It occurred to Buddy, then, that he had never seen a hydrant opened on his block; he'd seen them open on Paco's block, children playing in the gush, their parents looking on, shouting at them in good humor. Here, most of the adults wouldn't approve.

He might get in trouble for this. And anyway, he didn't want to play in the water, now. Not after seeing the red foam.

He turned and ran up into Everett's building, and nearly collided with Everett, who was coming out the lobby door. Everett's expression was the same dour mask, but now his eyes were hot and his cheeks feverish red. "Did you see?" he asked, "it is coming out, is it not?"

Buddy nodded, regarding Everett with a kind of awe. "How—uh—how did you do it inside the building?"

"The Blessed People."

"What?"

"Nothing. I mean: the basement. There is a special control in the basement. It is in the sub-basement."

"You have a sub-basement here? My Dad—um—he's a building super. He knows all about that. We used to have a sub-basement, but it's sealed off. He says they don't use them anymore."

"No one uses this one. It is empty. Part of it is dirt. There used to be a coal bin there. The elevator does not go down there for other people. It goes down there for me."

Buddy was caught up in the excitement. "You have a way to open hydrants from basements?"

"Do you want to, see this? Do you want to go down?"

"Yes-I-do-want-to-go-down-thank-you-very-much," said Buddy in a parody of Everett's funny way of talking. It would have made Paco and Larry laugh, and it should have made Everett angry, but he didn't seem to notice it.

"Come with me, Buddy."

Buddy hesitated for just an instant. He had the cold, tight feeling in his stomach again. The feeling he'd had when he saw the icky stuff come out of the fire hydrant. *What was that stuff?*

Rusty water, probably.

He followed Everett to the elevator. Everett was already waiting inside, his hand on the *Door Open* button. Buddy hesitated again. Everett had a look about him like an outlaw Buddy had seen on a *Bonanza* rerun. The outlaw had crouched alongside the trail waiting for Little Joe, his hands tight on a rope connected to a noose that was supposed to close up around Little Joe's legs and pull him down. The outlaw had waited, hands poised...

"Come on in, Buddy. I will show you and you can show the other kids next summer."

Buddy shook himself, and felt the excitement returning. This was something *different*. It was exploring a sub-basement. The sub-basement was probably off bounds to kids. It was, therefore, an adventure.

He giggled as he stepped into the elevator. But he cut the giggle short—because Everett didn't giggle with him. He just looked back at him as the elevator doors closed and they sank into the earth.

The light in the elevator flickered, and went out.

"Uhh!" Buddy heard himself shout. "Hey, it's—" That cold tightness was back in his stomach. The air seemed very close. And what was Everett doing, in his corner of the elevator, in the dark? "Ev—hey, Everett, the light!"

But he fell silent, startled, as the elevator doors opened and a rectangle of red light expanded in the darkness in front of him.

"It is all right. There is a light down here, you see, Buddy," said Everett.

Everett sounded like an adult, patiently explaining everything. It irritated Buddy.

Everett stepped out of the elevator, into a small gray-walled room. The red light came from a lamp with a brass shade-frame, though the shade itself was missing. The lamp sat precariously on the uneven dirt floor like the leaning tower of Pisa. It was probably Everett's lamp.

Stepping into the sub-basement, Buddy was surprised to find that it was hot there. But no furnace. Why should it be hot? The heat and the red light seemed to go together.

The lamp was near the middle of the little room, its plug wire running up to an outlet in the side of an empty ceramic light fixture screwed to a wooden rafter on the low ceiling. An adult would have had to stoop here. There was just enough light so that he could see the knot of hungry darkness in a spiderweb on the rafters, without being able to make out the spider clearly. The web looked red.

In the right-hand rear corner was a sort of low wooden corral, and after a moment he realized that it had once held coal.

A distant rumble was building up, becoming a rattling roar that brought sweat out on his forehead. He knew it was a subway train, somewhere nearby, underground. But knowing that didn't seem to help. It scared him anyway. He was glad when it died down.

Just the uptown subway, he told himself.

There was one wooden post in the middle of the room, held to the rafters by rusty square-edged nails. The rafters were two-by-fours, running diagonally across the concrete ceiling, penetrating the walls. The back wall was old, black brick. He had never seen a cellar so old before. He felt like he wasn't alive in his own time anymore. He'd gone to the sort of world where people hid in cellars like this, to avoid being caught. And never came out, because they were afraid. Died there, in the darkness, hiding.

He wanted to leave.

But Everett was watching him intently. Everett stood by the short wooden fence in the corner, the left half of his face in shadow, the right half, in the red light, showing up the diamond-shaped birthmark as if it had been drawn there just now in crayon. Like war paint.

Buddy moved closer to the lamp, squinting into the corners. He picked up the lamp by its squat wooden base; it was slippery in the perspiration of his fingers. He heard himself panting. Was it just him? He heard other panting sounds. Maybe coming from Everett.

Buddy carried the lamp, stretched out in front of him, to look at the walls, trying to find the metal wheel or whatever it was that Everett had used to open the hydrant from down here. He wanted to find it all by himself. He didn't want Everett to think he was the smarter one.

He didn't see any wheels. No pipes—except an upright one, with nothing like a wheel on it, in the left-hand rear corner. But at the base of that pipe was a cracked wooden crate containing three broken bottles. The bottles were empty, and they had yellowed, peeling labels with Xs across them. Buddy laughed. His voice sounded faint in the room. "Hey, Everett, you know what I think they used this room for, really? You know what bootleggers was?"

Everett didn't say anything. He was standing outside the ring of wavery pink light cast by the lamp. He made no move to come into the light. He was just a shadow.

Why didn't he come into the light? Anybody else would've come into the light.

Buddy walked toward Everett, holding the lamp high, holding it like a red-hot sword between him and Everett. The light in Buddy's shaking hand rotated the dark places like a kaleidoscope without color. No color but red and black. The shadows squirmed away like dirty thoughts.

Now Everett was full in the light of the red bulb, like an actor in a spotlight. His shadow flickered back and forth behind him with the wavering of Buddy's arm; the shadow split into two which seemed to open and close like great black flapping wings attached to Everett's shoulders. Someone had scribbled strangely on the wall behind him. Buddy was standing just three feet from Everett now, near the wooden rail in the corner. Something made a low, coughing sound from the floor inside the wooden enclosure. Buddy looked down. "*What?*" (That was Buddy's voice, but he didn't know it.)

There were two small heads on the floor, looking up at him with three tiny animal eyes. They had dirty brown fur on them. Just heads with pointy ears and no bodies, muzzles open, white tongues lolling, panting, panting. The gums of the tiny mouths were cracked and dry. They were the heads of small dogs. Pekingese dogs. He guessed with a sick feeling that they were Mr. Gribner's dogs. Buddy had seen Mr. Gribner walk them many times. They were buried up to their necks in the dirt floor, close together. Close enough so that they could chew one another in the frenzy of entrapment. One of the dogs was missing an eye; the other had chewed it out.

It was the ugliest thing Buddy had ever seen. But he saw something uglier a moment later, when he looked at Everett: Everett's smile.

Buddy realized with a small shock that he had never seen Everett smile before. Everett was smiling as he looked at the dogs. He had one hand in his trousers.

"Get them *out!*" Buddy said. He looked away from the dogs. "Let them *out* of there!" His voice was shrill.

"You want to know how I opened the hydrant, Buddy? I know you want to know." He took his hand from his trousers. His smile had gone away. He held something green and gleaming up in the red light. It was a tiny head carved of green stone, no bigger than a walnut. "The Head Underneath does favors for me. He opened the hydrant. I speak to him with this. I hear him between walls. A man gave this to me. He was watching me at school. He said, 'You will be a good one. You will be just right. You are going to have a friend come and live with you.' Then he gave me this."

"*Let them go!*" Buddy's voice was going out of control, like a little man made out of *scared* was inside him, shouting out through him. His mouth felt dry; he felt he was buried alive. He felt what the dogs must be feeling. It was so hot.

Everett just watched him. Buddy burst into tears.

Buddy dropped the lamp and, waves of tension shaking through him as he cried, dug under the dog's heads with his fingers. The dirt was dry, and hard-packed, and the dogs snapped at his hands. As he bent over them, one of them gave a wheezing sound, barked three times rapidly—and its head lolled to one side. It was dead. The other one began to bark—Buddy could hear, in the dog's weak rasp, its desperation, its last strength going, the dryness in its throat. He suspected that Everett had done something more than just bury them. As he dug into the earth, he came to a layer soaked with blood, and knew that Everett had cut the little dogs open.

Face sticky with tears and sweat, feeling buried himself, Buddy got to his feet and looked around for Everett. Everett was gone.

Feeling the room squeezing itself smaller and smaller around him (and knowing he was imagining it didn't help—somehow be was sure that imagining a bad thing strongly enough could make it happen), he ran to the elevator doors. The doors were closed. He couldn't find a button to press. He pounded repeatedly on the doors. He shouted "Everett!" And "*Everett!*"

He was quiet then He was very quiet, listening.

A nasty growl was coming from inside the elevator. It didn't sound like Everett. And then he heard Everett's voice, distantly. He couldn't be certain, but he thought Everett said: "*If I give him to you, will you let me come with you?*"

"Everett!" Buddy shouted. Somehow he was sure that Everett was keeping the elevator door shut.

Everett spoke again, and this time Buddy heard him clearly. "*Will you let me come with you?*"

There was another, lower, nastier growling in reply.

It came from the cellar. It came from behind Buddy.

The one dog that was alive began a frantic yapping. Convulsively, clapping his hands over his mouth, Buddy turned to look. He could see over the railing, to the right of the glowing red bulb, into the coal bin. One of the dogs was missing its head. Blood oozed from a hole in the ground. Buddy could see nothing else in the wooden square, except a dust-devil. It was just a wind, a wind that was kicking up coal-dust and dirt around the head of the remaining dog. But as he watched, that head vanished, as if it were a vegetable plucked from the ground by an invisible hand, then hidden within an invisible fist. A second hole spouted wet red.

The air quivered and waves of tingly heat came over him from that corner. He closed his eyes, tightly.

He saw it behind his eyes.

It was as if closing his eyes had opened a dark window. Through that gap in the world he saw something like the twisty reflection you could see of things in a glossy coat of black paint. The shape came closer, and he could see it more clearly. It was an animal made of red sparklers. That's the way it looked to Buddy. Like Fourth of July sparklers, sizzling, but very thick in its sparking, and bent into the bristling shape of a four-footed animal…made all of red outlines…He couldn't make out its shape perfectly…its shape wobbled and changed…but he knew that it was making the heat. He knew that it was the servant of the Head Underneath. And he knew that it had eaten the heads of the dogs. And he knew that it was hungry still.

FIVE

"Maguss?" The name felt funny in his mouth.

"That you, Lanyard? I'm waiting for your—"

"I sent it by express. This isn't a very good connection."

"What?"

"There's an example. I said, speak up." Voices gibbered in the background, voices made of sparkling and static crackle. Lanyard was afraid to listen to them.

"Well, what is it you want?" Maguss was shouting, but the voice came across hollow and distant.

"I've moved," Lanyard said. "I'm living at 507 East Sixth Street, apartment 5R. You got that? It's a sublet. Madelaine got it for me, through a friend of hers. I got sick of the Hilton."

"Repeat that address again. Can't hear." Indeed, the static was a blizzard. "Had three other calls to New York. They all sounded bad."

Lanyard repeated the address, and gave his phone number. And hung up without saying good-bye.

He sat on the couch, trying to orient himself. He was in someone else's apartment, someone he'd never met. Madelaine had arranged the sublet for him; the leaseholder, a woman named Melissa Wickett, was close to Madelaine and trusted her. Melissa had gone to Europe for a few months.

He glanced at the typewriter set up on the wooden table between the two living-room windows. The windows were dim with the thickening dusk. He had decided to write a book about his part in the investigation. And naturally he wasn't going to tell Maguss about the book. It was Lanyard's chance to break into another kind of journalism. Supposing, that is, he uncovered something conclusive. He took a notebook from the typewriter table and, returning to the couch, opened it on his lap. He was keeping a journal, as background for the book. He took a pen from his shirt pocket and wrote, in his neat, squarish hand:

I'm sitting in a stranger's apartment, in a neighborhood strange to me, in a very strange city, caught up in events strange to anyone. I'm part of a police investigation. Strange. I suspect Gribner's losing interest in keeping me on as part of the investigating team.

The apartment's shabby, but comfortable. The roaches are only occasional visitors. It feels funny to sit on a couch someone else picked out, to sleep in their bed, eat off their dishes with their silverware. I've been drinking some of her liquor. I have permission for all this, but it feels odd and intrusive all the same. Parquet floor. The walls are off-white. Way off. The only heat will come from a radiator. But this freakish weather makes the radiator unnecessary. The temperature has gone down today. It's still unnaturally warm, though. It's not like the usual Indian Summer, either, I'm told... The bathroom is miniature, the water pressure's almost nonexistent. And this morning (I moved into the apartment last night) when I turned the spigot and held my hands under, I got a handful of rusty foam! I'm drinking from a bottle of distilled water, now. The—

The phone rang. Lanyard put the receiver to his ear.

"Lanyard?" Lanyard winced: The voice was Gribner's.

"Yes. Uh—listen, Gribner, I can't—I have an appointment this evening—"

Gribner didn't seem to have heard. "Lanyard—uh—there's something I want to show you. It is worse than the others. There was no—ah—pentagram, but there were signs on the wall—the same sort—not much left of the kid. My dogs. The kid."

"What the hell's the matter with you, Gribner? You're not very coherent."

"It was in my building, Lanyard. My building!"

"Don't shout into the phone. Okay, I'll come and have a look."

"My nephew's gone. I was down in the basement looking for him. I had to break the lock on the elevator-control box to get down there. I don't know how he got down there. To the sub-basement. It's just a coal cellar. He disappeared yesterday. He left the jade head. I want you to look at that, Lanyard. I want you to—"

"All right, all right!"

"You got a pencil? Here's the address. You come to—"

Lanyard wrote down the address, hung up, and went to the door, cursing through it all.

"I HAD TO sell the cameras today. Well, I hocked 'em," Billy Krupp said. He was in one of those antiquated wooden phone booths, against the back wall in a bar so old-fashioned it had sawdust on the floor and a mildewed painting of a topless girl over the rows of bottles. There was someone in the booth adjacent; he could hear the man moving. He waited for his brother Reggie to say something. Preferably something like, "Hey, no problem—I can front you a little cash till you get another film in the can."

But Reggie only said, "Jeez. Thas a bummer. Lissen, I gotta go. Someuh these guys, they wait till they see I'm on the phone, then they try'n rip me off for stroke books, you know?"

And he hung up.

Krupp slammed the receiver into its cradle. He sat for a moment, despondent, on the little metal stool in the phone booth, staring at the urine-soaked newspapers on the floor. Absentmindedly, he read the headline: INFLATION SOARS.

"Yeah, tell me about it," Krupp muttered. He'd spent twenty minutes detailing his financial horrors to Reggie, who had listened almost silently, now and then mumbling ,"Jeez," and popping his gum in the mouthpiece.

"Fuck him," Krupp said more loudly. "Not like he hasn't made any money off my fuck-flicks."

Krupp pushed free of the phone booth and shuffled, with exaggerated pathos, toward the bar to spend his last twenty dollars.

Billy Krupp was the subject of a photo portrait, part of a series by a photographer who specialized in snapping the Times Square area. The black-and-white—Billy Krupp had never seen it, didn't know it now hung in a well-appointed SoHo photo gallery—was titled The Pornographer. It showed Billy Krupp very characteristically: in motion, leaning toward the bed over which the 16-millimeter movie camera brooded like a dour mechanical bird, obscuring all but the feet and ankles of the man and woman on the bed. Krupp's stubby arms were outstretched; he was bent at the waist, emphasizing the roll of fat overlapping his belt; he wore sweat-stained checked polyester shirt and high-water corduroy bellbottoms. His blond toupee, which didn't closely match the rest of his hair, was slightly askew on his head; his dandruff-flecked extra round glasses were low on a nose that was like the head of a ball-peen hammer. His jowly face was patched with missed whiskers. His mouth was open as he rasped directions—"No, pull it out when you cum so it shoots on her—"

Now he looked very much the same, dressed similarly, arms outstretched, leaning forward, mouth open, as he tried to get the bartender's attention. "Whiskey sour," he said. The bartender didn't hear: He was watching baseball on a ghosting color TV over the bar, "Whiskey *sour!*"

The bartender grunted and mixed the drink. "Shit-ass Dodgers," he said, slapping the drink down so hard a fourth of it sloshed onto the bar.

"Hey you're costing me money," Krupp said, reluctantly passing over his twenty.

He watched closely as the bartender made change.

There were only two other customers. He took note of them. An old woman whose tipsiness and toothlessness made her impossible to understand. The man beside her, middle-aged, face blank with TV-absorption as he watched the ball game, nodded now and then as if he understood the yammering old woman. They seemed harmless. Krupp kept an eye on the door. He still had twelve hours to come up with the eight hundred dollars he owed Ponti, but the bookie might've sent some muscle to *remind* poor forgetful Billy Krupp. Krupp hoped to avoid that. He watched the door, as his mind checked off the possibilities.

He couldn't borrow money from Eunice. He'd squirmed out of paying alimony. She could afford to loan the money, but she'd say, "Nope—it's a mattuh of *princ*-ih-pull."

His old man might muster a hundred. But it wasn't likely.

And Krupp needed eight hundred dollars. For starts.

He might get two hundred dollars for the car, but—

He flinched as someone sat down beside him. There were four empty stools to either side of Krupp. The guy wouldn't have sat beside Krupp, a complete stranger, unless he wanted something from him. Either he was a grifter of some kind or Ponti had sent him. But the guy was small. Nearly a midget. Little bald guy. Wisps of hair around his ears, not much more. Nice suit. Gold watch. Lots of rings. Didn't look like costume jewelry.

Cellars

"Your name's Billy, isn't it?" Friendly voice. But a voice with purpose in it. Krupp decided to be polite. "Yeah. Billy. Uh…" He shrugged. "We met?"

"Not directly." The little man smiled. "To be perfectly honest—and I'm always perfectly honest—I heard your conversation with your friend Reggie in the phone booth. I was in the next booth, trying to find a phone number in one of my pockets. Never found it. Maybe I found something more important: a business associate. You."

He smiled like an insurance salesman.

"Yeah?" Krupp smiled cautiously back. "What makes you think—"

"Hey, this is silly," said the little man. "I haven't introduced myself. I'm George Tooley."

They shook hands. Tooley's hands felt dry, feverishly hot.

He no longer seemed so small. His gray eyes seemed to grow. Krupp found it difficult to look away from those eyes. They were the color of a bank vault. As the little man talked in low measured, mellifluous tones, something in his voice hinting *Big Opportunity* and *Gain* and *Don't Blow This One*, he seemed to grow, in Billy Krupp's perspective. Not physically—not exactly. But, though he was half a foot shorter than Krupp, he somehow seemed to be gazing beatifically down on him from a height.

"Money is funny stuff," Tooley was saying. "It's sort of like ice cream. You can crank it like homemade ice cream and fluff it up and make it more. Or you can store it. But you got to be careful how you keep it—you don't keep it in the right place, it melts."

"Boy, it sure melts all right," Krupp said. In some part of him, a warning bell was rattling, like a burglar alarm heard in the distance. It was the internal alarm that warned him when something looked too good. But there was something so deeply *reassuring* about Tooley.

"And money is like something else. It's a form of energy, Billy. It's a hard thing to explain. But if you learn the right way to handle money, why you can make it come back to you on a circuit just like with electricity. You can use people for transistors to make it a stronger current. But you got to plug into the right places. You know what I mean?"

"Sure, you bet," said Billy Krupp, in utter dishonesty.

"Now, my organization is looking for someone to channel some of that energy into. You pick the right guy—well, you put money into him, you get

69

good money—good current—right back from him. If everything's done right. I think you might just be one of those guys. The *right* guy. It's funny how we just sort of stumble across them, now and then."

Krupp nodded numbly, fascinated.

"Did you ever wonder..." Tooley went on, slowly, philosophically, "how they do it? The guys with a knack for making the big dough I mean. You wonder—is it smarts? Or is it something else? Like maybe they're just the lucky types...."

"Yeah. That's the way I figured it. Some guys just sort of walk into it. They're the lucky types. Not many of them. But they're around, all right. Sure."

"You're right. There are guys who are just...lucky. Only, there's a trick to it. Of course. See, the guys who are lucky *had to learn how.*" Tooley paused dramatically, as the bartender finally came and took his order. He asked for a piña colada.

Krupp waited impatiently, trying not to seem eager.

Tooley smiled, toying with a swizzle stick, waiting for his drink, glancing at his watch, watching the bartender as if to be certain the drink was mixed properly.

The bartender brought the drink over but didn't ask for the money then and there. He wrote the amount on a bill. This irritated Krupp: The bartender had waited till Krupp had paid before handing over the whiskey sour.

Krupp cleared his throat. "You say—uh—the lucky guys weren't always—uh—"

"Prosperity luck is a form of energy. Because, like I said, money is part of an energy flow. It's society's blood flow, is money. Anyway—say you want to pick up another kind of energy, radio signals. What do you do?" He smiled inquisitively.

"Uh—you buy a radio."

Tooley chuckled. "I mean, suppose there isn't one to buy. You build a radio. You want to pick up that radio signal, you got to have the right equipment, work according to the right diagrams. Same with picking up prosperity luck: Got to have the right equipment, work with the right diagrams. You got to work for the right people. For the right *power.*"

Krupp was beginning to get the drift.

Tooley put his hand to his throat and drew a gold coke spoon into sight. A gold coke spoon on a gold chain.

"Who—uh—" Krupp began. He brought his glass to his lips—his throat was suddenly like an old boot—but the glass was empty.

"Bartender!" Tooley called cheerfully. "Another drink for this gentleman." The bartender seemed startled at this description of Krupp, but he brought a whiskey sour.

"Who," Krupp began again, "would I be working for, exactly? I mean—I have the impression you're offering me a job."

"In a way. I'm offering you a *chance*."

"Let me put it this way: Suppose I agree to learn whatever it is that brings this prosperity luck. What do I do for you? I mean, what's your—uh—percentage?"

"It's very simple. You'll be one of us. The more of us there are, the stronger we are. You'll understand later. After the initiation."

"Initiation?

Krupp began to wonder if he were being shucked into a Moonie cult. Or Jesus people. Moonies with coke spoons? Jesus people offering material wealth? "How do I—uh—how much do I have to *invest*?"

"Not a penny. Nothing to sign. No organization to pay dues to. It's not a religious cult, if that's what you're thinking. It's not a con scam. It's that rarest of pearls: genuine opportunity."

"You don't get something for nothin', friend," said Krupp. But this show of skepticism was only a kind of prod to induce elaboration from Tooley. Krupp had already accepted Tooley's word. You could tell when a fellow was bullshitting. Tooley wasn't.

"No, you don't get something for nothing," said Tooley, nodding approval of Krupp's perspicacity. "There's something you have to do. No expense to yourself. You simply have to lay out the luck—on the energy diagrams. And we'll show you how. Because the more people we help, the more we're helped by it. That's just the way it works. Ready to go?"

He said it as if his going were a given.

Krupp heard himself say, "I'm in."

Tooley silently paid his tab, tipped the bartender handsomely, and preceded Krupp to the door. Outside, the street was alive with wind. Whirlwinds sucked newspapers and plastic cups high overhead. There was an edge of damp-cold in the gusting; the sky glowered with clouds.

Krupp looked around in surprise. "Looks like the heat's done with. That crazy heat. Just like that, whammo, we got windstorms."

"The heat will come back," said Tooley, opening the passenger side of a blue Mercedes for Krupp. Krupp got in, admiring the leather seats, the inlaid wood around the speedometer, the smell of newness. Tooley got in and started the car. "How much do you suppose this little beaut cost me, Billy?"

"I hate to think!" Krupp tilted his head to one side and twisted his lips. "Um—thirty thou, thereabouts?"

Tooley shook his head. "Oh, it's worth more than that, easy. It cost me twelve hundred bucks. Friend of mine had to get rid of it. Tax problems. Needed to undersell it. I lucked into the deal."

"Lucked into it…" Krupp repeated dully.

They drove past Times Square. A black guy on the corner was trying to sell shish kebab from a portable grill. The wind stirred his coals and spattered his shirtfront with grease from the spit-roasting meat; stung, he leapt back, and Krupp could read his lips: "*Shit motherfucker!*" Krupp chuckled. Tooley pressed a button on the dashboard. Muzak soothed from a hidden speaker. A version of the Beatles song "Baby You're a Rich Man." Krupp nodded his head in rhythm. Hookers cruised the sidewalk nearby; Krupp eyed them professionally, thinking about hiring a few for some shooting once he got a grubstake together. Maybe he could go up to 35-millimeter. Class. Get reviewed in *Screw* magazine.

Krupp was distantly aware that he felt—well, *different*.

Like that time they'd given him Demerol in the hospital. Like everything was smooth going, everything was amusing. And he knew, dimly, that his sense of well-being was connected with Tooley. So he didn't ask Tooley where they were going. It just didn't seem right to ask too many prying questions. He tried not to seem as if he were listening in, when Tooley opened a panel on the underside of the dashboard, extracted a telephone, and made a call: "This is Tooley. We're going to want the Direct Line at Second Avenue and Houston. Two-thirty. Get it there sharp. And monitor the other trains this time, we don't want any more foul-ups....Don't worry about those, we're keeping them contained. Yeah. Beautiful. Later."

Tooley hung up, glanced at his gold watch, and drove peacefully on.

Krupp slid into a contented reverie, visualizing the parties in his honor at Plato's Retreat and the Valencia Hotel when his Big One grossed more long green than *Talk Dirty To Me.*

Tooley hummed along with the Muzak.

It seemed only a moment later, but it must have been at least twenty minutes, when Tooley pulled up in front of a delicatessen at the corner of Second Avenue and Houston.

Tooley opened the passenger door for Krupp. The wind burst into the car, bringing tears to Krupp's eyes, making him feel he'd just awakened from a pleasant dream into the cold necessity of a day's work. "Billy…" Tooley said. "Coming?"

"Hm? Oh…sure!" Krupp climbed from the car. Tooley shut the door and locked it.

A couple of tramps shuffled toward them, to beg for money—and stopped, at the same instant. Krupp looked at them, puzzled. The tramps were looking at Tooley, and muttering to one another. They backed away. Krupp glanced at Tooley. Tooley was walking toward a subway entrance; he seemed amiable enough. He wasn't waving a gun or anything. So why did the tramps back away like that?

Krupp caught up with Tooley halfway down the subway stairs. "Boy, that's some wind," Krupp said.

Tooley only nodded.

"We—uh—taking the subway to avoid traffic?" Krupp asked.

Tooley glanced at him. "You might say that. We're taking the Direct Line."

"That's a new wrinkle for me."

"You might say it's a *private* subway train."

"What? Are you kidding?"

Tooley took two subway tokens from his coat pocket and gave Krupp one. They went side by side through the token turnstiles and down grimy concrete steps to the platform. The platform was empty, here on the downtown side, except for overflowing trash bins and the graffiti that seemed to squirm restlessly when glimpsed from the corner of the eye. To Krupp the station seemed like a big garage that stretched on and on, measured with metal support beams. The wind soughed even here, intruding through some ventilation shaft. Krupp fought down a chill.

Tooley glanced at his watch.

Krupp stood beside him, thinking muzzily: *Maybe the guy's crazy. Hallucinating. No such thing as a private subway line.*

The objection was faint; and it was washed away in Krupp's growing sense of destiny. He felt like a piece of paper sucked through the air after a passing car, following down the street because it was caught in the car's air current.

Two bright lights glared from the right, deep in the shadow-face of the subway tunnel. Tooley looked again at his watch. He nodded. "There she is." He turned to smile reassuringly at Krupp, holding his wrist under Krupp's nose. "You see this? Rolex. How much you think that cost me?"

"Well, I…" Krupp was too logy to think about it.

The train shot into the station, swaying a little, sparks jumping under the massive metal wheels. The station boomed with its entry.

It was moving fast; Krupp was sure it wasn't going to stop. It was one of the old trains, out of service, layers of half-scraped spray paint making its metal hide piebald. "This one won't be stoppin'," Krupp shouted over the roar.

Tooley ignored him. The train made squealing, grinding noises and slowed. It stopped after pulling its tail alongside them. The doors of the last car opened. Only the doors of that car. The windows of the car were closed, and every one was opaqued by black paint. Krupp stepped into the car after Tooley, feeling like a burglar.

The doors slid closed behind them.

"It's like one of those old-fashioned railway cars…like the tycoons had, a private…" Krupp mumbled, looking around dazedly. How was it possible? The Transit Authority would never permit this.

He was standing on a thick red pile rug. Looked like real wool.

The original seats had been pulled. The straphanger's handholds had been stripped away. The ad racks were gone. The dark-paneled walls were lined with long, low, black plush velvet couches bolted to the floor. Small chandeliers swung pendulously overhead, tinkling, as the train lurched onward. Over the growing rattlebang, Tooley said, "Would you like a drink?"

Krupp nodded numbly. He sank onto a couch. It was soft.

Tooley went carefully—walking like a sailor, adjusting to the floor's shaking, the tilting and inertia when they took turns—to a wooden cabinet. Inside were rows of bottles, good booze, Krupp noted, in wooden racks, rattling with the motion. Despite the jerky ride, Tooley performed an almost acrobatic feat of drink-mixing. Without spilling a drop he brought Krupp a whiskey sour, and sat down beside him, sipping his own martini from a crystal glass.

Once again, Krupp began to feel dreamy, logy, sedated. And again time collapsed on itself, so that it seemed but a breath later—though he'd drunk his glass dry—that the train ground to a halt. "This way, Billy," said Tooley, as the doors slid open.

They stepped out onto a darkened subway platform. Krupp swayed in the dimness. The train's doors hissed shut and it rumbled away down the tunnel. Now the only light was from a single red light bulb in what was clearly an abandoned token booth. The light spilled tenuously across spiderwebbed turnstiles, tinting the platform the color of diluted blood.

Krupp realized he was still holding the whiskey sour glass. He set it on a bench. Something scurried away under the bench as he set the glass down. "Mouse," Krupp muttered, straightening. He squinted through the shadows at the walls. The street sign that should have identified the platform was painted out, consistently, everywhere. There were metal gates blocking the exits to the street. The station was entirely abandoned. "Whudduhfuck?" Krupp said groggily.

"Over here, Billy," said Tooley.

Krupp turned to look. Tooley was standing between the turnstiles, silhouetted against the red light from the token booth. Krupp moved toward him. "Tooley...?" Tooley must have a key to the street exit's gates. Krupp started to push past him through the out turnstile.

"Krupp," Tooley said. A single warning syllable.

Krupp froze. "Ah—uh-huh?"

"Not that way. Stick close by me." Tooley turned and began to walk down the platform, into the darkness.

Krupp picked his way nervously through the darkness. The shadows thickened around him. His foot struck a beer bottle and he stumbled. He recovered, cursing.

He caught up with Tooley. His eyes adjusted gradually to the darkness; he could see the girders and benches and the edge of the platform as gray outlines.

They reached the end of the platform. Blank tile walls. No place left to go. Tooley must have gone the wrong way.

And then he saw that Tooley was descending metal rungs, down to the bed of the train tracks.

Forty years in New York had habituated Krupp to staying well clear of the tracks. He pictured getting caught on the tracks as a train roared down on him. He pictured tripping and falling against the third rail and shaking to death in electrocution. He pictured stumbling and breaking his leg, set upon by swarms of rats....

Numbly, he followed Tooley down the rungs and along the track bed.

He was startled when Tooley switched on a small flashlight. It was a wan illumination, just enough for Krupp to make out the strip of water between the tracks, the muddy gravel, the tail of a rat disappearing into a hole in the concrete. The tracks looked very old, their supports half-rotted, so that Krupp thought: *We ride the trains over those every day? They don't look like they'd last a week.*

They walked along a moraine of gravel near the left-hand wall. Now and then Krupp glanced apprehensively at the third rail. It looked dark, dead. All that power rushing through that dark, dead metal. You just never knew by looking at a thing what was really in it. Like the streets and that deserted station.

Krupp stopped walking to listen.

There was a slow thunder building up behind.

"Tooley...there's a train coming."

Tooley said nothing. He maintained his measured pace, picking his way calmly but carefully, his pocket flashlight swinging at the end of his arm like the lamp of a brakeman.

"Tooley..." Krupp realized that he was whispering. He wondered why.

The roar was building.

Krupp glanced over his shoulder. Far down the tunnel, two white eyes glared and grew.

He turned back to Tooley. But Tooley was gone. The flashlight's beam was gone. There was darkness ahead and darkness behind—except for the lights of the approaching train. He could sense the train vibrating the tracks, though it was still far down the tunnel.

"Jeez," Krupp muttered. But he didn't feel half as frightened as he should have. He felt like lying down and—

"Krupp!" Tooley's voice. "What are you doing, my friend? Come on!"

Tooley was standing by a niche in the wall. He'd stepped into it when Krupp was looking away.

Krupp hurried to the niche and, following Tooley, stepped inside. It was a narrow passage half blocked by utility pipes, dripping with water, redolent of rust. Tooley sidled by the pipes; Krupp followed.

Tooley bent over a metal box, opening its padlock with a key from his key ring. The lock popped open just as the train roared by behind. The suction of the train's passage pulled at Krupp's coattail.

When the train had passed, Tooley handed Krupp a pair of gray overalls taken from the metal box. "Slip these on over your clothes. Keep you neat. And these…." A pair of gardener's gloves.

There were other things in the metal box, but Krupp couldn't make them out. Tooley relocked the box, and set his flashlight, pointing at them, on a brace. They each climbed into a pair of overalls, drew on the gloves, and, Tooley leading, climbed rusty metal rungs up a damp concrete wall over the box.

Krupp's heart was pounding. They were ascending into warmth. Sticky, itchy warmth. There was a light growing up ahead. The light was sulfur yellow and came from a rectangular gap, the opening of a horizontal shaft about three by four feet. Tooley climbed unhesitatingly into the passage; Krupp followed. They had to travel for about ten feet on their hands and knees. Krupp heard things scratching in the dark cracks of the concrete walls around him. He felt sweat trickling along his spine, making a swamp of his underarms. But with every inch he moved closer to the source of the light; and the closer he drew to the light, the more the sweet excitement grew in him. It wasn't like the excitement that came with stimulants, it was the excitement that came with drunken abandon, or with too many tranquilizers. And somehow he felt he was coming home.

They reached the end of the horizontal passage and emerged into a circular chamber; a heavy vertical iron pipe thick as three men together was clamped to the wall to their right. The chamber had no discernible ceiling. The huge pipe sank into the metal floor; in the room's center was a trapdoor.

Something moved toward them on hands and knees.

It was a tramp, getting to his feet, shaky, blinking in the light from the portable lamp clamped to a pipe brace overhead—a sulfurous-yellow lamp, not something the city maintenance men would have left here. The thick black cord for the lamp led into a passage half seen behind the huge pipe. "Say—uh—yo, par'ner," said the old man.

He was a classic Bowery bum. He was missing a shoe, his bare right foot was caked with grime, toenails bloody; his left eye was puffed purple, infected; the lower half of his face was lost in a mass of white whiskers stained yellow from food and nicotine; the whites of his eyes weren't—they were yellow; his clothing was a shapeless tumble. He was having trouble staying on his feet, and he coughed before every word. "Say, I dunno—uh—I don' mean nobody probl'ms. They—uh—"

"I told you people to stay out of here, didn't I." It wasn't a question. There was a metallic sharpness in Tooley's tone that Krupp hadn't heard before.

"Nobud' tole me—"

"I put the word out on the street. Everyone was told. No one is to go underground this winter."

Krupp looked at Tooley with surprise. Traditionally, New York tramps took refuge from the winter cold in the utility tunnels and sewage vaults and abandoned subway stations under the city. How could Tooley possibly keep them all from the places under the streets? And why would he want to try? "What—uh—" Krupp began. He cleared his throat. "What difference does it make if they—"

"It provokes the Stalker, and we don't want it prematurely excited," Tooley said casually. To the tramp he said, "You were warned. You wait here."

Tooley nodded to Krupp and led him to the door beyond the pipe. The tramp stumbled out of their way. As they stepped into the passage, Tooley stopped. He took a blindfold from his pocket and a roll of adhesive. "You'll have to be blindfolded after this."

He offered the blindfold.

Krupp took it. His hand was shaking. He raised the cloth to his eyes, and then hesitated. It was black silk. He lowered the cloth and glanced at the tramp.

The tramp was doing a strange kind of dance.

He was staggering back and forth, clawing at himself. He moved as if he'd stumbled into a swarm of bees, invisible insects darting at him, stinging viciously. Probably the old man was having some kind of fit. DTs.

78

But the tramp's screams expressed pure terror. They were the sounds a mouse makes as it's being swallowed whole by a snake—the same sounds, but amplified monstrously. The chamber echoed with the shrieking.

And there was blood leaking from the old man's trouser cuffs. And from his sleeves, from the gouge that—as Krupp watched—just *appeared* on the side of his face. The wounds weren't self-inflicted. Krupp was sure of that, because he could see more wounds ripping open as he watched. Strips of the tramp's throat were raked away, as if he were unraveling.

The old man wasn't alone on the round black metal floor. Krupp closed his eyes, to shut out the scene.

That's when he saw it. A creature made of nasty blurs like—

Krupp remembered a bestiality film he'd done two years earlier. He'd finally found a woman willing to be fucked by Bernie's trained wolfhound—and the damn editing machine had caught fire inside, a short in the wiring, and damaged the film. When he'd looked at the film on the screen, the image of the hound had been twisted up by the heat, warped and reddened and as nasty-looking. *That's* what this creature looked like...this creature glimpsed on the back of his eyelids.

He opened his eyes and saw the tramp flung backward, as if struck in the chest by an unseen two-by-four; he bounced off the wall and fell face down. And then his limp body was dragged by nothing, by nothing at all, toward the other entrance.

In a moment the room was empty and silent and nothing remained of the tramp's strange dance except the splash of blood on the black metal floor.

Krupp stared. His mind tried to click with an idea, and then backed away from it, and then tried to close with it again, and then retreated. A sort of mental record-scratch-repeat, never quite coming to the conclusion.

He wasn't aware that he was shaking and crying until both the shaking and crying came to a sudden halt. All of the fear and tension drained out of him, almost in one instant, when Tooley touched his arm. That's when Krupp understood.

He understood several things. He realized that his sensations—sweet excitement, sedation, acceptance—flowed out of Tooley, somehow. Out of Tooley personally; from his presence, his voice, his touch.

And he realized that Tooley was magic.

He understood, too, that what had happened to the tramp was appropriate and inevitable. Tramps were bad luck personified. Tooley was good luck personified. The tramp had disobeyed Tooley, who commanded the power of good luck; Tooley had sucked all the good luck out of the tramp, the little that remained, so that the old man was entirely at the mercy of the hatefulness that was bad luck. And that hateful energy had torn him apart.

Krupp knew this, because he was looking into Tooley's eyes; it was all written there.

Tooley represented the power of Good.

Krupp's eyes went to the gold coke spoon glittering in the yellow light; it hung like a sort of ankh on a tiny lovely chain around Tooley's neck, and it was the color of promises.

It was the last thing he saw before Tooley wrapped the blindfold over his eyes and taped it thoroughly into place.

Krupp allowed himself to be led through narrow places and low places—more than once he bumped his head, but it didn't seem to hurt much—and into a room he realized must be an elevator. He could feel a rising sensation in his chest.

After a while he was led by the hand into the smell of oiled leather and burning logs and oak paneling and the fragrance of expensive cigarettes.

Tooley peeled away the tape and the blindfold.

It looked like the basement rumpus room of a large suburban house. Only they couldn't be in the suburbs. There were no windows. He'd been right about the oak paneling, and at the far end of the long room, to his right, was a fireplace where logs crackled. Not a familiar sight in Manhattan.

The only light came from a single yellow ceiling light-strip and from the fire.

Just in front of him was a brown leather couch, dimpled with buttons; it smelled new. On a stand between Krupp and the couch, was a large color TV set, with its back to him. Tooley led him gently by the elbow to the couch. They sat facing the TV set.

Dimly, on the wall above the elevator doors through which they'd entered, Krupp could see a TV camera, the sort one sees in banks. The camera's monitoring light was on, its lens looking straight at them.

"Hello, Billy," said the TV screen.

Shaken, Krupp leaned forward on the couch to focus his bleary eyes on the screen image. It was the outline of a man. A round-faced man with hair that wasn't long and wasn't short. That's all Krupp could tell about him, for sure, because he was sitting in half-light.

"How do you feel, Billy?" said the voice from the speaker under the TV screen.

"Sort of sleepy. Sorta weird. But good."

"Billy—can you answer a few questions?"

"You want my life story?" Krupp felt silly. He felt like joking

"No. We have that already. We have all the facts on you, Billy, including your home address and the addresses of your relatives—should you be indiscreet."

"I gotcha."

"We'd like to ask you a question or two about your attitudes. To see if you're ready. You ever read a book called *The Art of Intimidation?* It was a popular book."

"Sure. I read *I'm Number One,* too."

"Good. Now answer this honestly. It's necessary to be very honest. If you were in a house fire, and the next-door neighbor's infant son happened to be in the same house, and by going into the next room and carrying him out you'd be taking a big chance on losing your life in the fire—would you?"

"You mean, if I had a clear way to get out myself?"

"That's what I mean."

"Uhh—"

"*Honesty,* Billy, or we can't help you. We know when you're being dishonest."

Krupp believed him. "Okay. I'd leave the kid. He ain't my kid. I'm just as important as he is."

"Absolutely. Suppose you were trapped in a house with your ex-wife—the latest—and you—ah—were told by the people who had you trapped there—people with big guns—that they wanted to kill your wife and they'd kill you if you didn't give her up to them."

Krupp felt reckless, and he could hardly speak for his giggling. "I'd shove her out the front door! And I'd thank 'em!"

The shadow on the TV screen chuckled.

"Now let me ask you this: Do you ever feel like just giving up and dying? Or maybe risking your life in a bank job? Because you're desperate and *they make it so hard for you.*"

"Yeah," said Krupp, quietly now. "Sometimes. They sure as hell make it hard. Everybody wants the money right now. Or too soon."

"Sure. I know just what you mean. You used to live pretty well. You made a lot of money, so now it's even hard for you to get welfare relief. But the spades—they get welfare, no problem, right? It's not fair, you ask me."

"Not fair…"

"So success—moneywise—is a matter of life and death. It's dog-eat-dog more than ever before, because of inflation, and recession, and—well, because of people like that bookie who's on your case. Do you think that's true?"

Krupp nodded. It was all undeniably true. "Life and death."

"It's you or them. A guy has to do what he's got to. Got to fight."

Krupp nodded. He was finding it hard to talk. The room was filled with smoke. Only, he knew the smoke wasn't really there.

The figure on the screen seemed to grow, to loom like a drive-in movie image.

"That's all I want to ask you. You'll remember the questions, and the answers."

Now the screen image had changed. It was a shape made of angles and lines, with little squiggly marks scattered around it. The marks looked like Korn Kurls to him. He giggled, faintly.

There was another shape in the mist. It was a female shape. A nice figure. Very nice. Nothing hiding it. He couldn't see it clearly, but it looked good. The woman knelt alongside the couch, and her hands moved to unzip his pants.

He sat passively. It must be a dream.

She slipped his small, purplish member into her mouth, and began to suck gently.

He enjoyed it, but he didn't become excited, exactly—though he was getting hard. It was simply…soothing.

Most of his attention was fixed on the things he saw on the TV screen. Until the fog thickened, blackened, and made everything gone.

Gone. Gone the woman, the TV set, the couch, the basement room. Gone Tooley. Gone the voices (many voices, speaking in strange languages…a gabble that even in New York he'd never heard), gone the half-seen man on the screen.

He was in his apartment, in his bedroom, and his head felt like the Liberty Bell with extra cracks and some vandal pounding it.

He sat up. He winced. He was hung over. He remembered the dream vividly. Dreamt he'd been in a bar. Man with a coke spoon—

Something golden was dangling from his bed post. He blinked away the last traces of the fogginess and peered at the shiny thing. A tiny gold coke spoon. Below it, on the mirror-topped bedside table, was a gram of what had to be cocaine, laid out in neat lines. There was a hundred-dollar bill beside it, rolled up and taped. Beside the hundred-dollar bill was a black leather case, cigar-box-sized.

Hands shaking, he opened the black case. On the red velvet inside were two bright surgical knives.

SIX

While Krupp was descending the gray stairs of the Houston Street-Second Avenue subway station with Tooley—was making that descent for the first time—Lanyard was at the same instant stepping from an elevator into the sub-basement of Gribner's apartment building. He stepped out into the light of police lamps—light given a bloody tinge by the shadeless table lamp sitting on the dirt floor in the corner of the oppressive, low-ceilinged coal cellar. An ugly reek made him wrinkle his nostrils. Something dead. His stomach felt as if it were curling up to die, too. Slowly, his eyes adjusted to the glare; he sorted through the shapes of the several men working in the room and picked out Gribner, facing him, arms outspread, face sagging with a defeated look that accused everything and everyone, as if the whole world had betrayed him. "Lanyard!" Gribner shouted. "You tell me—what am I, that this should happen here, to me? You tell me, what is—Lanyard, look at this...." He bent and laid back a corner of the sheet covering an oblong heap on the floor.

"Gribner, hey—I don't want to see any more goddamn—" Lanyard started to turn away. But his eyes went involuntarily to the shape on the dirt floor. "Damn it, Gribner." It looked like a skinned lamb.

Lanyard turned away, retching.

It wasn't a skinned lamb. It was a small boy. The remains of a small boy. He swallowed hard to control his gag reflex. The sensation subsided. He glanced over his shoulder at the markings on the wall, then stepped quickly into the elevator.

"Lanyard, come back here and—"

The doors closed on Gribner's shout.

Lanyard closed his eyes and took a deep breath. He opened them immediately. He didn't see anything, this time, in the darkness behind his eyes. Except the darkness. But that was enough. He didn't want to look into it. The boy had been mauled.

He found his way out of the building, down the street, into the Ukrainian bar on the corner. "Gin and seven," he said, sitting at the bar. The bartender made his drink, brought it over. Lanyard rose, and—drink sloshing on his shaking hand—went to a well-lit table in the corner. The jukebox was playing a polka. Twelve old men and two young ones at the bar chattered loudly in what Lanyard took to be Russian. He enjoyed the fact that he couldn't understand a word of it. It made him feel isolated. He wanted to be alone, with a drink. He was annoyed when Gribner came into the bar and headed straight for his table.

Gribner sat down, without speaking, without looking at Lanyard. A waitress came and Gribner ordered straight bourbon. When this was brought, Gribner and Lanyard sat silently drinking. Now and then Gribner, kicked at the sawdust on the floor, or rubbed his nose. Lanyard became aware that Gribner was trying to keep from crying.

After two or three polkas, Frank Sinatra singing "New York, New York," and two drinks apiece, Gribner's face seemed to harden.

He met Lanyard's eyes. "I remember, Lanyard, you said something about my being used to this sort of thing. About it not affecting me."

Lanyard shrugged. "I think people get that way after a while. But you were personally affected by this. You must be pretty worried about your nephew." Lanyard had to force the words out. He didn't want to talk about it.

Gribner snorted. "If I catch that little S.O.B., I'll send him to an asylum."

Lanyard glanced up in surprise. "Yeah?"

"I think he killed my dogs. My Louie and—" He had to stop. He spread his hands. "I must look like some sappy old bird to you, huh? Pissed about his dogs when that kid's dead down there."

Lanyard shrugged. "What makes you think your nephew killed the dogs?"

"He was a sadistic, sick little sonuvabitch. I knew that, but I didn't want to think about it. And he…Jeez, one night I thought I was going crazy. I don't know. I think he did it with some kind of ventriloquism. But that just goes to show how sick the little prick is." Gribner's voice, just then, was harsh enough to make people at adjoining tables look over, though they weren't close enough to hear what he was saying.

"Did *what* with ventriloquism?"

"The growling."

"What—"

But Gribner interrupted him. Vehemently. "Lanyard! Did you see the marks on the wall? Yes or no?"

"Yes. The same mix. Same sort of invocation. I didn't see a pentagram…but that isn't always necessary. There are always several methods for invoking the same—influences. But it didn't look like that kid was cut up in the same way."

"He wasn't. Looks like maybe a swarm of rats or a wild dog—how a big dog would have got down my basement—"

"You sure that kid's not your—?"

"He's not. Enough of his face was there. Hair's different. Lanyard, you think these people—the cultists—you think they did this to get me off their case? We don't have a damn thing. It's not like we're getting close."

"I dunno. Maybe. Seems a bit too obvious a tactic, and one that wouldn't be much use—they can't terrorize the whole police force when the city is…" He shook his head. "I take it you think that they approached your nephew… they involved him?"

"Lanyard, you know anything about a…a religious symbol that—ah—it's a skull with a long mustache?"

Lanyard blinked. He'd seen something of the kind. Somewhere. "I think— there are Persian charms supposed to invoke the healing power of a certain Persian mystic. A sorcerer who was supposed to have the secret of eternal life and luck. He dealt with appeasing Ahriman, while supposedly serving Ahura Mazda. And that's part of what his cult is into. Appeasing the personification of Evil with sacrifice, but otherwise living the 'Life of the Just.' It was a heavily rationalized built-in hypocrisy they had."

"What about the mustache on the skull?"

"You make it sound pretty silly. Ah—it's what the charm I mentioned looks like."

Gribner stood abruptly, accidentally sideswiping the table so it rocked and nearly overturned. Lanyard steadied it; his own glass wobbled but remained upright; Gribner's rolled onto the floor and broke.

Lanyard looked up. Gribner was already halfway across the room, heading for the door.

He's holding out on me, Lanyard thought. That's okay. I don't have to tell him everything, then. Maguss prefers it that way. And Maguss is the man seductively waving the Big Check.

But Lanyard wasn't thinking about money, really. "Like a skinned lamb," he murmured. His eyes were itchy with tiredness. Yet he didn't close them, except for the briefest possible moment.

MADELAINE WAS GLAD the reception wasn't at Minder's private club. The Valencia made her nervous; like Minder, it was fraught with hidden expectations.

The reception for the author of *Shake 'Em Down!!*, a musical about "good-hearted con men," was held backstage at Minder's theater, the New Orpheum. Minder was the show's producer. It was expected to open in early spring. Minder had called Madelaine personally to invite her to the reception. And he'd hinted that there might be a part for her in the play—not the lead, but a substantial role.

The curtains were down; the guests munched canapes under the ropes and pulleys and the stage lights crowding the ceiling fifty feet overhead. The rehearsal lamps were on, too brightly. The stage area was crowded by men in business suits and in black tie, a few in designer jeans and studiedly chic dyed-leather jackets. The women wore evening gowns or dark, tight-waisted suits...or studiedly chic dyed-leather jackets and designer jeans. Madelaine was in a jumpsuit. She accepted a drink from the red-uniformed bartender on the other side of the linen-covered table, and pretended she was pleased to exchange small talk with Lorna Sandina, the tall, catty Spanish actress who'd been cast as the female lead.

Minder, in a blue dinner jacket and bow tie, shambled through the crowd shaking hands and quipping. Even in blue he looked like a domesticated panda bear.

Madelaine instantly disliked the man Minder chivvied politely before him through the crowd. Minder introduced him strategically as Charlton Buckner, the author of *Shake 'Em Down!!* Buckner's nearly shoulder-length hair looked as if it had been dyed black and given a permanent; it contrasted absurdly with his middle-aged, lined face. He wore a gray suit-coat over a black turtleneck sweater and gray tweed trousers. He was an erstwhile Madison Avenue copywriter for cigarette ads.

She hadn't heard him speak, and she was picking up nothing from him via her Gift, but his gestures duplicated those of the scores of bantering authors she'd seen on talk shows. Crinkling his eyes with quiet amusement at the right moment; becoming temporarily serious when it was called for, then timing his comic relief.

Madelaine caught Minder's eye. He trotted ponderously over to her. "My lost lady-love! I can't see the forest for the trees; I've been talking to the other ladies and all the time looking for you!"

"You're an elegant liar," she said.

"Tell you what—I'm going to let Tooley handle this business for a while. My young author has got himself snakecharmed, anyway. I wonder if you'd like to take a drive with me to see my new launching pad—it's a pretty little townhouse on Gramercy Park. *Private* park—you have to have a key to get into the park in the square. Pretty elitist, huh? Classy stuff. Like to have a look?"

"Delighted," said Madelaine, though the word didn't describe her feelings.

Alone with Minder, it would be easier to talk about a part in the play. To talk about it very casually, of course. Fewer interruptions; better chance he'd bring it up himself. She took his arm.

Twenty minutes later, Minder's limo was pulling up in front of his Russian Renaissance townhouse. The driver stopped and parked, though Minder had told Madelaine they'd simply "swing by."

"What the hell," Minder said, "let's go in and have a look around."

Very casually. Of course.

"I've got some Colombian flake we can sample, before we hustle back to the reception. And we can talk about the part. It's not big, but it stands out. Its got its own dignity. Yeah, you gotta try this coke, one line of this stuff and..."

Nodding now and then, she followed him out of the car and up to the house.

It's not too late to make excuses, she told herself.

But she said nothing except, "Oh, thanks, gallant sir," when he opened the front door for her. And she stepped inside.

LANYARD LAY ON his back, staring at the water stain on the ceiling over the sofa. The water stain bore a resemblance to a Japanese demon-mask. A gnarled, almost clownish countenance. Red. Snarling.

He closed his eyes—and opened them quickly. The flecks behind his eyelids conspired to arrange themselves in patterns that were gnarled... clownish...red...snarling.

This time he was sure it was his imagination.

He stood, stretched, and went to the small portable TV set on the old wooden trunk beside the bedroom door. He switched on the set and watched the figures in the tiny luminous box expanding geometrically, taking on bloodless form. A newscaster. "Oh, *splendid* timing," Lanyard said. "Shit." But before he could switch the channels the newsman said, "...still no significant leads in the subway ritual murders of seven people. The Guardian Angels, a group of uniformed self-appointed subway patrolmen, have sworn to apprehend the subway killers. Meanwhile, ridership on the trains is down thirty percent, resulting in a greater use of private cars by commuters and unprecedented traffic jams...."

Lanyard switched channels after noticing the gruesome insignia the TV news program used to symbolize the story. In a small video-matted box inset above the newscaster's shoulder was a skull with a pentagram on its forehead and two sharp knives crossed under it. "Looks like a Hell's Angels armband," Lanyard muttered. It was as if the city unconsciously relished the horror taking place in its own innards.

On the PBS channel a self-serious, highly manicured commentator was saying, "We have to conclude, studying the imagery of current, popular gore-horror films objectively, that the emphasis is not on subtle terror, the sort that once reigned in classics like *Psycho* and *The Cat People*, but on grisly enactments of ritual murder, explicitly detailed and, often, shot from the viewpoint of the killer, so that the audience can satisfy its need to express hostility. Not since the Great Depression has the country been so pressured, have people felt so threatened. The growing Soviet presence, combined with the rising crime rate and rising prices, have given the public a huge need to express an anger that it has long kept suppressed—"

Lanyard hurriedly switched off the TV. "No fucking escape from it!" he said, shaking his head. He was startled by the loudness of his own voice.

He opened a copy of *The Village Voice*. The first thing his eyes focused on: "…all four black men were taken to the cellar room of the police station, separated, and threatened one by one with…"

Cellars, he thought. Underground. All the killings have happened underground.

Allowing his eyes to rove the page at random, he fixed on:

DON'T PAY US

Unless we produce something useful!

That's the offer made by Data Digs, Manhattan's most sophisticated data-collating service. Doing a term paper? Compiling information to use in applying for a grant? Detective work? Scientific study of human behavior? Consumer buying patterns? Our computer obtains its information from newspaper records, police files, media input of all kinds, and sources we're unprepared to divulge.

We can collate data for you on any subject. Call _____

Lanyard tore the ad from the magazine and laid it atop the telephone receiver.

He went into the kitchen and fixed himself a drink. He knew it was going to be a long, sleepless night. Because he was afraid to close his eyes.

As it happened, Lanyard fell asleep at about four in the morning, glass in hand. He awoke at nine, on his back, on the couch, dressed except for his shoes. The glass had toppled on his chest. His chest felt sticky. His head ached. But after a few attempts at falling back to sleep, he gave up. He got up, scowled, feeling his clothes as an itchiness, and went into the bathroom. He stripped, took a bath and five aspirin, and drank two cups of coffee. He dressed, looking out the window now and then. It was another windy day, clouds racing like frightened hippos, fat and gray.

He went to the phone and called Data Digs and made an appointment. Then he called Madelaine. She wasn't home. He left a message on her answering machine, asking her to have dinner that evening. He hung up, but before he'd taken his hand from the receiver, the phone rang, making his hand tingle.

He couldn't bring himself to lift the receiver to his ear. He was afraid to. He wasn't at all sure what it was he was afraid of. Was it Gribner? Gribner had to be dealt with sooner or later. Maybe he'd had a breakthrough. Lanyard forced himself to pick up the phone.

"Okay…Yeah—hello."

"Lanyard?" The voice sounded distant. High-pitched. Maguss.

Lanyard groaned inwardly. "Right."

"Lanyard, I've decided it might be a good idea if we met, face to face."

"What?" Lanyard was surprised. He sat up straighter on the chair. "You're taking a plane?"

"I already have. I'm in town."

"In town?" Lanyard felt a chill. "Sounds like a long distance connection."

"It's a car phone. I'm in an associate's car. Ah…can you meet me at my hotel for lunch? I'm at the Waldorf." He didn't wait to see if Lanyard was prepared to meet him. "At one this afternoon. All right? Suite 32Y."

Maguss hung up.

Lanyard sighed and went to the kitchen. He put two raw eggs in a glass, half a teaspoon of cayenne pepper, tomato juice, and a finger of vodka. He mixed it up, steeled himself, and drank. He shuddered. Then he slipped into his coat, and headed out to Data Digs, determined to read a morning paper on the way, no matter how sick it made him.

SCHMALTZ ELEGANCE, LANYARD thought, waiting at the door to Maguss's suite. He stared at the gold painted trimming on the white door and thought: *One step above the Valencia Hotel. But only one.*

The door opened. "Mr. Maguss, please. Tell him Carl Lanyard—"

"I'm the very fellow," said the little man. Lanyard had taken him for a servant.

"Oh," said Lanyard, at a loss. "Sorry." It wasn't the way Maguss was dressed that made Lanyard mistake him for a servant; the old man was wearing an expensive three-piece dusty-blue wool worsted herringbone suit, over a cotton shirt with barrel cuffs and a sporty dotted tie that was probably Yves St. Laurent. But Maguss was diminutive physically and diminuendo in tone, and at first he seemed shy and humble—a contrast to his phone personality. Which may have been why his employees generally were not allowed to meet him face to face.

And that face.

"William Burroughs!" Lanyard blurted.

Maguss raised a white eyebrow. "I beg your pardon?" he piped. "I don't resemble the man at all."

"I guess not," Lanyard said, feeling awkward. Privately, he thought that Maguss looked remarkably like Burroughs. The lined deadpan face was ashen, the lips thin, the eyes like stones of a sunken temple only just brought to light. Pale blue eyes, full of distance.

He was much older than Lanyard had thought. He was stooped, and his white hands, spotted with age, trembled slightly as he gestured Lanyard into the suite.

But Maguss moved with energy as he closed the door and sat at the table laid out with food in the center of the living room. The furniture was not antique, but was designed to seem that way; there were framed copies of Revolutionary War woodcuts on the walls. He sat in a wooden chair across from Maguss. "Go right ahead and have something to eat, my boy, before your stomach growls something rude at me." There it is, Lanyard thought. The old man's acerbic sense of humor. It grated on Lanyard.

Lanyard was hungry, but his stomach fluttered nervously. On the white tablecloth, symmetrically arranged, were covered china dishes. When he looked up, Maguss had somehow already filled his plate, and was eating rather greedily for an old man. They ate shrimp, liver pâté, and lemoned salmon. Somehow Lanyard expected servants. There were none, and he filled his wineglass repeatedly with the Chablis. Lanyard twitched nervously at the noises Maguss made with his fork against the plate. The clicks and ringings seemed painfully loud.

Worry about Madelaine nagged at him. She was never home when he called. He didn't trust Minder; the man was a born exploiter.

Lanyard glanced up at Maguss. The old man was now noisily eating his dessert. He still hadn't said a word.

What the hell does he want with me? Lanyard wondered. But he began to feel better, more relaxed, as the wine took hold.

So he only twitched a little when Maguss said, suddenly, not looking up from his mousse, "And how is our old friend Madelaine?"

Lanyard managed to keep himself from saying: *You've never met her, she's no old friend of yours.*

"She's fine, last I heard of her. I haven't been in touch with her."

"You've been dating her." He didn't say it accusingly.

"How do you know that?" And Lanyard was speaking accusingly.

"I have informers working for Joey Minder. Minder doesn't know they work for me too. They told me you were recently her escort to Minder's club."

"Informers? Why? Are you in competition with Minder? He's going into publishing?"

"No. And I'm not going into theatrical production or nightclubs. Let's just say that Minder and I are old competitors. We simply don't like one another."

"He's not someone I'd trust to scrub my back in the showers, either," Lanyard said into his third glass of wine.

His tired eyes were playing tricks on him. He thought he saw something sliding through the air like a flying eel; something glimpsed from the corners of his eyes. He turned to look at it directly and found nothing.

"Let's sit on the couch," said Maguss, rising. He stretched, and walked with energetic but mincing steps toward the sofa.

Lanyard sat in an armchair across from the sofa. He badly wanted a cigarette, and he almost hated Maguss when the old man said, "Cigarette?" He nodded toward a coffee table holding a carved-ivory cigarette case. The carving on the case showed the head of a Japanese demon, rather like the demon he thought he'd seen in the water stain on the ceiling over his bed. With a practiced flick of his thumb, Maguss opened the case and extracted a custom-made cigarette.

Lanyard shook his head slowly, watching enviously as Maguss lit up. The purple-blue smoke smelled like fine Turkish tobacco. Lanyard nervously fingered the dimple in his chin.

"I wonder if you'd be kind enough, Carl, to tell me a little bit about yourself." Maguss spoke languidly, staring at the ceiling.

For no conscious reason, Lanyard glanced up at the ceiling. For a moment he thought, again, that he glimpsed a gliding, elongated shape in the air. He'd experimented with psychedelics more than once; maybe he was getting a flashback.

His eyes watered; he looked away. Nothing up there.

"What sort of…what would you like to know? You know I'm divorced, and all that's in my files. I—"

"For instance: In what religion were you raised?"

Reminding himself that there was more than a hundred thousand dollars remaining at stake, Lanyard didn't say, *Why the hell do you want to know?*

"I was raised a Methodist," he replied. "A very liberal atmosphere, really. We didn't go to church regularly after I was thirteen or so. My mother was a painter. And my father was a gloomy, antisocial old cuss. He taught law at U. of C. Which is probably why I know so little about the law."

"Your father is still alive?"

"Yeah. We're not really in touch. My mother died and—"

He shrugged.

Out of the blue, Maguss asked, "Have you noticed anything new in the way of psychic phenomena around Madelaine Springer?"

Trying to smile, Lanyard asked, "Is that supposed to catch me off guard so I blurt out a confidence, or what?"

Maguss gave his rasping chuckle. Lanyard felt a chill.

"No, Carl, I was just curious. Professional curiosity. You may have quit the magazine, but I haven't."

"It's just that I thought you had given me different priorities now."

"I have, I have indeed. But my question about Madelaine is not necessarily irrelevant. I firmly believe there are psychic phenomena to be noticed when one is with Ms. Springer. I have, as I said, my sources. And if you are able to perceive those phenomena, then it could be that your block is lifting. *And—*" he paused to tap his cigarette on a marble ashtray"—if your block is lifting, then it could be that you will perceive in the way you were intended to, which would help us find the source of—"

"Pardon me," said Lanyard, rather more harshly than he'd intended, "but you seem to be talking to someone who isn't here. Because I sure as hell don't know what you're talking about."

"Good." Maguss smiled. "Then we're both confused. Lovely. Confusion makes things interesting. Just the other day I saw a confused man walk into a wall. He took a rather comical spill. I had a good laugh over that. Made the day more interesting."

Lanyard waited out Maguss' sense of humor in silence.

"What I was talking about," Maguss said, "was a report I read on you. It came from your grade school. It was old and yellowed, and if we hadn't rescued it, it would have gone to their incinerator. They were cleaning their files."

"What report?" Lanyard said, almost whispering.

"It was a report that said you complained about hearing voices. Hearing voices and seeing things. You pointed at things that weren't there. The principal was of the opinion that you were trying to draw attention to yourself. He accused you of that, and you lost your temper. You told him he was a—" Maguss paused to rasp a chuckle. "—a 'pimplebrain.' Very colorful description, I thought. He shouted at you and made you stay after school. Later, there is, in the same file, an angry note from your mother saying that you had to stay home from school because the school grounds hadn't been adequately policed and as a consequence you were rather severely beaten by two bigger boys after school."

Lanyard winced. "I will have that cigarette now, if you don't mind." He extracted a cigarette from the box and lit it with Maguss's bone-handled lighter; he inhaled and coughed. He wasn't used to it.

Maguss glanced to one side, his eyes narrowing. For a moment he looked like a cat following the course of a fly in the air. Lanyard automatically looked in the same direction and thought he saw something flutter there, something dark and slippery. Then it was gone. No fly. Something else.

The hand that held the cigarette trembled, shaking a few tiny ashes adrift on the air.

Lanyard couldn't contain himself. "I don't know who you bribed to get those files, and I don't know much about the law. But your reading them was an invasion of my privacy. I know that much."

Maguss spread his hands apologetically. "I'm sorry, my boy. But, you see, I'm a compulsive researcher. I had to research your childhood, once I began to suspect you. I'm the publisher of a magazine that, after all, is devoted to—"

"I don't really see what this has to do with psychic phenomena. I am afraid I'm not really following you." Lanyard's interruption was desperate. He had stopped thinking. He was pure defense. He felt he was under attack as surely as if a mugger had jumped him with a sawed-off baseball bat. "I think it would be more pertinent if we talked about the killings. You asked me to investigate them. You haven't said a damn word about them. I've put in some real work. For example, the one thing that links them all is the fact that they happen underground and of course there is the nearly identical methodology. The methodology—" Lanyard was speaking in machine-gun bursts, trying to keep Maguss from saying any more about the reports from his grade school—"indicates that the cult is interested in placating Ahriman and exchanging sacrificed life-energy for prosperity, good luck or what have you. The cult has its origins in a Persian tradition that stipulates its temple must be underground. So, I've gone to a data-researching place and paid them to collate anything that comes along concerning unusual events linked with the city's underground…anything involving subways, or cellars or—"

He stopped. He couldn't go on, when Maguss was so openly laughing at him.

The laughter was the silent sort, but it was real. As Lanyard rose angrily and turned to go, Maguss took a deep breath and said, "If you're through hedging now, Lanyard, I'll finish what I was trying to tell you. Let me see—"

Feeling limp all at once, Lanyard turned and sank into his seat.

Maguss was saying, "I believe I was telling you about suspicion. My suspicion of you. I suspected that your relentless skepticism about the occult demonstrated that you were afraid of it. Just as a homophobic man is probably a suppressed homosexual. You were afraid of the occult, of psychic phenomena. So you stuck with the magazine to have the opportunity to debunk it. You made yourself forget your boyhood 'hallucinations.' It was a trauma—and all of us cloud over the traumas in our lives."

Lanyard stared at him. "You sonuvabitch," he breathed.

"Yes," said Maguss thoughtfully. "I am. Anyway, I want you to know that your time for self-recognition has come. You have to recognize that at least part of your attraction to Madelaine is the result of your understanding that she is that rarity, the genuine psychic. Your Gift is trying to emerge in you—fighting off your suppression. Through Madelaine. Just a theory," he added airily. "You're a psychic, Lanyard. But your Gift isn't the same as Madelaine's. Because you can hear the Otherworld only occasionally. More often, you can *see* it."

Lanyard hardly heard him. He was distracted. He couldn't take his eyes from the black, sinuous forms writhing into being in the air over Maguss's head.

They almost took shape. And then they were gone.

"The process has only just begun," Maguss was saying. "If I know the pattern, it will come in fits and starts. When it begins to show itself in you more fully, you may be able to use it to trace the power currents. If you can trace the power currents, one of them will lead you to the temple of the people you seek. So you see, the subject was not irrelevant."

"I am of the opinion," Lanyard said in a monotone, controlling his voice very deliberately, "that you are a senile old man, suffering hallucinations. I seem to be having a few myself. I haven't had enough sleep." He stood. "I'm going to go home and get some. If you want to fire me for what I've just said, you can, of course. But if you don't, I'll continue the investigation...because, in all candor, I need the money."

"You're welcome to your opinions, Lanyard," said Maguss.

Lanyard realized that the old man was again silently laughing at him.

"And," Maguss added, "you're not fired, no. I brought you here to help apprise you of your situation. To pry your Third Eye open a little. I think you'll see that—"

"I'm not buying it, thanks. Are you going to stay here for a while?"

"For an indefinite period, yes. Right here." Maguss smiled.

Lanyard took another cigarette, lit it, moving robotically, and turned away.

In the elevator, going down, he felt overwhelmed. *I'll continue the investigation,* he'd said, *because, in all candor, I need the money.*

But he knew perfectly well it wasn't the money he was after, now.

GRIBNER TYPED OUT his report.

"I can find no evidence," he wrote, "that an animal of any sort, except for the victimized dogs..." He paused and said, "Hell."

He got up from his desk. The clatter of typewriters clicking and desk drawers banging and phones jangling from the adjoining room was abrasive. Sometimes the noise seemed to merge and shape itself into a single sound.

He opened his file drawer, and in the alphabetized section, under "C"— C for Consolation—he found a flask of brandy.

He poured two fingers into his instant coffee.

He sat at the desk, knocked back two quick slugs of this caustic brew, shuddered, clapped the cup down so that it sloshed onto the papers in the corner of his desk, and returned his attention to the typewriter.

"I can find no evidence that an animal of any sort, except for the victimized dogs..." he read, and shrugged. He added, "...was present at the scene. The basement floor, which was dirt, was completely free of footprints except for the boy's. I was the first one down there with a flashlight, and it's the first thing I looked for. Hell, I—"

He stopped and stared at the report. He'd written *Hell, I* on an official report. Hands shaking, he carefully erased it. He took another swig of his laced coffee, and wrote, "Additionally, the medical examiner found no trace of saliva in the wounds on the child's remains." He hesitated. Would it confuse the issue if he mentioned that nevertheless the examiner had insisted that the wounds were made by an animal's teeth and fangs?

It was then that Gribner made up his mind to be taken off the case. He wasn't sure what had made up his mind. He only knew he couldn't do the job right—not like this. He'd been looking for an excuse to quit. Screw excuses. He'd make them take him off the case.

He wanted to be relieved of the case so he could follow it. So he could pursue his own private, nonofficial investigation. So he could find Everett. "It's you, you little bastard," he muttered. "You're one of them."

"No, Miss CHANCERY," said Tooley, "it is not hypnotism. It is kind of—ah…"

"You're telling me it's not hypnotism? I start feeling like I should do everything you suggest. I don't really even remember coming here…and then you want me to sit and watch this TV…and I start watching it and—well, if it's not hypnotism, what is it?"

"It is," said Tooley, "merely a harmless and inexpensive means of teaching something complicated in a short time."

"That sounds like euphemistic boondoggle for 'brainwashing.'"

"No, Miss Chancery. We are not hypnotists, but we are limited by the same principle: that we cannot make someone do what they would otherwise be incapable of doing. We can only suggest what is already possible. Or release what is concealed."

There were just the two of them, standing, and the TV screen between them; the dark image that had filled the TV screen minutes before was gone. The TV was lit but dark, though there was something pensive and alive in its blue-white flickering.

Lily Chancery looked around at the basement game room, new leather-covered furniture, the windowless paneled walls.

"Too fucking harmless," she said.

"I beg your pardon?"

"Nothing." She gazed down at Tooley; Tooley's head didn't reach her shoulders. She was five-foot-eleven, willowy, with billowy blond hair, eyes the blue of ice found deep beneath the surface of a frozen sea; her long face, in its careful mask of makeup, was so modelesque it could have been stamped out on some Madison Avenue assembly line. The lines of her black suit were severe, but her high heels and lacy cream-colored V-neck blouse brought a kind of flirtatiousness to the outfit.

She was striking. She was a failed model.

She had the looks. But, as her agent had said, "I—ah—I guess they think that you're just too damn cold-blooded. No—uh—no warmth. They don't see the sexiness they need to go with the coolness. And warmth is coming back. It's a look."

She'd walked out of a shooting because the photographer had insisted on putting his hands on her. He was gay and no threat to her. And, though he carefully explained he had to manipulate her limbs at first until she relaxed enough to fall into the poses more naturally, she couldn't tolerate him—or anybody—touching her; unless she was very, very stoned.

But she rarely ever relaxed.

She'd been sitting rigidly in a corner at the party for the opening of a new line of designer jeans—a party she'd crashed, more or less, in her smug, matter-of-fact way—when Tooley had said, "Pardon me, but aren't you Lily Chancery? The model? You know, it's funny, we were just looking at your portfolio—Joey Minder and I—and we were talking about how underrated you are. I was wondering why you haven't—uh—been seen lately. Professionally. Are you going into acting, or—?"

How had she come from that party to *here*?

She couldn't remember. It had been underground, a train, and then an elevator…down. "We've just had the elevator installed," Tooley had said. "We put it in for important customers."

There had to be a way out. She looked from side to side, perceived no doors. The room was too dark to be certain, but instinctively she felt she could leave only if she gave herself over to them.

If she didn't give in—she'd never leave.

She sank onto the couch before the TV. "If it wasn't hypnotism," she repeated dreamily, "what was it?"

Tooley shrugged. "A harmless kind of possession. Just a temporary borrowing of your mental faculties. And we bring something special out…Let me put it this way: Everyone has inside them an instinctive personality that is just waiting to be released. It is the personality that becomes dominant when a person's survival is threatened. The one that takes over when that person needs to become completely selfish in order to survive. Sometimes it doesn't work, and people sacrifice for one another. But it's there, in the sacrificer, suppressed, unsprung, waiting. And what happens when it is released? You gain a new perspective on other people. They lose their so-called humanity for you. They become things to be pushed aside. Used. Or killed. Or toyed with in the ugliest way. And *it's a great liberation!* It's the purest delight, when it's developed. It is a triumph of the spirit of individuality, in a way. In its lesser manifestation, it is what makes it possible for people to shove through the crowds on the subway platform; in its greater manifestation, it allows one business partner to pull the rug out from under the other, destroying a colleague for the sake of controlling the business. It is what you need if you're going to get in touch with the power that makes things happen for people… the Strength we talked about before, the essence of *luck*. You've got to let that personality take you over thoroughly. What we really want is for you to realize yourself. Yourself. Yourself. Yourself."

"*Is she there?*"

"Yes, sir," said Tooley to the shadows. "She's tranced."

Lily Chancery stared fixedly at the images on the TV screen. The ritual in all its details. The words to be written, the words to be spoken. The marks to be made on the body of the Chosen. The cuts to be made within the marks. The opening. The rearranging. Simple though wet work. Not much more complicated than making a casserole, really. And similar somehow.

It would nourish her.

Her lips were parted and her tongue traced them.

"*She's a natural. I can feel that.*"

"Yes, sir."

"*You spoke her into it quite nicely. More cleanly than the speaking-into-place for Krupp.*"

"Thank you, sir. But it was easier, for her, once we got to the speaking-into-place, because she understands more. She responds in a more sophisticated way. She is, also, as you say, a natural."

"*I think she's going to be valuable. The sort of energy we can use. She can work in high places.*"

"Yes, sir. And I think she's going to enjoy her work."

SEVEN

"Madelaine? I—"

"You have reached Madelaine Springer. I am unable to come to the phone at the moment—" The voice on the tape machine sounded tired and far away. Lanyard pressed the receiver closer to his ear—he couldn't hear her voice clearly enough. "But I will be pleased to call you back if you leave your name, number, and a brief message."

He waited for the beep and when it came he said, "Madelaine, this is Carl Lanyard. I've tried to call you several times. I need your advice and I'd like to see you. Not necessarily in that order. Anyway...Shit!" The machine had broken the connection.

He checked the clock on the table across from the couch. Seven PM. He felt restless and decided to go out for a drink. Outside the window, pigeons were fighting the wind, trying to reach a perch on the tenement building across the junk-crowded backyard. The night sky was restless with breeze.

Lanyard stood, stretched, put on his jacket, and went out the door. He locked both locks and descended the five flights to the street.

Near the sidewalks the tenements reflected the bluish glow from the street lights; but above the street lights the façades rose into deepening darkness, so that the rooftops were almost lost in the night.

He walked west, away from "alphabet town"—Avenues A, C, and D—and toward the cluster of bars and restaurants on St. Marks Place. Overgrown silvery radios carried by young Hispanics blared at him as he passed.

He crossed the street, dodging through a fleet of reckless taxis, and passed a series of burnt-out, deserted buildings. Some citizens' group had pressed "tenement decals" over the boarded windows, contact-paper depictions of neat shutters and curtains and flowerpots. They were supposed to give the building the appearance of being occupied, to discourage squatters and vandalism. At best they were convincing only in half-light, and here most of the decals had peeled in bad weather to hang like torn skin, flapping in the wind. Between the decals someone had spraypainted: LANDLORDS ARE NOT LORDS OF THE LAND, THEY ARE SCUM OF THE EARTH.

A spatter of cold rain made Lanyard cringe into his brown leather jacket. He wished he'd worn a cap. A movement caught his eye, and he looked to identify it: a tramp shuffling toward him from the doorway of a deserted building. He'd camped there for days; the doorway was littered with empty pint whiskey bottles and quart wine bottles, and over the doorstep were flattened cardboard boxes, damp around the edges, where he slept.

Lanyard's first impulse was to look away. The neighborhood was rife with tramps, and one soon learned to "not see" them. But he forced himself to look. "You exist," Lanyard murmured, not expecting to be heard.

"You betcher I exist," said the old man as Lanyard gave him a dollar.

He wasn't as badly debilitated as many of the tramps. He had both his shoes, and they matched. He had a jacket—a torn ski jacket, once blue, now grimed to gray. Some of his shirt was tucked in. His white hair was like a thatch of frosted weed, and his mouth worked spasmodically between phrases. "I'm here, no earthly reason I ain't here. Betcher."

At last he thrust the dollar bill in his side pocket and extended his hand to Lanyard, this time for a handshake. "M'name, it's Finley."

"Finley?" Lanyard shook the crusty hand, gently disengaged, and wiped his hand on his trousers. "Finley—it's getting cold. What the hell you doing out on the street on a cold night like this? Be November soon. You ought to get out of this wind. Beginning to rain out here. Find yourself some shelter. Maybe go down in the subways or one of these buildings—"

"The buildings, they dangerous. Kids around here prowl aroun' in there, catch you with yer pants down, kick th' shit outta yuh fer no reason. Betcher. Can't go undergroun' neither." He looked at a sewer grating. "Wish I could. I was snug as a cricket inna thicket last year—down them utility tunnels under Grand Central. Hardly nobody going down there now…"

"Why not?" Lanyard found himself listening very closely.

"They won't letcha. An' you go down there, maybe ya never come back up. Big animal down there, it killed Dusty."

"Big animal? A rat?"

Finley shook his head. He turned away and moved toward the doorway.

Lanyard continued down the street. Half an hour earlier he'd written in his notebook:

> I've become convinced that the animal made out of red barbed wire—that's how I think of it, now—that I thought I saw in the cellar of that apartment building…I'm convinced it was a hallucinatory projection of my own terror and/or hostility…

And now he told himself: If the tramps are attacked underground, probably someone's dog found its way down there and got lost and grew wild.

But he hastened his pace. The street was darker here.

Another two weeks and it will be Halloween. Now what brought that to mind? It was almost as if a voice had spoken the words in his ear.

His mind was a carousel of anxieties. He would temporarily resolve one, and the next one to come around on the carousel would whirl into his thoughts. Madelaine. Madelaine and Minder. Minder and Maguss. (What was Maguss's relationship to Minder?) Gribner. The remains of the child in the basement. A news report he'd seen on TV: There were an unusual number of missing-person reports in the city lately, particularly on children.

He turned down St. Marks Place, into the bellow of the drippy wind.

The wet streets reflected traffic lights, chrome bumper gleams, and neon.

He sidestepped a bald, wrinkled black man who was orating to the lampposts. The man's gapped yellow teeth made his words whistle as he shouted, "Th' Pope he comes ovuh heah the motherfuckuh wantsuh fuck wid evvybuddy bud he don' want no pregincy pills 'n' he gets 'em pregint when he fucks widdim—"

The constant din of traffic noises drowned the man's voice as Lanyard left him behind, pressing through a bristling knot of krazy-kolor, leather and shiny-plastic punk rockers. They were laughing at something; Lanyard fancied they were laughing at him. He felt his ears redden. Farther on, when the street noises lulled, he heard, "Lanyard…walk in garden canyons and…" and what sounded like "Lanyard: Santeria and Macumba, they…." The voice faded. Lanyard stopped, glancing about irritably. Someone who knew him, hassling him for fun? He didn't see anyone he recognized. Probably he'd only thought he'd heard his name called; someone had said something that sounded similar, and his brain had processed it to the nearest familiar analogue: Lanyard.

"Santeria" and "Macumba" were religions related to vodun. He'd written an article on them. Nothing at all like the Ahriman appeasers. Except that they, too, made appeasement sacrifices—usually killing only small animals.

Lanyard looked around once more. A few people glanced incuriously at him and walked on. The street flowed busily with Saturday night traffic, tourists, laughing couples on dates crowding the sidewalks, portable radios calling dance themes.

He shrugged and hurried on.

It's loneliness, he decided. I need to talk to someone. That conversation with Maguss spooked me. Which is probably what the old fraud intended.

He thought he glimpsed a shape, eel-like and airborne, slithering through the shadows to one side. Just caught a flicker, from the corner of one eye. Probably an autumn leaf blowing by.

But he didn't turn to make sure. He hurriedly turned, instead, toward a bar. He didn't stop to notice the name or the sort of bar it was. It was a place with the tavern-style neon in the window, and as the door opened he could hear bottles clinking, glasses tinkling. That was all that mattered.

He was dimly aware that he'd shut off part of himself. He wasn't noticing much. Details seemed painful, no matter what they were. He tried to ignore his acid stomach too. *Psychosomatic*, he thought. He elbowed with uncharacteristic rudeness into a narrow crevice in the crowd at the bar, muttering, "Psychosomatic…"

The bartender misheard him. "Whuh? Sickoso? We ain't got that. The only kinda Japanese beer we got is Asahi—"

"No uh—I—Oh, okay, give me an Asahi beer. And a straight vodka with that. Take the beer as a chaser." He spoke to the air; he didn't really see the bartender. It was as if he were selectively blind. He saw only what he needed to. A bottle came into range and a shot glass filled with something transparent. He was willing to focus on the bottle and the shot glass. He automatically fished a bill from his wallet.

"You shouldn't ought to flash that stuff," said the bartender quietly, taking the twenty to make change.

Lanyard frowned. Flash *what?*

And then he realized that the bartender meant the wallet. The wallet still open in his hand. There was too much visible money in it. Nearly four hundred dollars. He'd cashed some traveler's checks. Had meant to deposit some of it into the checking account he'd opened, a bank near his new apartment.

He stared at the wad of money. In the open wallet it resembled something gone green in an untended wound. He winced at the thought. But he couldn't take his eyes off the cash. I'm staying in New York, he thought, and I don't want to stay here. I want to go away from the killings. I don't want to look at any corpses. But I'm staying here for this *stuff*: for the money Maguss is paying me. And for Madelaine?

He focused his attention only on the glass and the bottle. Maguss had implied (*The bottle, bring it to your lips, taste it, nothing else*) that be was interested in Madelaine because (*The glass! Knock it back!*)—

He coughed, the hard liquor searing his throat, further convulsing his stomach. To one side, someone laughed and said, "John can't hold it."

John?

"Carl," he murmured, trying to make himself laugh.

Relax. He took another drink.

It worked...partly. He stopped thinking about Maguss and Madelaine and the movements in the air—movements like a magician's hands disembodied, slicing....

Someone offered him a way out. "Yo, my man, whuh you wanna drink fo? That shit give you hangover, man." A young Hispanic with red-rimmed eyes whispering in his ear. Lanyard could smell strong, cheap after-shave.

Lanyard shrugged. "Drinking's the best I have at the moment."

"Hey checkitout, got some blues, top-drawer shit."

Blues? Lanyard was tempted. It was a way out. He didn't want to admit that he wasn't sure what drug blues were. "Uh—they good quality?"

"Pharmaceutical, my man."

A cupped hand below the level of the bar. No one seemed to notice. In the man's palm were four blue tabs.

"How much?"

"I leddem go for five each. Goodshit, checkitoud."

Lanyard didn't know the proper method of haggling. So he didn't haggle. He shrugged again. "You got it. I'll try anything tonight." He dug a twenty from a side pocket, handed it over under cover of the bar. The man dropped the pills in Lanyard's palm and slipped away.

Two pills Lanyard slipped into the change pocket of his pants the other two he swallowed—the bartender's back was turned, but it probably wouldn't have mattered if he were looking.

Fifteen minutes later, Lanyard was humming and looking for the jukebox. "Quarters, quarters," he murmured, squinting over the selection.

The jukebox glowed like a geode, purple and rosy in the bar's darkness. A subterranean egg of crystal. It was playing some undistinguished disco tune; black girls chanting *"You do that thang to me, makes me so dizz-zee, when you use that thang on me—"*

Lanyard looked up from the jukebox, trying to get a handle on the sort of place it was. But the bar had no particular decorative theme. Its ornaments had been culled randomly: On a plywood cabinet behind the bar was a murky aquarium containing a few gasping, piebald angelfish and up-ended plastic plants. A four-foot plaster model of a cigar-store Indian stood between the aquarium and a rack of low-cost liquors.

A woman sidled up to him and said: "Can I play a tune, babe? You put a quarter in and you didn't pick nothin'."

"Mm? Oh, hell *yeah*—play anything you like."

"Could you press the buttons for me? Play 'I'm Lonely Tonight'."

Laboriously he searched through the numbers till he found the tune, and carefully punched its code.

He expected her to thank him and walk away. But she asked him for something more. "Do you have an extra cigarette?"

He did, and shakily lit it for her. He lit one for himself.

"I went a year without smoking," he said, in an effort to make conversation. "I blew it yesterday."

"Did you? What happened?" She seemed genuinely interested. Something in her manner implied that she was concerned for him, that she wanted to help.

"Oh—uh—someone tempted me. I tempt easily."

"Yeah?" She smiled. She was dressed for partying. She wore a high-slit tight tan dress, tan high heels, tight peach-pink sweater (so much that was the color of flesh, Lanyard thought); she had wavy shoulder-length dyed-blond hair. Her eyes were dark, her skin olive.

Lanyard knew she was probably a hooker. But seeing her in the stained-glass glow of the jukebox and through the drugs, he didn't care.

Looking close, he could see she had acne scars on her cheeks; but somehow the scars were charming. Her teeth were crooked, but somehow this was endearing.

"Buy you a drink?" he heard himself ask.

They sat in one of the booths. She told him her name, Julie. A thin black man with three overcoats on, one buttoned over the next, came into the bar carrying a paper sack. From the paper sack he took a broken blender and a single stereo speaker, held one item in the crook of each arm, and said, "Blender works good, speaker works good, good price. Blender here; speaker."

The music from the jukebox had somehow merged seamlessly with the noise of the crowd, the clatter from the bar, the quasi-futuristic noises of the electronic games, so that it all became one wallowing liquid sound, washing over him in regular waves of drone.

He hardly noticed that he'd begun talking (now and then stopping, thinking he saw a shadow take impossible shape in the air, or imagining he'd glimpsed Madelaine in the shifting faces passing their table); his mouth had become a dam's spillway. "You can see whatever you like in the world, really, Julie, you ever think of that?"

"Oh, I know just what you mean," she said, just as if she did.

He went on, "I met this tramp—they're human beings. We walk right past them like they're pigeons with broken wings. You can see Bowery tramps filling with pneumonia on the streets when it gets cold. This is still, eighties or not, still the Me Decade. So we see their deaths as natural selection, right?"

"Uh-huh," she said, seeming interested, taking another cigarette from the pack he'd left on the tabletop between them.

Not till much later did it occur to him that he hadn't been speaking loudly, that she really couldn't have heard him clearly, that she was only pretending to be interested.

Not till the next morning, when he woke and found her gone.

He was in his apartment. His wallet was missing. His radio was missing. He dimly remembered bringing her back here. He didn't remember what happened after they'd arrived, except that she'd stroked him and cooed in his ear as they lay on the bed.

He'd awakened on top of the bedclothes, fully dressed. He was fairly certain they hadn't had sex. And he realized that she hadn't come onto him in the bar, hadn't talked money. She'd known that robbery would be more profitable than hustling. She'd gotten four hundred dollars cash, and by now she'd have purchased some expensive things, with the aid of a male friend, using his credit cards. Then she'd ditch the cards and sell the furs, the shoes, the—

He thought: *Oh, Christ. Madelaine.*

KRUPP WAS AFRAID to answer the phone. It would be the phone company with a last warning. It would be the bookie. It would be his ex-wife demanding and demanding. It—

It might be the police. He'd thrown the knife into the river and burned the pants soiled with the girl's blood, and the next day he'd walked past the newsstands with his eyes closed, knowing nevertheless that thousands of people were reading NEW SUBWAY HORROR: CULT KILLERS TAKE 8TH.

But he answered the phone; Tooley had told him to keep in touch, to wait for their call.

It wasn't Tooley, or the cops, or his wife. It wasn't his bookie. It was his brother, Reggie. The cold-blooded lowlife prick. "Hey, pal, you get over here and pick up this damn lottery ticket and you take it down to that office and *collect!* The ticket's registered to you, and you know damn well I can't use it. Shit, when you left it here for collateral, I laughed at you. Who coulda guessed? Now you owe me four hundred bucks and—"

"Just shut up," Krupp interrupted. "Shut up if you want to get your money."

His brother shut up.

"How much?" Krupp demanded. "For God's sake, how much did I—"

"You bought the damn ticket, you know how much it's—"

"How *much?*"

A pause. "You won seventy-four-thou, what you think?"

"Seventy-four thousand dollars?" Krupp was almost as disappointed as he was elated. But it was enough, sure it was, yeah. *Yeah.* Enough so that Lydia Backstrom wouldn't laugh when he asked her to do the film with him. Shit, it was enough so she'd fuck him on the side, too. It was enough to pay off the bookie and to pay off—

"Hey—" Krupp said suddenly. "You didn't say anything about this to that *bitch*, did you?" Meaning his most recent ex-wife.

"No, Christ, no, what kind of bastard you think I am?"

"The bastard who turned up his nose at me more'n once," said Krupp impulsively, realizing he didn't have to be nice to his brother anymore. He'd always hated the lowlife prick anyway. His brother was using a genial tone now, ingratiating himself, because the money was there, hovering like a golden goddess in the air between them.

"Ha, ha," said his brother, pretending that Krupp was joking. "I guess you can help me out with that financing that annex to the shop. You know, the bank wouldn't lift a finger to keep God Hisself from going under, and—uh…" He paused, working up his pitch.

Krupp wanted to say, *Fuck you.* And hang up. He had Tooley's Organization with him now. He didn't need the shithead anymore.

But his brother still had the lottery ticket. He had to get it from him. If he pissed the guy off he might drop it in the Cuisinart or something. "Oh, yeah, sure, I can help you out," Krupp said. Let him believe it for now. His brother rattled on for a few minutes more about his plans for the annex, and other ingenious ways he had for spending Krupp's money, and Krupp was thinking: *I'll get a gram—no, three grams—of coke and maybe a Toyota, get my cameras out of hock, make that big one, talk to the mob about distribution, and—oh God what if the police come, what if they find out, what if Tooley calls, what does he want me to do?*

He mumbled an excuse, said he'd be over to pick up the ticket, and hung up.

He sat staring at the gold coke spoon on the mirror laid flat over a table beside his bed. His right hand clenched the imitation zebra bedspread. His left reached tremblingly for the gold bauble. He thought: *What will they want me to do next?*

He picked up the spoon and the coldness of the metal seemed to travel along his fingertips and into the veins of his hand and into his bones and up along his arm and into his shoulder and his spine until his back was prickling with the chill of gold, the cold of gold. "Gold," he muttered, "is cold stuff."

He knew the cold was fear.

What scared him, what really bothered him deep down, was that the ritual had worked. He had generated luck by killing. Doing the ritual, he'd felt that Thing around. The Head Underneath. He felt it send its pet and he'd run to get away from the kill site, the night air making the sweat that covered him feel like a coat of ice. He'd run to be out of the subway. No one had seen him. He'd gone up the stairs, crossed to the uptown side of the station, all out of sight of the token-booth operator. Not a soul around. He'd paused on the uptown platform to look across the tracks at the person—a once-person, now less than a person, a piece of meat in a crazy splash of paint—and he'd glimpsed the red-flickering animal that was there, and wasn't there….He'd seen it poised over her, snuffling at her like that dog he'd seen—as a kid he'd seen a big dog corner a kitten. A German shepherd. The dog had the little big-eyed kitten cornered against the bole of a big Douglas fir tree in the park of his hometown. No one was around then either. He knew the dog was deranged; the big boys who owned the dog tortured it and chained it up a lot of the time. You could see it in the dog's manic eyes, its muzzle all slathery and grinning, the way it zigzagged across the park, looking for trouble, hoping someone would try to pet it. Showing its teeth and grinning. Then it saw the kitten—two months old, nearly half grown—and the dog lowered its head, stopped its zigzagging, and started moving in a straight line for the little furry thing—

He'd been scared. He looked around for someone to call. When he looked back the dog had the kitten in its mouth and he was snapping it back and forth. The dog's testicles jiggled to the right when it jerked its head to the left. Five or six of these obscene wagglings, the kitten's body kicking, whipped like a rag caught in a racing car's grille, the squealing was submerged under the dog's half-hysterical growling. And then it snapped the kitten's back. The dog glanced at the young Krupp and raised a leg to piss, as if to suggest its indifference to the boy's presence, its awareness of the boy's impotence.

That's how Krupp felt on the platform, seeing the red whirly toothy thing, the pet of the Head Underneath, poised over the body he himself had carved. Seeing it dart down, the way the German shepherd had gone for the kitten.

That's how he felt now, too. Thinking: It's too late for me now. Because it works. That means it could be anywhere. It has that much power. And it knows about me. I'm part of it now.

I have no choice. I have to do exactly as it says.

EIGHT

"There's always a choice," Gribner said, jabbing his index finger at Freeberg, "especially when the guy has no gun showing."

"I had no *choice*," Freeberg persisted. "I had to shoot, and that's the way it was. You weren't *there*, Lieutenant. You had to see the suspect's face to know. It was kill it or it would have killed me."

"*It?* What do you mean, *it*, Freeberg? We're talking about a *child* here. Maybe fourteen years old at the most. Still a child. A human being. A boy. A *he*. Not an *it*. Am I getting across to you?"

Gribner was shouting.

"Cool off, Lieutenant," Captain Lubbuck told him. "I told you—you are not going to be relieved of this case, and your shouting during a debriefing is not going to change my mind. You think I don't know what you're doing? You're on this case, Lieutenant. So stop looking for trouble; that won't get you off. You understand? No one asked you come uptown for this briefing. You came on your own. Understand?"

Gribner snorted and looked away. *He thinks I'm faking. But for the first time in my life I think I understand rooftop snipers.*

The four other men in the captain's office were giving Gribner much the same look of quiet disbelief they'd given Freeberg an hour before.

An hour before, about six PM, Officer Freeberg had given his oral report on a shooting. He'd shot a teen-age boy, who so far remained unidentified, in the utility tunnels under Grand Central Station. Freeberg wasn't a transit patrolman but he'd been walking his beat just outside Grand Central, on Forty-second Street, when a burly, "strong-looking" black man, a tramp wearing grimy army-surplus clothing and rotting tennis shoes, ran screaming out of the station with the left side of his face torn away. He'd collapsed, bubbling blood and sobbing, at Freeberg's feet. Freeberg used his walkie-talkie to call a patrol car. The patrol car pulled up and took the tramp, pumping blood from a gash in his neck as well as the ragged face wound, to a hospital. Freeberg, a gangly, blond-mustached, ambitious young officer, had meanwhile plunged into the station.

For two weeks he'd been trying to catch a team of teen-age purse snatchers who had been working his beat, always a step ahead of him. The tramp had babbled about "a bunchakids, all buggy weirdshit...inna lowuh tunnels...." The *lower tunnels* were seven levels beneath the streets, and contained mostly heavy power and steam mains. They were a filthy, rat-infested but relatively warm haven for wintering hoboes. Freeberg was supposed to report his suspicions to the Transit Authority cops. It was their turf. But he was bored, and he wanted the bust for himself.

He'd pushed rudely past the crowd on the down stairways; the stairways seemed endless. He pounded downward, level on level, till he saw the sign he was looking for: AUTHORIZED PERSONNEL ONLY. At this point, the transcript of his oral report read:

I looked at my watch. It was eight PM I went through the door. There was no one around. I think they should have someone watch it, it was too easy for me to get in. They ought to lock it. Then maybe this would never have happened. It was a construction site in there, ladders and paint buckets everywhere. And on the other side was a metal stairway. I went down and I'm prowling through the tunnels and they got these overhead lights there and...I didn't have a flashlight on me...every third light was out. Now and then there was like a little place where there was some light, and—uh—I noticed there weren't any tramps or any bag ladies down there. And usually, the way I hear it, there would be. I figure these kids scared them away. Anyway, I was going through a stretch of darkness, real jumpy, I could hear the rats running around, and I was crouching down a little, see, because the ceiling was so low and this big rubber pipe filled with power lines, I guess, was next to me. I glanced under it at one point and I saw these eyes. So I'm backing up and the kids, they're coming out from under the pipe at me, so goddamn dirty it's unbelievable. I didn't have a flashlight with me and it was real tight in there and the only source of light—there was a bend up ahead—the only light was about forty feet behind me, so I'm backing toward it and the little bastards come at me and they're…some of them are like seven, eight years old. The oldest one—well, he was coming at me ahead of the others, he had his face painted up in some marks, I didn't know what they were. He was saying things in some language and then he would switch to English and say these things….I suppose I should tell you what he said, to explain my feeling about him….but I can't. I can't tell you just now. I can't think about it too much. He said things that made me want to kill him to keep him from saying anything like that to anyone else. But that's not why I shot him. I'm—I'm making myself talk like he was a human being, but he—at the time I thought of him as an *it*. Because he was shaped like a human but he was acting like an *it*. It was the way he was backing me up, snarling at me, and saying those things. He was coming along at me in a sort of walking crouch, his head moving from one side to the other, almost. The way he was moving his hands too, like they were cobras, almost like he was a dancer….He ignored my gun, he looked me right in the eyes, and I kept backing up till there was enough light—

GRIBNER: Enough light for what, Freeberg?

Enough light to shoot. I knew I had to shoot him. He wasn't no purse snatcher. He was—I had no choice! If you'd seen him, you'd know, if you'd seen the way he acted…I had no choice.

That's where Gribner had said, "There's always a choice."

"He was outnumbered," said Lubbuck, a little later, sitting in the captain's office opposite Gribner, Freeberg between them. "They probably had knives."

"Oh, I know, I know, more than you people do, that that kid was dangerous," Gribner said. "But I don't think you should have shot him, Freeberg. The officer who called me from your precinct, *that* guy knew the connection, he could see that the little bastards you ran into are mixed up with the subway killings. You may have shot our only lead. And anyway, that kid didn't know what he was doing—he wasn't himself. You were killing his body, and someone else, the someone who controls him, whoever's running this cult, *he's* getting away scot free."

"Oh, Christ," Lubbuck said, "he's giving with the mystical stuff again. 'Killing his body'…'Controls' him, Gribner?"

And Freeberg was staring at Gribner in open horror.

The captain sighed and said, "Lieutenant Gribner, take a break, okay? We've got no reason to believe this is part and parcel of the subway killings, and that's what you're supposed to be—"

"*What?*" Gribner snorted. "Are you joking, or what? Didn't you hear the part about the marks? They have the symbols painted on their—"

"Gribner," said the captain warningly. "Take the rest of the day off. That's an order. I'll call your precinct captain to get that order confirmed with him if you want…"

"That won't be necessary…*sir*," said Gribner sarcastically. He was older than Captain Lubbuck.

He left the office, thinking about the small warm friends who'd died ugly in the cellar of his building, of the boy they'd found in that cellar, of the nephew still missing, and that would be the time, right, *just* the time that S.O.B Lanyard would call.

"You Gribner? Call for you…"

"Gribner? They said you were at this number, I hope you don't mind I chased you down…I called the Ninth Precinct twice…"

Gribner sat on the corner of some absent officer's desk, talking to the black instrument that people called a telephone, staring at the dirty green ceiling, saying, "Now what is it you want to know, Lanyard? You're talking too fast, gimme a break here, I got a pain you wouldn't believe, trying to get something done, and these people—what?"

"I said, I want Minder's address."

Gribner hesitated. "Why?"

"Because…" Lanyard's voice became falsely blasé. "Because—well, it's a long story, but I was invited to a dinner there, and—uh—I have to meet Madelaine there, and—uh—I lost my invitation. It has the address."

Gribner felt sure that Lanyard was lying. "Tell you what, Lanyard, I'll believe that story and give you the address, if you talk to this guy I've got here. I want him to describe some symbols—oh, wait, here's the report. He's already drawn them out here. Now, one is an inverted pentagram with a skull face in the middle, some smears on the skull that might be a sort of antenna or…or mustache."

"Yeah. Those symbols come from the same cultural set as the ones we saw in the subway and in the cellar…." Lanyard's voice seethed with impatience.

But he said, more slowly, "What were the circumstances in which the symbols came up?"

Gribner described Freeberg's encounter under Grand Central.

"Huh…" Lanyard sounded far away. "Gribner, maybe you ought to talk to the people at Public Utilities. Sewage workers, utility workers of all kinds. Subway techs. Maybe this thing is more connected with the tunnels than we thought. I mean, I always assumed the killers were just going down into the subways and cellars and…and then coming back up again. But maybe they—some of them—live down there."

"That's the way the kid looked. The others—after Freeberg fired the shots, the others ran away like frightened rats. He carried the kid's body up, and I had a look at it. Filthy, like it lived down there. The face 'paint' from Magic Markers. Like graffiti."

"Yeah. But I've been doing some research, Gribner. I'm convinced this thing somehow is rooted in the underside of the city. I mean that literally. You mentioned Grand Central: seven levels underground there. A forty-acre area, mostly underground. The city's sewer system is sixty-five-hundred miles long. There are sewer mains, telephone and electricity lines, water mains, storm sewers, water tunnels, and the damn subway—the damn subway covers *two hundred and thirty miles!* And in all that there are lots of places to hide. Hundreds of deserted tunnels. Unused, closed-down subway stations…there are two hundred sixty-five stations in use, but—"

"Yeah, yeah, and New York produces thirty thousand tons of garbage per day! That's a fact, too. So *what?*" And then Gribner understood. "You're saying we're going to have to systematically search all that underground, maybe? If those people are living down there…"

"Can I have the address now?"

"Gramercy Square. Number seven. Just below Twenty-third and Lexington. Private park with a locked gate, townhouses. You'd *better* have an invite—"

"Thanks." Lanyard hung up.

Inexplicably, thinking about his wife at home staring at the TV, trying not to cry, Gribner's unconscious chose that moment to spring a leak—

He burst into sobs.

LANYARD PAID THE cabdriver, again overtipped in his nervousness, and climbed out. He stood on the sidewalk, looking up at the townhouse. A chill wind made him cringe. The wind whipped his wet hair. He stared up at the gray stone townhouse; its face was ornate, with carved figures he couldn't quite make out in the darkness, the shielding blue-white of the anticrime street lamp glaring down at him.

There was a gray-green wake of decapitated rose bushes on either side of the building's aggressive, unwelcoming prow.

A pay phone stood at the corner. Maybe that one would be working. He couldn't bring himself to crash Minder's place without trying to call Madelaine once more. She might have come back while he was in the taxi. He walked past the front of Minder's townhouse, trying, without craning his neck too much, to see past the shuttered windows. The house was mute; no noise of partying, no bright lights whirling at the upper windows. But then, the building was five stories. And it probably had a basement.

He winced as a fire truck raced along Lexington, a block away, its warning horn blasting with a noise like the earth's crust sundering.

He dialed the number and heard, dimly over the traffic noises and wind, "You have reached Madelaine Springer. I am unable to come to the phone at the moment...."

He hung up. He hunched deeper into his coat, fists balled in the pockets, and turned toward Minder's house.

Lanyard...Carl..."And I could not laugh with the Demon, and he cursed me because I could not laugh..."

He ignored the voice.

He heard it, picked it out clearly from the background tapestry of sounds. But refused to acknowledge it. Some mutinous brain cell informed him: The voice quoted Edgar Allan Poe.

He ignored it, just as he ignored the eel shapes flickering around the eaves of the house.

But he stopped at the black-iron gate, his hand on the cold metal as he gazed at the building. It wasn't really that it was a forbidding sort of place. It wasn't Gothic, or particularly grim: It's windows were trimmed in bright blue, its shutters sea-green. The roses must be quite cheerful in the summer.

But still, when he looked at it, he had an odd sort of feeling.

It was an elusive feeling. He'd had it before. It's a feeling you get when you're driving down a highway and the highway's horizontal plane becomes vertical, in your mind's eye, so that, you feel for a moment that you are no longer driving cross-country, but pitching headlong into a lighted shaft, a deep, *deep* pit whose walls are inexplicably marked like a freeway....

It's the feeling you get when you see an old man sitting utterly *alone* in the lobby of a flea-bag hotel, his toothless mouth drooping, gazing out at the world traipsing indifferently by, making you wonder why he had to live his whole life just to come to this.

It's the feeling you get when you realize, really know for the first time, that yes, definitely, someday you are going to DIE.

The first time Lanyard had the feeling he was a little boy. He felt it just before he'd tried to tell some people what Mrs. Connely told him from the Otherwhere. No, he corrected himself: What he *imagined* Mrs. Connely told him.

Later, he'd had the feeling after a dream. In the dream he'd come upon a bottle with a cocoon in it. As he watched, the cocoon split open and out of it crawled a tiny golden skinned little man. The little man had two glittery wings on his back. Wings of lacy black sparkle, beautifully articulated feathers. The little man's eyes shone with beams of light. The golden man had escaped from the cocoon but he was still trapped in the bottle. He pounded at the glass of the bottle, in some distress, trying to break out. The bottle was uncorked, but the neck was too narrow to admit the tiny man to the world. Young Carl had known that if he broke the bottle to let the little man out, he might accidentally hurt him. The little man was obviously fragile. But Carl didn't know what else to do.

He couldn't get the tiny man's attention because he was fluttering madly about in the bottle, hysterical at being trapped. Overwhelmed with pity, Carl tried to break the bottle, at one end, with a rock. But his effort was indelicate; the whole bottle was crushed, the tiny man impaled on glass shards. That's when Carl woke up with that feeling...that odd, hard-to-define *feeling* of...

He shook his head. He still couldn't define the feeling.

Every second you live brings you closer to the time you will die, Carl.

You're not hearing voices, he told himself. Those are auditory hallucinations from your bad night, and what happened with that bitch and you're splintered with worry about Madelaine.

He opened the gate and walked up the flagstones, trying to frame his opening lines for whoever came to the door.

He stood on the porch, thinking. *Some bald-faced lie. That's what I'll have to do. Make up some outright lie and hope she plays along.*

It was always possible that she wasn't here. His suspicions might be silly. Or she could be out with Minder somewhere.

But somehow he knew she was there. Realizing that, he had that odd, indefinable feeling again.

He fished a cigarette from his coat pocket, put it in his mouth—and changed his mind. It wouldn't do to smoke when he was trying to get inside. They might have rules against it. He put the cigarette back in his pocket, took a deep breath, and pressed the doorbell.

He stood a long time waiting, wondering if he should go.

At last the door opened. The man who looked out at him might have been a husky second-year college chemistry student, with his large round glasses and his gray sweater, the collar of a blue work shirt neatly overlapping the sweater's crew neck. His black hair was fashionably long, but not too long. He appeared to be waiting for Lanyard to exhibit some sign that he was either *Type A* or *Type B* of something. He was *big*. He could have crushed Lanyard's head in the crook of his arm. He said nothing; he waited.

"Lanyard, Carl Lanyard," said Carl Lanyard, smiling and businesslike. "I was to pick up—ah—Madelaine Springer. Mr. Minder called me—"

Apparently the man at the door—clearly a bodyguard—had sized up Lanyard as a *Type B: Not Admitted.* "I don't think so," he said. "It's my understanding that Ms. Springer is not to be disturbed. She's studying her part for Mr. Minder's production."

"You studied *that* part well," Lanyard said. The door closed in his face. He heard the big man's footsteps recede.

Lanyard was insulted: The man hadn't bothered to remain to make sure that Lanyard went away. By the sound of it, he hadn't even locked the door. Alarming overconfidence, in New York City. Lanyard tried the knob. The door opened easily. Moving as quietly as possible, picturing himself in jail for breaking and entering, he stepped inside and closed the door softly behind him.

He was standing on a polished hardwood floor. The Ivy League Juggernaut, as Lanyard thought of him, was nowhere in evidence. Lanyard padded to the left, breathing shallowly, a rippling of warning moving through his chest. He entered a high-ceilinged room furnished with antiques; the undyed woolen pile rug sank deeply tinder his feet. The Early American furniture was in excellent shape. The furnishings, the yellowed oils, the antique clocks, the bronze mantel sculptures—all chosen by a decorator.

Passing beneath the chandelier of the dining room, Lanyard realized that these were essentially showrooms. Not much dining done in the dining room.

So, Lanyard wondered, what's all this a front *for?*

A grandfather clock ticked. Its ticking seemed too slow, maddeningly sluggish.

Lanyard was, unconsciously, holding his breath. The crackle of a dead leaf blowing against a shutter made him freeze, until he identified the sound. He moved on, down a short flight of stairs to the kitchen, half below street level.

There was something cooking in a pot on the stove; it smelled like Italian food. Probably the cook would return any moment.

Surrounded by all this domesticity, Lanyard felt for the first time like a burglar. An intruder.

But the sense of danger connected with Madelaine was too acute to allow him to feel actually ashamed. Still, he knew that his tactics were foolhardy. He was in hot water. He was in deep shit. He was—

He was staring at a door at the far end of the long kitchen: Somehow he knew the door led to the cellar.

He hurried toward it, his eyes fixed on it, seeing nothing else—not seeing the chrome dog dish on the floor; he struck it with his right foot, then leapt back, bit his lip to keep from shouting at himself in anger. It went clattering against the wall, loud as any burglar alarm, nastily spattering dog food in an arc across the tile floor. "Shit," he muttered. He hurried toward the cellar. He heard the sound of a large dog barking from the front hallway. He could hear its nails clicking on the wooden floor of the hallway, the sound of its barking growing louder, coming at him. *Jeezus fucking Christ,* he thought. *An attack dog.*

He yanked at the cellar door. The knob wouldn't turn. He looked frantically around, his breath coming in noisy gasps. He heard someone yelling from the dining room.

"I dunno, I—" The Ivy League Juggernaut's voice.

"You dolt, you left the front door unlocked—"

"I'm not used to this place, I thought it locked itself when—"

Lanyard felt his fingers close on something small and metallic beneath the knob. A key in the lock. He turned it, fumbled with the knob, snapped the door open, just as the dog bounded into the kitchen behind him. He didn't see the dog; he felt the vibrations of its coming in the floor, and his back went up with its aggressive snarling. He slipped through the door and slammed it shut, his heart's pounding almost louder than the thuds the dog made leaping again and again at the door.

He remembered the dog that wasn't a dog, the thing made of red-hot wires he'd glimpsed on the back of his eyelids in a cellar furnace room.

He turned and descended the stairs. The concrete stairs had recently been painted bright blue. The ceiling was covered in a rug. Why? For sound absorption? The way was well lit by fluorescent bulbs.

The walls were paneled wood. It was a perfectly ordinary stairway—except that it went much, much deeper than it should have.

Lanyard hadn't quite reached the bottom when the door above him opened. He leapt down the last few steps shouting, "Madelaine!"

Someone was pounding down the steps after him. He heard the dog whining, snuffling, as it came along behind.

He sprinted along a short, mirror-walled hallway and turned a corner. And stopped cold.

Madelaine was sitting on a plush red bench, in a small dimly lit alcove, leaning against silver-velvet wallpaper; the kitschy wallpaper depicted valentine cherubs. To one side was a curtained doorway; the curtains were of coral beads, and they swayed slightly as if someone had just passed through them.

Madelaine looked weary, her hair had been hastily brushed and tied back— it was still partly disarranged. She wore a black kimono. Nothing more.

Lanyard didn't care for the look on her face. It was a look that said, *Oh, great. After all I've had to put up with. Now you...*

"I—um—thought you might like..." Lanyard began. All his badly contrived excuses shattered when he was wrenched from his feet by what felt like thick iron pipes catching him under the armpits. The pipes were the Ivy League Juggernaut's arms. Lanyard was short, the bodyguard was tall; he lifted Lanyard off the floor with the armlock and whirled him about.

Lanyard found himself facing a black Doberman that rocked back on its haunches, looking as if it were about to spring. Lanyard's feet dangled off the floor; in his shoulder blades he could feel the bodyguard's massive heart thudding. Lanyard squirmed uselessly. The dog's jowls slavered, its eyes were hot, its teeth bared. It leapt at Lanyard and nipped at his kicking feet. It seemed to understand that—though a short leap could take it to Lanyard's throat—it wasn't to rip into him till the bodyguard gave the signal.

Lanyard struggled against the bodyguard, whose muscles were as hard as the steel bumper of a Cadillac. Lanyard could feel the bodyguard's breath on his neck and he could feel the dog's breath on his ankles and now and then the spiteful pinch as the dog nipped him and pulled back. He looked down at the dog's face, shouting "Heel!" and "Down!" in an attempt to intimidate it, all the time writhing in the air, caught in the big man's arms like a moth stapled to a wall.

Insinuated into the sounds of the dog's barking and snarling, the rasp of the bodyguard's hard breathing, and Madelaine's shouts at them to *"Stop it and get out of here!"* was something more…Woven in with this grotesque tapestry of noises was the Voice—not necessarily the same voice—laughingly advising Lanyard, *"You know all about the Head Underneath. They kill underneath, in the dark places under the city, because it's closer to Hell…"*

Ten seconds of this, between the bodyguard's lifting him over the dog and the last words of the Voice, *"because it's closer to Hell…"*

Two more seconds, then, for the flicker of remembering. He was ten years old and running across a deserted playing field until: *Carl tasted dirt and there was a funny ringing in his ears. He thought he would break in half from the pressure on his back. Frank banged the back of his head…No more hearing, no more seeing, except the dirt under his nose….*

The dog's snarling seemed to crowd into his ears, then, so that everything else was drowned out by it, so that it filled the world with its tearing; it was all the ugly noises he knew, combined and whetted: the sound of a bone breaking (though no one had broken his yet) and the sound of cartilage ground into slivers (though no one had yet crushed his face) and the sound of glass breaking and the sound of claws on metal and the sound of a scream in the subway overcome by the roar of an incoming train.

All this was gone, in an instant, reduced to panting, when Minder's voice boomed at the dog: "Down, Ronnie! Get down, sit!"

The dog obeyed and the bodyguard quickly came to heel, lowering Lanyard to the floor, when Minder said, "Let him down."

Lanyard stood gasping, waiting for the hammering in his chest to subside. A high-pitched whine seemed to come through the bones around his ears. He leaned against the wall, unable to take his eyes off the dog. It sat on its haunches, now and then washing one of its front paws. It was sleek and shiny, its short coat seemed almost reptilian. It turned to look at Minder when he spoke again: "Lanyard, I think, isn't it? They tell me you called earlier today, looking for Madelaine. You didn't mention that you would be burglarizing the house in order to find her."

Lanyard said, "Maybe, strictly speaking, it was—" He paused for a breath, and to glance at Madelaine. She had her head in her hands. "Uh—it was breaking and entering, but I'm not sure your bodyguard's attempt to feed me to that warped creature you call a dog is a legal means of dealing with—"

He stopped, choking with anger, because Minder was laughing at him.

"*Lan*-yard! You act as if I'm going to turn you in to the police. No, and"—this next seemed to be in answer to an inquiring look from the bodyguard—"I'm not going to punish you in any other way, either. I'm glad you dropped by. Gave me a chance to chat with you again. Saved me the trouble of arranging for a limousine for Madelaine. I was just going to send her home...."

He stopped, his eyes flickering-to the empty air between his left hand and the wall.

But the air wasn't empty.

Lanyard was staring at the spot, and Minder had noticed him staring.

"See something my housekeeper missed, Mr. Lanyard?" Minder asked softly.

Lanyard's vision was blurred with sweat, and his eyes didn't focus properly. So, he reasoned, he might not be seeing the eel shapes whirling, chasing their own tails, in an obscenely sinuous column in that space to Minder's left.

Lanyard shook his head and turned to look at the dog. "No. I don't see anything."

"Come on, Ronnie, I think you're making the man nervous." Minder turned and, the dog at his heels, climbed the steps. The bodyguard bent to whisper to Lanyard, the man's lips close beside his ear, "Not ever, not ever again. Piece by piece next time. Don't you ever come here again for anything. And don't you fucking linger about now." The Ivy League Juggernaut turned his back on Lanyard and climbed the stairs.

No witty comeback occurred to Lanyard. He felt only an inward churning. The churning was relieved, as the minutes passed, by a hollow sense of exhaustion.

Lanyard waited as Madelaine changed her clothes in the room down the hall.

She was ready with unusual speed; she came out dressed in a blue-black business suit. She seemed wobbly on her high heels. Her makeup was still smeared.

The atmosphere between them was somehow sensitive. He chose not to speak, just then, though he wanted to ask her: *Have you really been rehearsing all this time?* and *Why were you wearing nothing but a kimono? Is it only because you were waiting to change for a dress rehearsal?*

He preceded her up the stairs, wanting to leave the cellar badly, his exhaustion momentarily forgotten as he took the steps two and three at a time. He found the kitchen door slightly ajar. Half afraid the dog would jump him from somewhere, he stepped into the kitchen, blinking in the brighter light, and looked around. No one around. Voices came from an adjoining room. He waited at the top of the stairs, watching Madelaine climb them. It was as if he were looking down a throat that was swallowing her, frustrating her efforts to clamber out; the stairway seemed endless and for a while he thought she wasn't going to make it free. She climbed slowly as if her legs hurt.

Her face was white with strain when she reached the top. She smiled at him, blinking away small tears, and pressed past. He followed her out through the kitchen, up the stairs into the dining room, and hurried past her to act as insulation between her and the others, into the hall, all the time afraid that at the last moment Minder would rescind his pardon and the dog would come leaping at him from behind. Just as he put his hands on the front door, the dog would come.

He put his hand on the doorknob. A bark of laughter came from behind, and for a moment he froze. He turned the knob, it rotated in its collar, and then the door swung open and he stepped into the tingling night air.

He took her by the hand—the hand seemed limp and there was no discernible affection in her touch.

He hailed a cab, and the driver ignored them. He hailed another, it stopped and, enigmatically, the driver shook his head and drove on again. A third cab stopped for them.

"I'd like to go home, please," she told Lanyard. "I need to spend a night alone. I mean—I'm really tired. And I think it would be easier to sleep if I were alone."

"Sure," he said, puzzled by the vacuum between them. She hardly seemed to be there.

She gave the driver her address. The trip went by in silence. Silence, except for the drone of the motor, the rattle as it bumped over the badly kept Manhattan streets, the unintelligible braying of a deejay from the driver's radio. And the silence was broken, too, by the snarling Lanyard still seemed to hear, the dog snapping at his heels as if he were a biscuit held enticingly by its trainer. Lanyard trembled with suppressed fury. Visions of blowing the bodyguard's hamlike biceps in half with a shotgun came to him.

"This is it," Madelaine said, startling him. She spoke to the driver: "My friend is staying in the cab, he's going home from here."

"Shookay, lady," said the cabbie.

She climbed out, rather laboriously. She bent and peered into the cab at Lanyard long enough to say, "Hey, thanks and everything." Then she closed the door.

.

NINE

"Special messenger," said the tinny voice on the intercom.

"Special messenger from *who?*" Lanyard asked. He had not moved from his apartment since coming home the previous night after "rescuing" Madelaine from Minder. He hadn't slept much. He was afraid he'd find himself, in his nightmares, back in the grasp of the bodyguard, dangled over pink-gummed white-toothed jaws. He was irrationally afraid that the "special messenger" was actually someone sent by Minder. With Madelaine not watching—he had assumed Madelaine's presence was the only thing that kept him safe from Minder, the night before—Minder might well decide to come down on him.

"Messenger from Data Digs," said the man irritably.

"Oh! Damn!" Lanyard pressed the button to open the door. "Come on up."

"You got to come down for it," said the messenger.

"Just leave it in the hall, I'll pick it up shortly," he told the intercom.

He paced, glanced at the clock. Wait at least fifteen minutes, he told himself. They'll get tired of waiting and go away.

It was seven-fifteen PM The radiator whistled a keening note of alarm. Ticking sounds came from the pipes in the kitchen. He looked around. The apartment came into focus for the first time that day. It was a mess. Dirty clothes were piled in a heap by the bed; his coat lay sprawled across the couch like an animal drained of blood. The papers on which he'd tried to record his theories about the subcity killings for Maguss and Gribner were scattered about the floor.

He glanced at the clock and decided: *Ten minutes more.* He paced. And then, "Oh, to hell with it." If it were Minder's boys, he would deal with them.

After all, he had the gun.

Like something obscene, the gun was guiltily concealed, tucked under clothes half spilling from the wooden bureau to the right of the desk.

He had bought it on the street. Carrying it could net him jail time. But after the bodyguard had dangled him over the dog, helpless and humiliated, he could not bring himself to go anywhere without a gun. He went to the bureau, took it out, and looked at it. It was so nakedly *specialized*. He put on his jacket and tucked the cold, snub-nosed revolver in his jacket pocket.

He went to the door—and hesitated.

Lanyard was afraid of something more. He was afraid he was going mad. The Voices couldn't be what they seemed to be. If he was hearing voices, he was experiencing some of the symptoms of classic paranoid schizophrenia. A paranoid schizophrenic should not carry a gun.

He told himself: *You are not insane. You have to protect yourself.*

He opened the door and clattered down the stairs. He felt dizzy, today, going down them for the first time in twenty-four hours. He had a sense of forever, of being caught in an endless spiral staircase. Descending endlessly. He counted the floors. Fourth. Third. And—he stared in frozen horror at the number above the landing: 4. But he'd already passed four. He'd passed the third. This should be the second floor.

It was going to go on forever. He was caught in an existential whirlpool. He wanted to scream. And he nearly jumped over the banister in shock when the high-pitched giggling came from behind. He turned around, his hand closing on the pistol in his pocket. He had a glimpse of small children—rather dirty small children, with their faces oddly painted—disappearing into apartment 2A.

But 2A was on the second floor. He reached out and touched the number 4 on the wall; it slipped away, fell scraping to the floor. It had been loosely taped to the wall. The children had played a joke on him. That was all. He was on the second floor.

Shaking with relief, he descended the last flight and looked furtively around. No one in sight. A large manila envelope was leaning against the wall atop the metal frame around the double rows of mailboxes. Half of the mailboxes were deeply cored at the locks; three were hanging open, permanently broken. The mail was routinely stolen.

Glancing around once more, he bent and retrieved the envelope and took it upstairs with him.

Cellars

When he'd locked himself in the apartment, he decided that it was late enough for a cocktail. He poured himself a bourbon on the rocks and sat at the table to inspect the contents of the envelope.

There were photostats of police reports. How had Data Digs acquired them? There were also copies of newspaper clippings and a sheet of statistics (drawn from where?) that he didn't at first understand.

He glanced at one of the newspaper articles. Then he frowned, and reread carefully. Feeling an excitement that was both unsettling and euphoric, Lanyard fetched his notebook from the living room, returned to the kitchen, and sat down to paraphrase the article for his report to Maguss. He wrote:

A family of three: Mario Escondido, Sally Escondido, both twenty, and their daughter, Julie Escondido, two years old. There was, in a way, a fourth: Sally was three months pregnant. They were driving along Avenue B in a 1958 Pontiac sedan, on their way to Mass at an unspecified church, when they swerved to avoid a sack of garbage, a very large plastic sack, which for some reason was in the middle of-the street. According to witnesses, when Escondido came out of the swerve, returning to his own lane, the street "broke open under him...like when ice breaks under somebody on a river." The front end of the car dove into a hole that was later measured as nine feet wide, twenty feet long. The people on the street were at first afraid to approach the break in the street, afraid something would explode—a gas main?—or the street might collapse further. As they watched, the car sank further into the street till its rear wheels were lost from sight; a painfully loud grinding noise issued from the hole "like the car was getting all blended up in a blender." Over the grinding noise, the screams of the car's occupants were faintly heard. Smoke rose from the break, and exhaust fumes. And then a burst of flames announced that the gas tank had exploded. Smoke rose up thickly from the hole. At that point the screams ceased.

The city's maintenance crew set up a derrick to pull the car from the hole. When it was cranked up, creaking on its heavy chain harness, the wreckage was empty. There was no trace of human remains, except a little burnt blood on the dashboard, across the stopped clock. Nothing else.

The street had collapsed into a closed-off manhole which, "for unknown reasons" had been widened "by unknown persons." As if to accommodate something as big as a car. A passage led down to an unused water main. "Presumably, the Escondidos found their way down the manhole and into the empty water main, and got themselves lost in the tunnels." The search for them has so far been unsuccessful.

Lanyard stood, took another swig of his bourbon, coughed, and went to the telephone. He dialed Madelaine's number, and he was greatly relieved when she answered.

"Hey-lo, hey-lo," she said, sounding rather more giddy than usual, "this is not a machine speaking. This is a Madelaine speaking. Hello."

He smiled. "Hello. I'm glad you're not a machine."

"Who's this, pray tell?"

He was hurt that she didn't recognize his voice. "Carl Lanyard, Madelaine. Think back now. You remember. Hey, you okay? I mean, physically?"

"Sure...why?"

"Oh, I don't know, I—You just didn't seem well when I saw you last."

"I was just—tired. And upset because that guard was roughing you around. But you know, Joey has to be careful, crazed actors are always threatening to come and commit hara-kiri if he doesn't give them parts and—uh—all kinds of people try to nail him with lawsuits because they know he has money—"

"I see he's given you the whole rationale. So I guess it's okay with you that his bodyguard tried to feed me to—"

"No, no, the guy was an asshole, but—he says he just wanted to scare you."

"Oh, I'm sure he *did* want to scare me. For starters."

"Yeah, well, you brought it on yourself, Carl...I mean, I appreciate—uh—" She gave a noisy sigh. "Oh, never mind, I don't know why I'm bothering-to try to explain it. It was just an ugly misunderstanding. I have to hang up, Carl, I have to do some hard work on my script—"

"Did he give you a good part? What's it like? He—"

"Yeah, uh-huh, it's a good part, but really, I have to go. Thanks for calling, we'll get together—"

Lanyard groaned inwardly. How had he made her so defensive? He'd alienated her. "Look I'm sorry, Madelaine, if I—"

"Doorbell's ringing. Got to run."

Lanyard closed his eyes. "Okay. Talk to you later." He hung up, then dialed the Ninth Precinct. As he waited for Gribner to come to the phone, Lanyard carried the telephone into the kitchen and put it on the table next to the spread of papers sent him by Data Digs. When Gribner answered, Lanyard immediately launched into the story about the Escondidos.

"What, you think I don't know about that? I don't think there's any connection—"

"Are you kidding? No connection? Someone undermined that street. People are living down there somewhere—and this demonstrates that they're malicious, that they're playing vicious games with us. I think there may be a whole community of them. They're creating an atmosphere of terror because it suits their—"

"*Lan*-yard, boy, you're talking sensationalism, not sense. Living down there? Why should they do that? You said the rituals were designed to make them rich, to bring them success, right? So in the meanwhile they're living in the goddamn *sewers*?"

"I don't know why, *yet*, except that it may be necessary for the full effect of the magic—what they think of as magic—to come to pass. Or the people living underground might be the—uh—henchmen, for lack of a better term, working for the people who would benefit by the rituals. But in the particular magic tradition I believe is responsible, there is a belief that the god who bestows riches actually dwells in the rock underground. After all, that's where gold and jewels and other valuable ores come from. Therefore, they—"

"Lanyard, I haven't got time. I—my wife is very upset because of what happened with that boy. We never found him. She feels responsible…And our dogs…She—I have her staying at her sister's. She's frantic. I've got to go see her. I can't stand around right now—I was at work at seven this morning—uh—I can't stand around listening to your theories. Write it up for me, okay?"

"But *listen*—there's *another* report here that says that, in a part of the Upper West Side where rats are almost never seen, a woman was attacked by more than two hundred of them when they just sort of *poured* from a hole in the ground. Now the city pest-control people say there's some kind of underground disturbance, like maybe a tunnel fire or a wild dog lost in the utilities tunnels that drove them out—"

"Lanyard, write it up and—"

"And there are two reports of tramps being found mangled by 'wild dogs.' Now, what does that suggest to you? Maybe if you locate the specific places the bodies were found, you'll know where it is that the tramps came too near to—"

"*Lanyard!* Forget it! Write it up! Gowan, knock yourself out with it—" Gribner's voice was cracking. "Good-bye." Click.

Christ, Lanyard thought. Everyone I know is falling apart.

FOR A MINUTE after she spoke to Lanyard, Madelaine stared at the telephone blankly. She wanted to call him back; But it would mean having to explain *everything.*

There were things she didn't want to think about.

"I guess I'm just not the type," she'd said, smiling apologetically at the four nude men and three nude women on the vast, almost oceanic waterbed in Minder's basement.

She was still dressed, then; Minder had brought her down, had introduced her to the seven people on the waterbed just as if they were in a restaurant, and not nude and fondling one another. She tried to be casual, mildly indifferent, as if she were turning down a cigarette: *Oh, no, thanks, I don't smoke; you go ahead.* She didn't want to seem priggish. "Hey," Minder had said, "there's no pressure on you here. Come on, you don't have to do anything...but look, let's just you and me hop in the hot tub down here, to the right, you can put your clothes in this locker—and—uh—relax and—"

"I can do that much," she said, laughing lightly. She'd made it with Minder before. It was like having sex with a giant sponge, but it wasn't intolerable. In fact, he had a certain flair, at times.

And after the hot tub, he'd given her three lines of the best cocaine. And just a *little* heroin to take off the rough edges. And after that, a towel wrapped around her, she went with him easily to the orgy room, nearly flying there, not thinking, working *hard* at not thinking about it, and just as she entered the room they all looked up to give her the same look. Their expressions were so uniform from one face to the next that it was as if their seven heads were extensions of a single creature, a hydra of tangled human flesh. (And the disco ground away urgently in the background, never ceasing, panting the euphemisms.) Their expression was *knowing*.

None of them had yet touched her, but they looked at her as if they knew her when she screamed in orgasm. As if they'd watched secretly her every intimate moment; as if they'd watched even when the gynecologist had tied her tubes. The look wasn't a leer. It was recognition.

Later she told herself it had been the coke and the heroin and the cocktails that had made her melt for them when they'd risen to surround her.

But really it had been that expression of *knowledge*, though she'd never seen them, except for Joey Minder, before that night. And she knew somehow that all the time that man Tooley was watching, watching and masturbating, from a room where the mirrors around her were really a window.

She had gone down on every one of them. She couldn't remember their names.

And then they'd done some more coke and the two dark olive-eyed women had taken the little Italian with the close-clipped beard and tied him, as he giggled, to his chair. And beat him with leather straps and toyed with him. "It's all right," the little man with the beard had said, when she'd burst into tears. He'd smiled at her from between the two flaps of the leather mask they'd tugged over his head, inanely piping, "It's all in fun and performed with love." One of the women put her cigarette out on his leg.

So Madelaine had tooted more coke, and chased it with a smaller hit of heroin, and felt herself carried on a whirlwind into a place where there was no differentiation between fantasizing and doing. None at all. She'd let the two women tie her up; olive-eyed women, sisters, dark sisters, their hair swirling strangely in the red lights. Madelaine's breasts were remade by a tight black rubber brassiere with its tips cut out so that her nipples extruded in globular deformity. The third woman, the tall slender blonde, used the butt of her riding crop to probe…at first it was probing. Then it was digging, prying. It didn't hurt, at first; Madelaine was massively stoned. And she was spread-eagled, gagged, wriggling in a drugged continuum where all her sensations were as remade and deformed as her soft flesh under the tight ropes and straps, the black rubber brassiere.

Only much later, after Carl had arrived and taken her home, did she see the blood. It was funny—but she hadn't felt it. She saw it running down her leg, and it might just as well have been someone else's blood, someone else's thigh. The doctor had told her it was a mild uterine hemorrhage, and by the next evening the pain had become a distant throb.

But now there were other kinds of hurts. Loneliness and fear. She missed Lanyard. She couldn't talk to him, without explaining her behavior toward him. And she just couldn't explain. And fear? She was very much afraid the psychic flashes would come back.

Joey had told her that cocaine would insulate her from the flashes, and he was right. She'd had a gram he'd given her—he'd slipped it into her purse so she'd find it later—and she'd been snorting it, little by little, all day.

He'd given her coke—but so far, no contract for a role, no script. She regretted lying to Lanyard about the script. But she was sure that soon, any day, tomorrow perhaps, Minder would give her the part.

She sat staring, depressed, and snapped her head around to scowl at the kitchen sink when the damn pipes began to wail. She'd written to the landlord twice about the noisy pipes. The super said that it was a pressure problem that couldn't be repaired without a new pump, and the landlord would have to pay for that. Which wasn't likely. But the whining of the pipes was sometimes so loud it woke her out of sleep. She seemed to feel the keening—in her sinuses; she rose and padded into the kitchen to turn the faucet handles. She let the water run for a while, and the pipes' wailing subsided into a low, disappointed moan. She found herself staring at the drain in the sink. There were sodden, multicolored scraps of food clinging to the chrome lip of the drain; she brushed the garbage hastily into the gurgling hole, and watched the water sweep it away.

She put a plate over the drain, so that the water rattled on the china.

The drain. It went down, through all the building's stories, and down farther to the basement, and farther than that; it went into the secret places under the city's skin where tubular infinities of liquefied civilization pumped through crumbling pipes, gurgling.

She went to the dressing table for another toot. The gold vial was open, the gold coke spoon on the glassy tabletop beside it. She knew her depression was made worse by crashing from cocaine. She knew that more coke would make her feel worse, in the long run. She'd have trouble sleeping, at the very least. But she went to it without hesitation and performed the act automatically.

She spent the next hour cleaning house; tidying always made her feel better. It was as if she were putting the components of her life in order. In her sparely furnished rooms it didn't take long, and she was almost disappointed when the place was clean. Thoroughly clean, almost painfully spick-and-span. Ah—but there was dust coating the white crucifix on the white wall. She found a clean rag, put it to the tiny Jesus face, and screamed. Screamed, when the flash hit her—it came to her through the fingers touching the crucifix. She somehow that something, not God, was punishing her for the crucifix. Was claiming her. *You don't belong to Him, but to Me...*

Madelaine was on her knees, screaming, when the door opened.

(In some part of her she thought: *But I locked that door. Where did he get a key?*) Joey Minder and Tooley came into the living room and helped her to stand. When he touched her the maddened flashings in her head—ceased. Instantly. His touch was like water extinguishing flame. Her scream became a relieved whimper.

She let him enfold her in his soft, heavy arms though. His aftershave was so pungent she thought she'd gag. Her ears were ringing; there was a thudding in her temples. But she had come back from the brink. Minder had pulled her back. She could learn to like his after-shave.

"Hey," Minder was saying, "what's going on? What's wrong? We were just going to drop in on you and we heard you yell...." He was uncharacteristically solemn.

How had he got in without the doorman announcing him?

She was too exhausted to challenge him. She was afraid he might let her go, and the howling in her head would return. The howling, and the pictures of people in pain. *A girl in restraints in a madhouse, chewing away her own shoulders; an old lady starving to death in an unheated apartment because she was afraid to go out; two ambulance attendants sodomizing a woman with a broken leg and dumping her in an alley.* Somehow, Madelaine knew she'd seen things that were real.

What sort of God let all this suffering go on? And on and on?

A small boy tied to a bed, dying of rabies. Anesthesia doesn't work against rabies. And after two weeks of unspeakable pain, as his brain explodes inside its skull, the boy convulses in death.

She sobbed, burying her face in Minder's cushy chest. The pictures no longer came, but the memory was fresh.

"You'd better come with us," said Joey Minder. "What do you say, hm?" Some of his jolliness was restored. He helped her into her coat and led her out the door.

TEN

SHE'S TRYING TO *talk herself into joining us,* Krupp thought. *All this other stuff is bull. Just playing coy.*

There were five of them in the refurbished subway car. The car was stationary, the air a little close; they'd pulled into a deserted side tunnel, once used for emergency repairs.

Krupp watched Madelaine Springer closely, and listened raptly. He felt the same way she did, but he hadn't known how to say it. Now she was saying it all for him. She was putting into words all the gnawing maybes and what-ifs floating in his head since he'd come to realize who owned him.

Minder and Tooley were there, too, and a woman, a skinny fashion model of some kind he'd recognized from the last group rite. He wondered bow real her blond hair was. She sat coolly smoking a Virginia Slim and now and then sipping a gin and tonic.

Krupp thought: *Why us?* There were more than a dozen Blood Initiates. Why did Minder call *us* here, why us three?

Maybe we're the ones he has doubts about.

"It's the long-term consequences a person has to think about," Madelaine was saying. "They're what get you in the long run, man." She spoke in a monotone. She had a blank, sad look on her face. "But on the other hand," she went on, leaning back against the couch, her eyes on the small chandelier anomalously dangling from the old subway car's ceiling, "I can't stand it much more. The screeching in my brain."

"Is that really what it is?" Tooley's voice was soothing. "Let's put our cards on the table. You have a career you're concerned about. You want to be an actress. You want to be a *big* actress. That's never easy. You need every break you can get."

"Not the kind..." Now there was a little heat in her tone. "Not the kind that comes with the things...with killing."

137

"Americans who complain about the morality of selfish killing make me laugh," Minder said, chuckling. "Never mind Viet Nam, never mind Hiroshima. There are people starving to death right now, in various parts of the world. If the morally snobbish are so upright, why don't they send, say, two thirds of their income to the people dying of hunger? They could get by on the remaining one third. They would have to do without their second color TV and their daily cab fare and their new stereo with the special noise-reduction components and their weekends on Fire Island. But they'd never consider giving up their luxuries for the hungry. Middle-class liberals sit in their brownstones shaking their heads about cutbacks in the antipoverty programs—but right below their windows old ladies are poking through their garbage can, sniffing at wax paper, looking for a morsel. The liberals know those people are out there. Do they go out and offer them something from their overflowing refrigerators? Maybe some of their gourmet *fromage chimérique?* Maybe, once a year, they write a check for fifty bucks to United Way."

"A person can't take responsibility for the whole world. But you can at least attempt to keep from making it worse," said Madelaine wearily.

Smiling, Minder shook his, head. "Frankly, I don't think it could get much worse, short of nuclear holocaust. Do you know how many people starved to death in Cambodia a year or two back? Circumstances cut off the flow of food to the cities there, and hundreds of thousands of people had to try to walk to Thailand. And most of them starved to death. The deaths from violent crime in New York last year—well, life is cheap. Life is truly cheap, Madelaine. People are insubstantial as soap bubbles, and they're drifting through a hostile universe. It's *worse* than dog-eat-dog, most places. In El Salvador the government troops perform mind-boggling acts of butchery on anyone who looks at them funny; and the guerrillas do monstrous things to the families of those who collaborate with the government."

Madelaine took a deep breath and closed her eyes.

Minder finished quietly, "And that's what kind of world this is, Madelaine. But we in the Fraternity don't believe in hurting people unless it's necessary for the rites...."

Madelaine shook her head. "No, you can rationalize it any way you want. But that doesn't make it right. It's all for nothing, anyway...."

"All for nothing?" Tooley sat up straighter and spread his hands. "What about all this? Just one example: Do you have any idea how much it cost us to acquire and conceal and refurbish this subway car? Do you think the money for that comes from Joey's investments? It was given to us. Through the Strength. *He* is that strong, and *He* is stronger. You've felt the Strength. You said so. You felt it in the air. Why do you think none of us have been caught? Because as we give Him strength, through the rites, He multiplies it, and uses it to control events in the upper world. Luck can be manipulated. And that alone should remove any immature notions you have about 'justice.' The only justice is in Strength. Those who have the greater Strength *make* things Just—*for themselves.*"

"Do you know what sociobiology is, Madelaine?" Minder asked suddenly.

Madelaine nodded. "Sociobiology…I read about it in *Time*. It's the notion that almost everything we do, all of our behavior—uh—has some basis in instinct."

Minder was nodding, smiling gently. "You see, every behavioral impulse has—something to do with…with survival, the survival of the species or, more likely, of the individual. It's something instilled by nature. And what is this 'nature'? It's Life Itself. It's DNA, yes—but that's just the bottom line of Life Itself. And what else is there, really, that is God, if not Life Itself? So if you deny the voice that tells you to survive at any cost, then you disobey the edict of Life Itself. And so you disobey God, Itself. *Life* is God."

"I think there's more to it than that. I don't see why making yourself rich and successful with human sacrifice is something you do 'for survival'."

"You don't?" Tooley asked, pretending surprise. "But life is very uncertain. Obviously, the more money and power you have, the more likely you are to survive—you can hire the best doctors, you can hire bodyguards, you eat the best food and live in the safest, cleanest places, and you have fewer worries and less stress. You are simply more free, and more happy—never mind that asinine poem about Richard Corey, that's bullshit. Richer people are generally happier people. And the happier you are, the healthier you are. And so the more likely to survive."

How likely am I to survive? Krupp wondered, watching Madelaine, admiring her wavy fall of dark hair, wondering at the sadness in her; he could see her defenses crumbling, although her face showed no expression at all. As if that blandness on her face were her last, thin bulwark against giving in.

A low rumble built up in the car, at first entirely sonic; then they began to feel it in their fingers, their teeth, in the walls around them, until the chandelier rattled and the bottles clicked in the liquor cabinet. It was just a train passing somewhere nearby, but to Krupp it was the voice of the Head Underneath, arising from the hidden place, rumbling a warning through His realm. A sound that was part sob and part sigh escaped Krupp, and his hand tightened on his glass. He closed his eyes and swallowed, trying to nerve himself up. *You're a rich man, and you've got powerful friends,* said the rumble, diminishing.

When Krupp opened his eyes he saw that Minder and Tooley and the blond, modelesque woman were watching him. Madelaine was staring at the ceiling, her head tilted back onto the cushion, her neck arched oddly backward.

There was a grating but translucent tension in the rectangular chamber; for a moment Krupp thought that the tension was strongest in Madelaine, as if it had moved to dwell in her; she seemed close to bursting into tears. Her hands were clenched on her knees; looking at her black-Danskin-covered knees, his eyes were drawn to her thighs, thighs gently deformed by the seat, just glimpsible under the skirt of her soft blue-cotton dress. He found himself picturing Madelaine masturbating on a bed, in that same dress but without underwear, her legs spread for his whirring camera.

The image disturbed him; he felt what he supposed must be shame. He couldn't recall the last time he'd felt that way.

Maybe it was the steady, calm gazes of the other three.

They were making him self-conscious. That woman—what was her name? Miss Chancery, Tooley'd called her at the rite—she was the one who disturbed Krupp most. She was blond and long and slender and her features doll-perfect. But the look in her blue eyes…he saw no warmth there. He could imagine contempt in her eyes, or dull disrespect—that was what she held there now. As if Krupp didn't rate contempt.

Krupp somehow feared her more than he feared Minder and Tooley.

She wore a red taffeta ball gown, gushy, lots of fabric, right to the floor, with a semitransparent bodice to show her small pointed breasts.formally.

"Something wrong, Mr. Krupp?" she said suddenly, smiling without amiability.

"No, I—uh—I was just thinking about all what was talked about here. I didn't really follow a lot of it." He smiled sheepishly. "But—it's interestin'."

"Oh, it's *interestin'?*" she said, tilting her head, her smile widening till he thought she would burst out laughing at him.

He knew then that he hated her. You fucking cunt, he thought. You'll get yours. With the rest of us. He cut the thought short.

"The rite," said Minder softly, addressing Madelaine, "will be at eleven-thirty sharp. The preparatory makeup should be applied by eleven."

"I don't care to attend, thank you," said Madelaine, blankly.

The rumble went through the car again. But this time there was no train passing. The rumbling receded.

The Strength is real, Krupp thought. I have to do… what it says.

A picture flashed through his mind, and to keep from seeing it again, he went to the small refrigerator by the liquor cabinet where Minder kept ice and snacks. "Mind if I get some munchies?" he asked nervously, avoiding their eyes, bending to open the door and peer inside. He wasn't hungry, but he thought if he had a little something to eat it would ease the nervous fluttering in his stomach. He often ate when he was nervous. Or afraid.

"Help yourself," said Minder.

"Anyone else care for a snack?" Krupp asked, trying to be relaxed and affable.

"No," said Madelaine softly. She hadn't taken her eyes from the ceiling.

"No. No, thanks," said Tooley, rattling the ice in his glass with a swizzle stick.

"No," said Miss Chancery, as if turning down an invitation to wallow in mud.

"Cut me a slice of that cheese there, friend," said Minder, to Krupp's great relief.

Krupp made a small plate of crackers and grapes and cheese. There was a butter knife on the cheese tray; he decided to add some sausage to the snack tray. Kneeling by the half-console refrigerator, he pressed the dull knife-blade through the waxy skin of the sausage. The sensation it brought to his hand sparked an unwelcome memory: He was kneeling in the subway in the spray-painted magic circle, over the body of the girl, trying to concentrate without looking too closely at what he was doing; carving her, pressing the knife through her skin. At first the knife seemed reluctant to penetrate the flesh of her abdomen; it made a deep dent but didn't cut. He put his weight on

141

it, and the blade slashed through, transmitting to his fingers the resistance-and sudden-release sensation that meant he was breaking skin, sliding into the spongy inner tissues...Nearly the same sensation he experienced now when he forced the butter knife through the skin of the sausage. The sausage: ground-up cattle, butchered in a slaughterhouse, squalling.

He jumped back as if he'd touched a live wire.

"Ungh!" he said, standing now, shaking, staring at the quivering butt of the butter knife in the meat. Tears burned in his eyes.

He knew the others were staring at him. He didn't look to be certain. He knew.

"You get an electric shock?" Minder asked evenly.

Without taking his eyes from the butter knife—the quivering slowed, as Krupp's heart gradually slowed its thudding Krupp nodded, said, "Yeah. Must be a...loose wire in the fridge."

"I'll have it checked."

As if still afraid of an electric shock, Krupp gingerly picked up the snack tray, closing the refrigerator door with his foot. He put the tray in the empty space on the couch between him and Minder. Neither of them touched the food.

For the first time, Miss Chancery addressed Madelaine. "I suppose you think you're a little too spiritually pristine to come to the rite?" Miss Chancery said. "You weren't so pristine the other night when we used the—"

"No need to get mean, Miss Chancery," said Tooley in his friendliest tone.

Miss Chancery raised an eyebrow; but she smiled and nodded. "Sorry if I came off that way. But—I think people are silly who pretend they aren't completely self-serving. Everyone is, but they cover it up. I mean, why do the saints do things like starve themselves or spend their lives with lepers? Because they want recognition. Maybe from people—but mostly from God. That's a selfish motive."

"People who are afraid to be punished for what they do are either afraid of society or God's vengeance," Tooley put in. "We have no fear of society. Because of the Strength."

Madelaine continued to stare at the ceiling, hardly blinking, ghostly pale.

"No fear of society," Tooley repeated. "But what about God? Let me ask you this—do you believe in God, Madelaine? Do you believe in judgment and punishment for sins? Or in *karma* perhaps?"

At first Krupp thought she wouldn't answer. *Why don't they leave her alone?* he thought desperately. He wanted to scream it. He sat with a smile frozen on his face, now and then mechanically taking sips of his drink, tasting nothing.

"I don't know," Madelaine said, straightening her neck, looking at each of them, one by one, as if she were seeing them for the first time.

Minder was laying out cocaine on a mirror tabled across his lap. Madelaine's eyes fixed on the cocaine, and she kept her gaze there as she spoke: "When people found out about my Gift, they used to ask me if I could communicate with 'higher spirits'—they called them things like that. And if I heard something from those 'higher spirits' about God. Had I met God? They actually asked me things like that. I couldn't believe it. I had to say something neutral because I didn't want to disappoint them. But the flashes I get are incoherent. Sometimes they foretell, and sometimes they're leaks from someone's mind. Sometimes I think I get fragments from the afterworld. From my father. I used to like to believe it. It *felt* like him. But it might have been something out of my unconscious. I never got a glimpse of a higher order. Or of God, or of angels. There were other...other *things*. Creatures who aren't exactly in this world. But I don't know what they are. I don't think they're divine. In fact..."

Her mouth buckled. She *was* going to cry.

Minder set aside the mirror and moved closer to her, put his arms around her. She sobbed against his heavy shoulders.

Miss Chancery rolled her eyes and lit another cigarette. She looked bored.

After a minute, during which Krupp fixed himself another drink, Madelaine quieted. She sat up straight and wiped her eyes. She looked at the mirror.

Long glittering white moraines of cocaine. Two good lines for each of them. The best.

Madelaine had hers first, snorted through a hundred-dollar bill. Then Miss Chancery, then Krupp, then Tooley.

Krupp felt better. For a while. His nerves sang along the cocaine continuum. He was excessively optimistic about everything. His wife was going to let him alone about the money, he felt sure—even though his sonuvabitch brother had told her about it—and the police weren't going to find out and they had the Strength behind them and even if that thing, that Head Underneath, *was* the Devil—was that so bad?

Maybe the Devil, like all successful people, had been slandered over the years.

Krupp's high was roaring, and he rocked along on it. But a strong high brings a strong crash. And when he crashed, the sexual fantasies that had flowered in him like bursting fireworks cooled into a rain of sulfurous ash and he felt leaden, heavy with depression. He wanted more cocaine but he was afraid to ask.

And now the train was moving. They were on their way to the rite.

The lights flashed on and off. Krupp groaned and shut his eyes tight.

The trip to the hidden place took only ten minutes. Krupp used the time to get as drunk as he could, and still stand. His nerves sparked like the third rail. Minder and Tooley and Miss Chancery were quietly talking, laughing, at the other end of the car, braced against its swaying. Madelaine was lying on her side, on the couch, an arm over her eyes.

Every jounce of the subway car made him grit his teeth with irritation. As he drank, the alcohol smoothed his jagged nerves; he became suffused with numbness, except in the hollow place in his gut, the place that was like his personal internal domicile for the Head Underneath. He visualized the Head Underneath in his gut, gnawing him with its lipless mouth. He drank till the image faded.

The drink soothed his nerves, but deepened his depression.

When it came time, he followed the others out of the car, all his attention zeroed in on trying to walk without stumbling. He shuffled along the deserted, twilight-dim subway platform, a little behind the others. Madelaine walked between Tooley and Minder, clearly restrained by them though they made it look as if they were supporting her with comforting arms.

They went to the padlocked men's room and stood in the cone of light under the funnel-shaped shade on the light fixture above the door. Tooley used one key from a crowded ring of keys to open the padlock, which he pocketed. They went into the men's room; it was unnaturally, clean for a subway-station restroom. Even the graffiti were gone. A yellow light bulb burned overhead. In the left-hand wall were blue-metal elevator doors. An elevator looked out of place in the tile-walled men's room. So did the man waiting there for them, a man Krupp muzzily recognized from *New York Post* photos. Who *was* the guy? A city councilman? Krupp couldn't quite place him. He greeted Minder cordially, whoever he was. He was some high mucky-muck—Ah, Jerry Bourbon from the Transit Authority.

Krupp wondered what had become of the workmen who'd installed the elevator here—it looked as if it had been put in recently. It was new to him, anyway. Who had put it in? Surely Minder hadn't let them live? Unless they belonged.

The damn affair was too big. There were too many dead already. The more people who were killed…the more had to be killed. To be silenced. Damn Minder. Damn Tooley. And Billy Krupp. Damn Billy Krupp?

He laughed, a sharp bark of nervous hilarity, and Miss Chancery glanced over her shoulder at him as if to say, *Really, have some taste.*

Krupp followed them into the elevator. They went down. He stood close behind Madelaine, so close he heard Minder whispering to her: "We need you, Madelaine. Your Gift means you can be a channel. You can help us with— with something special. We need you and we don't want you to be an enemy. But we can't force you to join us. You have to join us of your own free will—as much as anyone has free will. If we threatened you into it, your conversion would be insincere. And we couldn't trust you, then. Then, well…then He would use His strength and you would be hurt. Hurt until you were dead. Slowly hurt; repulsively dead. Okay? There's no God that you know of, you admitted that. So who's to judge you for joining us? Who's going to say it's wrong? No one will ever know, I can guarantee that."

Leave her for God's sake alone, Krupp screamed inside. A scream that shivered through his spine but never escaped his lips.

"We can't force you," Minder was saying, "but we'll make you a present to His pet, tonight, if we can't have you with us. You've got to change your mind sincerely, inside, because if you pretend, *He will know.*" His tone was that of an amiable lawyer explaining the terms of a mortgage contract. Just business, nothing personal. But.

The elevator doors opened and they were in the room Krupp had been taken to originally. The leather couch, the big TV. They passed through that room, and entered another, paneled in mahogany, dimly candlelit; the concrete floor was freshly painted with the pentagram, the weird writing they'd taught him. Painted in red.

More than a dozen people stood about the circle. They stood in assigned places, swaying slowly in the slow dance, to lugubrious drums and fuzz-guitar from a hidden tape deck. And there: the jade vase to one side, in the altar niche. Krupp hoped he wouldn't be assigned a spot standing near the vase, tonight. He hated being near it. He could always hear the papery noises and the squeaking that came from it, no matter how much noise the others made.

Minder and Tooley and Miss Chancery and Krupp went into the dressing room, next door to the ritual room, to apply the scents and paints. Everyone was solemn. The laughing and the other thing would start later.

Tooley had to help Krupp undress. "You shouldn't be so tipsy," Tooley muttered, as he painted Krupp's sunken breastbone with the signs. "Not now."

Tooley left the dressing room first, and then the others. Krupp looked up as Miss Chancery, nude and almost little-girl slender, passed him, moving like a ghost to the ritual room. Her blond hair trailed behind her; her eyes had gone wild, and the delicate sneer was no longer on her lips. Still, she held herself as if she weren't stark naked and painted with wiggly lines, the eyes in the triangle below a dog's head. She moved as if she wore a gown designed for a *Vogue* cover. Krupp thought: *Smug bitch.* He wanted to trip her, to rattle that cruising aplomb; but he didn't dare.

When he came out of the dressing room, it hit him. The Strength was in the air; he felt it tugging him toward the circle. From the urn came the papery stirrings, the squeaking, and then a low, throaty growling.

He stood just outside the dressing-room door, facing the door into the "orientation room." To his right, the congregation stood at the candle-flickering circle, whispering the foreign words—words they understood subverbally, if not literally. Krupp didn't look at them. He knew he could be drawn into it. He knew he *would* be. But he'd half made up his mind that this time…

He looked up as a rumble went through the walls. Tooley, his outlines wavery, a figure of power, standing with one hand on the urn…There was something about his head, at those moments—you'd look at it and he would look as usual, and then it would be a different head, for just a split second, almost no transition—pop!—the head of a snarling dog, but a dog with the eyes of a man. And then—*snap, click*—the human head again. And you'd wonder—the vision had been so brief—if you'd seen the other head at all.

Krupp's eyes adjusted to the dimness; he saw a big man he vaguely recognized as Minder's bodyguard carrying Madelaine—who didn't struggle in the least, damn her—in his arms, like a Muscle Beach regular carrying a drowned girl. But she was alive; she opened her eyes as he laid her on her back in the center of the red circle, within the seductive symmetry of the congregation swaying around its edges.

They're going to carve her, Krupp thought. She's refused them. So she's going to be the one.

That's just the way things *are*. That's all.

They held her down and the big man raised the wrought silver cudgel with the beast-head on its knob, so that it flashed for a moment over his naked, sweat-shiny, muscle-rippling shoulders preparing to stun her so that she wouldn't fight the ritual cutting.

But he froze, cudgel uplifted, when she began to chuckle and shake her head, sitting up and smiling like an actress who's blown her line and exasperated the director. Her laugh was lighthearted and sane.

"No, it all comes together now," she said, nodding slightly, not at all as if she were desperate for an out. "I've made up my mind. I'm with you, and with you inside. I'm tired of being a freak. I want to live. And I want *to make it.*"

The bodyguard looked questioningly at Minder. Minder bent and looked into Madelaine's eyes. She looked straight back at him.

Minder nodded. "Let her go," he said, smiling like a proud father. "And bring in the other one."

By the time they'd brought the alternate sacrifice, the Escondido kid, from the chains at the secret pool (the pool where He rested, dormant, dreaming) below the ritual room, Krupp had slipped away. He pulled on his pants, his shoes without socks, his sweater, and deserted the remainder of his clothes.

He was careful not to look at the circle, or the jade urn, as be passed through the ritual room. He stopped for a moment, vacillating, at the door to the room with the elevator, feeling the Strength tugging at him, and drawn by the secret implications in the voices of the chanting congregation. They were tranced; no one looked at him. Except Tooley. Tooley always knew, and Krupp could feel his eyes on him as he walked out. *He won't want to ruin the ritual,* Krupp thought. *He'll let me go. Maybe I'll have time.*

147

He hurried to the elevator. The elevator doors were still open. He flung himself inside, panting with relief, and pressed the *Door Close* button. It might respond and it might not. Five seconds of nothing, as the chant and the crackle of power built from the ritual room.

The elevator doors slid shut. He held his breath and punched the button that he hoped would take him to the deserted subway station. Another ten seconds of nothing. *It won't respond for me!*

Then, a distant click—the elevator rose.

Somehow, he'd been able to live with it, when he'd carved the teen-age girl. And when he'd seen what happened at the group rite. He had almost managed to block from his mind the vision of what lived in the red pool below the ritual room. But there was something deeply, ultimately brutal in Minder's manipulation of Madelaine. Minder had reached into her and deformed her soul under his fingers. And that was far worse than carving her up on the circle.

Krupp just couldn't live with it.

I'm with you, and with you inside, she'd said. "They're not going to get that part of *me*," he murmured, shutting his eyes.

FORTY-FIVE MINUTES LATER. Where? The typewriter-chattering, phone-clanging back office of the Ninth Precinct police station. A young rookie on office assignment came into Gribner's cubicle and said, "Lieutenant, there's a guy here says he read about you, wants to see you, nobody else. Says he knows who's doing the subway killings." The rookie shrugged.

"Another crank," Gribner muttered, hardly glancing up from the report he was reading. And trying to suppress a leap of hope. "What's his name?"

"He claims his name's William Krupp," said the young snot. "The young snot" was Gribner's mental tag for the rookie; he could never remember the kid's name. The young snot was moon-faced, with sandy hair and a sandy, bushily uneven mustache; he had a manner of spurious camaraderie, as if they'd been through hell together, that never failed to annoy Gribner.

"So where's the background on him? He got a file or a Social Security number or—you have anything...?"

"Uh—" The young man sucked at his mustache and gave his head a quick shake, chuckling like a bad actor. "Damn. Procedure is to get all that before coming to you, right? Sorry, I guess I—"

"Never mind, I'll talk to him now," said Gribner, feeling shaky with the rising excitement.

He thrust his hands casually into the pocket of his rumpled brown suit-coat and sauntered as unconcernedly as he could back to the interrogation room. The room was locked only from the inside. He turned the knob and went in, annoyed by the scraping of the metal door. (How many times had he requisitioned to have it reset on its hinges?) The gray-walled room contained only a drain in the concrete floor, a steel desk and chair, used simply as an authority prop, and a folding metal chair, on which sat a stubby little man he took to be William Krupp. Seeing Krupp, Gribner's heart sank. The man had all the earmarks of a crank. The guy had shoes on, but no socks; a sweater on inside out. He had a phony-looking blond toupee, slightly askew. He was roly-poly and nervous, and looked as if he disliked himself; just the type to seek attention and media recognition by pretending connections with a series of famous murders.

He was the third that week.

"Oh-kay, so give me the whole schpiel," said Gribner, sighing, sitting down at the desk; the desk was empty except for a clipboard and pen in the bottom drawer. He discovered that there was no paper in the clipboard. "Goddamn it."

He looked up, feeling the pressure of Krupp's gaze. Krupp sat with his hands clasped on his knees, shaking perceptibly, breathing as if he'd just finished a long run; his face was blotched with red, his forehead sweat-runny. Gribner could smell liquor, and even from where he sat, a yard and a half distant, he could see a residual white dust crusting the man's nostrils. Probably drunk and coked up. Delusions of grandeur, for sure. Gribner shrugged.

The little man cleared his throat. "Um—you're not Lieutenant Gribner, are you?" He seemed disappointed.

"I'm not? I sure as hell am. So what did you expect? Kojak, maybe?"

"I'm sorry," Krupp's hands fluttered. He glanced at the door. "Um—I know where they are. I know who did it. Most of it, anyway. And, I guess it's going to come out: I did one. About four days ago. In the mezzanine of the West Fourth Street station. I bashed her there and dragged her down to the lower level. It was four in the morning, nobody around...I had a stocking mask on...I tossed the mask on the tracks...." Stuttered, blurted, and out in ten seconds.

Gribner sat up straight. "Why—why'd you take her to the lower level before—uh..."

"He says we got to have it a certain distance below ground...."

Gribner nodded, slowly. Lanyard had said something of the kind. But what made Gribner want to jump up and bang the desk with exhilaration was Krupp's phrase: "about four days ago in the mezzanine of the West Fourth Street station." The department had carefully lied to reporters about the actual location of the killing, so they'd have a way to screen out the phonies. Krupp had given the right location, which only half a dozen cops knew. Oh, it could have been leaked. But Krupp knew about the stocking on the tracks. Two spots of the girl's blood on it. That had been left out of the newspaper reports.

Instead of jumping up and banging the desk in exhilaration, Gribner leaned back, crossed his legs, and, taking his pipe and tobacco pouch from his coat, began to tamp.

"Where," said Gribner, his voice shaking only a little, "do they hold their... meetings?"

Krupp licked his lips. He turned and glanced at the drain in the floor. The room had once been used as a drunk tank.

"And who else is involved?" Gribner went on, wondering: *Should I get the sergeant to do a videotape of the confession? Or I could cell in a stenographer.* But it was a delicate moment; bringing other people in on it might jar Krupp into defensiveness. He might clam up and demand an attorney. Gribner needed names.

Krupp was gazing fixedly at the drain, and shaking his head. His voice was a squeak when he said, "Uh-uh. Not till...I got to have protection. I mean, I want two armed men with me. And a priest. I don't know if the priest'll help, but I got to try. 'Cause I seen what the Strength can do. I seen it turn guys into the Blessed People."

"What?"

"The Head Underneath looks at you and decides if you're more use to Him in the upper world or the lower place. Some people, He changes them, man, He—I didn't get that far. I didn't get taken to Him, so He could decide. But the Director, he said I'd work in the upper world. So I never worried about—"

He was chattering on so quickly Gribner could barely make out what he was saying. But the phrase the Head Underneath seemed to ring in his ears.

"Who is the Director?"

Krupp shook his head bard. "Could I have a glass of water? I—"'

"Just as soon as you tell me."

Krupp swallowed. He shook his head, more slowly. "Not till I get the guards, and the priest. I know it sounds dumb, but I ain't safe here. And it's got to be in a room that hasn't gotta drain…"

"Why?" So, maybe the guy *was* insane. But that didn't mean he wasn't one of the killers. They had to be crazy, to do what they did.

"Because He can reach me that way. And they know if I'm betraying them, man. They know, no matter who I'm talking to…"

"You can have whatever you like, once you—"

Krupp shook his head. "I'm fucked up on all kindsa shit. But I'm not going to tell you any more till I get what I want—" He cracked his first smile. "And until I can get a good lawyer in here. I want my phone call now, man. I got to call my brother. He knows a lotta slick shysters."

Krupp was now trying on a false bravado. *He knows a lotta slick shysters.* As if he were in command of the situation; as if he had strings to pull. Krupp was, Gribner realized, genuinely scared.

Gribner caught himself looking at the drain: remembering Everett crouching in the bathtub, Everett fondling himself mechanically; pallid little boy growling in response to the ugly noise from the bathtub drain.

Gribner puffed his pipe alight and stood, trailing ashes. "We'll take care of you." He used a key on the chain extending from his belt to unlock the door, and opened it to shout, "Hey, send in a couple of patrolmen—ah—and… yeah, you…" He spoke to the young snot. "And bring me in a telephone. That one, it's got a long cord. And bring us a glass of water. And—" He hesitated, glanced over his shoulder at Krupp, then spoke to the young snot again. "And bring me a priest. There's a referral number for clergymen on my desk, taped to the top drawer."

"A priest, Lieutenant?"

"Right. A Catholic—" He turned to Krupp. Krupp was staring at the drain. "Mr. Krupp?"

"Yeah?" Krupp jerked his head up with a snap.

"A *Catholic* priest?" Gribner asked.

"Oh, yeah, sure, any kind. Any Christian kind."

"Yeah. Right." He turned to the rookie. "Yeah. A Catholic priest. Start by bringing the telephone."

KRUPP WAS AFRAID to drink the water in the paper cup, though his throat was dry. He sat in the metal chair with the phone on his lap, the receiver pressed to his ear, listening to the ringing at the other end. He was alone in the little room; Gribner had been unable to turn up two spare patrolmen. He seemed shifty about telling anyone what the special guards were for. No priest yet, either. He had the water and a telephone.

But he hadn't touched the water.

It was tap water, from a spigot. From under the city. They knew all the pipes, and all the watercourses. They could get to anyone's water supply. And they knew, by now, what Krupp had done.

He found out everything you did, once you became one of them.

Only now was it beginning to dawn on Krupp: His chances of survival amounted to a dewdrop in a blast furnace.

Unless—he could stipulate to Gribner that he be interrogated away from the city. Far away, upstate. Even there, his chances weren't good. He'd been drunk, and stoned, and feeling sentimental about the Springer girl. Maybe he could call Minder instead and explain all that and ask forgiveness—and they would get him away from the police before anyone made him talk. (And while he wondered, the phone continued to ring, and ring.)

But even then, they'd kill him. They'd feed him to the pet, or make him, at best, one of the Blessed People. Since the night he'd glimpsed one of the Blessed People after a group rite, Krupp had worked industriously to forget what he'd seen.

He felt sick to his stomach, and weak. He wanted to lie down somewhere. But he couldn't sleep (Why the hell didn't Reggie answer the phone? He was at the store, Krupp knew he was) until the guards were posted. No, not even then. First he'd have to make Gribner take him far away. He glanced at the drain in the floor. It was completely rusted, and one of its pinning screws was missing; the drain-screen had been scuffed by some careless foot, swiveled to one side so that half of the actual hole in the floor was exposed in a shape like a quarter moon; a dark moon.

"Yeah, what?" Reggie's voice on the phone.

"Reggie—this, hey, this is Billy. Lissen, I gotta problem. Now, you know that check was cashed an' I got the money in the bank and I'm gonna use some of that prize money to help you build that annex on the store, okay?"

"Hey, you know I'm good for it and anyway you got that scratch gratis—"

"Yeah. Well, anyway, I want you to do two little things for me and then we'll call it clean and you don't have to pay me back. First, I want you to get me a damn good lawyer, a criminal defense attorney, and I'm talking the best. I'll use alla that prize money—'cept what I give you for the annex—to pay him off if I have to. You get him down here, I'll make arrangements to get him some cash in advance, I'll get the Lieutenant to—"

"Now goddamn it, Bill, slow down! You're babbling like a motherfucker. Where are you, anyway?"

"I'm at the Ninth Precinct police station. I'm accused of offing somebody and that's all I'll say about it."

"Oh yeah? Was it…was it Eunice?"

"Eunice? Why the fuck should I kill Eunice? I don't give her alimony and we don't live together—" He cut himself short. "Why? Something happened to Eunice?"

"I tried to tell you. I tried to call you. I—she found out about your prize money a couple of days ago. She wanted to get an attorney to put a claim on it for her, she—well, she was acting prit-teeee weird, boy. Flipping out. I guess finding out about that money really got under her skin. Made her crazy to think she was going bankrupt and she didn't get a penny from the divorce and—"

"Hey, that's bullshit, she got some blood outta me, pal, believe me. Now get on with it—what the hell happened to her, Reggie?"

"They say she drowned herself in the bathtub. Suicide. Her boyfriend found her and…well, he had a hard time getting in because there's no window in that bathroom and it was locked from the inside. But I—"

"She's *dead?*"

Reggie didn't reply. There was a brief interval when neither of them spoke and the telephone seemed to whisper to itself over the lines.

"What makes you sure it wasn't an accident?" Krupp asked. "I mean—why suicide? Maybe she slipped and fell."

"Well—she was acting so *weird*, and she kept saying, 'It isn't worth living, to have this aggravation, these people trying to hurt me.' That kinda shit. And three times she called her boyfriend and two other times she called the police and she told 'em that someone was in her basement. She said she heard squeaking sounds down there. And growling noises in the drain, and she was sure they were trying to poison her. She wouldn't drink the tap water. And I forgot to tell you: When they found her in the tub, she was on her knees with her face by the drain, you know, and there was a towel rack she'd pulled off the walls in her hand, you know, and she'd jammed it down in the drain....Kinda hard for a big woman like that to drown herself accidentally in the tub—she had to have held her head underwater, right? Or *somebody* held her head underwater. She had her hands wrapped around that towel rack when they found her. Weird shit."

"Yeah, well...I didn't have nothing to do with Eunice's death or..." Sobering, he said, "Or this other thing either. They set me up to make it look—"

"Yeah. Well, I'll get you a lawyer, buddy, don't you worry."

"Like right *now*, if you want that money, Reggie. Don't think I don't know what you were trying to pull. You went to Eunice and told her about the money to see if you could work a deal with her to get it out of me so you could get a good cut on it. So you do as I ask, pal, or you won't see a fucking penny. I'm at the Ninth Precinct. Send somebody quick. Promise him anything."

He hung up.

Slowly, he turned in his seat to stare fully at the drain in the floor.

Tooley said they'd protect me, he thought. *They killed Eunice because she was going to take away the money they got for me.*

He ran for the door. "Hey!" he shouted. "Hey, get me outta here!" He tried the knob. It was locked, the bastards had locked him in. He pounded on the door. Then he froze, his hands clammy on the metal surface of the door. He stood rigid, listening.

There was a noise. It was a noise like the squealing of a train's wheels as it comes to a stop. Or like a city bus hitting brakes short on brake fluid. A noise that was a combination of squealing and grinding, with an undertone of growling.

The noise was coming from the drain, behind him.

He tried to find his way to calmness, so he could think, decide what to do.

But the only thought that would come into his mind was: They won't send the pet of the Head Underneath. I'm too far above-ground. It can't come up here. But the Blessed People could. He remembered fragments of the chant:

These are Blessed, for they have become part of Him.

The growling from the drain became a roar. Krupp recommenced his pounding, shouting, "What the hell are you doing out there?"

...become part of Him; Ahim Ahriman Maz; these are Blessed, who eat when He eats, for they are His mouths...

A bubbling made Krupp turn around, and look. The mouth of the drain was erupting red foam. Rusty water? But it had a phlegmlike cohesiveness, and came in frothy dollops. No, not rust. And now there were red buckets of it, geysering like a burst water main, higher, a column of bubbling red high as his waist, bringing with it another noise, a noise like a soundtrack run backward at high speed.

...for they are His mouths, and they speak as He speaks, and by His hand they are transfigured, they who were once only men...

The crimson geyser subsided; the floor was inch-deep in slimy red liquid; the air choked him with the stench of a thousand dead rats. Gagging, he fell to his knees, trying to remember the invocational words, hoping to gain favor. He couldn't remember a thing. "I didn't tell them anything!" he shouted.

The red muck on the floor congealed in seconds, as he watched, becoming something like a layer of gelatin; gagging, shouting without words, he tried to climb onto the desk.

He couldn't reach the desk; he couldn't move an inch. The stuff had hardened around his shoes, had moved up to grip his ankles.

He screamed and tried to jerk his feet loose—

Krupp tripped and fell face down. The stuff felt awful against his cheek, and under his fingers, it was like gelatinous skin. He held his breath so he wouldn't have to breathe the stink of the red membrane. His head was only two feet from the drain; his body pointed toward it. His arms were outstretched in front of him, close together, as if he were diving into the drain; he lay flat, hardly moving for a moment, gasping, laughing now and then (*why? at what?* he didn't know).

The right side of his face was pressed to the red slick, the living mucilage; he could not tear himself loose; the contact burned, and he could feel patches of his skin sizzling where it touched acidic pockets.

"*Uhhh...*" was all he could manage. The membrane moved.

He was being drawn toward the drain. He tried to lift his head; he managed a half inch, and felt sections of his face ripping away as he made the effort. The red membrane spread out around the drain like a monstrous, ugly poppy petal; the floor sloped slightly toward the drain, and the membrane entered the hole in the floor evenly, leaving a round gap in the middle, like the female part of a flower. A great, stinking flower of flesh drawing him toward its stem, as if closing itself for the night. And just the way a bubble appears in the chamber of a bubble pipe, growing from within, the glossy top of a head appeared in the drain, expanding from within the pipe, emerging even as the red membrane drew itself downward; it was as if the withdrawal of the membrane caused the extrusion of the rubbery head. Krupp knew that it was the top of a head, because he had seen the Blessed People once before, conjured by Tooley at the edge of the hidden pond—the pond in which *He* lived. The Blessed People were the issue of His blessing.

Flexible, semitransparent, hairless and slick like the head of an oversized tadpole.

...they who were once only men, they move like quicksilver to do His work, they squeeze sleekly through the city's veins...

Krupp had just a glimpse of the thing's eyes before the membrane sucked him flat again. Sucked him flat, and began to flow over his face, to shut off his breathing. He had a distorted view of the room as the slick crimson skin covered his eyes; he saw the little room and the desk, untouched by the membrane, all wavery and red-tinted through the translucency. Krupp knew the shape of the emerged once-man, one of the Blessed People rippling quicksilvery by, its boneless, see-through body moving like a whiplash, its head snaking on the stretchable neck, the neck extruding farther and farther from the body like the stalks of a snail, its fingers moving independently of one another, bending themselves backward; curling up against the knuckles, impossible boneless wrigglings.

After that, the red membrane gave a great shudder, and righted itself over the drain so that it was as if Krupp were standing on his head, arms outstretched, feet pointed at the ceiling, suspended vertically, the membrane wrapped around him, upthrust like a tropical bloom closed for the night. And after that he couldn't tell one thing from another, because all shapes were absorbed into the white-hot crackling of pain as the red skin, its texture somewhere between artificial plastic and natural skin, tightened and closed, tighter, tighter, squeezing inexorably, twisting itself like a wrung towel, and descending. Screwing itself down into the drain. Breaking everything hard in him. He heard a sound like the note an opera singer makes that breaks glass, but more abrasive. SCREEEEEEEEEEEEEEE.

Pop.

The red membrane screwed itself into the drain, taking the pulped, liquefied remains of Billy Krupp with it.

"UH—YES, SIR, there was a helluva commotion. I beard this big splashy sound; and then a groan from in there. I figured he threw up. Well, they got the drain in there, so I didn't worry about it because I was taking a call from a fella reporting a burglary in progress. So I got that information, Lieutenant—uh—to the dispatcher, and then I was passing Interrogation and I heard this weird, long squeaking sound and a growling underneath it, sort of, and—well, it didn't sound right. So—uh..." The young snot paused to marshal his excuses.

Gribner waited. "Yes?"

"So I went to open the door. Couldn't get it open. Someone was holding it shut." He shrugged, embarrassed.

"Holding it shut. But—you're much bigger than that little man in there. He couldn't have held it shut against you."

"Not just against me, sir. I called Windy and Leibowitz and we all put our shoulders to it—all three of us couldn't get it open. It didn't feel like it was jammed. It was like there was... something...I...And—uh—finally there was this squealing, and then a squishy sound. And then the door just came open, like it hadn't been blocked, and he was *gone.*"

The young snot ran his fingers through his hair, his face scarlet.

"The hell you say!" Gribner, holding his kerchief over his face to diminish the stench that rolled over them from the interrogation room, stepped inside.

His eyes watered as he looked around. The room was as he had left it, except that it stank like a maggot's belch. And—Krupp was gone. Something more: There was a ring of red, like a bathtub ring, around the walls, about an inch off the floor; it was slightly damp, and crusty. A sort of high-water mark.

The, room had only one door. No windows. No way out but the drain. "Get the lab…" Gribner said slowly, "to test that stain on the wall. See if it's blood. If you can find medical records on the guy Krupp, see if he has the same blood type. If that's blood, I think I know what it is. We've been hearing…Ah, and…search the building. Maybe someone let him out. And the door was stuck. Right. Sure."

Gribner hastily left the room. He was halfway down the hall, heading toward the locker where he kept his overcoat, when the young snot caught up with him. "Sir…"

"*What?*" Gribner turned on him, shaking with fury. He knew perfectly well that the rookie wasn't responsible for Krupp's disappearance. Something had held the door shut from the inside? Yes, Gribner believed it. But he needed, badly needed, to blame someone.

Rubbing his temples with one hand, the rookie said, "Uh— I thought I ought to tell you what I saw when I opened the door. I mean, it probably was nothing or my eyes were seeing things funny because I'd been pushin' on the door and I used to see spots when I exercised hard—"

"*What the hell did you see?*" Gribner was white, rigid, cold inside.

"It—looked like rubber gloves."

Gribner just stared, waiting.

"I mean, sir—like a pair of rubber gloves with something heavy and wet in them. Going down the drain…the fingers part sticking upward. And then it just got sucked down. And I heard this big noise. Like a crashing, crunching, growly sort of noise. From the drain, sir."

"And what are you suggesting?"

He hesitated. "Nothing." He was becoming angry. "I thought I ought to tell you."

Gribner slumped. "I'm going for the day. I'm sick of staying late for this shit. They don't listen to me. I told them where to look." The fury had gone out of him. Self-pity was speaking now, and he knew it.

"Yes, sir. Shall I tell them to call you at home if this guy Krupp turns up?"

Cellars

"He won't turn up… I'm not going home. I'm going to temple."
"Where?" The rookie blinked.
"To synagogue, schmuck."
And maybe he wouldn't come back to the station, ever.

ELEVEN

Lanyard waited as the doorman tried the intercom for the third time. "I know she's there," Lanyard told the little Asian in the brass-button uniform. "I just called her. She said she'd be there."

"She's not here," said the little man, adding, "In fact, I doubt she's been home all this afternoon."

Lanyard was close to losing his temper. He restrained himself from punching the doorman. "Just try it one more time and I'll leave," Lanyard said, his voice straining with leashed anger. Thinking: *I'm making a fool of myself.* He'd felt better, that afternoon, though he hadn't slept much. He'd been almost optimistic. The Voices hadn't come back; he hadn't had the hallucinations. He was bleary-eyed but cheerful. He'd called Madelaine. His spirits had soared even more when she'd agreed to see him. And now this.

The doorman shrugged. "It's a matter of no concern to me," he said. "I'll try it once more." He pressed the buzzer and spoke into the intercom. "Miss Springer?"

"Yes?" Madelaine's voice. Lanyard's heart leapt.

"There's a man here to see you. His name is Lanyard—?"

"Oh. Okay. Send him up."

The doorman sighed, perhaps disappointed that she hadn't said, "I don't know any Lanyards."

Lanyard shrugged and went to the elevator. Automatically, just before entering, he glanced at the mirror snugged in the upper left-hand corner of the elevator, a convex triangle of chrome placed to reveal anyone who might be hiding inside. Lanyard stopped short. Wasn't there a figure reflected in it? Someone pressed against the wall near the floor-selection console? A narrow figure, almost sexless, who seemed to be wearing a rubber suit or a sheath of

161

plastic; the head was bald and the color of long-dead fish; the shape of the head reminded him of Munch's painting, *The Scream.* The figure was clearly inhuman. Probably it was an illusion, a trick of the light, or someone had left a raincoat and hat on a hook in the elevator.

Still, Lanyard stepped back and allowed the elevator door to close.

He was not at all surprised to see the floor indicator over the elevator lighting up B. The elevator had gone down to the basement.

I'm sleepy, Lanyard thought. Dreaming awake. It happens to people that way: They don't get enough sleep, their eyes distort what they see. There was nothing there—a blur, is all.

"Something wrong with the elevator?" asked the doorman.

"Uh, no—someone inside wanted to go down." Lanyard's instincts warned him against trying to explain. The little man would want to call the police. The police! Lanyard chuckled.

The doorman looked at him suspiciously, eyebrows raised. Lanyard's chuckle had seemed sinister. Lanyard pressed the button again.

The elevator returned and squeaked as its doors opened. Lanyard studied the mirror. It reflected nothing but the opposite corner of the elevator now. Still, he looked around cautiously when he stepped inside. He pressed the button for Madelaine's floor. The elevator ignored him: It went down.

"Shit!" Lanyard muttered.

The elevator sank. It was taking longer than it should. No—his imagination made it seem that way; when one was afraid, time protracted. And when one was afraid, Lanyard remembered, one noticed peculiar details. Like the red crust around the floor molding of the old wooden-walled elevator and the access hole for some kind of utility panel in the floor. It was emitting peculiar sounds. Gurgling.

His hands were clenched tight, now.

He heard a buzzing, a distant whispering. He wrenched his attention away from that. From the Voices, coming back.

The elevator stopped moving. Was he trapped between floors?

The elevator door opened onto the basement. A clean, white-tiled corridor; a long fluorescent light overhead, giving off buzzing sounds, as if it were conversing with the gurgling hole in the elevator floor.

"Hello?" Lanyard called tentatively. "Someone going up?"

His voice echoed along the corridor. He couldn't hear a washing machine going; he thought he heard a burring sound, from the right, the sort of sound a furnace makes when its thermostat turns it on.

It should have been a comforting domestic sound. But he didn't like it just then. He pressed the button for Madelaine's floor again. The elevator clicked, but did nothing else. He waited nearly three minutes. The elevator doors didn't close. "Damn rickety old elevators," Lanyard said, stepping out into the corridor. He was trying to believe this was a mechanical problem. He looked up and down the white hallway. To the right were two doors, almost facing each other. He sauntered toward the one he guessed to be the entrance to the stairs, laughing softly at himself: *The clutching in my gut, the prickling, it's all left over from the memory of the basements I visited with Gribner. That furnace room with the little boy laid open, his insides redistributed like condiments set out on a table.*

He was adjacent to the door to the furnace room. It was half open.

But the noises at the back of his mind rose like the sound of surf, a surge of white noise. One can hear anything in white noise. One can seem to hear Voices.

"Carl!"

And that was Madelaine's voice. Heard clearly, as if she were standing behind him. He was almost past the furnace room door.

A cold hand closed on his wrist, from behind. He whirled, wrenching away.

Madelaine was there. She was really there. She wore a short white cotton shift. No shoes. Her hair was up in an untidy bun; her eyes looked out wearily from lavender sockets. She'd lost weight. Her face was rosy; she was breathing hard. Had she *run* down the stairs?

"How—how did you find me?" Lanyard asked, his voice shaky.

Once more she took his wrist in her damp hand. "You didn't show up. I called the doorman and he said the elevator went down and got stuck in the cellar. I came down the stairs." She raised a thumb to point behind, over her shoulder. Lanyard looked. He hadn't noticed that door, at the far end of the hall in the shadows.

"So *that's* the stairs."

She was looking just past him, through the half-open door of the furnace room.

Her eyes widened.

He began to turn, wondering what she saw behind him. A rat, probably.

She clenched her clammy fingers about his wrist and pulled him toward the stairs, toward the shadows, away from the furnace room. He hadn't time to look. "Anything wrong?" he asked.

"Hm? No, I just don't like it down here." She smiled, and for a moment she was her old self again. She inclined her head toward him and did a barely recognizable imitation of Boris Karloff as she said, "It's too *spooh-key-eeee here!*"

He laughed. Always the actress, he thought. And somehow the thought disturbed him.

She was still breathing hard, and that prompted him to ask, "Did you run down the stairs or what? You sure got here fast."

"Oh, yeah," she said softly, suddenly serious. "I was in a hurry. Yeah."

They climbed the steps, Madelaine's bare feet slapping on the concrete, Lanyard's shoes clacking out echoes.

Madelaine glanced down, past Lanyard, more than once. She never let go of his wrist.

She fumbled at the door to her landing. "In my own fucking building," she muttered, sniffing. "In my building."

"What? Oh, the elevator breaking down?" Lanyard was puzzled.

"Yeah. You might say that." She tugged the door open and led him to her apartment. She had left it unlocked, the door slightly ajar. Lanyard was amazed. Leaving an unoccupied apartment open was most uncharacteristic of any New Yorker. She *had* been in a hurry.

He followed her into the apartment. She didn't offer to take his coat; she didn't ask him, at first, if he'd like a drink. That was unusual for her, too. She seemed depressed. The apartment was the same except that, if it were possible, it was even cleaner and barer than he remembered it. The white crucifix was gone from the wall.

She locked the door behind him, and even connected the chain. She went to the small living room's single piece of furniture, the white couch, and sat down, saying nothing. There was a sealed manila envelope on the cushion beside her.

"So," he said, in an effort to fill the gulf of silence between them, "what's the part Minder gave you?"

"The part?" She looked at him vacantly, calling her mind back from some place distant. "The part. Oh yeah. Here, let's see…" She spoke in an undertone. She tore open the manila envelope, murmuring, "I dunno, he told me what it was. But I guess—I forgot."

She *forgot?* Her first major part and she hadn't looked at it yet? He sat down beside her, shaking his head wonderingly. "You sure you're okay, Madelaine?"

One corner of her mouth twitched. That was her only reaction to his question. She drew out a sheaf of papers. "Um—the play is *Shake 'Em Down!!* Two exclamation points yet. And I am to be the con artist's lost sister, who he is stealing from, because he doesn't know she's his sister." She shrugged. "Drivel."

He sat well apart from her on the couch. He could tell, though, by something in her posture, maybe the way she was hunched forward, a little defensively, the way she kept her arms close to her body, her knees together, that she didn't want to be touched just then. He ached to touch her. Suddenly he felt tired. He yawned. "I'm sorry…." he said. "I'm half asleep. Had some trouble sleeping."

She snorted. "You and me both."

He glanced at her and tried to smile his warmest, "I hope you lost a little sleep over me. Did you miss me at all?"

She rubbed at her eyes, sniffed, and nodded. "Sure. I missed you." As if admitting to the telephone man that she hadn't been home on installation day.

"I—guess there's something wrong with your buzzer…"

"Yeah." She pursed her lips and nodded vigorously. "I guess so."

That's as good an explanation as any, Lanyard decided.

"Well," she said, as if gathering herself together, "let's listen to some music." She went to the small stereo in the bedroom and turned on the radio. It played a Beatles tune. Something about *"Love, love, love, all you need is…"*

Lanyard stood and, as she returned, impulsively took her in his arms. At first he thought by her stiffness she would push him away. But she slumped, and her arms went around him. She passively allowed him to squeeze her; she dutifully tilted her face up for a kiss. She kissed him back, but her lips were as clammy as her hands, and no warmth passed from her to Lanyard.

"Hey," she said, "Joey gave me a little present." She gently broke free of him and went into the bedroom. "Come on." He followed her to the dressing table.

165

A small heap of cocaine was laid out on the mirror. Beside it was a gold coke spoon on a tiny chain.

"Oh—no, thanks," Lanyard said, feeling odd. "I don't much care for cocaine. I don't like it when you come down and feel yourself wanting more."

She laughed. "Oh come off it, it's not that you don't like cocaine." As she spoke she used a single-edged razor to chop the white crystal more finely. "You don't like Joey Minder, that's all. And this came from him. Listen, you don't have to be jealous of him. I let him flirt a little, but, uh…" Her voice had become almost too soft to hear. "But that's all…."

"Oh, no, really, I'd rather just talk than do drugs, I haven't had a chance to see you and—uh…"

"Come *on*, Carl, this will help us talk. It'll…" She laughed, too loudly. "It'll have us talking too much."

Lanyard sighed. Anything to get closer to her. "Okay."

"Here, use this A hundred-dollar bill, rolled and taped into a tight tube. Where had she acquired a hundred-dollar bill? She was on unemployment, last he knew. Minder must have given her an advance.

"Yeah," she said, between sniffs of white powder, "I've—" Snuff. "I've been—" Snuff. "—sort of depressed. I wasn't in the mood to talk, frankly, but I think this'll help. Here, I'm going to lay out some more. A massive hit…"

Lanyard snorted his two lines, wincing at the pharmaceutical taste, but feeling more cheerful almost immediately.

The radio was playing "Little Triggers," an old Elvis Costello tune. Lanyard found himself swaying to the music. For a moment he felt foolish, thinking: I feel good now, artificially. It's like pushing a button on a machine to get a certain programmed reaction. To make the elevator go up. We put the chemicals in ourselves and we're elevated. Automatically.

But in a moment another wave of drug exhilaration crested in Lanyard and washed the doubts away, and he again encircled Madelaine with his arms. This time she was pliant against him, moved to caress his chest with her breasts, the small of his back with her fingers.

He started to speak, but she closed his lips with a kiss, despite her promise that they'd be able to talk more easily after doing cocaine. She was making love more aggressively than he remembered, and he suspected that she wanted to use sex to avoid conversation. But she broke away from him rather abruptly when a newscast came on the radio: "…unconfirmed reports of a reliable witness to the subway killings who later disappeared from the Ninth Precinct police station. Police denied allegations of a cover-up, although sources said—" Madelaine moved to switch channels so swiftly she might have been running to hit a fire alarm.

Lanyard was about to say, *Hey, I'd better listen to the news, I'm supposed to be investigating the killings.*

But he didn't want to hear the news, really. He wanted something else entirely. For a time, his weariness and his fear had melted away from him. *Magic potion,* he thought.

The radio now played some mindless, assembly-line, softpop tune.

She came to him and fell to her knees and, with no hesitation at all, unzipped his pants, reached into his underwear, withdrew his rigid organ, and popped it into her mouth.

Lanyard was too amazed to question her behavior. He focused on sensation.

When he came he felt like a spool unwinding its thread all it once. And he was unraveled. Spent.

He disengaged. She sighed and said, "Whew…" But it sounded false. She turned away from him so he could move, as clumsily as he'd anticipated, to pull up his pants.

"At least," Lanyard said five minutes later, when they sat together on the couch, his arm around her shoulders, gin-and-tonic in hand, "we broke the ice."

She laughed at that, and her laughter seemed almost genuine.

Lanyard went on, "what would you like to do for Halloween? There must be some great costume parties in Manhattan. That's this Saturday, you know, and I thought there might be a party—anybody's but Minder's. I haven't worn a costume for years, but I thought it might be fun." He let his voice trail off, disturbed by sudden sadness in her. "What's the matter?"

"Nothing." She shrugged. "My moods change quickly, I guess. I've always been a bit manic-depressive." She added softly, "I won't be able to go out this Saturday. I have a meeting. A business thing."

"On Saturday night?"

"Yeah. A business dinner."

She quickly changed the subject. "Hey, there's an article here, 'in this envelope somewhere. Joey put it in, says it has my name in it. I haven't looked yet."

She opened the manila envelope again, took out the script, and beneath it she found a clipping from the theater section of the daily New York Times.

Looking at the script, Lanyard remembered that last time he'd called her and she'd said she couldn't talk because she was studying her part; but today she spoke as if she were seeing the script for the first time. Maybe he should confront her with the discrepancy. A burst of honesty might do them both good. The cocaine and the alcohol made him feel capable of blurting almost anything. He decided against it. Too soon for a confrontation. He sipped his rum; the drink alleviated the ennui and the crash from the coke.

"Here it is, one great big line: 'Madelaine Springer, formerly a member of Minder's cast for Nero, will play the part of Edwinna, the con artist's sister.' What a dumb name Edwinna is—oh hell, wouldya look at that!" She'd spat out the last five words loudly, as angrily as someone catching their cat urinating on a mink stole.

Jarred, Lanyard said, "Uh—what's the matter?"

She was oblivious to him. She was staring at a glossy color photo stapled to the clipping. It showed a tall, gaunt, icy-blue-eyed blonde modeling fall fashions: a dark-brown dress and black wool jacket. "Well, she got hers," Madelaine muttered. "Her little present."

"You know that model?" Lanyard said, irritated at being ignored.

"What?" She snapped her head up. "No—oh, sort of. She's a bitch. I can tell you that much."

Sensing that once more the time had come to change the subject, Lanyard said, "Has your 'Gift' been bothering you?" He was tempted to tell her about the Voices. About his boyhood. About Maguss. He was on the point of doing so when she said:

"No!" She gave him a hard look and stood, snatching his glass too briskly from his hand. "I'll get us a refill." Though he'd only drunk half of his gin-and-tonic.

He watched her movements as she padded into the kitchen; the pleasure of watching her mingled with his growing weariness and a sense of disorientation. Already, the brunt of the cocaine up was long gone. Lanyard felt sure she was going to bring out the drug again. He wasn't sure how he felt about that, either.

A crash-and-tinkle of breaking glass came from the kitchen. His thoughts abruptly changed lanes—he jumped upright and hurried to Madelaine.

She was on the kitchen floor, huddled with her knees drawn up, pressing her breasts out of shape. Her face was contorted like an infant about to burst into a long, hard crying spell, but the tears never quite burst free. She seemed to be trying to hold something in and keep something out all at once. She rocked on her haunches, her face partly hidden by her curly black hair. The cocktail glasses were shattered, in a small brown puddle, under the sink. The sink rattled low to itself.

"Madelaine! Should I call—an ambulance? You have too much coke, or—?" But he knew it wasn't the cocaine.

He touched her shoulder and recoiled; her skin was hot, so that his fingertips tingled painfully, and her flesh was hard as carved wood.

At his touch she jerked her head spasmodically to stare at him in abject terror. She wasn't pretty, just then, her face deranged by frightened disbelief and confusion, her mouth slack, chin wagging up and down, nose wrinkled, eyes alternating between opening too wide and crinkling almost shut. "They want Carl too," she said, and he knew then that she wasn't seeing him. She was looking at something behind him, above him, beyond him.

They want Carl too…

Lanyard suppressed an impulse to leave the apartment and run like hell.

SHEBOP AND BRIZZY stood outside the Backstage Social Club, Members Only, West 110th Street, just as the street lights came on, and as if that were some kind of signal, the unmarked patrol car came swinging around the corner going so hot it fishtailed. Before Shebop could say anything more than, "Who those motherfuckers fuckin' wid now?" The yellow sedan nosed into the curb, pulling up with a jerk, and three plainclothes cops piled out. The car was a familiar sight in the neighborhood. Everyone knew about it. The man selling works on the corner crossed the street slowly, careful not to seem in a hurry but hurrying anyway; the pussy broker on the stoop above the deli lit a cigarette and studied the cloudy sky as if wondering about the weather: he wasn't holding and his girls were all out on tricks; the sidewalk dealers stepped into their buildings' front hallways, not too quickly. But the cops—in suits or jacket and jeans, all three of them pink-skinned as a rat's tail—they came strutting straight for the Backstage Social Club. For Shebop and Brizzy. Brizzy said, "Shebe, get yo' black ass in gear, nigger." Because they *were* holding, they'd just bought. They turned to run.

Someone was coming out of the social club, two teen-age boys, possibly brothers. They both had the same big eyes, and the same skin tone, black as midnight, and both of them were on roller skates—they'd been practicing roller-disco moves for the contest. They saw the white guys in the suits running at them—Brizzy and Shebop between them and the cops and they saw the guns popping from the white guys' coats, and they both naturally thought (Shebop guessed): "Some kind of mob action, better get the fuck outta here." So they tried to split, too, skating off down the sidewalk. And Brizzy ran not far behind Shebop.

When the bullets hit Brizzy in the lower back it felt, at first, like the impact of hard, cold snowballs. It didn't start hurting till he'd been lying on the sidewalk a half minute, shaking and trying to make his legs work, trying to get to his knees—and then it hurt, it hurt, it hurt like a son-of-a-bitch.

The car sounds, the gunshots, the shouting, the screaming, the weeping—all of it she heard in her brain. She heard it just the way Brizzy heard it, because she was picking it up through Brizzy. Why did they call it a "Gift"?

Brizzy rolled onto his back so he could use his arms to protect himself against the boots of the man kicking him. He could see that Shebop was down too, and he could see two men standing over him pumping shots into Shebop, and he could imagine the cops explaining, "The suspects attempted to escape...." And then he saw the big cop with the red face hide the little pistol in Shebop's jacket. He heard shots and screams, from out of his line of sight: the other cops gunning down the two kids on roller skates, who would later be "accidentally caught in our line of fire." And then he heard someone, a woman's voice, someone's mother, shouting, "What the hell you animals think you doing shooting those boys down? Them two boys on the skates, they good boys, I know those boys, they—"

"Suck my white cock, you nigger cunt," said one of the cops and the others laughed and then Brizzy was gone for a while. He came awake long enough to realize he was bumping through the streets in the back of an ambulance, feeling every bump in his wounds like a baseball bat slamming him, and he heard the cops tell the driver, "No, that fucking hospital's practically around the corner. Go to the one uptown. We'll tell 'em the wounded niggers asked to be taken to that one. Give 'em time to bleed, I don't wanta have to listen to these assholes lie all over the witness stand...."

And that was the last thing Brizzy heard—

Madelaine screamed again and this time she clawed at her ears.

—because after that Brizzy was occupied with listening to the roaring sound that came to fill his head when his heart gave out from lack of blood pressure and he tried to yell for his sister Tess because Tess took care of him since Dad got busted and—

Madelaine tore her clothes away, trying to get at the wounds that she knew were bleeding her life into nowhere, though she wasn't bleeding, and by then Brizzy, in another part of the city, was already dead.

"Joey keep them out....Keep them out!" Madelaine gurgled, her face hidden by the shift she'd dragged over her head.

"Okay—if you'd be more comfortable without your clothes," Lanyard said, "I'll help you get them off....There...." He pulled her dress off over her head. "Now lie still, and I'm going to call an ambulance."

"Uhh—uhhh—UHHH-UH!" A crescendo of shouting as she dragged her nails over the skin of her belly, her rib cage.

Lanyard stood over her, paralyzed by recognition. Her hands were moving in deliberate patterns, making a specific design, clawing the same lines over and over on her quaking skin. The red appearing on her belly like smeared lipstick to make the configurations of the cutting.

The cutting Lanyard had seen again and again, on the victims of the subway killings. Their bellies cut open, in just the pattern, though bloodless now, as if only in blueprint, that Madelaine dug with her nails across her skin.

Joey, she'd said. Joey keep them out.

Lanyard nodded slowly to himself.

She was lying on the floor, alternating convulsively between two positions: stretched out rigidly, legs together, feet pointing at the door, arms crossed on her chest, trembling with tension; then she snapped her knees up to her chest, her hands over her ears, her eyes screwed shut as she screamed, "Out, OUT!" Lanyard bent over her, trying to hold her still, afraid she'd hurt herself. He tried to pry her grinding jaws apart so he could slip a pencil, which he took from his shirt pocket, between her teeth, in case she'd been taken with an epileptic seizure.

But suddenly she went slack in his arms, the tension drained from her, and the pencil was no longer necessary. Her lips were parted, her eyes shut, her face was more placid. She was breathing shallowly, her white skin blotched with rose. He hugged her close and helped her to her feet:

"You okay, Madelaine? You…are you on some kind of medication I can get for you? Are you supposed to be taking Dilantin? What happened, honey?"

She leaned on him, her head bowed, blinking, wobbly, heavy drops of perspiration from her chin splashing his arm.

"My God," he muttered. He helped her to the living room and sat her on the couch.

"I'm going to call an ambulance," he said firmly, looking for the phone.

She shook her head adamantly. She took a deep breath, and forced a smile. "Uh-uh. No. I'm better now. Had some bad flashes. My Gift—I get some ugly pictures, sometimes. That's all I get lately. And clearly, more clearly than…I wonder why they're doing it to me? To force me closer to them?"

She was calmer, but seemed confused, almost delirious. "You need a doctor."

"No, please. No. But you know what I do need? A drink. Really and truly. Boy, do I ever. Okay? Some cognac. In the kitchen, the cabinet over the fridge."

"Sure!" He wiped the wetness from the corner of his eyes, feeling weak himself. For a moment, he heard the background sizzling sounds that led to his hearing the Voices, the whispering, and seeing the squirming darkness. *Ignore it,* he told himself. *It's not there.* He kept it repressed with maniacal firmness when he was with Madelaine. He tried not to wonder why, and went into the kitchen, blinking in confusion. Where was the refrigerator? He was still shaken, not thinking clearly. There, and above it a white wooden cabinet. He stepped over the broken glass at the sink and took the quarter-full bottle of Courvoisier from the cabinet above the refrigerator.

I hope a drink is the right thing for her, he thought. *Maybe it'll make her feel worse.* He couldn't find the shelf where she kept her drinking glasses. Finally he elected to wash the single coffee cup in the otherwise spotless sink. He poured three fingers of cognac into the cup and returned with it to the living room. To find her gone.

The closet in the entryway was open, one of her long coats missing; the front door was ajar. Her purse was gone. The radio played an old Janis Joplin tune; Janis said she felt a ball and chain weighing her down. Hands shaking, Lanyard set the cup onto the floor—and then he picked it up, drained it, threw it down.

Then he ran to the door and down the hall to the elevator. He waited impatiently—then remembered that it had broken. He ran to the stairs, and took them, down and down, three at a time. He burst out into the lobby, puffing. She wasn't there. The doorman scowled. "Where did she go?" Lanyard demanded.

"Miss Springer?" As if he didn't know.

"Obviously! You must have seen her!"

"She went out. She was wearing a coat and *no shoes*. I think you had better talk to the building manager—"

"The hell you say!" Lanyard muttered, shouldering the doorman aside.

She was not on the sidewalk. The traffic was dense with every sort of vehicle, especially long shiny Caddies and Lincolns intent on blocking one another as they angled testily into the street. The background noise was building to a hysterical pitch, presaging rush hour.

Lanyard wondered what to do.

He made excuses for her: She was embarrassed by the fit. Maybe she was an epileptic—there are various kinds of epileptic fits—and ashamed of having been seen in seizure. She just had to get away to avoid his pity, or his disgust.

Nah.

Well then, she'd had too much cocaine, probably a great deal of it before he'd arrived. And some drug-inspired impulse drove her from the apartment—she probably forgot he was there. She might have felt the need to get outside, to walk…

Maybe.

More likely, she had gone to Minder.

Lanyard stood on the corner, stone-faced, thinking: It's not her fault. If she's treating me like I'm a nothing, walking out on me, pretending there was nothing wrong in the way I was treated at Minder's, it's only because of the drug, because she's become dependent on Minder for it.

Oh, sure.

They're twisting her around somehow. Minder's doing something to her…*because it just wasn't possible that she'd become one of them.*

No?

He thought of Maguss, Who knew Minder. It was time he gave Maguss his report, anyway.

He took a cab home, chewing his thumbnail, reading and rereading the little yellow signs that said Driver Not Required To Change Bills Larger Than $5 and Not Responsible for Forgotten Valuables. There was a scratched pane of bulletproof glass between Lanyard and the driver. When they arrived he pushed a five through the small metal PAY HERE drawer in the window. "Wait—here's an extra couple of bucks to cover the time…I'm just going to run up the stairs and grab some papers and run back down, take me two minutes…

"Okay."

When he returned, in just over two minutes, winded and red-faced from taking the stairs so quickly, the cab was gone. He swore and tucked the envelope under his arm. He set off, west.

Lanyard walked toward Astor Place, at intervals trying to hail a cab and failing. The sky was darkening, and in the distance the mist was becoming fog. He stopped at a pay phone and called Minder's.

"Mr. Minder's residence, may I help you?"

Too urgently, Lanyard said, "I need to talk to Madelaine Springer, if she's there…"

A pause. "I'm sorry, sir. She's in rehearsal."

Lanyard banged the phone onto the receiver and, on impulse, dashed down the subway entrance, thinking, *It'll be faster this way, I'll avoid the street traffic.*

And found himself pressed onto the uptown local in the midst of rush hour. Deep underground.

Lanyard had bought his token and passed through the turnstiles without really looking around, until he found himself swept up in a single-minded throng into the train. "Let 'em out, let 'em out!" shrieked the public address system, trying to tell the people eager to get aboard the train to let those debarking through to the platform; the order was for the most part ignored, and the doorway was a bottleneck jammed with human bodies in twisty currents, some edging and elbowing in, some edging and elbowing out.

Lanyard was forced to walk in silly, mincing steps because there was so little room in front and behind him. He found a corner of the car and hung onto one of the spring-hinged metal handholds.

The doors tried to shut; a black newsboy was caught in between.

"Geddaway from the doors!" the P.A. voice shouted.

Two people inside forced the doors open, and the black kid plunged into the train. The doors rattled, as if petulant with the delay, and squeaked shut. The train gave a great heave and everyone inside was wrenched about on their straps or in their seats—they showed no change of expression during this lurching, though they were bounced one against another.

Then they were barreling down the unlit tunnel, taking the corners at a harrowing rate so that the wheels strained to leap the rails; now and then, without explanation, the lights cut out, and they were plunged for five or ten seconds into total darkness.

When the lights came back on, no one had altered their expression. The car was crowded from back to front; the air was close, and though a few people chatted above the apocalyptic racketing of the old train, Lanyard sensed that each rider was intent on mentally maintaining a sense of personal space— mentally, since it was impossible physically.

They stopped at four stations, taking in more people than they let out ("*Leddemout, comeon, leddemout…Move away from the closing doors please don't block the doors…*") so that Lanyard's arms were crushed hard to his ribs by the pressure of commuters: careworn shopkeepers and hard-eyed secretaries and proud young blacks in speckless business suits gripping monogrammed briefcases; everyone clutching their purses, their packs, their wallets protectively.

They rocked to a stop at Grand Central, and an old woman accidentally poked her umbrella into Lanyard's thigh; he bit off a curse, and she scowled as she withdrew the umbrella from him, as if he'd been trying to steal it.

As they paused in Grand Central Station, Lanyard looked out the window, bending to see past the graffiti on the glass, and thought he glimpsed Madelaine in the crowd, buying a magazine from a newsstand. He couldn't be sure. The woman stood with her back to him, and people dashed back and forth in his line of sight, running to or from a train. It looked like her hair—but she was too far for him to tell. The woman wore a long, tan coat. He couldn't see her feet.

He pushed frantically through the crowd, eliciting "Hey whoyuh shovin' azzhole," and flung himself through the door, onto the platform; he nearly fell flat, and the doors rattled shut behind him. He threaded the crowd, making for the newsstand. The newsstand contained one of the stumpy, cap-wearing, cigar-chewing, bulldog-faced men that Lanyard was sure were bred in some secret kennel, probably in the wilds of Long Island.

The woman—Madelaine?—was no longer at the newsstand. He saw her climbing the stairs under the paint-flaking wooden sign that said MAIN TERMINAL; she was just one more figure in an endless chain of others climbing the stairs, part of the crowd flow and almost indistinguishable from it. He still couldn't be certain.

Two hundred people occupied the forty-foot space between Lanyard and the staircase. The trains roared their musty wind into the station, and people, more people and more, pushed past him, glaring because he was standing still, because he wasn't going somewhere and therefore he was in the way....

He weaved through the crowd, moving against the confluence with painful slowness, plowing through an ambience of synthetic clothing and defaced wall-posters for stage musicals and horror movies and rock bands, feeling that he was gradually being buried under the incalculable weight of the station itself, the tons of concrete around him somehow adding their fulsome gravity to keep him from reaching Madelaine before he lost her in the crowd. "Madelaine!" he shouted, and could hardly hear himself over the pandemonium. He had lost sight of the woman. He reached the stairs and was forced to ascend them one at a time, one every two seconds because the way was packed and to go faster he'd have had to walk over their heads.

When, at last, burning with frustration, he reached the top, he found himself at forking hallways. Had she gone to the left or right? The ceiling sagged above him; insulation and rotting support frames and rusted pipe hung down; the signs indicating his whereabouts were patched over with cheaply printed posters warning about the Rockefeller Conspiracy, or the Consequences of Sin or the Consequences of Nuclear Power. Again he hesitated and again he was buffeted by the impatient crowd flow. A nun sat on a folding wooden chair at the crossways, holding a cup for money on her lap, her eyes hidden behind dirty wing-tip glasses, her smile frozen; as he watched she dumped the change into a leather pouch, replacing the empty cup on her lap. "Guh bless you," she said, when someone dropped a coin into her metal cup. "Guhblessyou, Guhbless."

Lanyard picked a direction at random; he allowed himself to be shunted to the left. Funneled down the populous hallway, he felt like a chunk of gravel in a cement mixer's dispenser, forced down by the weight of the medium in which it was embedded, part of some subterranean foundation for a construction whose purpose was alien to him.

Now he found himself in an underground mall, passing shop fronts of all kinds—clothing stores, gourmet-cheese stalls, hot-dog stands, knish-and-hot-dog stands, fried chicken-and-knish-and-hot-dog stands…

And without warning he was in the grand concourse, standing with his back to a wall, gaping to the right and left, lost and buried. Buried not only under the weight of people, but under their multiplicity of purpose, the fact that they were all strangers to him and all bent on different goals and not one of them really cared whether or not he found Madelaine. He was surrounded by media, sales pitches in the form of photo imagery big as a building on the huge walls of the concourse, and the electronic lettering trying to sell him insurance, the scores of bored leafletters hired to pass out glossy invitations to high-priced massage parlors or camera sales.

Grand Central, stacked level on level, covers forty acres; the main concourse, rows of ornate vaulted arches layered atop one another, high narrow windows, the distant ceiling painted gold with astrological signs, is a great echoing ballpark of a room vast enough to contain a hundred thousand people, and perhaps more, at once. And now, it seemed, at least half that number swarmed the broad floor, bustling every which way. Here and there the floor space was studded with flower stalls, and in the center was an information kiosk with brass fixtures, containing an ornate antique clock. Around the edges of the room were entrances to train terminals, a bar, a bank, and long rows of Off-Track Betting windows.

He thought he glimpsed Madelaine—there! Near the very center of the great, templelike room.

He dashed toward her, shouting, "Madelaine!" his voice lost in the surf sound of footsteps and hidden beneath the Olympian voice announcing Amtrak departures. The human maelstrom whipped about Lanyard, shifted and broke, and she was in sight, twenty feet away. His eyes were blurred with sweat as he ran up to the figure in the tan coat and, puffing, laid his hand on her shoulder; she turned. It was a harridan, a woman probably not as old as she looked, her face sunken and purplish; she wore a curly black wig, its elastic showing clearly at her temples, her toothless mouth opening to cackle, her hooded colorless eyes blinking back tears. "Baby, dat you?" she asked, shrilling over the din like a brake squealing; she reached for him, the fingernails on her shaking yellow hands caked in filth.

Lanyard reeled back, repelled, but also saddened by the look of disappointment on her face as it came home to her that he was not, after all, going to acknowledge her, that she was going to spend another day speaking to no one but herself. He turned away. She was soon lost in the crowd.

TWELVE

Lanyard stood by the window, one of Maguss's expensive cigarettes in his left hand, a glass of Chablis in his right; he sipped the wine to soothe his jangled nerves, and tried to keep his attention on the traffic moving like luminous flotsam in an underground river, far below. The window of Maguss's hotel suite was lightly glazed with reflections of city lights, lights softened to vague haloes by a thick, masking fog. The night seemed to have gathered intensely wherever there were shadows, and the lights were muted, as if afraid to anger the darkness.

Looking down into the crevasse between the high buildings to the haze-distorted street, Lanyard felt as if he were gazing into a shaft leading into the bowels of the earth.

Now and then he glanced over from the window when he heard Maguss turning a page. Sometimes he thought that the rustling sound was really Maguss himself; he was such a dry, papery-looking old man.

Lanyard half expected Maguss to close the notebooks, put aside the Data Digs reports, and say, flatly, "Carl, your conclusions are utter baloney."

So he turned sharply on his heel when Maguss said, "Well, Carl—"

"Well?" Lanyard demanded, crushing out his half-smoked cigarette and instantly lighting another.

"I think you're on the right track. And of course you're right about Minder. It's him, all right."

Lanyard stared. "What do you mean, 'Of course you're right'? You talk like you knew all along." Maguss ignored the remark. "I have found some papers I thought were lost...some letters Joey Minder wrote back when he was a very young man. He wrote the letters to me. Joey and I knew each other well. I was much older than he, almost twenty years older, and I was a sort of father figure to him for a while. He was a teen-ager when we first met. That was in

San Francisco and I was publishing *Mystic Mages* magazine, which was really just a scam so the so-called Mystic Mages could scalp the guileless. Young Joey was a subscriber, and came to see me when his troupe was in town. He was traveling with a carny that had a sort of vaudeville programming to it. I liked him, and I could see that he was intelligent and earnest, and I found myself confessing that most of the Mystic Mages cult was a money scam, if not quite an outright fraud. He was appalled. Then angry. He asked me if I believed in what he called 'the serious investigation of the paranormal.'" Maguss laughed, his hooded eyes like burnished glass, and then became abruptly solemn. "I said, yes, I believed in it, in principle. But I didn't know anyone really doing it. He accused me of promoting bunkum and giving psychic research a bad name, and he practically burst into tears. I confess I was moved. I had been offered another job, editing a Sunday supplement, and at that moment I decided to take it."

He smiled sadly. "He was idealistic then. He has lost most of that, of course. At any rate, we kept in touch, and I published an article he wrote-I had to edit it rather heavily—about an institute for psychic research, an organization which Joey took very seriously. I was a little dubious about them, because they specialized in 'the study of occult artifacts,' which is to say objects supposedly invested with supernatural influences. Like the Crystal Skull, various chunks of the 'True Cross' that were supposed to heal, and so forth. Joey became obsessed with a jade urn that was purported to contain the head of an ancient Persian priest. A priest in the cult of Ahriman—"

"What?" Lanyard leaned forward attentively.

"I have here a photocopy of a letter Joey sent me. Here, read the part circled in red. He was at this time still with the carny show, of course, but while they played New Orleans he found out about the organization, which had its so-called headquarters there."

Lanyard read:

> Simon, the tedium of the road is more than I can bear. I forecast that very soon I will transcend this grimy, tacky life, and find my way through the Hidden Doors...

Lanyard paused and looked up, forehead creased. "Is he kidding with this stuff, or what? This doesn't sound like the Joey Minder I know."

"You've got to remember that this was written years ago, Carl. He was a foolish boy, and he had a habit of reading pompous Theosophy texts. He's evolved a new style for his—uh—show-business connections. Skip ahead to the bit I outlined in red."

Lanyard shrugged, and found the place marked:

I was disappointed by all the artifacts I examined but one. The one that did indeed emanate a kind of numinous presence was a jade urn, on which, in relief, were figures depicting the Persian god Ahura Mazda in his dual manifestation, and an image of a dog-headed demon which I believe is the Persian demon Ahriman. I was drawn to the urn almost immediately. It was as if I heard it whispering to me. It is sealed at the top, and the archaeologist who found it, a Mr. Soames, claimed that it has never been opened since it was sealed centuries ago.

…There are various estimates as to the date, but its manufacture is generally placed at about 200 AD. It is "emerald" jade, with a few swirls of butter color in it. It seems to be carved of a single piece, two and one-half feet high. Soames refuses to open it, so we cannot confirm as to whether it, indeed, contains the severed head of a priest in the Cult of Ahriman…

Lanyard paused in his reading. His eyes hurt from lack of sleep. He seemed to be seeing the words as if they were raised from the page, blue lines of scribble floating in the air; and between the lines of twisty script swam miniature black worms, threading in and out, squirming…

…Lanyard closed his eyes and shook his head violently. "I don't want to read any more," he said.

"You don't look well, my lad."

"And I don't feel so goddamn well."

"You're worried about Madelaine. They need her—so they won't hurt her."

"Won't hurt her?" Lanyard shot Maguss a look that made the old man, usually beyond intimidation, sway back in his seat. "Maguss, she was on the floor clawing herself, dammit! And you're trying to tell me she's in good hands?"

"What do you want to do? Go to the police? They could search Minder's place from top to bottom and find nothing. If you could get them to search. He's a friend to the police. An influential man. A moneyed man. Now—" He tapped the letter on the table between them. "Now you know how he became a powerful man. It's all there in the following letters. He became obsessed with the urn. He met a man who had traveled in Persia, who was himself an occultist, and who gave him instructions in the rituals. A gent named Daniel Oswald. Ten years ago, the jade urn came onto the collector's market. I tried to buy it myself—I thought we could do a feature in *Visions* about it—but someone else bought it first. Someone who took great pains to remain anonymous. I have reason to believe, however, that it was Minder's associate Daniel Oswald who bought the urn—he had been born into a large fortune, and he could afford it. Oswald was soon dead, drowned in his bathtub. By accident, supposedly. I think Minder had him killed and stole the urn. The urn is a focusing object, at the very least. It is a link between our world and the entity in question. It could be—"

Lanyard snorted. "Bullshit. Madelaine is the victim of hysteria. And drug abuse. And maybe even brainwashing."

Maguss smiled superciliously. "Oh, *certainly*, Carl. Believe what you want. But, after acquiring that urn, Minder's fortunes turned. He became monumentally successful in less than a year. Let's put aside the notion that some supernatural entity actually assists those who sacrifice to it. Let's suppose that, instead, those who perform the ritual achieve success because they really *believe* they will—perhaps it's a form of mind over matter. The human brain generates electrical power—that's a proven scientific fact. Maybe that power can be directed at influencing events in the external world. Hm? Is it so impossible?"

"How can something as diffuse as this 'mental energy' would have to be— how could it influence events? Make a man rich, and—uh…"

"*If* mere mental energy is what it is—well, imagine a person's life-course through time as the rolling, bouncing of a pinball. You can influence the way a pinball moves by strategically tilting the table, to set up the best shot. That's all the power we're talking about does: It tilts the table, the plane, the subjective continuum through which we move, to favor our preferred course. It rolls us a little to the left, or right. Or it causes us to roll into the pit…if we're the subject of someone's hostile influence. Which is one reason no one seems to happen on the killers, no one successfully traces what few clues there are—events are tilted, by the power of the sacrifices, to favor the killers."

Lanyard looked at him, wondering if the old man were serious. "So—they must know by now, since I barged in on Minder's place, that—uh—I'm suspicious of them."

"They know with other means. They can *feel* you out here."

"So—why don't they kill me with their 'power'?"

"They can't tilt the plane for you so easily. It's difficult for them to touch you, because you're charged."

"I'm what?"

"I told you before. You have the Gift, however repressed. You can Hear. You can See. They might get a nasty shock if they tried to touch you, psychically...But they may well elect to kill you. To simply walk up to you and..." He paused, apparently enjoying the dire pronouncement. "And blow your brains all over the wall with a big fat black gun."

"And what's stopping them from doing that?"

"People with the Gift are useful to them."

"I assume you're pulling this 'Gift' business on me as some means of— uh—manipulating me. You paid me, and I work for you. That's enough."

"So then...what do you suggest we do?"

"We'll have to find their temple. Catch them in the midst of one of their rituals. It's got to be underground somewhere. Under the city. Maybe in an abandoned subway station."

"And then call the police once we've found it? Possibly. He's concealed it well. There's not a trace of emanation I can pick up—"

"Oh, stop with the quasi-mystical claptrap—"

Maguss went on as if speaking to drown out the voice of a babbling child. "So we'll have to find it another way. Now...I have a name of a gentleman I want you to visit. His name is Jesus."

"What?"

"Jesus Merino. He lives on Clinton Street, just south of Houston. Lower East Side heroin supermarket. In fact, he is a drug dealer. But he is also—or used to be—a spiritually powerful man. A practitioner of Santeria. In order to see him, you will have to go on some pretense—he prefers not to discuss his 'religion' with white people. You'll have to go to him ostensibly to buy drugs. And then, play it by ear. If anyone would know how to find Minder's temple, he would. He can feel things moving in the dark places. Here is his address, and the name of a man who will introduce you to him. The man can be trusted. But Merino cannot."

ONCE BEFORE, IN San Francisco, Lanyard had accompanied a musician friend on a trek through the Mission district to cop drugs. Lanyard had been doing an article on the band; he'd gone along on the connection out of curiosity. "You just gotta have the right attitude when you're looking, and you don't buy from anyone off the street," said his friend Locust. "You got to buy your smack and your coke"—they were looking for both heroin and cocaine because Locust wanted to mix the two to make a "speedball"—from somebody selling out of an apartment. If you buy it off the street and you don't know the guy, four times outta five they'll sell you a little bag of talcum powder. If they inna apartment, man, then you know *they* know you can find them if the stuff is a burn. Right?"

"But you said you don't have a connection lined up. How you going to find the stuff?" Lanyard had asked nervously as they'd sauntered with artificial casualness along the boulevard.

"Oh, you got to think about drugs, and pretty soon their street man, he comes up to you and asks you what kind you want and tells you the prices and then tells you what building it is and you go in. It's easy, but you got to be thinking about the shit, and lookin' for it. Because they always know, man."

And it was the same now, in New York. Lanyard and Jo-Jo, the man Maguss had recommended, were walking down Avenue B, thinking: *Where do we cop dope?* It wasn't telepathy that told the street connections what they were after; it was something conveyed in body language, and a sense of seeking in a neighborhood that offers nothing else. Even the whores were farther uptown.

It was a wet afternoon three days before Halloween. There was a cutting wind from the East River keening between the tenement buildings and through the trash-choked alleys. Lanyard shivered in his leather jacket; Jo-Jo, a hollow-eyed Puerto Rican wearing moldering tennis shoes, a smudged blue ski jacket, floppy corduroy pants, wet at the cuffs, and a black knit cap, walked rapidly beside Lanyard and seemed to feel the wind not at all. His jacket was open, his hands balled in the pockets. He stared straight ahead as he spoke. "So, my man, you know you shoon't come out here widduh piece, you know?"

It took Lanyard a moment to translate; Jo-Jo was telling him he shouldn't be carrying a gun. "I didn't think you could see it."

"They can see it frommuh way you' hand's in you' pocket acrossuh fucking street, man. They suspicious then, they think you rip 'em off for the dope or maybe you the heat or some shit."

"I didn't think it was safe to come into this neighborhood without a gun."

"Safer without one. You askin' for trouble. For one thing, the cops frisk you, they run your ass to stir for carryin' a piece."

"So is this gonna fuck up the connection?" Lanyard asked, trying to sound streetwise.

"I dunno. I dun think so, no. But you be cool when we go see Papa Merino, okay?"

"Okay." Lanyard shrugged. The streets were uncrowded; loiterers stood just inside, out of the wind, at nameless grocery stores, Chinese restaurants, combination Chinese-Spanish restaurants, and combination Chinese-Spanish and East Indian restaurants. For every business that was operating, three more had shut down; the street was pocked with boarded storefronts, failed shoe-shine parlors, "social clubs," countless trashed restaurants, their windows broken in, soggy cardboard and broken glass spread over the counters, over broken stools. Every third building was gutted, the wind whining in its ragged sockets. The street was nervous with windblown scraps; heaps of wine bottles spilled from deserted doorways and vacant lots, exuding a layered stench. They traversed Houston, a four-lane crosstown street, ignoring the lights, dodging cars, and jogged onto the below-Houston extension of Avenue B; the street action was almost dense here; every forty strides were groups in ski jackets or army-surplus gear, each face with its mustache and its darting assessment and its final indifference, standing about rusty oil drums, warming their hands at fires dancing red from the pitted metal. Now and then someone spoke to Lanyard, or made a move toward him, probably thinking: *Dumb whiteass; easy to hustle.* With buddy-buddy asides, "Hey got your good dope, try it before you buy it, lookin' good green-tape, get you two for twenny." But Jo-Jo shook his head in a way that said *This one's mine,* and they turned back to rapid-fire conversations in street Spanish.

They passed buildings without doors where men squatted, muttering; they passed a church from which clean and formal families passed, leaving Mass;

in the same block an almost fleshless man in a sailor cap chanted, "Get the good works here, your clean works, t'ree dollars for chew' buddy, good points, nobody use, clean works..." And just beyond him they passed a laundromat where sweating, stocky Latin housewives fanned themselves in the steamy interior and laughed and gossiped. Lanyard and Jo-Jo passed a long, dark car in which two black men in suits took turns counting a fat roll of bills; and they passed a group of children playing tag, shouting "You're it—" in Spanish.

Then they stopped in front of a high stoop, the stone chipped so that some of the steps weren't quite there; to either side Spanish Marxist posters were peeling from the façade; posters for rock bands, posters for Latin music shows, posters for discos, posters overlapping and muting one another the length of the block, between doors; the trash cans stood, bent and blackened like giant cigarette butts in ashtray groups near the rusting NO PARKING traffic sign.

Across the street black men and a mulatto woman stood passing reefer around in the front door of the Suffolk Social Club, Members Only. At intervals along the block shopkeepers rolled metal-link door covers down to block the storefronts for the night, locking them twice.

Jo-Jo tilted his head toward the stoop. Lanyard leaned against a brick face in his best imitation of nonchalance. "So," said Jo-Jo, "Papa Merino, he's up there. Now, this is what the old man"—Maguss—"say we do: They got a shooting gallery up there too, right? So we go up, we buy the shit, some works, then we go in the shooting gallery and do up a little; that way we're inside. Then they see we're cool, we're not cops, we're doing it up. So then maybe if I give the green, then maybe we gettuh see the Papa. I talk to 'em for you, then you talk to the Papa. He speaks good In-glish. Right?"

"I've got to shoot the stuff up?" Lanyard whispered. "I can't do that. I've never done it, and anyway I've got to be able to think clearly."

"It's cool. I be makin' your hit for you, my man. I give you a hit of water, nothin' but water, an' it won't hurt you. No dope in it. They won't see. An' I'll do you up, guys here they do each other all the time. I just hope they don't ask to see your tracks. I show 'em mine. Sometimes they want to see your tracks if they think you might be a pig, right?"

"So let's get it over with."

Jo-Jo said, "Come on," and led him up the broken steps. Endless scenarios of catastrophe were staged for Lanyard's inner eye: he and Jo-Jo make the buy

Cellars

just as the police raid—the police raid only when a pusher hasn't paid the precinct bagman—and Lanyard goes to prison for possession; some clumsy movement causes his gun to fall from his pocket, and the nervous junkies inside take him for a hit man and descend on him with lead pipes; someone insists Lanyard shoot up where they can see it, so they know he's all right, and he's forced to mainline a heavy hit of China White, after which he pukes and babbles; they are set upon and robbed and murdered and dumped in the East River. All credible possibilities.

Jo-Jo and Lanyard stepped inside the doorless hallway lit only by an unshaded bulb on the landing above. The hall reeked of piss, the floor sagged; the wallpaper was indistinguishable from graffiti, and phantasmagoric whorls of mold. A man with a beard and thick glasses—the right lens was cracked—blocked their way, stepping from the shadows beneath the staircase. His mouth drooped, showing blackened teeth; a half-empty Coca-Cola bottle in one hand. Lanyard's fingers tightened around the gun in his pocket.

Jo-Jo said, "Yo, wha's happenin'," and continued in telegraphic bursts of Spanish. The two conversed for three minutes; the bearded man now and then indicating Lanyard and asking questions. Then he shrugged, and opened his hand, palm up. There was a moment of awkwardness, as Jo-Jo waited for Lanyard to produce the money and Lanyard waited to be told to produce the money. Was it the right time?

Jo-Jo turned to him and said, "Wheresuh green, man?"

"Uh—how much?"

"Forty for two good bags, six more for two sets uh works. Right?"

"Yeah."

Lanyard took the money from his left-hand jacket pocket and, carefully detaching his right hand from his gun, counted forty-six dollars into Jo-Jo's palm.

Jo-Jo counted the money out for the street connection, who went down the hall with it. He knocked on the door of the only apartment on the first floor. There was a hole cut in the door, at eye level, the size of an apple. A panel slid back, and someone looked through the hole; another interchange in Spanish. Then the bearded man passed the money through the hole. The panel shut. They waited two minutes more. From somewhere came the sound of water dripping in an upper hallway. The halls were unheated, dank; Lanyard gradually became aware of noises, from the upper stories; Latin music, people laughing, the shuffle of feet, a woman shouting at someone, the someone shouting back in gruff male tones, a few Anglo-Saxon expressions, like "cunt" and "fuck off," mixed with Spanish.

The panel slid aside again; two foil packages closed with green plastic tape were passed to the bearded man. He waited, and then two finger-length paper-wrapped sets of syringes were thrust through.

With a jerk of his head the man with the beard led Lanyard and Jo-Jo up the stairs; sometimes they had to step over gaps in the wooden staircase—where there should have been stairs there were rectangular holes into darkness. Lanyard had had only a few hours' sleep; for a moment he thought that the darkness in the stair gaps was somehow thickening, rising in tendrils like mist off a subterranean lake to entwine his legs.

He shook himself as they reached the third landing. Exhaustion was catching up with him. He felt as if he were struggling through layers of tepid liquid wax.

Down a hallway with a floor so raked it might have belonged to a funhouse, and at the end, a metal door with a peephole opened to inspect them. The bearded man spoke something that might have been "Open sesame" in Spanish, for all Lanyard knew, and the door swung inward. Lanyard resisted the impulse to put his hand on his gun as they went in. A haggard middle-aged woman stood by the door, looked each of them over once, and moved aside for then. She didn't seem surprised to see Lanyard, though he was the only Caucasian there.

Through a barren hallway, into a barren central room, a turn to the right through a sagging doorway, and into a long, narrow bedroom—the "shooting gallery." *You need someplace to get off, man? We got a place you can go, cost you just two bucks more.* The place? Splintery wooden floor. No furniture. Boarded-over window. One person using the room, a woman who sat hunched on a blanket against the far wall; part of the tree-patterned, once-blue wallpaper had peeled and curled protectively, like a palm frond, over her bleached-blond head. Her face was hidden in her drawn-up knees; she rocked slightly, her scarred arms locked about her shins. She wore red pantyhose and black stiletto heels and a sweatshirt printed with a slogan he couldn't see. Her works, the syringe in a water glass like a spent insect, were on the floor beside her left foot. The pink baby blanket was sealed to the floor at one corner by a dried puddle of vomit. Lanyard was relieved no one else was in the room. They sat on their haunches in a corner opposite the girl. The haggard woman left them. Hands shaking only slightly, working with thrifty expertise, Jo-Jo opened the packages, balancing the syringes across the open top of an aspirin bottle of water he took from his coat pocket. From the other pocket he took a spoon and a bit of dirty cotton; he frowned over the cotton, "Fuckin' cotton is too dirty innyway." He tossed it aside, then carefully opened the foil wraps of heroin; he glanced up to see that no one was looking in the door. The girl was still nodded out across from them. So Jo-Jo slipped one of the foil packages into his coat pocket, and filled Lanyard's syringe with water; he recapped the syringe's needle and handed it to Lanyard. "Hold dat, man," he whispered, "cover up the inside with your hand so they can't see it ain't got nothin' but watuh." Lanyard nodded, took off his jacket, rolled up a sleeve, and took the syringe in his hand, cupping its chamber.

As Jo-Jo used a cigarette lighter to cook the yellow-flecked white powder in his singed spoon, Lanyard watched the girl across from them; she was beginning to lean to the right, and looked as if she might collapse entirely. She might be more than nodded out. She might be overdosed. Lanyard thought about calling an ambulance. But that would jeopardize the meeting with Jesus "Papa" Merino. And there were a great many more lives to be considered. How many potential victims? Thousands. Because if Maguss were right, if the ritual worked—or even if it only seemed to work—there were numberless people, hordes and hidden armies of people, who would be willing to sacrifice a stranger if they thought it would turn their fortunes. More people than would ever admit it. It could become a national disease, like Nazism had been for another country, once.

Jo-Jo had filled his syringe, had tied up with a piece of lamp wire that lay on the floor for just that purpose, and now a tiny red splash, oddly like an attenuated nuclear-blast cloud, blossomed into the chamber as he worked the needle into one of the few unscarred veins on his forearm. He'd struck blood.

Lanyard looked at the red blossom, and remembered the blood he had seen on the subway platform and in the cellars, blood splashed on women and little girls, and wondered what the connection was; somehow he knew there was a connection with the blood in the syringe.

Jo-Jo was pressing the plunger home. Lanyard looked away. It was too personal to watch. He sat on the cold floor, feeling the chill seep into his buttocks and spine, and waited. He could have fallen asleep, except for the cold.

He heard water trickling from a drainpipe somewhere outside the boarded windows, and sounds from another apartment: music and laughter. This one was so barren...everything that could be sold had been. *"You gimme a dollar for this chair, man? Okay, a half-dollar. Okay, a quarter."* Jo-Jo was nodding beside him, murmuring to himself, head drooping. Scratching his face, scratching his crotch with lazy motions of his dirty-nail fingers, Jo-Jo squinted at Lanyard through deep-set eyes. "Soon," he said, to Lanyard's unspoken question. And then, "Take the cord, tie up."

Gingerly, Lanyard unwrapped the wire from Jo-Jo's biceps, and, trying not to think about it, wrapped it about the biceps of his own right arm. He tightened the cord, and pumped the arm to make his veins bulge. Moving slowly but deliberately, his rush over, Jo-Jo took the syringe from Lanyard, uncapped the needle, shook it for bubbles, spritzed a little water from the glistening point, and probed Lanyard's arm. Lanyard hardly felt the puncture. Jo-Jo was smiling; he took his time, enjoying it, apparently, when Lanyard's blood formed the tiny mushroom-cloud in the chamber.

There were footsteps in the hall; the tired-faced woman, overweight, wearing a soiled blue-flower-print muu-muu, leaned against the door frame to watch, just as Jo-Jo pressed the plunger home. Lanyard shuddered as the cold water dispersed in his veins. He waited, half afraid that Jo-Jo had put something in it after all—and perhaps a little disappointed when it was clear he hadn't. He pretended to nod, drooping slightly, not wanting to overdo it.

The woman went away.

Jo-Jo removed the needle and set it aside. He took out the second foil package and started to unwrap it.

Lanyard glanced at the woman across the room. She'd fallen to her side, her left cheek on her arm, her face exposed now. A gaunt face, pocked, familiar.

"Julie," Lanyard murmured. The woman who'd taken his money. The woman who'd seduced him when he was lonely and stoned, had pretended to befriend him. Had used him. Had sacrificed him, in a way. She'd used him to get money for junk.

An anger Lanyard had held-in check for a week rose in him. He put his jacket back on, feeling to be sure the gun was in place. He stood and walked directly to her, hissing, "Julie—remember *me?*"

What would he have done? Would he have kicked her? Would he have pulled the gun and threatened her, maybe shoot her kneecap away? Would he have slapped her? Would he have tried to drag her down the hall to the police? Would he have simply shouted at her, tried to humiliate her, to give her a sense of the humiliation he'd felt when he'd awakened and found himself ripped off?

What would he have done if he hadn't found that she was dead?

She was blue: one of her eyes was open, crusting as he watched; the other was shut, and sticky-edged. Blood and vomit leaked slowly from her half-open mouth. She was quite dead. He could see the lettering on her sweatshirt now: THE EMPIRE STRIKES BACK.

And Lanyard was ashamed. When she'd stolen from him she had been just a machine, programmed by drugs, beyond compunctions. Just another victim. And he'd been seriously considering kicking her in the kidneys.

Gagging, he turned away—and found Jo-Jo cooking up another shot of heroin. Lanyard strode across the room and kicked the dope aside. He drew his gun, and with the other hand put a finger across his lips. "That's *my* money you're shooting," he whispered. "And if you do it you won't be in shape to help me. Maguss said you were reliable. I think he knew you before you were strung out."

Jo-Jo was staring at the spoon on the floor, the splash where dope seeped between the floorboards. He made a small sound in his throat. He looked up at Lanyard, blinking, his face twitching; he stood, slowly. Lanyard took a step back.

Jo-Jo teetered, and took a deep breath. Mechanically, he rolled his shirtsleeve down. Scratching his face, his arms, his crotch, his face again, he said, "Pudduh gun away an' we go see Papa."

Lanyard slipped the small pistol back in his jacket pocket. But he left his hand in the pocket, and the angle of his wrist made it clear to Jo-Jo that he kept the gun ready. "Take me to see him. Hundred dollars fee, right?" He had to repeat the whispered question; Jo-Jo wasn't hearing clearly.

"Three hunnerd."

"Bullshit. Maguss said we could see him for one hundred."

"We try it. One hunnerd." He held out his hand.

Lanyard shook his head. "No, you just make the deal and I give'em the money."

"Hey, you know I better…"

"I said forget it."

"Shit, I don' care." He scratched his nose. His cheek. His neck. His crotch. His nose.

He shuffled out the door. Looking as needled-out as he knew how, Lanyard went with him; he didn't look at Julie's corpse, but out of the corner of one eye he thought he saw eel shapes swirling in the air above her, whirling to converge…

The haggard woman in the shapeless dress and mules sat on the floor in a corner of the front room, reading a Spanish language newspaper, *El Diario;* her chunky arms were bare, and Lanyard saw no track marks on them. He supposed that she didn't live here, that she wasn't into junk. She was an employee. Whose?

Jo-Jo spoke listlessly to her, nodding toward Lanyard. She shook her head and said a word that sounds the same in Spanish, English, and French: "No."

Lanyard sighed and slid five twenties from his pants pocket; he crouched to count them out for her on the floor. She made a cone of her lips, thinking, and for the first time he noticed that she wore bright red lipstick and dangling seashell earrings. She grunted, swept up the money with one pudgy hand while tossing the newspaper aside with the other. She took a set of keys from her bodice; they hung on a leather string about her neck, She pointed to the door. They waited for her in the hall as she locked the door. She led them down the stairs, muttering to herself obscurely.

They went outside, and to the basement. She took them down the stoop and down into the stairwell to the right of the stoop, below street level; a walk-down basement flat. The woman knocked on the door. It opened a crack, a chain dangling between the door and the frame. She spoke to someone Lanyard couldn't see, and handed the money through. The door shut again. They waited another minute in the drizzle and the shadow from the stoop; the street lights had come on while he was in the building.

Lanyard thought about Julie. The shadows seemed to thicken in the stairwell. "*The Empire Strikes Back,*" he muttered, ignoring the quizzical looks from the other two.

The door opened, unfolding a yellow fan of light onto the concrete step at Lanyard's feet. The woman from upstairs gestured briskly for Jo-Jo to leave, for Lanyard to enter. He went in alone. Inside, he faced a slender young woman dark as the black-iron fence around the stairwell, wearing an indigo wrap resembling a sari, a red scarf over her kinky black hair, and no shoes. She spoke to him in what he supposed was Haitian Creole. He spread his hands to show his incomprehension, smiled, and said, "Papa Merino? Can I see him?"

She said something else he did not understand and pointed down the hallway. It was a shock after the desolation of the upstairs. The walls were well painted in dull gold trimmed in red. The crushed-glass-coated ceiling fixtures were new; the earth-umber rug was clean and thick. Lanyard walked down the hall, toward a tinkling of soft music, the girl just behind him. To his surprise, the music was an "easy listening" FM station playing from a desk radio in a room that he thought of as an "office." The woman motioned for him to wait there. She moved silently from sight, down the hall to his left, leaving the door open. There were no chairs, no place to sit but the floor. He stood, stretching, rocking on the balls of his feet, his gut tightening with uncertainty.

The walls were lined with bookshelves filled with as many paperbacks as hardbound books, of all varieties. There was a shelf of leatherbound books, their spines printed with a lettering he didn't recognize, as foreign to him as Sanskrit.

A desk against one wall was the only item of furniture. He felt exposed in the light from a tall stainless steel floor lamp beside the desk. The plastic radio on the desk top cooed a watered-down version of "I Got You Under My Skin." Behind the steel bookshelves, the walls were cork. The concrete floor was bare, painted white. Here and there were red smudges, as if chalk lines had been hastily wiped away. The floor sloped slightly toward a white-painted drain. For catching blood? Santeria practitioners frequently got in trouble with the ASPCA for sacrificing animals. Mostly chickens and rabbits.

The old man who came into the room was so short he would not have intimidated a midget. He was carved of black walnut, handsomely offset by his cream-colored suit, white silk cravat, and white shoes. He hobbled forward on his light aluminum cane, pausing to peer balefully at Lanyard with eyes yellowed like old dice, hobbled forward a step or two more, pausing to size up the stranger again. His voice was musical, almost as lilting as the Muzak

version of "The Way We Were" coming from the desk. "You have gone to a
great deal of trouble to see me, sir."

"Maguss sent me to you. My name is Lanyard. He seems to think you
might be able to help us find..." Lanyard searched for words. "...find the
people who are the enemy of us all. So that we can stop them."

"You are a very direct young man. You are also not doped. They told me
you were doped and that it seemed likely, therefore, that you were not police.
Stupid of them to assume that the police don't take dope." His accent was
faintly Caribbean. "Are you the same Lanyard who wrote 'Animus Rites of the
Lower Cameroon' for *Visions?*"

"Yes!" Lanyard blurted, pleased.

"Then you probably know a little bit about me and my people as well. So
there is no point in pretending."

"Pretending what, Mr. Merino?"

"Pretending you don't believe. I perceive in you a fanatical skepticism. But
you are drawn to us—to write about us, people like us—for a reason. I know
a man who believes but does not want to believe."

The old man studied him like a biologist identifying a species of lower
anthropoid.

"Maguss must have spoken to you," Lanyard said, thinking aloud. "He told
me that he couldn't. That you two are not friendly, and that you couldn't be
reached except in the way I did it. But you sound too much like him. You
and he are setting me up for something." His head buzzed with pain and the
rushing, whispering background was coming to life again. He felt distanced
from everything around him, as if he were seeing the little black man and the
room on a home-movie screen, detached and two-dimensional. Merino's voice
came to him from a long ways away.

"You really ought not to leap to conclusions," said Merino, looking at him
quizzically. "The fact is simply that your Mr. Maguss and I see you the same
way, because we both perceive the same truth about you. There are skeptics
who are genuine, who debunk in an effort to expose fraud, and then there are
skeptics like you, who believe deep in their hearts."

Lanyard was finding it hard to breathe. The air swarmed with dark
ribbonings, like ticker tape come alive; he noticed, now, that their movements
took on definite patterns in particular areas of the room, and around Merino

they swarmed at a respectful distance in a sort of in-and-out dance, as if they were trying to reach him, wriggling toward him like sperm. They were repelled, then returned a moment later only to be driven back again.

"You are more than a believer," said Merino. "You are charged. I see that now."

There was fear in Merino's voice. He began to turn away, saying, "I have nothing to tell you. I would not help Maguss, no matter who I am helping him against. It is all the same. And they are too strong. Too deeply rooted." He turned back to Lanyard. "I will tell you this: *Leave the city.* I hear Him breathing at night. His breathing is excited. He is aroused. He is well fed. They feed Him to feed themselves. But He is never quite full." He turned again to the door.

But now the door was shut.

The old man raised a trembling hand to the knob. The dark things swarming the air congested near the doorknob. It would not turn for him. "Ryonna!" He shouted, rapping against the door with his cane. "Open it!" And something more in another language. From beyond the door came a prolonged, low rumble which built in volume and rose in pitch to become the shriek of an infuriated beast. The snarling, grinding sounds that followed, along with the whispering in Lanyard's head, almost covered the scream of the girl Ryonna.

Carl…My daughter…Madelaine under…Madelaine beneath…

Lanyard clapped his hands over his ears. But the Voices resonated from the bones of his skull—resonated in sympathetic frequency with the bone in a thousand fleshless skulls, skulls lying empty under rocks and soil and in the throats of caves, echoing behind their dusty sockets with Voices.

He closed his eyes, and wind swept by his face. His eyes flew open when the great thump went through him. The room had tilted askew. And then he realized that he'd fallen, that he was lying on his side, his palms still clamped over his ears. He lay just beneath a book shelf; he tried to wriggle closer to the wall, to hide in the shallow space under the shelf, as far as possible from the living darkness that possessed the air itself. He was almost blind with it. It looked as if beetle-black maggots were eating holes in the stuff of Space, crawling in and out and in and out, so densely he couldn't make out the details of the wall on the other side of the little room.

John Shirley

*Carl, voilà, chéri...je t'ai délivré de tout ce qui te geneaité...Il faut dormir...
Demain...*

Lanyard wondered if he'd been drugged, after all. He preferred to believe he was hallucinating, when he felt the wetness on his arm and looked up to see the red foam vomiting from the drain in the floor, rising like a crimson fist and forearm, foamy but gelatinous, spreading, filling the floor in seconds, giving off a smell that made bile rise in his throat.

He was nearly blind with the black swarmings; he couldn't see the old man. He could hear him shouting, invoking weaker gods, over the buzzing, the whispering, the rasp of his own labored breathing.

The red muck had covered the floor—except where Lanyard lay. It touched him...and drew back.

It hardened like batter in a hot pan—and the room was hot, the heat soaked the strength from him; and now the light was reduced to a distant glimmer, blurred and frightened, filtered by the dark swarming in the air. There was something deliberate in the motion of the eel shapes, the blackness flowing into channels that coursed about the room, dipping to taste this and that, retreating, shaping and reshaping...coming, now, to hover over Lanyard, darting tendrils at him, recoiling.

The power currents encircled the sputtering drain; the drain was the eye of the hurricane.

Through the smoky swarm Lanyard made out the old man on his knees in the thick, glistening red muck. Merino's face was hidden by a thickening of the black swarm; Lanyard could see that he was shaking violently, snapping from the waist, backward and forward, fighting something unseen, spasming with an elasticity that should have been impossible for so old a man.

He was moving horizontally, too; dragged slowly, like someone pulled on a rug. Toward the drain. The red fountain had stopped. In its place, a single glossy bubble was rising from the hole in the floor. As it expanded from the drain, it took on a coherent shape. It was a bubble shaped like a head. Or a head with the texture of a bubble. But it wasn't so fragile as a bubble. As the body of the thing came into sight Lanyard was reminded of a novelty-store snake springing from a can, its inner spring forcing it out—but the body came in slow motion, now, unreeling. Somehow he knew it was a *strong* body. When the head popped completely free of the drain it bounced a little on the thin neck, repulsively rubbery. The rest of the body came swiftly, rising to man-height over the drain. It shouldn't have been able to fit in the drain at all.

You're Carl Lanyard, don't forget who you are, hold on.

He recognized that voice. His mother's voice. A calm descended on him, and he watched with renewed detachment. It was all on a screen somewhere. He wasn't part of this. The red membrane on the floor was wrinkling up, closing around the old man like a sea anemone—but that was part of the dream. The rubbery thing, whose fingers were moving without respect to bones or knuckles—nobby nailless fingers, each one with a life of its own—that thing was walking toward Lanyard and standing over him and opening its mouth. In the dream.

Not because it was happening to him. Not to Carl Lanyard.

It was happening to someone else.

You're here with me, Carl. You're okay. But you've got to live with the world when they've gone away.

The Blessed People, said another voice. *This is one of the Blessed.*

The Blessed One stood over him like a skeleton molded out of the stuff of slugs. It was almost transparent, and like the exotic fish in aquariums whose entrails are visible, the Blessed One's insides were all there to see: a beating heart that was like a thing of lemon Jell-O, an esophagus like a glass tube leading down to a stomach of rose quartz within which was a silhouette: a severed human hand.

The Blessed One's genitals were colorless, inhuman, and depended from its crotch in four whipping, seeking, oozing feelers like the whiskers of a catfish. Dripping yellowish phlegm.

The swarm wheeled behind the Blessed One, like a weightless snakepit. Like a lamprey mouth. Like a suctioning whirlpool.

The radio, somewhere remote, played a Muzak version of "Send in the Clowns."

The Blessed One stood with its splayed feet, toes fused into duck-foot appendages, planted to either side of Lanyard's head; the pus dripped from its quivering four-part genitals to splash by his cheek. He lay on his left side, gazing up at it, paralyzed.

The Blessed One remained rigidly upright—but its head, alone, came down to visit Lanyard.

To pay him a little visit, chuckled one of the Voices.

Leave him alone, let him withdraw! His mother's voice again.

The Blessed One's head lowered itself from its shoulders, neck unreeling to a five-foot length, the head drooping on it like a heavy swamp blossom on a long slack stem; the head was still solidly attached to the unmoving shoulders on an upright torso. The head tilted on it so that the face—blackbutton eyes, lipless mouth, a nose that writhed like the fingers and genitals—within an inch of his own. Its cold, lidless black eyes looked into his eyes.

There was a recognition in the eyes that made him want to hide forever from seeing, and from thinking. Mentally, Lanyard recoiled. The Blessed One withdrew, encompassing with the little man trapped in red—and methodically crushed as he was drawn to the drain. The black swarmings fell away too; the room shrank to an image the size of a dime against a great field of night. And finally was gone altogether.

He had time for one thought: *If this is death, I hope it's final.*

The last thing he heard before losing consciousness was the radio playing a Muzak version of David Bowie's "Changes."

THIRTEEN

"Morty, my good friend, how is it for you?" Gribner's cheerfulness was forced. Morty could detect the false note.

"Cyril, you don't look so good. I heard they took you off this subway-killing business. It's some nerve I got bringing it up, but maybe that's what's bothering you? I mean, I've never known you to be taken off a case. It's politics, my friend, that's all."

"They took me off? That's what they say. I say: I quit. I'm retiring from the force altogether. I need this aggravation? I don't need it."

They sat at the bar in the China West, a Chinese restaurant and cocktail lounge on Delancey. There were two other people in the room, Chinese businessmen talking in their own language over tall, multicolored drinks at the far end of the curving leather-padded bar.

Morty Abramowitz, New York City Assistant Utilities Commissioner, was overweight by a good ninety pounds, and too short to carry it well. He wore a glistening layer of Vitalis on his gray-black hair, and there was something of the same glassiness in his wide-set black eyes. He shifted in his suit, and undid the top snap of his trousers to ease the pressure, as he ordered a second round of Tom Collinses. Morty was an earnest but humorous man, and Gribner had always liked him.

Gribner glanced at his Timex. It was 7:45 PM. Morty had said he had a meeting at nine. He supposed he should tell Morty why he'd asked him to the bar. Morty knew it was business. They were making small talk till the right moment came.

But Gribner didn't much want the right moment to come. "So you remember when you were on the force, Morty, or did you manage to forget yet?"

Morty gave the little toss of his head and the grunt that he used for laughter. "It's as far from my thoughts as I can make it. But sometimes I think about that slob Strieker. He says, 'Who are you guys? You ain't cops, we paid the cops yesterday.' You got to be a bagman to be a cop, he figures, right? So then he tries to offer us shoes! *Hot* crates of shoes! He was a resourceful man. You know, my kid, eight years old then, came into the station once and he sees Strieker in the cage waiting to be booked, so—so Strieker tries to offer him a candy bar for the keys on the desk and the kid says, 'How low-class you think I am? I should spring creeps for candy bars?' Eight years old!"

"How is the little guy, Morty?"

"Ten years older, Lieutenant." Morty was suddenly solemn. "He's got draft-age worries. Going to school."

"Right, yeah, studying veterinary, right?"

"Yeah, he's a good kid. So how's the old lady?" He brightened. "She still goes to the Madame Sees-It-All or Madame Fortune Cookie, or whatever—?"

Gribner chuckled. "Madame Tanya. The old fraud. Sometimes I think I ought to send the bunko squad around, save myself some money. But the old girl's got to have something to...I guess you heard about the dogs."

"I heard. Some people ought never to have been born. To do something like that. Any word on the kid? Your—what was he?"

"What was he? I don't know. But if you mean was he my relative, he was my nephew."

Morty glanced at Gribner sidelong, the creases around his eyes deepening. He waited. The time had come.

"At first, Morty," Gribner said (as the sad-eyed blonde at the piano bar began to play "Love Is Blue"), "I wanted to resign from the case, myself, my own idea. I begin to get a picture what's going on here, deciding I got to do it my way. A kind of private investigation. Because they're not listening to me. But they wouldn't let me quit. So yesterday I went and told them what I really thought was going on. I told them about the growling in the pipes—"

"What?" Morty seemed startled.

Gribner looked at him. "What I said maybe brings something to mind?"

Morty hesitated. "Uh—we had to fire some guys. They wouldn't go down in 216 and 217; that's where they found those ripped-up bums. And they claimed they heard some growling noise coming from the pipes. And one of 'em says he saw a ghost. A guy you could see right through. We thought, maybe you inhale methane fumes, it can cause hallucinations, am I right? And—uh—"

"You read my report on the kid under Grand Central?" Gribner's voice was suddenly crisp. He leaned back in the bucket-seat chair.

Morty nodded. "Sure, Cyril, I'm not going to read your report? Natch I read your report. I think this guy, this patrolman, I think he shot too quick, myself. I'm with you on that. He got spooked down there. He said he'd gone there when he was a kid and got scared, right? So it all came back, and he spooked and started seeing things. Like the way he claimed those kids were acting."

"I don't think he was 'seeing things,' Mort. That kid he shot—we didn't get a chance to look at the body. Not much. It disappeared from the morgue. There was a red crust on the drain in the morgue, and around the walls, near the floor—same shit we found when this man Krupp came forward, and we lost him—" He lowered his voice. "You heard about the other stuff, so maybe you heard about this Krupp, too?"

"I heard."

"The stuff on the walls was blood—but blood from lots of people, mixed, dried, and with something else in it—some kind of organic soup."

He waited, tapping his glass, watching for Morty's reaction.

Morty shrugged. "Some sewer backed up. Sometimes we get a lot of blood in the sewer, from lots of different sources...slaughterhouse, meat packers..."

"This was human blood."

Morty stiffened. "Okay. Stuff builds up in some sewage leakage pools in layers, and there could be a layer of blood backing up...maybe from a hospital. What—uh—?"

"What do I think? I think it has something to do with the subway killings, and I don't know what yet. I think there's something smart down there that's not human, and you know I've been on the force a long time, I'm not going to jump to wild conclusions. And I think those people have their temple underground—if they are people—and I think some of them live down there. And we're not getting anywhere. I mean, clues dry up overnight. It's unnatural for a case with so many killings to have so many dead ends. It's unnatural...."

Morty was studying his hands, looking very unhappy.

"Morty," Gribner said in a friendlier tone, "on you is the look of a man who has to tell a friend something he doesn't want to tell him. Like, 'Cyril, you're getting senile,' or 'Cyril, you worked yourself into exhaustion. You're snapping.'"

Morty let out a long slow breath. "Some of that occurred to me. But we been getting stories…things that make me wonder. I guess you heard about the new guys on the MTA board?"

"What? No, I thought the Transit Authority was sealed up for at least a year—"

"Hollins and Bourbon both had a run of unbelievable bad luck. It's—unnatural. Like you said. Both at the same time. Hollins, his wife died, his son's a drug addict, all his investments dropped to nothing, and he has a nervous breakdown. He had to quit, to go to work selling real estate again, try and recoup. And Jerry Bourbon tried to shoot himself."

"What? Jerry Bourbon? You'd have thought the *Post* would have splashed that—"

"Keep your voice down. They don't know. The guy almost overnight went into suicidal depression. Anyway, we got these two new guys on the board, appointed by the Mayor's Emergency Committee, and uh—well, they know each other too well, these guys. One, I don't know what he knows about mass transit or what makes him qualified. I mean…his name is Tooley. And we had an investigation going into the Outside Train thing—"

"Whoa, slow down. You got all the dirt on my department, but I heard nada and nil about the Outside Train thing."

"It's—" He spread his hands as if to say *Who knows?* "It's a train that's completely unauthorized, with all the windows blacked out, that somehow gets clearance from the dispatchers—and they're so fucking innocent about it you know they're on the take from somewhere. It runs up the East Side, according to the story—I mean, maybe it's bullshit. But it's causing delays and all kinda confusion in the scheduling. That and the pest damage."

Gribner stared, waiting.

"You haven't heard about the pest damage, either? Way more than usual I mean. Rats or dogs or something chewing through some of the power lines… and a whole section of the subway blacks-out of power. Only happened twice, and people are so used to late trains that no one noticed much, but it's getting harder and harder to find them, and repair them in time…."

"Let's go back to the…the Outside Train, you called it? Where is it spotted?"

"Mostly between Delancey and Grand Central, on the East Side. An *old* train."

Gribner nodded. "That's the area I want you to search."

"So that's what this is about…but they took you off the case…"

"I'm investigating on my own, So, I want you to search mostly in the area between Gramercy Square and Grand Central. Utility tunnels, drain-off mains, subway tunnels, search anything big enough for a man, and most especially if it's not being used much. Old basements…even old mine shafts if there are any. Caves if you have access to those—a systematic search."

"This is my department you're talking about? We're going to do this search? Hah! And where are we going to get the personnel? Our budget could be printed on a bubblegum card. We haven't got the men to patrol for sewage leaks, gas-line leaks, power-line breaks—we're already overextended. We got five boroughs to cover, Cyril—"

"Tell them anything," said Gribner, as if Morty had already agreed. "Tell them to look for anything unusual—and tell your boss they're looking for what you said, power breaks. But find some excuse to concentrate them in that area. The more men the better. Because that's the area where we're getting the most reports of things seen under—well, it's too much to go into. There was that Escondido thing. They still haven't found those people. I don't have the authority or the push anymore to get the force to do it. But this thing has to be stopped. The uniforms are too trigger-happy now, anyway, I can't trust them."

"Yeah. I heard about—"

"Why is it you got all the dirt on my department, Morty?" Gribner asked, grinning.

"I got the connections," said Morty with mock smugness. "I was just going to say, that I heard about those plainclothes blasting away uptown, the kids at the social club. On some bullshit excuse. There was nothing like that when we were working together. You didn't draw that gun without filling out five forms first. Now they're shooting innocent black kids."

Morty was a little tipsy. He worked every other weekend at a neighborhood reclamation project as a vocational trainer, mostly with black kids.

"Hey, I know how you feel, but let's not talk loose about it," Gribner said instinctively, "till it's been investigated. And anyway, you're just changing the subject."

Morty smiled widely enough to show his yellowed dentures. "You got me—take me away, officer!" He raised his hands as if in surrender.

"C'mon, c'mon." Gribner dug his elbow into Morty's ribs "What do you say?"

"I'll do what I can. But if this little twerp Tooley hears about it he'll be all over my ass. He's trying to get us to reduce our inspection force—" He snorted in disgust, "—just when everything's breaking down. Is that logic?"

Gribner didn't reply.

He was thinking about his wife. *Better she stop taking the subways for a while,* he thought. *I'll give her cab fare. Which may give her heart failure.*

He smiled wearily.

LANYARD WAS TRYING to wake up. It was strange to have to *struggle* awake. His limbs weren't screwed on properly; he couldn't operate them, but he could feel them there, heavy, twitching in a mindless effort to respond to his directions. *Flex, arms, and help me to sit up. Flex, fingers, and reach to pry open my eyes.*

But he felt as if his body were in a metal sheath of some kind, vaguely man-shaped and deep underground, like a buried suit of armor, held unmoving by the weight of the whole city atop him; and his consciousness, his sensations and sense of himself, were combined into the man trapped in the suit of armor, struggling to break out, hearing the faint, pitiless creak of the metal at each useless effort....

He couldn't open his eyes.

When he saw the beast of hot red wires bounding toward him across the ashen negative landscape—the dark world behind his closed eyelids—he fought to open his eyes, galvanized by terror. *This time it's coming for me.*

He felt something rip free, and for a few moments the weight lifted from him. His eyes snapped open.

Out of ashes into whiteness: white walls, white doors, white ceiling.

An unpleasant sound, a high-pitched *ah-ah-ah-ah-ah* came from somewhere in the room. After a moment he realized it was a sound issuing from his own lips. He was trying to breathe. A wave of prickliness ran through him as he drew air. He lay gasping, looking around. A hospital bed, a hospital room.

Now the room came into focus. The walls weren't completely white—they were badly smudged, and in one place smeared with bloody fingerprints. What he'd blurrily supposed was a wall to his right wasn't a wall at all, it was a white curtain on a railing, separating his bed from another; the room was

Cellars

small, his section no bigger than a walk-in closet. Out of the corner of his eye, he could see the aluminum IV stand with its up-ended bottle and dangling hose. He looked away from it; the rubbery, transparent hose brought ugly associations to mind. He didn't want to think, now. Thinking made his head hurt. His limbs ached, and the sounds of an old man coughing wetly and nattering senselessly on the other side of the partition made Lanyard want to plug his ears. The sounds seemed unnecessarily *organic*. And they made him think of another old man wrapped in red membrane...the crunching as the membrane clenched.

But Lanyard couldn't plug his ears; he couldn't move his arms. He'd been strapped to the narrow hospital bed. There was a sheet over him, though he could feel that he was fully clothed beneath it. What was he here for? Why hadn't they undressed him, if he was to be a patient?

Where was he, really?

He was strapped down in some unidentified hospital, surrounded by strangers, forced to listen to ugly noises—from beyond the closed hall door came sounds of women crying, a baby squalling, a security guard shouting at someone to get *the fuckoutorshuddup*. His nerves tautened and frayed with every sound. And he couldn't move.

He knew where he had to be. They'd taken him *down*. They'd taken him to hell. He was thoroughly and sincerely convinced of it. He really believed it. This was hell, the Christian hell, or another more modern hell. He hated hospital emergency rooms, he'd always been miserable in them, even if he'd come there on someone else's behalf. And when the nurse came in, a platinum blonde with halitosis and a grisly case of eczema, he was doubly convinced. He was in hell...it said so on her nametag.

Just under the Dynalabel, *Melonie Tutz, RN*, were the words for hell in the local vernacular: Bellevue Hospital.

He was in the emergency room at Bellevue.

He screamed.

He struggled, and Nurse Tutz called for an orderly."Shid, Bennie, c'mmere, gimme a hand widis guy, he's wrigglin' outta the straps." She pulled back the sheet. "Where do you think you're goin', dumbshit?" she asked Lanyard, spraying his face with septic spittle, her eyes almost crossed with aggravation, radiating sheer hostility.

205

The orderly was black, reeking of marijuana, his white uniform spattered with something yellow. He nearly wrenched Lanyard's arm from its socket trying to jam it back under the strap. He cursed Lanyard, and Lanyard cursed him back, and the nurse cursed them both.

"Better givim a downer," said the orderly.

"He's some fuckin' junkie jus' doin this shid to get some tran-kill-izer," said the nurse. "I ain' givin'im shid."

"Gowan, givetim, I don' wanna hold 'im down all day. Whus 'e here fo'?"

"Some guy brought 'im in, said he was in shock or something, said he wasn't breathin'...Okay, I'll give 'im a shot of this shid...he won't get no fun out of it; makes you feel like shid when you wake up. But it sure puts you out."

The orderly grinned.

"Hey don't put me under, you don't know what I see, when—" Lanyard fought to keep the needle from his arm.

The orderly rapped him across the face. Lanyard, more astonished than stunned, lapsed into quiet, staring in disbelief. The man had *hit* him.

"But then," he murmured, as the darkness of the injection came, "I forgot I was in hell."

Unconsciousness came like mudslide silt into clear water, a falling curtain of black stickiness.

The dream came rising up out of the black stickiness, as if it were some underwater creature disturbed, nosing upward, opening its mouth to engulf him.

Children on a subway platform. Children on a subway platform at the Battery in early evening returning to their own neighborhood from a field trip to the Statue of Liberty. Accompanied by a tall, thin lady teacher.

Lanyard, invisibly, was there watching. Was there, and wasn't. It was one of those dreams that mockingly announce themselves, where something- tells you: You're dreaming and there's nothing you can do about it.

There were nine children, first graders, he guessed. He tried to speak to the teacher—an angular woman in a badly fitting gray wool dress and blazer; her chin was a little weak, her black hair shaped as if she were carrying a spherical black basket on her head. She had a pretty, pointy noise and large green eyes. Lanyard liked those. He tried again to speak to her. She couldn't hear him. Or he couldn't make a sound; he wasn't sure which.

They peered down the tunnel, waiting for the train; the children were tired, cranky, kicking at one another, asking the teacher silly questions. Seven of the children were white, two were black, all the boys dressed in jeans and polyester shirts; two of the three girls wore frocks and miniature, stylish blazers, not much different from the teacher's. The tallest girl, black, with her hair cornrowed into wooden beads, was dressed like the boys, but wearing a sweatshirt that said THE INCREDIBLE HULK. Repeatedly, the teacher called the children away from the edge of the platform.

A large crowd was building up behind them, pressing them toward the track. Now and then a commuter with a briefcase glared at some child scurrying underfoot; one boy chased another to throw an apple core from his lunch bag.

The train was coming. It screamed that it was coming. It wasn't the usual train sound, though it was similar. It was shriller, and more animal. The children could see the train's glaring headlights far down the tunnel. Like an animal glowering from its hole in the ground. And funny—this train's headlights weren't white like the others. They were sort of…golden-red. The train shot into the station, bringing with it a foul wind, moving so rapidly its details were blurred. It ground to a stop, and Lanyard thought: It looks streamlined, must be one of the new ones, rounder than they usually are, almost worm-shaped.

And where were the windows? Where were its wheels?

Doors opened in the side of the train. They didn't slide open sideways, the way most subway train doors did; they irised open. Wetly. And it was dark inside. There were sticky white filaments around the edges of the door, like cobwebs, trembling as the train breathed.

The children backed away, whimpering. But the crowd behind them, unable to see the train clearly, moving according to habit, bulling to get into the train before the doors closed, forced the children and the teacher toward the damp-edged doors and the red darkness.

The children were thrust into the train.

It wasn't a train. The great worm, big as a subway train, closed the half-dozen mouths in its great, glassy hide and crawled off, picking up speed, down the tunnel, having eaten the children and most of the people on the subway platform, and Lanyard tried to run but he hadn't a body to run with.

He was only dreaming.

CHILDREN ON A subway platform. Children on a subway platform in the early evening at the Battery, returning to their neighborhood from a field trip to the Statue of Liberty. Accompanied by a tall, thin lady teacher-whose black hair was like a globe on her head, whose chin was weak, whose nose was pointed, whose eyes were green, who wore a gray blazer.

There were nine children. Mrs. Chilroy, first-grade teacher, was divorced. But she still went by Mrs., chiefly because she didn't want the other teachers to know her husband had left her.

Mrs. Chilroy was annoyed to see that the little boy who had followed them along the docks was waiting on the subway platform. He was a grimy little boy, and not her responsibility, and she frankly wished he'd go away. He'd refused to answer her questions, except to say, "Oh, I'm on my way home, too." But he stayed with her group for blocks, trotting the sidewalk just behind them, down into the subway station, jumping the turnstiles, following onto the platform, just as if he were part of the field trip.

Mrs. Chilroy called Rocky and Nancy back from the edge of the subway platform, shuddering as she pictured what could happen; so easy for them to fall off, to lie stunned on the tracks just as the train barreled into the station. How far down to the tracks? Four, five, six feet? It would be hard to get a child back up in time.

So many things could go wrong.

"You kids come over here, stay near the bench," she called. "Donny!" Donny was the tall black girl, repeating first grade, intelligent enough but psychologically unable to concentrate on anything but mischief.

"Yo, lady teacher, I'm gonna go up the street 'n' take a cab!" she yelled from the exit gate, pretending she was about to leave so that Mrs. Chilroy would have to go and fetch her. Mrs. Chilroy did, collaring Donny by the back of her Incredible Hulk shirt, just as the train came rocking and squealing into the station. It was an old train, with layers of highly stylized graffiti; the magic-marker graffiti on the windows made them almost opaque, but Mrs. Chilroy could see that the cars were quite crowded, people standing, swaying with the motion of the train as it ground to a halt. The children dutifully lined up behind her and she led them into the car that seemed the least crowded, near the train's rear. She had to count them three times before the doors closed to make sure everyone was aboard. She wished the school budget hadn't been cut again: no buses for field trips. She wished they'd taken the city bus. But she'd been in a hurry, and now the children were wending in and out of the crowd in the subway car as it gathered speed, sometimes literally underfoot, as if playing in a woods, eliciting "Lady, control yuh kids willyuh?" Most of the kids, at least seven of them, were bunched up at the end of the car farthest from her. Mrs. Chilroy had taken hold of a stanchion near the door; she was reluctant to let go her support. The car was packed; there was nowhere to sit, and barely room to stand; the riders, all colors, all economic strata, swaying as if in some communal dance, everyone to the left now, when the train took the curve. The train, as usual, felt like it was just about to jump the tracks. And then they rushed into another station.

As the train rocked to a standstill, she took advantage of the temporary stability to plunge through the crowd. "Excuse me, pardon me, excuse me, oh I'm sorry, pardon me, I didn't mean to step on—"

But when she reached the other end of the car, only one of the children was there. Rocky, a small blond-haired boy with thick glasses and rumpled, oversized ("You'll grow into it") clothing, squinted up at her, his eyes distorted through his lenses. "Where are the children?" she asked in a hushed voice, and the *thunkathunkathunk*-grind-and-rumble of the train's starting seemed appropriate to her growing intuition of catastrophe. "They're in the last car." Rocky shouted, as she leaned close to hear. "That kid, he said some bank robber left some money in there, and that kid, he showed 'em some money. He had a hunnerd dollars in his hand! So they all went back there. That kid Everett. But I don't like that kid. He smells bad, and—"

"Come on." She took Rocky's small wrist and with her other hand pushed open the heavy sliding door between trains, walked through the rollicking passageway, pressed through another crowd, nearly falling as the train lurched. She apologized endlessly, dragging Rocky, who had inexplicably burst into tears.

They labored through another precarious linkage between cars, and into the last car.

The car was almost empty. There was no one in it but the children. Donny was listening raptly to the grimy little boy—Everett?—who had his back to Mrs. Chilroy. She couldn't hear them clearly over the train noise; she heard only, "...if that is what you want, He will give it to you, and when He plays with us it is just like we own everything...."

And Donny replying, "I want a motherfucking color TV with cable and Betamax."

Mrs. Chilroy looked at the children with amazement. They were clutching money. There was paper money on the floor. It looked like real money.

Her first thought was to turn back to try to find a transit cop.

She turned—and saw the train receding, dwindling in the distance, swallowed in the darkness of the tunnel, its lights getting smaller and smaller. The lights went out. The children screamed.

Their car had become detached from the rest of the train.

It was still moving, rolling, slowing, swaying more than usual as it shuttled around the curve. *Another train will come up behind*, she thought. *They won't see us in time. They'll hit us.*

Gradually, the train thunkachunked to a stop, and they were alone in the darkness of the tunnel.

That boy, she thought. Somehow he broke the last car loose. *But he's such a little boy, he must have had help.*

And now she couldn't tell the children apart, in the murk.

She turned to try and organize the children into a group. "Quiet down, please, children, we're going to be all right. There's something built into the track that tells people we're lost from the train and they'll send someone—"

She stopped, looking around, peering through the darkness. The car was moving again. Very slowly.

Who was that crawling down the walls?

The children had gathered near Mrs. Chilroy, and some of them clung to her; they hid their faces in her skirt when they saw the blue-white rubbery men outside the windows. Naked men. There were dozens of them. And children, too, discernible in the light given off by the rubbery men—the rubbery men seemed to glow faintly in the dark. You could see through them, but they were solid, and their fingers, leaving slick trails on the train's windows, moved independently of one another. Like worms. Their heads were below the window, now—their hands reached up to rake the glass. Pushing.

They were pushing the car into a side tunnel.

And now they were opening the doors. Forcing them open with their glowworm fingers as the children screamed. But Donny didn't scream, nor did Ben, nor did—there he was, Everett. Donny and Ben and Everett helped press the doors aside.

And then they—they, with their white fingers leaving glowing smears on the window, with their peanutshell-shaped heads, and the human children beside them—they who were recognized from nightmares, who could not be wearing masks because you could see the dank bricks of the opposite wall through them…they climbed up, into the car.

The children they brought with them surrounded her own and began to herd them out. Some of her own children began to giggle, and others continued screaming, and some gaped in horror—but all of them screamed when they saw the rubbery see-through men up close, very close, and felt their sticky touch.

She looked into the black-button eyes of the rubbery men, and she looked at the dead-white flesh of the grimy children painted with geometric symbols, some nude, some dressed in rags, their fingers caked with blood—whose blood?—and she felt them surround her, tugging and pulling her to the door, and some deep-rooted instinct, awakened by the semidarkness of the subway tunnel (so like a cave, like a place where her ancestors had cowered and sacrificed and worshipped) told her that she had been ensnared by the bottomline basis of all evil, and that it was, really, Everett's fault, there was no one else to blame. And before she lost herself to babbling she felt in her purse till her fingers closed around a long, sharp nail file. And just before they pushed her down onto the gravel—she caught a glimpse of one of the children, her favorite, redheaded Marlene who wanted to be a singer when she grew up, Marlene running, trying to get away, the children with the painted faces tackling her, pitching her against the third rail, whooping and slapping palms as they watched her spasm, watched her sparking and smoking, charring—she gripped the nail file firmly and thrust the shiny metal sliver deep into one of Everett's laughing eyes. He crumpled, and she supposed that he was dead, and she felt glad about that. And then she felt some other things, because of what the rubbery men did to her. That's when she started babbling.

Never mind what they did to her.

FOURTEEN

WHEN CARL LANYARD was a boy, not long after he stopped listening to the Voices, just two weeks, in fact, after the bigger boys had left him face down in the dirt of the playing field, his parents had taken him to visit his Uncle at Bert and Mandy's farm just east of San Diego.

It was a hot day at the end of fall, and they'd all gone down to the pond for a swim.

Carl had felt craven, since that day on the school playing field, and he brooded, saying very little. The trip was supposed to "put the bloom back in his cheeks," as his mother said. But Carl spent the whole time sulking, unable to explain why he was withdrawn, but enjoying the attention his quiet misery brought him. His cousins and his parents and Uncle Bert splashed in the shallows of the broad green rush-bordered pond, under a dusty blue sky and a hot, yellow sun. They dived off the old, weathered dock and Carl watched, shrugging and trying to seem mysteriously tragic when they called for him to join them. "I wouldn't go in neither," said his youngest cousin, Clemmy, coming up behind. Clemmy was seven, tanned, his red hair always mussed, his blue eyes always wild, his mouth always popping open and shut as if he were singing without sound.

"Why wouldn't you go in?" asked Carl vaguely, shading his eyes to look over the olive expanse of water. The water was unruffled, and somberly reflected the yellowing transplanted stand of birch trees on the far side. Here and there it rippled when a frog surfaced to snap at a fly. The water looked friendly, and Carl was uncomfortably hot; he wanted very much to go in. But swimming and splashing were not part of his No One Understands Me scenario. Most introspective children go through a No One Understands Me phase, but Carl's was unusual: He was right. No one understood him. He had the Gift, and they didn't understand it. Now, it was pressed down deep inside him, at the muddy bottom of his own mirror-surfaced pond.

"I wouldn't go in that pond," Clemmy was saying, "because that's where my mom is."

Carl turned to stare at him. And then he remembered. Mandy had disappeared, and it was generally agreed that she had left Bert for a rancher up the valley who went bankrupt and sold his own wife's jewelry to run off to Mexico, taking Mandy with him. It was a story Carl was not supposed to know. But maybe that story was wrong. Maybe Clemmy had seen her drown herself in the pond. "What makes you think she's in there?" Carl asked softly.

"There's a slimy thing in there that grabs you and pulls you down. It took her and et her." There was very little grief in Clemmy's tone. He seemed to relish the notion. Mandy had been a notoriously bad mother.

But now Carl looked at the pond with new interest. It had become a symbol of tragedy, its mystery redoubled.

For a moment, he was tempted to listen, in the inward way, to see if he could hear Mandy's voice. Maybe she was haunting the pond.

But he seemed to feel the weight of two vicious boys on his back, and he shook his head, hard.

Clemmy walked away...and Carl trotted down to the dock. He ignored the children diving off the piles, his mother throwing a beach ball at his father in the muddy shallows. He went instead to a narrow gray wooden raft, cobbled together of two-by-fours and half a barn door, floating on the shady side of the dock. He untied the raft, lay out on it flat, belly down, and began to paddle out toward the middle of the pond.

"Carl? Where you goin', boy?" Bert's voice.

"Gonna dive off the raft out in the middle. I'll be okay. I can swim good," he called over his shoulder. Already his arms were aching. The sun drew moisture from the back of his legs—he wore ragged cut-off jeans, T-shirt, and tennis shoes.

He'd felt a coward, since the day he'd been crushed at the playing field. Maybe now he could regain himself. Show he had some nerve. Not that his family would understand.

He ignored their calls for his return. His arms chafed against the wood as he paddled, and his chest heaved against the nail-studded boards. He squinted as he moved into the open pond, where the sun reflected brilliantly.

Near the center of the pond, almost winded, he got carefully to his knees; the motion brought water slopping over the edge of the raft. Determined not to hesitate, not to stop to think, he stripped off his T-shirt and shoes, took a deep breath, shut his eyes, and dived in.

He was amazed at how cold the water was. It had felt warm against his arms…and then he realized that the sun only warmed the upper foot or so of the pond. The deeper he dove, the colder it got. Colder, and darker. He swam down till the glow of sunlight was completely swallowed up, and the pressure made his head feel near bursting. And then he opened his eyes.

He might have been floating in interstellar space. No stars here, no moon above, a glimmer of light, a few wavering rays slanting down. He heard a long, low sound like chuckling. Probably noises from the shore, or frog croakings, deranged by the water. He had reached the lowest point of his dive, and for a moment he floated, going neither up nor down—so far as he could tell—his head pointing to the surface, his feet dipping to try and touch the bottom and withdrawing from layers of slimy chill. His movements disturbed something, so that bubbles streamed up, crawling past his legs; some of them, along with the cold water, seeping under the cuffs of his cutoffs, nuzzling horribly at his genitals. And suddenly he had to be away from there. He needed air. Light. He needed *light*.

He kicked upward. But he couldn't be sure he was making headway. The surface seemed to get no nearer. His lungs begged—begged with fiery aching, pounding—to let go.

Panic closed in on him. He remembered stories that some ponds had connections to underground grottoes, causing people to be sucked down into a kind of whirlpool, drowned by a current no one would expect to find there.

And Clemmy had said, *"There's a slimy thing in there that grabs you and pulls you down. It took her and et her."*

He looked wildly around. The bubbles streamed up between-his legs, tickling his chest and neck, accompanied by the drawn-out chuckling. Just bubbles. But bubbles exhaled from what? From something rising from the darker places to take him by the ankle—and he did feel a slithery touch on his ankles. Just a tadpole. Just a frog. Just a fish. Just a weed. Just the corpse of Aunt Mandy animating her rotting fingers to drag him down with her so she wouldn't be alone.

The Voices were forever stilled in him. He'd seen to that.

But now… he thought he heard, now, from the other darkness, the dark inside his head: *Carl, give to us and we give to you. Come to us. Now or later. By sacrificing or as sacrifice: you'll come.* Then he saw the face. He saw it rising up toward him out of the gloom. Coming clearer and clearer as it ascended. For a moment, in the gloom, he thought it was a pallid woman's face. Dead Aunt Mandy. In the next moment he kicked convulsively toward the surface, trying to outreach it, as bubbles tickled up his crotch, his chest, to pry at his lips, to force his mouth open so the black water could get in—his limbs were numb from the cold, his arms and legs were leaden.

He looked down again. He saw the face more sharply this time, and the foggy outline of a skeletal blue-white body glimmering faintly with an inner phosphorescence. The head was shaped like a summer squash, but almost transparent, and its lidless black eyes were like the eyes of a flatworm, and it reached toward him with wriggling boneless fingers that trailed the sort of light given off by rotting things in swamps

He screamed soundlessly and raked water, trying to climb a ladder that wasn't there—the air burst in a geyser of bubbles from his mouth, and the pond, with its flavor of a million growing and dying organisms, forced itself between his lips, its liquid fingers choking him—

He burst into light and air. Coughing out water, gasping, he splashed toward the raft a yard away. Sure that at any second gelatinous fingers would close around his ankles and drag him down again, he flailed, whimpering, till he dragged himself onto the rocking slab of gray wood.

Recumbent, face down in the warm air, he wondered if he'd swallowed minnows or water insects, and he wondered: *How long was I under the surface?* He asked his mother, later, and she said, "I watched for you after you dived. You were down, oh, no more than ten seconds." It had seemed like ten minutes.

And after a while, after soaking up the sun for a few minutes, he managed to convince himself that the face he'd seen in the underwater gloom had been a distortion of the murky light.

Twenty years later, Carl Lanyard was fighting to ascend through the same cold gloom. This time it was entirely inside his head. He was once more trying to awaken, again mysteriously held back. His struggle for consciousness was mixed with snapshot images of his terror in the pond as a boy, the memory of the face, the livid rubbery subhuman he thought he'd seen, the bubbles tickling along his ribs, the small slimy creatures brushing him....He seemed to feel them now, as he fought to open his eyes, to sit up in the hospital bed, once more gasping for air. Clawing to escape the cold, dark, water—

He burst into light and air. But this time, instead of the friendly blue sky and the warm, rocking raft and the distant waving figures of his family on the dock—this time he saw Joey Minder and the Ivy League Juggernaut.

Lanyard was no longer in one of the temporary-assignment rooms of the emergency ward. He was in a regular hospital room, alone, with a bowl of fruit under colored cellophane on the table to his right, and beside the fruit a vase of freshly cut roses. There were windows here, the blinds drawn. "What time is it?" he asked blearily, squinting. His head spun.

He sat up, unencumbered by straps. This room was cleaner, he noticed, trying to look at anything but Joey Minder and the bodyguard.

Sitting up hurt his stomach; he felt like he'd taken a sledgehammer blow to the gut. But, just now, the Voices were silent; he was seeing no patterns of black squirming in the air.

"It's seven AM," said Minder. "We've been up all night, with one thing or another. It's not even visiting hours. We had to bribe the desk personnel." He chuckled. "You look half drowned, boy."

Lanyard shuddered. What made Minder say drowned? The dream was already fading...something about a giant worm in the subway, some children...then, the pond.

"They knocked me out," he said. "Wherezumwater?" Pain rebounded like a hard rubber ball inside his skull as he turned his head to look for water. The bodyguard—the man in the horn rims and neat sweater, the very man who'd dangled him over a ravening attack dog—filled a glass for him at the sink and held it out to him.

Lanyard took the water and sipped cautiously. "Uh—I feel...awful."

Sitting on a chair beside the bed, like an old friend settling in for a convivial visit, Minder said: "You lost consciousness at Merino's— I suppose because the power currents were too thick. They can be paralyzing. And you say someone else knocked you out? The nurses, I take it? Probably the sedative has given you a hangover, to boot. You have my sympathy." He put his large hands on

217

his knees and looked Lanyard in the eyes. "Lanyard—the room where you met the late Reverend Jesus Merino contained something else. Did you see?"

Lanyard nodded fractionally.

"The Blessed One would have killed you, of course"—he spoke casually, but with the verve of a sports enthusiast talking about the action of a baseball game—"if…if Madelaine hadn't prevented it. And, for your information, it was Madelaine who told us where you were and what you were up to. She says you have Gifts, Lanyard. She monitored you for us."

"The old man wouldn't have told me anything. He refused." Lanyard took another sip of water. His tongue was thick; it was difficult to talk. He felt he was in a dream; Minder wasn't quite real. Lanyard, at that moment, had no fear of him.

"He might have changed his mind about talking to you," said Minder reasonably, tilting his head and smiling. "And anyone who controls the power currents, who is not our ally, is our enemy. No one is neutral. You saw what happened, Lanyard. You know you weren't hallucinating. You are a believer now."

Lanyard was beginning to realize that this wasn't yet another dream. It was real. And Minder could do what he liked with him.

Lanyard tensed, forgetting his aches for a moment, wondering if the door was locked. And where were his clothes? And could he dash past the Ivy League Juggernaut?

Minder was right. He was a believer now. The Voices were real.

"Where's Madelaine?" Lanyard asked quietly, looking at both men with as friendly an expression as he could manage.

Minder smiled. "She's waiting for you in the Temple. Just come to me, at my home, and tell me in sincerity that you want to be one of us—you have *talent*, Carl, you could be a great help to us, you could grow with this—uh—corporation. Just come and tell me, and we'll know if you're sincere. And if you are, we'll take you to her. And if you're not, we'll take you to her in a different way, and you'll never see the light of day again. And if you don't come to us—well, sacrificing or as sacrifice: you'll come."

Lanyard stared.

Minder stood, buttoned his overcoat, and moved toward the door; the bodyguard went ahead and opened it for him. Minder paused at the door and turned long enough to say, "You'll be released from the hospital as soon as you feel well enough. We've given them all the pertinent data on you. We've even paid your bill. You see? We take care of you." He grinned, and for a moment he radiated boundless love for Carl Lanyard.

"I'll think about…what you said," Lanyard murmured.

"Whatever your decision, Carl," Minder said gently, "we'll know. And if you decide the wrong way—you couldn't possibly get out of the city."

His aura of compassion never wavered. "I know you'll do the right thing."

"The right thing," Lanyard repeated, as the door shut.

They left him in the white hospital room, alone.

SHE COULD FEEL the heat rising. The very stone exhaled it. The autumn rite was near, and His pet, the hungry one, the stalker, was pacing restlessly below, awakened by the upsurge of power currents.

She could feel the madmen, bound and caged in the asylums of the city up above, pacing restlessly, mimicking the stalker, made nervous by the upsurge of power currents. The mad could feel it too.

She knew, also, about the children gathering in the basement of their grade school, at that instant, nine PM the night before Halloween.

There were thirteen children; and they'd broken into the school easily enough, smashing a pane, unlocking a window, descending in darkness, giggling, holding hands, led by the eight-year-old black girl, Donny, and a blue-eyed boy who had killed his parents in Jersey to come here and paint his face and play in hidden places.

Thirteen children going to the basement of the school, to play with matches.

She could feel them moving about up there, like rats in an attic, above her.

Once, Madelaine had asked Tooley, "What does He want the children for? He doesn't seem to use them in the upper city; they don't perform the rituals." And Tooley had replied, "He loves children. They are close at heart to Him, by nature. He plays with them, He enjoys their games. He finds that he can cultivate them easily, once they are below, and once they have played with Him. He loves children. He is really just a playful child Himself."

She didn't ask Tooley anything, now, because at the rite he had dropped his semblance, and she had seen his face in its actuality. Now, whenever she looked at him, she seemed to see that face mingled with the face they called "Tooley."

She didn't ask questions of anyone. She didn't speak. She felt what she had to, but beyond that tried to feel as little extra as she could, to maintain a layer of insulation.

She simply sat in the mouth of the cave, below the rooms where the group rites were held. She sat there, hugging her knees, her eyes half open, refusing food, refusing water, refusing wine, waiting for the rite. She wore only the black silk kimono, tied at the waist with a strip of red; no underwear, no shoes.

The cave had a low ceiling; when Minder and Tooley entered, to find her in the shadows just inside the mouth of the cave, they had to stoop low. Minder swore when he bumped his head. He crouched beside her. "Madelaine—" He took her hand. It lay limply in his large, meaty, damp paw. "Madelaine, I've brought you some fruit juice. It's cranberry juice. I remember you said you liked cranberry juice. Drink a little for me, okay?"

She said nothing. She stared straight ahead. She blinked, once, her eyes dimly visible in the indirect light coming from the sub-basement room outside the cave.

The cave was artificial; it had been chipped here, half a century before, by immigrant workers using steam-driven diggers. They had stopped their digging when they'd come upon the hidden lake. Now, the way to the hidden lake was blocked by a heavy stainless-steel door, in the unlit tunnel to Madelaine's left.

Minder squeezed her hand. No response. He let it fall. A shudder went through him and, momentarily enraged, he smashed the bottle of juice on the rough stone floor. The red juice spread, amoebalike, from the jagged star of broken glass, reaching one tentative tendril to her bare foot; the juice was cold, but she didn't curl her toes away from it. She monitored the sensation and ignored it. Just as she ignored the sharper sensation when Tooley slapped her across the face. "Come out of it, woman! Stop playing games!"

Minder reached out and clamped his fingers around Tooley's wrist, preventing the smaller man from giving her a second, more powerful blow.

The two men exchanged glowers. Tooley's eyes smoldered; his pupils could be seen clearly, despite the dimness, as if, like the thick smoked-glass windows in a furnace gate, they held back an inner fulmination.

"I didn't tell you to hit her, Tooley."

"She's hiding from us. And from Him."

"From Him? Here at His very gate?" Minder shook his head. "I think she's communing with Him somehow." They both knew it wasn't so. "You said yourself you couldn't get through to her. You don't *know* what she's thinking. She might be in transformation, in some way. Just don't you touch her without my permission, little fella, understand?"

"I do His work. I do what I feel is—"

"*You heard me. I gave, and I gave to Him. He gave you to me. You are my* servant. You were told to do as I say. That is all you need to know. If I am out of line, then He will punish me. Leave her alone, until I tell you different."

Tooley looked away, and shrugged. "For now, I am your servant."

She heard Minder thinking: *What does he mean by that? But then, I won't be in this world after the rite. Once I've transcended, he'll be in charge here. He can have the whole fucking scene.*

"It's getting hotter in here. They're noticing it up above, again," Minder muttered. "They're calling it freak weather. They're blaming microwaves." He seemed exhausted. "I feel like I'm in a microwave oven here. Feel like I'm getting cooked. I'm going upstairs. I don't like to leave her here—she could become dehydrated—but I'm afraid to tamper with her. Did you ask Him about her?"

"He is silent, when I ask." Tooley left the cave. Minder, dripping sweat and huffing, followed him out.

She was glad they were gone. But she wasn't alone; She was never alone; she could never be alone again, as long as she lived. The Voices rose and fell in volume, but they were always there, mixed up and clamoring, or whispering earnestly to her; and she could not help monitoring the pictures. Nothing kept it away now. Not Minder's touch, not Tooley. It was always there. *Watch, and don't feel: That is survival.* So she watched and felt nothing when the children burnt the infant they'd stolen, in the school basement.

She no longer tried to interfere; she warned no one. Not even Carl.

She watched and felt nothing when she saw Carl Lanyard climbing the stairs of his apartment building; Carl Lanyard didn't know about the one who waited in his apartment for him.

THE VOICES, ALMOST inaudible, and the eel shapes in the air, returned as Lanyard reached the third-floor landing of his apartment building and turned to climb to the fourth. It was almost as if in reaching the third floor he triggered something; as if the last step before the landing contained a hidden lever. It struck him all at once, and he reeled, for a moment clawing at the air, to keep the eel shapes from darting at his eyes.

Ignore it, he thought. It'll go away.

Lanyard, the Voices whispered. *Ahead is behind, attack is retreat...*

He walked on through the crowded air; the elongated black squirmings parting for him, never touching him; and probably he'd have been unable to feel them, if they had touched him, unless they concentrated themselves.

He shivered, suspecting that he was beginning to understand them. He knew that he was seeing something that was always there, but usually invisible. He sensed intuitively that the slithering black strokes could be read, as tea leaves allegedly were read. He could see for himself that the squirming lines moved into coherent patterns, like iron filings on a magnet. And now, as he reached the fifth floor, he saw them arrayed around his door, nosing in toward it. As if it attracted them. For a moment he felt he was underwater again, in murky waters, drawn on a current that plunged through the spillway that was his door; the squirming lines were like free-floating strips of seaweed sucked on the current to his apartment; they passed through the door as if it were not there.

Lanyard stood staring at the door. He was afraid to go in.

He listened to the Voices, trying to glean a warning. There were only whispered fragments. "Mother?" he asked, tentatively. No reply. Had he really heard his mother's voice in the room where Jesus Merino had died?

He was sure he had. He tottered; the impact of what had happened was only now making itself felt in him. His whole world-view had changed—overnight—literally. The earth was shifting its axis for him.

He was still blurry from the drug they'd given him at the hospital. Blurred, too, by anger. The nurse at the front desk had shrugged when he told her how he'd been treated by the emergency room personnel.

Minder had threatened him. And Madelaine was lost to him.

The anger propelled him forward. He turned the knob, not surprised to find the door unlocked. He pushed it inward with his left hand, his right closing on the pistol, still unused, in his jacket pocket.

Dirty dishes in the sink. The window was wide open; an unseasonably warm and sticky breeze blew the dirty beige curtains.

Cellars

He tried to picture a burglar, perhaps with a long knife in his hand, waiting flattened against the wall to the right of the entrance into the living room. He didn't believe it. The black currents writhed in their ropy course, wending into the next room, something there attracting them. Nothing as pedestrian as a burglar.

Hand tightening on the pistol, he stepped into the living room.

The airy eel shapes, quivering, flowed to converge on a single figure seated on the couch directly across from him, so thickly they almost hid her. And then they drew back from her, fading a little, like a dark curtain opening to show her on stage.

Her. He tingled, gazing at her. A lanky blonde, racy with angles, holding a mirror on her lap, a small black velvet rectangular box on the mirror, her long white hands, immaculately manicured, nails pearly-pink, folded on the box.

Her eyebrows were sharp brown arches, almost elfin, plucked and penciled without seeming plucked and penciled. Her mouth was thin and sulky, given succulence by peach-blush lipstick; her hair cascaded in golden waves over her creamy bare shoulders. She wore a tight strapless black gown, exposing skin stretched translucently taut over her delicate collarbone. Her legs were demurely crossed, but the skirt was slit to the thigh; she wore black stockings and red garters. Tight red garters. One of her high heels was dangling from the toe of the overcrossed leg; the other nestled like a feeding infant in the mink wrap coiled suggestively beside her on the cushion.

Lanyard's pulse raced. His blurriness began to melt away.

Christ, her eyes were blue. The hint of a dimple under her high cheekbones...the diamond-stud earrings...the look on her face, as if she'd been dating him for ages, and she was awaiting him in a suite they'd booked together.

For a moment the black squirmings in the air radiated from her in a halo of restlessly alive exclamation points. A radiance of negative divinity.

"This is just the beginning," she said, spoiling the effect. She was a bad actress. Her voice carried no conviction. But he wanted to believe in her and in the promise that was tacitly suggested by her presence, her pose.

The Voices had gone silent, as if hushed in awe.

"You—you look familiar," he murmured. He'd seen her in a magazine ad. "You're a model."

Her smile was also unconvincing. There was something dead about her eyes.

But Carl Lanyard wanted this woman. All the loneliness, all the backed-up skin hunger and sexual frustration and sense of betrayal (hadn't Madelaine betrayed him by submitting to Minder?) came together.

The gown was tight at the bodice, and sheer; she wore no brassiere, and her nipples were clearly outlined in the clinging silk. As he gazed at her, the air's black squirmings, the power currents, began to fade. In a moment, they were gone: hidden.

"Sit down, Carl. I have gifts for you." She smiled, and the smile was no more than a sophisticated variation of a whore's leer. That's what Lanyard liked about it.

But he made himself say, "I don't feel so good today. Joey Minder sent you. Minder can fuck himself. What do you want? Tell me and then get out of here."

"You don't feel good?" False sympathy. "Come and sit down." When she patted the couch beside her—close beside her—he noticed the diamond-crusted gold ring on the slender index finger of her left hand. She returned the hand to the black box. "Why are you so hostile? We're not enemies. We're allies. You've got the talent. That means, really, that you're one of us."

"You," he said with conviction, "are a murderer. Or at least you are in complicity with murderers. With butchers. You're one of the people who specialize in taking away the humanity of other people so that they become sacrificial pigs. You are a pig yourself." He felt a peculiar thrill, talking to her so abusively. He knew the thrill was perverse. In his jacket, his hand reaffirmed its grip on the pistol, and he slid the index finger in his right hand into the trigger guard; with the thumb of that hand he switched off the safety. He decided his chances of killing her with one shot were good—he was only six feet from her.

She seemed faintly amused by his diatribe. "Come off it, Carl. Everyone is capable of anything, under the right circumstances. 'Nothing is true, everything is permitted.' Come and sit down."

"Who are you?" he asked, struggling with himself. He wanted to come and sit down. But...

"My name's Lily Chancery. That's my real name. You see, I'm candid with you. I'll tell you anything you want to know. Anything at all. It won't seem so awful when it's all out in the open. You'll see how routine it is."

Cellars

"You'll tell me anything?"

"Sure. You are going to ask me the location of our temple? Only a few know the exact location. The rest of us are taken there in the special train. We can't see where it's going. I can take you there, any time you like. I'll tell you anything I know. Because you won't talk to anyone about it. If you try, we'll kill you—or people you care about depending on the method He decides on. So we're not afraid. Ask and—" She uncrossed her legs—she was wearing no underwear; her labia were pink as rabbit's eyes, and clean-shaven, not a trace of stubble; the dampness gleamed faintly under the black silk. "Ask and you shall receive," she finished softly.

He wrenched his eyes from the pink cleft between the red garters...

"So tell me...where's Madelaine? She's at the temple?"

"You just answered your own question, clever fellow." She had kicked off the other black spike-heeled shoe. Her feet were planted well apart on the floor. The scene might have been set up by Helmut Newton; the incongruity of an urbane lady of fashion posing with pornographic availability. "I'll take you to Madelaine. She's a little...out of touch lately. You might be just what she needs. Next question?"

"What does Minder hope to gain from all this? Sheer power, more money? What?"

She grinned and tilted her head to the right. "He wants to kill Death."

"What? He wants immortality?"

"No. Even while you're alive, you're always dying. You get tired. You get a high—but then you come down. You're still alive but you feel beat, right? You fall in love, but love fades. You live for years—but you grow old, your vision fades. You get an erection, you have an orgasm, you slump—and that's all. Then you feel ennui. Nothing good lasts. And all the down stuff that comes after the good stuff, the low point of the cycle—that's an increment of Death." She chuckled. "He loves to lecture about it. He says death is like Creeping Socialism. Sneaks in bit by bit...nothing pleasurable lasts. The pleasure fades and dies. And then, if you had a lot of pleasure, you go to hell for a while: hangover, cocaine burnout, postcoital ennui, what have you. So, Joey reasons, jolly old Joey, he figures: Maybe you could freeze Time Itself in one of the moments of pleasure—like say in a combination of drug and sexual ecstasy, when you've had plenty to eat and you're comfortable, and everything feels good. Before it has a chance to go away, you freeze it, or at least you stretch out that one moment so that you experience it for an eternity. And since your thinking is all stretched out with it, you don't get bored. He claims that's what heaven is: eternal pleasure with no morning-after, no downer, no crash. But to obtain that, you have to transcend to a place outside of Time. Or—it's a sort of paradox I don't understand too well—where one segment of time never comes to an end. It's just stretched out and out forever."

"Locked into one blissful moment....And how is butchering children going to get him this?"

She ignored his acid tone. "The sacrifices bring power, and Joey gives that power to Him. The Head Underneath. The one who lives in the secret lake. And He..." Her eyes had glazed, she was talking as if tranced, as if chanting a holy litany. "He will reach out and change Time, to make it possible for Joey to transcend, so that what Joey is experiencing at the moment of transcendence he will experience forever, without it going away in the least. Enough of this dry stuff...okay?" Inept sexy wheedling.

"So—Joey gives the...the Head Underneath the—what? The life force of the people he sacrifices? Their souls?"

"Sure. Souls, so-called, are just energy fields. Energy is power. We send it to the Head. He gets stronger, and reaches out with His power currents, and changes things for us. He got me my career back. He can tilt things, so good luck slides right into your lap. You name it, He can get it for you, Carl."

She looked him in the eye. He began to breathe heavily. "Carl...come here. Look what I've got for you."

She opened the black box on the eight-inch-square silverframed mirror. Fitting perfectly into black-velvet insets were a long glass bottle of white powder, probably cocaine; a pair of capped syringes, side by side; a surgeon's scalpel; a small vial of water; an ornate silver spoon. She took the spoon out first, laid it on the mirror, carefully filled it with water from the vial, capped and replaced the vial, extracted the syringes, sucked the spoon's water into one of the syringes, extracted the coke container, unscrewed its cap and tipped a generous amount into the spoon, set the container, open, on the mirror, squirted the syringe's water into the spoon, dissolved the cocaine, drew the cocaine solution into the syringe, flexed the muscle of her right arm, expertly found the vein with the needle and—

Cellars

Lanyard looked away. "I haven't shot up in a while," she said, "because the track marks show. This oughta be good—ooh...it's good...yeah it's good..."Her hands shaking, she set the empty syringe aside and looked up at Lanyard, flushed and transformed. Her pupils dilated and shrank, dilated and shrank, as wave on wave of pure pleasure coursed through her.

"It's like nothing you ever experienced," she said, rocking and writhing, speaking through chattering teeth."It—Carl—try it. *It's not like snorting coke.* It's a whole different thing. It's a five-minute orgasm and—more. It's indescribable. And it removes all—all inhib—bi—all inhibitions, Carl, all—" She had spread her legs wide, was toying languidly with her clitoris...an invitation of flesh.

"Carl..." She opened her eyes and looked straight into his. "I have some here for you. I want you to feel it. This is just one of His gifts...Car...Carl, come here and fuck me..."

She wasn't faking it now; the drug opened up some secret mental orifice; everything repressed was pouring out.

He drew his gun, his hand trembling. "I think, I think I ought to kill you. Because the cops won't believe. And...if I let you go, you'll help them sacrifice someone else. I think the right thing to do would be to kill you. To take my chances with the police."

She was laughing. "Look at your gun—it's as limp as your dick!"

He looked at the .45. It was bent out of shape; the chamber was crumpled, the snout was bent downward. The Blessed One had taken it from his pocket while he was unconscious, had crushed it and replaced it. It was useless. He let it fall from his fingers; it bounced like a toy on the floor.

He felt drained, defeated. But the hardness was still there between his legs. He found his eyes straying first to her glistening crotch, and then to the syringe in the velvet box. He took a step toward her, and then hesitated. He thought: *Why not? Madelaine went to them. She betrayed me. The Gift will drive me mad, anyway. Maguss is a sonuvabitch. Using me. Gribner ignores me. The cops are corrupt bastards. Everyone's out for what they can get. Why not?*

Still, he hesitated.

He listened, inwardly: The Voices were silent.

He gazed at her; she was on her back, on the couch, legs spread, knees cocked, feet flat on the floor, her fingers holding her labia apart...her warm, wet, inviting—

227

"Never mind the foreplay, Carl...oh, I'm rushing just...Carl: *Come here and fuck me.*"

Unbuttoning his shirt, he moved toward her. And stopped, frozen, staring.

The squirming black lines were manifesting, and they seemed to pour from her crotch, to fly outward from there.

But his eyes were locked on something else, and his stomach turned flip-flops.

There were four glistening, transparent, rubbery tendrils gradually extruding from her vagina, wriggling like the antennae of silverfish; beckoning, dripping yellow ooze.

He opened his mouth to scream, but his throat was clenched too tight to let the scream out. He backed away from her and just managed to turn, to open the door, to stumble down the steps....

A HALF HOUR later, in the phone booth of an uptown bar, he listened to a clerk telling him, "Mr. Maguss has checked out, but he has left a message for a Mr. Lanyard. Is this Mr.—"

"Yeah, yeah, it's Lanyard, what the hell is the message?"

Unruffled, the clerk said, "I am to tell Mr. Lanyard that Mr. Maguss has moved to an apartment at 2323 Park Avenue. Number 44B. You are to seek him out there as soon as—"

Lanyard hung up and reeled toward the door of the bar.

Everyone he passed pretended not to notice that he was crying like a baby. He was thinking: *They've done something awful to Lily Chancery. What are they doing to Madelaine?*

GRIBNER, ALONE IN his apartment, packing his wife's porcelain knickknacks in a box so he could take them to her, paused to answer the phone. "Cyril? This is Morty," said a tired voice on the other end.

"I'm not going to know your voice after so many years I'm embarrassed to say? I know it's Morty. So, Morty, did you do what I asked—"

"Cyril, listen, you got to get over here...you got to come over my place. You know those men I told you—that Tooley, that other guy...the new guys on the Transit Authority—"

"Yeah, yeah, what about them, Morty?"

Cellars

"Some of us tried to have them removed for reasons of special interest. Gaddis at the *Times* was going to write an editorial backing us up. They found Gaddis dead tonight. Staked out like some kind of skinned animal in the basement of his place on Staten Island. And you know what? They think his *kid* did it. His nine-year-old kid. They can't find him…they can't find the kid, Cyril, and his sister said he—"

"Morty, cool down now." Gribner was talking to himself: He needed someone to tell him to cool down. He sat down on the couch and took a deep breath.

He looked down at the little white figures packed in newspaper in the cardboard box beside the couch. They looked, at that moment, like tiny corpses in burial shrouds, and somehow it was appropriate that their burial shrouds should be old copies of the *New York Post*.

"Morty—you're afraid for your life?"

"You bet your ass I am, Cyril. I'm home alone here. I'm going to the door to take out the garbage, right? I'm on the bottom floor, you remember, and I open the door, and I look out, and the street light's been busted out. So the block is all dark. And then I see these little kids all crowded on the stoop. They got crisscrossy lines painted on their faces. And I'm hearing these weird noises from my drains. Now you can laugh, but I—"

"I'm not laughing, Morty. Did you call a roller?"

"What am I going to tell these precinct patrolmen? That I'm scared of some little kids? Anyway, I talked to some detectives about Gaddis's death this evening—they aren't doing but nothing, Cyril. But nothing. I think they're infiltrated, Cyril. I think—I know how it sounds."

"You're afraid to go out?"

"Alone. I want—I know I sound like an old woman, Cyril—but I want you should come over here and we leave together. Maybe we can collar a couple of these kids."

"I'll come. Right now."

"Cyril…"

"Yeah, Morty?"

"Cyril, don't take the subway. Even if it's faster. Take a cab."

"Morty—ah—okay, I'll take a cab. Stay in your living room. Don't go into the kitchen or the bathroom. Or outside. Don't go where there's a drain."

A few moments of quiet. Then: "I guess I don't have to convince you?"

"No. No, you don't have to convince me. I'll be right over."

He hung up, ran to the coat tree, unslung his gunbelt from the hook and fastened it over his shoulders. He put his gray suit jacket on over that, and went out into the evening.

It was Halloween night, seven-thirty PM It was hotter than it should have been. It was like an August night. And the heat felt *funny.* And—it felt like it was coming from underneath.

From the streets themselves. Or from beneath them.

THE PARK AVENUE apartment was, so far, sparsely furnished. There were only two chairs, a glass dining table, and an antique clock ticking on the mantel.

Lanyard and Maguss sat across from one another at the glass table, the map spread out between them. Lanyard was almost sober. He sipped black coffee, feeling the first twinges of a headache.

"It has to be *tonight,* Carl," Maguss said emphatically, studying the map through bifocals. "They'll have so much power we won't be able to stop them. They'll influence events in any direction they choose. That's what the power currents are for. In sufficient concentration they can manipulate people directly, like puppets—"

"You've almost dropped the mask, old man," Lanyard interrupted sharply.

He watched Maguss's seamed face for a reaction. The old man's eyes opened fractionally wider; that was all. Maguss chuckled acidly. "Maybe under this 'mask' I'm really…" He leaned confidentially forward, making his face a caricature of the sinister. "Walt Disney!"

"You hoping for a laugh? Forget it. I'll laugh at your funeral."

"And won't you be surprised when I sit up in the coffin and laugh with you!" Maguss replied brightly.

Lanyard swallowed. "You must have known what would happen when you sent me to Merino. That old man was killed unnecessarily. And I might have been killed."

"That old man was a heroin pusher and a very successful murderer. Mere death was too good for him. You don't know him as I did. And no, you were in no real danger from Minder. They want you. You can see the power currents so damn well…better than I. You can find the temple where I cannot. Using your Sight….Go to the neighborhood circled—" He tapped the map of Manhattan's substructure, overlaid in blue dotted lines with streets and avenues. A large section of the Lower East Side was encircled in green pen. Red and solid black lines indicated subway tunnels, used and unused, and water mains. Orange lines showed sewage mains. "Plant the explosive in the right place, time it as per directions—it's as simple as following directions for baking a cake, Carl—and you can bring the streets down on top of them."

"And maybe cause some buildings to fall? Fires to start? Gas mains to explode? Maybe cause the death of—'

"Maybe, yes. And it's regrettable." Maguss nodded solemnly. "But it's better than letting them go on. Did you hear about this man Gaddis? He was a well-known newspaperman. But that didn't stop them. No one will catch the boy....There haven't been any subway killings in two weeks, Carl. You know why? They're waiting for Halloween. Tonight their power will peak—it is a time of optimum acquisition for them. It's as if they were buying and selling at the right moment for maximum profit in the stock market."

Lanyard studied the map. "Why—why a sewage main?"

"The sewage mains, the bigger ones, converge in just this area—here." He tapped the map again with a withered, tobacco-yellowed finger. "The temple is somewhere in that area. And it is, according to magical ritual, to be a specified depth below the surface. It should be just under the sewage mains. Now, the sewage travels through those mains at hundreds of miles per hour—at a pressure exceeding that of Niagara Falls. If its current struck a man directly, it would smash him apart. It would fill up a large underground room in no time. You've got to set the bombs, using your common sense and the maps, and get out fast—once you've got the urn."

"You said you want the urn so you can destroy it. Why not let the explosion destroy it?" Lanyard watched the old man's face closely.

"Because it would survive. It would protect itself. It has to be *ritually* destroyed. *Bring it to me.*"

"Where the hell did you get the plastic explosives?"

"One of the cardinal rules of Life in These United States is that a rich man has almost unlimited access to the tools of mischief, Carl."

Lanyard leaned back, and tried to sieve the Voices, churning, like background static, in the back of his head. He couldn't locate a familiar Voice. Only occasionally did anyone from the Other Side speak coherently.

An ancient, papery voice whispered, "*My joke's an iron, and the joke's on you.*" Lanyard shrugged. No help there. The power currents weren't visible, just then. Maguss had shown him how to tune them in—and out.

"I am going to do a stupid thing," he said thoughtfully, slowly, deliberately. "I am going to do a very stupid thing, because I don't know what else to do. I'm going to do as you ask."

FIFTEEN

The street was dark. The cab rolled slowly to a stop in front of Morty's building on the Upper East Side, Sixty-sixth and York. "Wha' happened th' fucking street light?" the cabdriver mumbled. He was black, and tired; the cab reeked of the reefer the driver had stubbed out when Gribner got into the car. "Somebody done busted out the stree'light."

"Yeah…" The meter said $2.90. Gribner gave the driver a five and a one and said, "Wait here, and I'll tip you double the fare when we get to the next place. I'm going in to pick up somebody."

The driver looked around nervously. "Street's so damn dark, man. I dunno."

Gribner sighed and gave him another five. "Okay?"

The driver shrugged. "Okay, man. I wait. Don' be long."

Gribner opened the door and climbed out. The shadows danced in the heat waves rising from the street. Gribner shifted his shoulders in his jacket; his shirt stuck to him. Sweat. Unnatural heat. And, strangely, the heat made him shiver.

The street was deserted, except for a single big-eyed cat prowling along under the parked cars, weaving in and out of the garbage cans and the squat green plastic sacks of trash. He saw none of the children Morty had mentioned.

Gribner climbed the stoop. He pushed the outer door open-and stopped, staring. The inner door had had a glass pane from waist level up. It was smashed; the glass lay on the carpet in the hall beyond. He pressed the doorbell button for Morty's apartment. He waited, throat tight, sweat trickling down his cheeks and crawling like spiders along his backbone.

No answer.

He reached through the broken pane; opened the door by turning the inside knob, and stepped through, over the glass.

Some of the glass fragments were edged with fresh blood.

"Morty!" he shouted, the sound coming from him involuntarily. He sprinted down the hall to Morty's door. It was unlocked. He pushed through, remembering that the apartment had a side door that led into a narrow alleyway.

The front room was dark; a single easy chair was overturned. A .22 pistol, Morty's, lay on the rug. He picked it up; it was faintly warm. It had been fired. He looked through the old bachelor's bedroom and kitchen; nothing else was in disarray. But Morty wasn't around. The side door, in the kitchen, was unlocked. Something glistened on the black-and-white tile floor there. Like a snail's track, but wider. It shone faintly in the room's darkness, just a suggestion of phosphorescence. The track, if that's what it was, led in a smear out through the kitchen door.

Gribner tucked the .22 in his pocket, drew his own .38, and nudged the door open with his foot. He looked up and down the narrow alleyway, below the short flight of wooden steps. No one. But the quicksilver track glimmered faintly on the steps, and down the blacktop alley, toward the street.

Honking sounds from the street. The sound of children laughing. Smashing glass.

Gribner was down the steps and running, puffing, toward the street where he'd left the cabdriver...

...who was being dragged from his car, thirty feet away, by eight grade-school-age children. Two black children, the rest white. One of them wore a skirt of rags; the others were nude, skin painted brightly in signs he recognized from certain cellars, certain subway walls. The driver was limp, his face obscured by blood. There was a cinder block on the driver's seat, Gribner saw, as he moved nearer—he moved more slowly now, crouching, hoping the children hadn't seen him yet. The windshield of the cab was smashed through, on the driver's side; the door hung open. The headlights were broken out. There was an open manhole four feet in front of the car—it hadn't been open before. The lid lay to one side. Gribner sprinted, seeing the children drag the unconscious cabbie toward the hole. By the time he reached the rear of the cab, they'd dropped the man into the manhole, head first.

Cellars

Gribner froze in his tracks, listening.

The children, too, were quiet, hunkering around the manhole, listening, their faces illuminated with a ghastly blue light from beneath, a light from the manhole.

From the manhole came the sounds of low growling, then snarling then ripping, then crunching…

As one, the six children burst into hysterical laughter. They joined hands and, tiny genitals flopping on the boys, the girls lifting their rumps, danced around the manhole, chanting something in a language no one alive was meant to understand.

Gribner leveled his gun, with every intention of shooting all of them, right there.

But the shout from behind made him turn—he'd heard Morty's voice.

He turned and, squinting, made out a dark figure silhouetted against the light from the next block, at the corner. It looked like Morty, proportionately. But the figure was slumped, and it shouldn't have been possible for him to stand that way, leaning back. Looking closer, Gribner saw the outline of the thing that was holding Morty up. Holding him up for Gribner to see.

A rubbery, glistening thing, skeletally thin, with a misshapen head. So translucent it was almost invisible.

Gribner turned and began to jog toward it. The children's chanting stopped—he glanced over his shoulder. They were climbing down into the hole, whooping, vanishing one by one.

He turned back toward the corner where he'd seen Morty. Morty was gone. The rubbery man was gone, too. But he spotted the shining slime trail on the asphalt, almost in the middle of the street. He followed it. It led to the corner—this one lit, street light intact—and turned left. He followed. The track curved left again at the next corner. He began to run.

Three minutes later, he glimpsed the rubbery man across the highway from him, shimmering faintly in the shadows of the narrow riverside park. The street light for the strip of greenery had been smashed.

Gribner waited for a lapse in traffic, and sprinted the roadway. *Getting old,* he thought, gasping, hearing his heart pound in his ears.

He dodged between bushes, in the edge of the park, and lost sight of the rubbery thing. It was dark going. He almost tripped on a snoring wino.

He circled a park-keeper's outbuilding and found himself on the sidewalk alongside the river bank. There was a spiked fence beyond the sidewalk; the fence was high as his head. And on the other side of the fence was a drop-off to the East River. Someone was awkwardly recumbent atop the fence, silhouetted gray against the black of the river.

Gribner came closer, breathing hard, shaking as he became certain it was Morty. Morty's body. Impaled on the fence. Lying on his back, arms akimbo as if crucified. The spikes had gone all the way through his body and punched wetly out from the white shirt at Morty's belly, and from his throat, and the fence ran red, a puddle stretching across the walk, the hot blood giving up its steam to join the steamy night air.

Gribner got close enough to make sure Morty was dead. Morty's face was turned toward him, and his mouth was open. The eyes were missing from their sockets. Morty's eyes were intact, however. They had been moved. They looked out from Morty's half-open mouth, now.

Gribner sank to his knees, wracked with silent sobs. He rocked there, chanting a prayer he'd learned as a boy, his eyes squeezed shut, the .38 pressed to his chest, flat against his breastbone, gripped in both hands as a mourner of another faith would have clutched a rosary.

"Cyril…" A woman's voice coming from the right. The voice had sounded like…

"Cyril!" The voice was his wife's.

He took a deep breath, and then another, and opened his eyes, and looked to the right. A light shone up, out of the ground.

Wobbly, he climbed to his knees and staggered toward the light. To the right of the sidewalk, between the concrete and the grass verge of the park, was a black, hard-edged ironbarred grating. A drainage shaft? Ventilation for—what? The light, phosphorescent blue, flared from the grating over the shaft. The grate was square, three feet by three, and screwed down with heavy bolts.

Shaking, his gun hand quivering like a branch in the wind, he approached the shaft. The light was tenuous, and divided into narrow strips by the bars. He stood near the grating, choking to hold back sobs, afraid to look down.

"Cyril, help us!" It was her voice. He leaned, and bent his head to look. The shaft was only about eight feet deep, and concrete-walled. She was there. She and the two dogs. Randi and Louie. The Pekingese, alive and well. The little

Cellars

bastard Everett must have stolen them and killed someone else's dogs just to make it look as if he'd killed Gribner's friends because—thank God, there they were and—*how did Trudy get down in the shaft?*

The dogs were perched on her shoulders. She wore her usual housedress. He couldn't see her face very well. The light hurt his eyes. Light came from— from *her.* He fell to his knees. *"Help me!"* she called. He could see her mouth moving. But the lips moved a split second after he heard the words, like in a badly dubbed foreign movie. *"Cyril!"*

"I—I'll get you out, I'll get help, I'll get you out—" He couldn't see what she was standing on. It was all blue light and foggy there. "How did you—?" It didn't matter. He'd get help.

"Cyril—wait, don't go—just reach down and take my hands...I'm so scared...." He could hear the terror bubbling in her voice. In two places, the bars had been pried apart, just enough to admit a grown man's arms, a chest-width apart. He tossed his gun aside and fell flat on the grating and, not thinking, his tears falling to her, to his dogs, his babies, his Trudy, he reached through the widened places.

Stretching his arms down to her. She reached up and closed her fingers around his wrists.

And began to pull.

And began to *change.*

But he'd known it wasn't her, not *really* her, as soon as she'd touched him. As soon as it had touched him. The fog cleared from his eyes, and he saw the thing that had him by the wrists. The Blessed One. Rubbery. Prehensile, impossibly strong, its boneless, transparent fingers unyieldingly tightened around his wrists. He screamed and tried to pull away.

It gazed up at him with black button eyes and moved its rubbery lips, making a sound like balloons rubbed together; the dogs were gone, and the things on its shoulders, in place of the dogs, took shape—rats. Big rats, stretching snuffling snouts to gnaw his arms.

The Blessed One began to pull him down. Gribner strained, screaming so loudly he couldn't hear himself, trying to wrench free.

His screams woke the wino. The wino's name was Finley. "Whadduhfug?" he belched, standing, swaying. He was still drunk. He weaved through the bushes, curious about the noise, but mostly looking for a place to piss, somewhere far enough from his sleeping mat. He remembered a grating, some kind of drain, near the sidewalk. He made for that.

He stopped, blinking, twenty feet from it, watching as Gribner was pulled through the bars.

Finley didn't believe it. DTs again. Time to check into Bellevue, dry out for a while. So he laughed at what he thought was a hallucination. You can't pull a man between bars like that, like he was cheese. But that squealing sound. That crunching sound. That screaming.

Finley shook his head and turned away. "Pizz somewhere else...Can't do that to a man—like a slice-'em-dice-'em slizes innything."

He laughed. And then his laughter ceased, abruptly, when the children came running out of the bushes and knocked him down, and dragged him toward the wet red bars where the pieces of the man remained....

AT NIGHT, THE black squirmings, the power currents, gave off mild inward flickers like static electricity—for those who could see them. Lanyard could see them clearly, over the crowd's heads as he walked west down Houston Street.

He was following the flow of the power currents. The currents, made up of the glimmering blue-black strips, like yard-long party crepe come alive, wriggled through the air at about seven feet over the sidewalk. It was a hot night, a weirdly hot night, and lots of people were on the streets, passing bottles, competing for loudness with their enormous radios, clustered on corners or strutting in groups down the street; most were Spanish or black, though here and there were chichi rockers on their way to clubs, and children in Halloween costumes, laughing behind plastic skeleton masks, Spiderman masks, even Ronald Reagan masks; the masks bobbed on their rubber-band supports as the children ran along the sidewalk, clutching bags of candy.

The power currents followed the course of the crowd, more or less; sometimes a whirlpool formed around someone, and the eel shapes reached down to snap at the head of a white teen-ager with matted blond hair—he stood on the street-corner shouting gibberish.

Lanyard guessed that the power currents manipulated some of the people; others they seemed to pass by. But the currents flowed, more or less, in one direction. He followed, knowing they would lead him to Minder. To Madelaine. To the Head Underneath.

Cellars

At Second Avenue, the stream of flickering eel shapes dipped and entered the subway station. Lanyard descended the steps. He wore a backpack, and in his hip pocket was a map. He fished a token from his pocket, passed through the turnstile, and followed the power currents onto the platform.

At the end of the platform, he removed his backpack and took a long silvery flashlight from it. He replaced the backpack and, flashlight in hand, ignoring the curious stares of the few people on the dirty gray platform, he leapt over the brink and landed, wincing, on both feet between the tracks. He found a narrow strip of concrete to the right of the tracks and walked into the tunnel, switching the flashlight on.

He could still see the power currents, alive, squirming overhead, darting into the tunnel. He followed the currents to their source.

Madelaine could feel them moving, up there. She felt Lanyard, moving closer, having left the subway tunnel, following the power currents along the route Krupp had once taken. Lanyard climbing ladders, crawling through drainage pipes, sweating in the growing heat, shaking with the effort at controlling himself: He was scared to the bone. She knew that, and felt it distantly—but she was unaffected. She couldn't allow herself to be affected.

She sat in the mouth of the cave, occasionally licking her cracked lips, swooning with heat—never moving.

Tooley entered the tunnel, alone. Walking in a crouch, he moved past her and unlocked the steel door. He swung the door aside, then came back and took her by the wrist. She allowed him to tow her—she was half walking, half stumbling—behind him, into the deeper places, the tunnel curving to the left and opening into the cavern.

Here they were able to stand. The pool shone with its own blue light; they could see the cavern quite clearly.

The underground lake had been here before the Indians had sold Manhattan. Until recently, it had been an empty sump, inhabited only by blind fish. It was about seventy-five feet across, almost perfectly circular. The ceiling was high and toothy with dripping stalactites, glimmering with the bluish light.

It was peculiar, the light being blue—because it was given off by the underground lake, and the lake was red. Rusty red, edged with foam at the shores. Part of the underground lake had developed a red membrane, a rubbery skin around the edges, and studded at intervals in the membrane were the heads of those undergoing transmutation, destined to become the Blessed People, their bodies, below the neck, hidden in the pool. One of these she recognized as Charlton Buckner, the author of Minder's production, *Shake 'Em Down!!* His face twitched, and his head twisted on the neck— distantly, she wondered what he was feeling. There were seven men and two women trapped, up to their necks in the red membrane, in various stages of transformation; one of the women was almost transparent; her nose was nearly gone and her hair was mostly fallen out. Two of the men, middle-aged men who'd once worn expensive suits and who'd once driven expensive cars and who'd once sat behind expensive desks, called plaintively to be released. Tooley and Madelaine ignored them.

But then, Madelaine ignored everything; she saw, and recorded, but reacted to nothing.

Like a pond where the edges have turned into ice while the center remains open water, the membrane extended only thirty feet, all the way round, into the lake. The center roiled, bubbling; as *He* rose into the uncovered area, the red liquid surging, parting for His great bulk.

He came in response to Tooley's silent summons.

Forty feet high, He reared from the red pool, dripping, glistening, pulsing with light and cancerous life. He sat on His haunches, stunted arms drawn up to cross His chest, His unfinished hands as always caressing the oversized male genitalia, always erect, that rose nearly to the chinless jaw of His grossly oversized head. He was an embryo. He was an embryo, in some ways outwardly very human, big as a house. His eyes were always closed, but the orbs moved behind the translucent, heavily veined red-blue lids.

Where a human embryo—seven months along—would have had a forehead, He had a great yellow boil; dimly seen seething in the boil were a million snaking, wriggling shapes. Worms. A special sort of worm. The boil always seemed straining to burst.

From the boil radiated the power currents, the airborne eel shapes, manifesting for Madelaine—and then vanishing as she willed the sight away.

She didn't care to see them.

Tooley gazed rapturously up at Him, and snarled.

Cellars

She didn't have to look at Tooley to know he'd undergone the transformation. His head was no longer in its human semblance. It was the head of a wild, rabid dog with the eyes of a man. The demon called "Tooley" snarled again. The Head Underneath opened its lipless mouth, and the cavern echoed with a long, low growl like the growing rumble of imminent earthquake.

Tooley turned to Madelaine, and his head had regained its human aspect. "He says you're to live, for a while. He says I'm to have a new master. He says you're a gift for the new master."

He waited for her reply. She closed her eyes. That was all.

He took her by the hand and led her back to the tunnel, through the steel door, and up into the temple.

All the while, she felt Lanyard coming closer. Someone was helping him. An old man. Maguss. This man Maguss…this man's thoughts were closed to her. She could feel his influence, however. He was bending the power currents to conflict with Minder's control of them. He was using them to protect Lanyard. And Lanyard was getting closer.

SIXTEEN

L anyard had discarded his shirt; his bare back was chafing under the straps of the backpack. The utility tunnel, slanting down at a ten-degree angle, was murky with steam. The heat stung his fingers when he reached out to brace himself against the curved metal walls. He moved along in a crouch, duckwalking on the heavy sewage pipe that took up the lower half of the tunnel; the pipe vibrated with the thunderous pour of its contents. It was lead pipe banded with iron, and three feet in diameter. His flashlight played over the walls and down the length of pipe as he looked for the appropriate place to plant the last of the plastic explosive.

With one blackened hand Lanyard wiped sweat from his eyes and peered through the steam. It was harder to see the power currents here. Now he made them out, shimmering, quivering strips of blue black, rippling with sparks near the curved ceiling. Sticky with sweat, Lanyard struggled down the narrow utility tunnel.

The currents continued down toward the place where the tunnel forked. There, they wound to the right. *"The currents can pass through doors, but not through walls,"* Maguss had said. *"They can only go where a man could go; they are, after all, the emanations of a man. They follow the path of least resistance, most of the time."*

For the dozenth time, Lanyard paused to rally himself, taking deep breaths, almost choking in the hot, sewage-foul air. He sat straddling the pipe, feeling its contents sluicing, vibrating between his legs. He listened—and heard it again: high-pitched laughter from behind him. He twisted on his hips to squint down the tunnel, the flashlight beam wavery in his shaking, dirty hand.

He saw his shirt dangling in midair where he'd left it. It was a yellow long-sleeved cotton shirt, discolored from sweat. It jumped about, arms outstretched, its back to him, dancing on the pipe as though the Invisible Man had removed everything but his shirt and gone into a mad caper. He half expected to see Claude Rains appear.

Dancing, the shirt turned, exposing its front side to him. Now he could see what was inside it, holding it up. Two huge albino rats. On their hind legs. Albino? No, furless, their gray skin rubbery, almost translucent. More of Minder's toys. Each rat bigger than a large cat.

The rats chattered, their miniature, oddly human arms holding the shirt over their narrow heads like shaman dancers in an animal skin, hopping toward him, two pairs of red eyes gleaming in the flashlight beam, their mouths opening pink and wet like Lily Chancery's—

"Get away from me!" he shouted. He tucked the flashlight in his right armpit, unslung the backpack, dug through its side pockets till he found the Luger that Maguss had given him. Holding the flashlight in his left hand, he flicked the gun's safety off with his right. The rats' claws clicked on the pipe. Closer.

He shone the flashlight back along the tunnel. They came at him. Twisting backward, firing at an awkward angle, he squeezed the trigger four times; the pistol's bucking hurt his wrist. The gunshots rang and boomed down the tunnel, and one of the rats burst open, spattering the gray-black walls with its thick yellow blood—*yellow?*—and flipped over backward, falling out of sight below the curve of pipe.

The other rat dodged and turned tail, dragging his shirt away down the tunnel, tee-heeing like a funny cartoon animal.

Maguss had promised to protect him. His protection was waning, as Lanyard neared the temple. Soon, perhaps, the pet of the Head Underneath would come.

He tucked the gun into the pack, slung it on, and pointed his flashlight.

Lanyard began to hump along the pipe toward the fork. That method was too slow. He climbed on top of the pipe, his head scraping the concave ceiling, shaking sweat from his eyes, and stooping low, duckwalked down the tunnel. The position hurt his ankles, his thighs, the inside of his knees. In his right hand he held the flashlight, and in the beam, at the place where the tunnel split, a pallid, prepubescent face grinned at him.

Spotlit, face wreathed in steam, was a boy with shaggy black hair—perhaps six years old. His yellowed eyes were wide, his mouth grinned so widely it seemed a rictus. The boy's face was narrow, ratlike—had it always been ratlike?

He held something in his hands.

He held it up—"Lookie look!"—for Lanyard to see. It wasn't a shirt. It was a portion of a human head. Like a section of jack o' lantern...part of the skull remaining, the skin clinging to the facial fragment, the eyes gone. But there was enough so that Lanyard recognized Gribner's face.

He turned the flashlight aside; the boy laughed from the darkness.

Lanyard became aware of the darkness, the palpable density of the subterranean city around him, the endless, labyrinthine stretch of tunnels.

And it was so damn hot. Giggles from the darkness.

"Leave me *alone!*" he bellowed.

*Alone...alone...alone...*his voice echoed down the tunnels.

ELECTRIC MUSIC IN the background. The lights fluttered low. The room was hot.

She watched impassively, from her place at the magic circle, as Minder and Lily Chancery painted the signs on one another with the blood of the woman they'd laid open, staked and shrieking, at their feet. The Blessed People were there, and the children, and the accountants, and the admen, and the rock stars....

The temple was a place of flickering twilight, from tall candles on braziers at the corners of the big room. There were almost fifty of them, gathered for the autumn rite, chanting, nude, gaudy with makeup and geometric arcana; their faces bestial in the shifting candlelight, their bodies, every kind of body, glossy with sweat; the floor was sticky with sweat, the room heavy with His heat. The stalker, the pet, the beast of red wires, fed noisily (seen and then unseen) on the body of the sacrificed.

She watched, and recorded, and felt nothing.

Not even when Lanyard came up behind, and took her by the arm, leading her around the edge of the transfixed crowd. No one seemed to notice; all eyes were on Minder and Lily, now mainlining cocaine in the center of the circle, in preparation for the transcendent moment, the minute of Time that would be protracted for them forever.

The room slithered with sounds; acolytes chanting, taped music thudding.

On the altar, just above the magic circle, was the jade urn.

Lanyard took it in the crook of his arm. No one so much as looked up. Madelaine was not surprised: *"There will be a change of masters,"* Tooley had said.

Lanyard whispered urgently to her, "You're dragging. Hurry *up*. Maguss has them confused or something…no one is looking. But we've got to hurry, we've got two minutes…."

She looked at him blankly, and he compressed his lips, dragging her by the wrist. She came along, not hurrying.

Distantly amused by it all.

She could feel the power currents converging on the magic circle behind them. She could feel the very arches of Space Itself creaking; she could hear the squeal as Time was rerouted. Minder was receiving his reward. He had paid his premiums, in sheer life energy delivered to the Head Underneath, Ahriman's earthly manifestation. Now his investment was paying off. Minder was achieving transcendence, climbing to a place outside the flow of Time, a place designed to reproduce a minute in Minder's life, over and over, again and again. And Minder had chosen the minute: He had it timed so that the transcendence would take effect in the next minute; one minute—while he was rushing on cocaine, locked into copulation with Lily Chancery—stretched into Forever.

One minute in his life—one minute from now.

The room shrilled with the ecstatic yowls of the worshippers; the walls writhed with vibratory imagery, as the power of the ritual built, climbing for that one minute of transcendence.

Madelaine passively allowed Lanyard to tug her by the wrist—the jade urn crooked in his other arm—out of the temple room, across the reception room, past the leather couch and the color TV console and into the elevator. He pulled her close to him and pressed the button. The doors hushed shut; the elevator began to rise.

They had just stepped out, into the deserted subway station's men's room, Lanyard wearing his shoes and jeans and no shirt, Madelaine wearing her kimono, when the floor rocked from the detonations.

Cellars

Six explosions. Plaster dust settled from the ceiling as Lanyard ran for the exit.

MADELAINE RAN WITH him. But mentally, in the involuntary reflex of her Gift, she monitored the events in the chamber below them, and if she hadn't worked for so many hours on detachment, on feeling nothing about what she witnessed, she would have screamed.

She saw from the viewpoint of one of the children. In one moment, the boy—he'd taken on a new name here, they called him Taker—was dancing, hardly hearing the keening electric music coming from the hidden loudspeakers. He was dancing to the throb he felt in his gut, *boom-boom-boom-I'm-With-You*, the Head chanting from inside him somewhere, *boom-boom-boom-My-Strength-in-You, Boom-boom-boom-Take-and-Drink-and-Feel*. He felt the rush, the surge of hot pleasure in his spine and his throat and most of all in the place between his legs, the pleasure coursing in through him in time with the *boom-boom-boom* of the Head's throb, the chanting of the others, the rhythm of the dance.

He laughed, seeing the comical Blessed Ones quivering, rooted symmetrically about the room, never dancing, but just...quivering with him.

Taker was enjoying himself.

He felt *good*. He'd enjoyed the way the woman had spasmed, suffering, when the knife had started digging into her—really *digging* in, not just nicking like they'd done playfully on the street before he'd come below—and most of all he'd enjoyed the fact that everyone else was enjoying her pain, too. So they approved of his enjoyment, because they shared it. And that felt good. It meant everything was all right—it meant everything, anything, was right. As long as the Head Underneath made it possible, it was *right*.

He didn't have to care. He was glad his dad was cut up. Bob Gaddis, big-shot reporter. Big shot. *Fuck you, big shot, you took away my knife when you saw me carve those initials on the furniture and you told me you wouldn't give me the minibike.*

Nothing was bad and that felt good.

And all around him was action, and color, and people laying on other people near the edges of the circle, men spearing women with their hard pricks, and everything was—Everything was coming down on him.

The ceiling was coming down. Ripping noises, and dust, and bad smells.

Big chunks fell on Dervish and Who-So and Grabber and Cutidoff and on the Blessed Ones and smashed them into jelly.

Something was killing the Head's people—but *He* was laughing. Taker—tottering, falling, crying—could feel *Him* laughing at them all, *enjoying* the smashing, the broken bones, and then the *spluchh* sound—

A big gray fist smashed into the room, and people were bouncing all around him like toy army men blown up with a firecracker, so fast he couldn't tell one thing from another anymore, it was blurred together and then it was covered up by the gray-brown sludge that was everywhere, knocking them down, filling the room. He threw up. He was in over his head in sewage. He...

MADELAINE WHIMPERED. She almost screamed. She managed not to feel. She withdrew. But not before glimpsing what had happened to Lily Chancery and Joey Minder.

ONE MINUTE. One minute of sexual ecstasy and drug rush, to be stretched out forever. The ritual would come to consummation so that whatever Minder was doing, at the ritual's climax, was to be his experience for an eternal moment.

But he hadn't known about the plastic explosive on the sewage pipes above the temple. The ceiling imploded and hundreds of tons of sewage, coming with the force of the falls at Niagara, smashed the congregation against the walls, spattering brains, drowning those who survived the impact.

Minder was one of those who survived the impact. But he began to drown, his lungs filling with all the best-forgotten things that are in sewage, in the one minute allotted to him by the Head Underneath. The one minute that was to stretch into an eternity, *no matter what happened then*. And it went on and on. While the cocaine rush made him feel it *intensely*.

Joey Minder and Lily Chancery drowned in sewage, forever. And Forever.

SEVENTEEN

"Hey, boy, it's crazy, this weather, huh?" the Greek cabbie prompted. The lower half of his broad, perspiring face was dominated by a black mustache. "Boy, I don't blame you, dressing in...so little."

Cabdrivers see it all. New York cabbies are not likely to be shocked by the sight of a woman dressed only in a black silk kimono tied at the waist with a red sash, her eyes glazed, her face full of silence, and a shirtless grimy man carrying a stoppered jade urn. Especially if the man standing on a street corner, girl beside him, is waving a twenty-dollar bill.

Long as the guy has the fare, what the hell. But maybe the cabbie was annoyed that Lanyard said nothing, not a word, when the driver said, "Whoa, whatchoo thinka that?" as over the radio came word that a section of the subway had collapsed. And the entire East Side's sewer system was "apparently sabotaged by some as yet unknown terrorist group." And two trains were derailed—all as a result of explosions under the city, just south of Second Avenue and Houston. "Can you beat that?" the cabbie asked rhetorically. It was his last attempt to prod conversation from the grimy man in the back seat.

Lanyard hadn't heard much of the radio newscast; he was limp with exhaustion, his head bowed and bobbing with every pothole they hit. The jade urn was on the floor, held in place by his feet. Madelaine sat passively in the crook of Lanyard's right arm.

They bumped in silence to Maguss's Park Avenue address. When they arrived, Lanyard looked up, yawned, and gave the driver the twenty. "Keep the' change," he mumbled. "For good luck."

Lanyard climbed from the car, the urn in his right arm, tugging Madelaine behind him with his left hand, towing her across the sidewalk, through the sticky Halloween night, and into the cool, air-conditioned lobby. He set the urn on the rug and tried to smile at the doorman.

Looking Lanyard up and down and cocking his head, the black doorman said, "You got to be Lanyard. He said to let you in no matter how you looked. This part of some Halloween costume, huh? Mr. Maguss said to give you this here." A white business envelope.

Lanyard tore open the envelope as Madelaine slumped against him. Reading the printed note inside, his tired exhilaration changed to mild alarm.

Have purchased two apartments. Second is in basement. 1B. Meet me there. Maguss.

Lanyard shrugged and, grunting, picked up the heavy jade urn and moved stiffly to the elevator, supporting Madelaine on his left arm. He heard the doorman say to a janitor, behind them, "Jesus, she must've got into some good downs."

Lanyard sagged against the back wall of the elevator, wishing that he weren't going down. He closed his eyes.

He opened them a moment later when he heard the elevator doors open. The first thing he noticed were the power currents, surging in the air over Maguss, flowing down the corridor to the right, behind him.

The black writhings reached tenuous fingers down to caress the jade urn; other wriggling strips fluttered about Lanyard and dipped at Madelaine, drawing back. He repressed the urge to take a swipe at them.

Maguss was staring at the urn. "That's it," he said wonderingly. "I can't believe it. I never thought—well, that's it then." He smiled apologetically at Lanyard. "You look beat, son. You and the lady both. Permit me to assist her—I presume this is Madelaine Springer? Is that who you are, dear?" he asked, patting her arm. She looked at him and said nothing. "I see," Maguss murmured. He wore a black pinstriped three-piece suit, a black tie tucked in a flat-black vest.

"You look like you're dressed for a funeral," Lanyard said, watching him.

Maguss didn't answer. He was leading Madelaine down the hall, taking her soft white arm between his dry blue-veined hands. He crooned to her almost inaudibly.

Picking up the urn, swearing, his back creaking, Lanyard followed.

Since leaving the tunnels, Lanyard had felt dizzy, giddy with triumph and exhaustion. The Voices were almost silent, his Gift blessedly muted. And he walked through the world noticing very little, wanting to deliver the urn for exorcism, to take Madelaine to a doctor, to let the last of his responsibilities slide away. But now he found himself scrutinizing his surroundings carefully, and listening for the Voices.

Perhaps it was his sense that in the heavy jade urn he carried in his arms— just big enough to contain a man's head, whole—he felt something stirring. And he wondered at the quality of Maguss's power currents—so much like the currents Lanyard had traced to the hidden temple.

Maguss led them down a spacious hallway, past the doors of other apartments—some of them open and clearly vacant. It was a new building, and most of the apartments hadn't been sold yet. The square plastic light fixtures were not yet flyspecked; the blue pastel plaster walls were not yet smutched at shoulder level on the corners. The smell of new paint was everywhere.

Number 1B was a corner apartment; its high basement windows looked out on intersecting sidewalks; beyond the antiburglar bars over the window was an endless parade of legs, seen mostly from the calf down, a confused parade in which the participants marched both ways.

"Interesting view, isn't it?" asked Maguss, closing the door behind them. "You see square-toed boots marching along with single-minded determination and three-hundred dollar Italian shoes mincing and alligator shoes lifted high—"

"Why did you take a second apartment?" Lanyard asked, setting the urn on the rugless concrete floor. "And what's the curtain for?" He nodded toward a dark-red curtain that divided the living room; the other half of the rectangular main room was completely concealed from him. The curtain hung floor to ceiling on a metal runner that looked as if it had been recently screwed into the plaster.

"I took a second apartment," Maguss said, with a touch of reproach, "for personal reasons. The curtain is part of an experiment—I'm sorry the room is so unfurnished. But do sit down, Carl."

Lanyard tingled with suspicion; but his legs were unsteady with weariness. He sank into the room's only furnishing, a curvy aluminum chair with a black vinyl seat. But he sat up straight when Maguss led Madelaine toward the curtain. "Where—"

"*Just* taking her to lie down on the couch, on the other side. Oh, *do* calm down, Carl. You're as jumpy as a cat in heat. The young lady has clearly had some sort of awful shock." Madelaine went along in utter docility. Her expression of faint curiosity hadn't changed; her lips were cracked, her hands and feet dusty. "It's nice and dark and cool in here. She can rest and then you and I will talk."

They passed through the slit in the curtains—and then were hidden from him.

Lanyard glanced at the urn; the figures on it seemed to shift, to buckle. He looked away.

Behind him was a hallway presumably leading to the bedroom, kitchen, and bathroom. He felt filthy recalling the look the doorman had given him. He could ask Maguss if he might take a shower, but he couldn't bring himself to leave the living room—not with Madelaine behind that blood-red curtain. He shifted nervously in the seat.

He could hear Maguss maundering meaningless endearments at Madelaine, as if she were a child he was putting to bed.

Lanyard checked for the power currents. He couldn't see them, now. Inexplicably, their disappearance shook him.

"Maguss?" he called softly, not wanting to disturb Madelaine. What was taking the old man so long? "Maguss!" he called, more loudly. "Hey, are you there?"

No reply. No reply, that is, from the material world. But someone else responded, in words beyond sound.

Carl...his mother's voice.

A thrill of elation ran through him. "Mother?"

Carl, they—

But he lost contact when Maguss parted the curtains, stepping into view and quickly drawing the curtains shut behind him.

"What's the problem, Carl?" he asked. But his eyes were on the jade urn.

"I—I was just wondering what was taking you so long...." What *had* been wrong? He wasn't sure.

"You've been through a lot today, Carl. You're understandably jumpy." Maguss walked over to the urn and went to his knees beside it. He touched the figures carved in relief, traced the milky swirl; his ancient, trembling hand—trembling more than usual—lingered on the dog-headed demon-figure. "You can feel it...." he murmured.

Cellars

Never before had Lanyard seen Maguss so obviously *moved*. The old man traced the seal plugging the urn, with his tobacco-yellowed fingers. "Do you know what's inside this work of art, Carl?"

"I know what's *supposedly* inside."

"Oh, it's *there*, all right. The cult that Minder revived was once, centuries ago, very powerful. And its priest was very powerful. A certain king was afraid of the priest's power. Afraid his monarchy would become a theocracy. So he had the priest killed, and had his head placed in this urn, which he used for a footstool." Maguss smiled at Lanyard; tears glittered in his eyes. Tears of happiness. The sort of tears one sees in the eyes of relatives at reunions, when years have passed since the last meeting. "He was—that priest—he was a sort of ancestor of mine....So much I don't remember..."

Maguss straightened and turned his back. "When you get old you get silly about your hobbies, your nostalgia." When he faced Lanyard again, his face was solemn, the tears gone. "Cigarette, Carl?" He brought out the ivory cigarette case.

"Thanks." Lanyard nodded, and Maguss lit one for each of them. Lanyard took the cigarette and inhaled; his jittery nerves buzzed less loudly.

He enjoyed the fact that there was no place for Maguss to sit. *Let the old S.O.B. stand,* he thought. Then, once more, he wondered at his own hostility.

He glanced at the curtain. "What's wrong with her? She's aware, I can tell. But she doesn't...respond. She doesn't speak. Have they got her—uh—mesmerized in some way?"

"I think, Carl, that they have driven her a little mad. I know for a fact that she never joined them, really. She pretended to, but she's a good actress, and Joey fell for it. She's just withdrawn into herself. She'll come out of it."

Lanyard squinted at the curtain doubtfully. "She—never participated? How can you be sure?"

"I'm sure. She's an innocent."

Lanyard would have pursued the question, but Maguss interrupted: "Carl—you have, I suspect, been thinking of writing a book about all this. An exposé sort of thing." His lips curled into the sort of smile that celebrates irony. "Still going to do it?"

Lanyard felt a small shock. Was he still going to write about it? "No, I don't see how I can. I blew up those pipes, I—" He laughed. But he felt his face draining. "I killed people. I must have caused millions of dollars in damage."

It was as if he were coming out of a drug delirium, remembering what he'd done with horror and embarrassment. And fear. His gut contracted.

"Yes," said Maguss pleasantly; his right hand cupped his left elbow, the upraised hand held his cigarette poised near his face. "It seems you're in big trouble."

Lanyard's jaw muscles bunched. "You set me up, again and again. You knew what I'd see at Merino's—"

"I had to trigger your...your acceptance of the Gift. Of the truth. It was—"

"For my own good? Right. And you set me up for this—"

"Frankly, I didn't think you would come back alive. I was rooting for you, of course. I wanted the urn. It makes everything easier."

Lanyard flipped his cigarette to the floor, a gesture of contempt. Maguss failed to react. Suddenly, shirtless in the air conditioning, Lanyard was cold.

Maguss gazed at Lanyard speculatively. He said nothing.

Lanyard stood, preparing to move toward the red velvet curtain.

Maguss held up a frail hand in warning. Lanyard could have broken the hand in his own, but Maguss was practiced in the exercise of authority. Lanyard hesitated. "Carl...we have agreed, I think, that you're in trouble. If I want, I can turn you over to the police. I can do it without implicating myself. Believe me—I've got it all worked out. They're just dying for someone to blame, Carl. You left an awful mess, you know. Literally. Whole sections of town are health hazards now. They even smell bad...." He laughed for a moment. "Worse than usual, I mean." He took a drag on his cigarette, then blew a smoke ring, and blew a smaller one through the first. "And then there's the fact that a lot of people died down there. I know they died. Horribly. I was following the whole thing from my end."

Lanyard shook his head in amazement. "You knew where their temple was?"

"Oh, yes. But I needed *you* to get there, to pick up the urn. I had planted someone in the cult, but—I only barely managed to keep them from discovering him. You were able to walk out with the urn, just like that. No one touched you. It was His will—because he intended you to bring the urn to me. So they couldn't hurt you. Not that you can't be hurt."

Lanyard looked at the red curtain. "What are you getting around to?"

"I can make you strong. I can teach you how how to really use your Gift. I can make you rich. I can—"

"You're not going to destroy the urn?" Lanyard's voice sounded dead in his own ears.

"By no means. That would be…well, suppose NASA blew up the space shuttle they worked so hard for, on the eve of the launch? Now, why would they do a silly thing like that?"

"I'm not going to help you. That thing down there—I don't care what happens, what the side effects are—that thing was growing down there. *They* were growing. Minder was going to put the whole city through a meat grinder, one way or another. I can explain to people—"

Maguss cocked his head. "Are you joking? If you try to explain, I suppose you might get off with the security ward at Bellevue, as opposed to life in prison. But that would be the best you could hope for."

Lanyard looked at the floor. He tried to look through it. "I could feel that thing growing down there—the Head Underneath. I'm not going to help you bring it back."

"Oh, it's still alive. The physical manifestation, in its nice warm embryonic pool is, I'm afraid, crushed, buried under tons of rock. You were a big hit: You really brought down the ceiling." His eyes twinkled merrily. "But He can't be killed. He will reappear somewhere else. He grows wherever greed grows and wherever the self-serving thrive."

"I'm not going to help you."

"Lanyard—you can't win. We are genetically programmed to selfishness. Nature conspired against anything 'good' in us. Nature defines us and we must define what is 'good' according to Nature. And Nature—our instinct—tells us that self-preservation is good. Over and above everything. And if you work with me, you will have not only survival—safety from the police—you will have success in everything. We'll see to it. Give to Him and He gives to you."

"You've been one of them all along…." Lanyard stared at the old man.

"No. No, indeed. Not one of them. *They* were impostors. Minder was an upstart. He stumbled onto the urn, and that gave him the power to conjure the thing he called 'Tooley.' And that made it possible for him to open the door to Ahriman. But he was a bungler. As evidenced by his current status—I had a *lovely* vision of it. We enjoyed it awfully. My son and I both saw it: Minder drowning in raw sewage forever. Never quite dying completely." He shook his head affably, as if at the antics of an eccentric friend. "What an oaf. What a bungler. And what an impostor!" His tone became very serious as he said, "I am the rightful priest of the Order of Ahriman."

"I'm not going to help you. Because—because if people act as if nothing matters but their own welfare, then life becomes hell for everyone. Sooner or later, it catches up. Maybe there is no objective Good and no Justice and no real morality—but we've got to act as if there is."

"Ho *ho!*" Maguss' laughter was a little forced. "A shining speech! The sort made by losers in this world." He looked at Lanyard with eyes ancient as the stones on the bottom of the sea's deepest trench. He looked at Lanyard from that deep, dark place, as if considering what he would do if Lanyard fell overboard, into the trench…down where he could reach him.

Carl, run, get out of there now. The Voices. His Mother's voice. *Carl, hurry, run—*

Lanyard was shaking with rage. "I'm not going to help you!" he shouted, brushing Maguss aside. He strode to the curtains and flung them apart.

The Ivy League Juggernaut stood there, mountainous, now wearing a black skin-tight T-shirt, yellow boxing shorts, and sandals. And the horn-rim glasses. His arms were one moment loose at his side, an eyeblink later whipping out to strike Lanyard in the chest. Lanyard's breastbone cracked and he was flung backward; the room's details were smeared together—he struck the aluminum chair, stumbled over it to tumble facedown on the floor, gasping. He was unable to move for several seconds, wheezing.

The bodyguard came and took him by the neck and jerked him to his feet. The pain in his chest doubled. Lanyard yelped. The bodyguard brought Lanyard's head close to his massive chest, both hands around Lanyard's neck, like a basketball player about to snap-pass the ball to a teammate. He snapped his arms out straight, propelling Lanyard into the wall. Lanyard struck with his shoulder blades, screaming his hurt; the impact jerked his head back, smacking the base of his skull on the wall. The darkness spread out from there and he was unconscious before he hit the floor.

Cellars

"It is still possible," Maguss was saying as Lanyard came achingly back to awareness, "that we can save our friend Lanyard from ruin. We may well have to knock sense into him, but I'm sure his instinct for self-preservation will take charge. Perhaps it already has. Oh, put him down, Harold. The poor man is quite limp, he's harmless. Get us some garbage bags for the girl, please. I don't want her remains found. The doorman saw her come in."

Lanyard was surprised to find that he was on his feet—until he realized he was being held there. The Ivy League Juggernaut—Harold—held him up with a familiar technique, his hands in Lanyard's armpits. Lanyard could feel hot, thick blood running down the back of his neck. He was weak. Too weak to fight. The pain rose and fell in shimmering waves.

Nausea rose to gag him, to spill over from his lips when he felt Harold lowering him to his knees. He finally made himself look at what they'd done with Madelaine.

"Oh, gosh," said Harold, behind him, in a tone that suggested he was offended, "he's throwing up on himself. He'll drip on the—"

"It doesn't matter, the ritual is quite done. You can go. The bags are in the kitchen somewhere. I'm not sure where—rummage around."

Lanyard heard Harold walk away.

Kneeling, his eyes shut, Lanyard took a deep breath to calm himself. It didn't work. He forced his eyes open and looked once more.

The pet of the Head Underneath had been there. Madelaine's breasts had been chewed away. Other tender parts of her were gnawed ragged. The places where Maguss had laid her open were neat-edged, cut with a practiced hand. Madelaine's remains were blue-white, splashed red, her head pointed away from him, her legs spread, her bloodied crotch opened to him.

Strange feelings passed through Lanyard. He felt as if the blood in him had turned to ice crystals, had freeze-dried, and he was empty of anything soft; he was a man of Styrofoam in a shop window.

What remained of Madelaine was spread-eagled, her blood almost obscuring the magic circle—blood drying on the signs and ancient writings skillfully calligraphed on the floor in red and black. The candles had burned down to stubs. The light was dim, here. Lanyard heard no Voices, saw no squirming power currents. He felt blinded.

The red curtains were drawn; the windows, on this side, were shuttered. Across from him, standing between her thighs, was the jade urn.

"Harold," Maguss was saying, "is my son. I think I told you I had someone planted in Minder's organization? Yes. Of course, he wasn't there tonight with you planting bombs. I wouldn't want to risk his life more than I already had. He's very dear to me. We're very close. You mustn't think I'm heartless, Carl. I'm really quite sentimental. And loyal to my friends. Tooley and Minder were, you know, already suspicious of Harold—it's hard to hide anything from Tooley. But of course he'll be working for me now. He's something you can't kill for long....Harold, do bring those garbage bags. Will you? I want to clean up."

Lanyard realized that the bodyguard, Maguss's son, was not in the ritual room. He was probably in the kitchen. Lanyard and Maguss were for the moment alone. Lanyard's strength was just a spark; he fanned it with the breath of rage. He looked for the sacrificial knife, blinking fog from his eyes. The knife lay to Madelaine's right, pointing toward her.

Lanyard stood, gathering his nerve and marshaling strength.

Carl. His mother's voice. In his head. Bringing with it a stab of pain. It was hard to hear it. *Carl, destroy the urn.*

Lanyard breathed deeply, tensing.

"Carl," Maguss said paternally, "you're in here, seeing what you're seeing, because I wanted you to look at her body and adjust to the sight. She's not suffering, Carl. It's just a mass of cells. Nothing more. You need to face it, and realize that it's not so awful a reality after all. Movie audiences regularly salivate over much worse sights. Face it, accept it, and forget it."

Lanyard trembled. The spark had become fire. He took a step and, ignoring the howling pain in his chest and head, bent and lifted the urn, for a flicker-moment surprised at how light it seemed.

Carrying the urn, he plunged through the curtains as Maguss shouted for Harold.

Lanyard made for the unshuttered windows. He raised the urn over his head—for a split second he hesitated, hearing a low growling issue from it, seeing the power currents flicker down to caress the demonic figures in the jade, listening to the contradictory voices in his head: *Smash it! Hurry!* against *Put it down carefully, listen to the priest, what you give to us we give back doubly* against *Run! Hurry!* And wasn't that one Madelaine's voice? *Yes. Smash it!*

He flung it at the window. It smashed easily through the glass and struck the curved bars outside. The urn broke into two large pieces, wedged between the window frame and the bars.

It had come apart all the way around its larger upper half; a glutinous yellow-brown liquid gushed from the break, sluicing with it an irregular gray lump not much bigger than a fat grapefruit: a human head, withered but uncannily preserved, retaining most of its skin and hair. Its eyes were missing; a long gray mustache trailed to either side of its bitterly clamped mouth. It lay on its side, glaring sightlessly at Lanyard through the jagged hole in the glass.

Harold and Maguss, forgetting Lanyard, ran past him to the window to retrieve the head and the urn fragments. Carl turned and walked stiffly toward the circle on the floor enclosing Madelaine's torn body. To the knife.

I can still kill these bastards, he thought.

The street noises came loudly through the break in the window. And someone was shouting, "Shit, lookit that, that's a goddamn human head! Call a cop—hey, there's a patrol—"

Lanyard skirted Madelaine's body, careful to avoid looking at her, and picked up the knife. It was a bone-handled dagger, slippery with blood. He gripped it hard, the blade pointing downward.

A shadow loomed over him. He turned. Harold was stepping over Madelaine, reaching for him. And Lanyard had a glimpse of Maguss, in the background, stuffing the severed, mummified head into a plastic bag, weeping.

Harold closed his fingers on Lanyard's throat. Lanyard lifted the blade high overhead, plunged it deep into the Ivy League Juggernaut's throat, and yanked it out again.

Harold screamed and gurgled, clutching at the wound—the gash squirted. Beautifully. Lanyard laughed and drove the knife into Harold's chest, experiencing a deep satisfaction at the meaty parting.

He pulled the knife free as the big man toppled backward. Harold fell across Madelaine's remains, dying.

Lanyard looked up, searching for Maguss. The old man had left the room, probably to hide the thing he'd taken from the urn.

The apartment's front door burst open. Two large, freshfaced young cops came in, waving guns haphazardly.

They saw Lanyard standing over the corpses. One of the cops retched.

His partner pointed at the symbols on the floor. Visions of medals danced in their heads. They saw Lanyard turning toward them, the upraised knife dripping blood, blood splashed on his bare chest, his mouth opened to explain—but they didn't know that he was about to explain. All they knew was that he was blood-spattered and toting a knife and he already had two victims at his feet and his eyes were insane. And as they cocked their guns they heard Maguss coming from the hall behind them, shouting: "For God's sake, stop him before he kills anyone else! Shoot!" The younger one had already squared off and drawn a bead. He squeezed the trigger. They shot Lanyard three times apiece.

"THANK YOU," SAID Maguss, his voice trembling as one of the cops helped him to the door. "He was renting the room from me—my son and I heard strange noises—we came to investigate and caught him at—well, you saw. We—we had no idea. And he—*my son!* He killed my boy…."

He began to sob.

"It's going to be okay, Mister," the younger cop told him, moved. "We got the man who killed your son. He's dead. He won't hurt anyone else."

Thank God," Maguss said weakly, face in his hands, sobbing convincingly. "Thank God you've killed that madman."

EPILOGUE

L anyard was surprised to wake up.
He'd thought the darkness that had flowed over him at the third gunshot was complete and final and forever. But here he was: in a prison hospital, chained to a bed. In great pain. Remembering the sight of Madelaine's flayed body...

Wailing for someone to send him back to the darkness.

They did—with tranquilizers. But it was a broken darkness, sharded with dreams, visions. His mother's face. Her voice. Maguss on his knees whispering to a withered human head. Madelaine smiling, telling him it was going to be all right, just hold on. Children screaming in a deep black pit...

* * *

THE NEXT TIME he woke there was a round-faced doctor, smelling slightly of bourbon, leaning over him, grunting to himself as he saw Lanyard's eyes open.

So you're back. Been in a coma. Cops almost did for you."

"How long?"

"Weeks—almost three weeks. You're healing, though. Had a collapsed lung, a bullet pressing the aorta, but you were lucky..."

"Lucky..." Tilting the plane. Lucky. He laughed, wheezingly. It hurt to laugh so he stopped.

"How about some morphine?" the doctor asked.

"No," Lanyard said. "No drugs..."

"Suit yourself."

* * *

FORENSIC EVIDENCE SUPPORTED Lanyard's story. There were others who'd investigated—who knew ritual murders had been going on. They knew he couldn't have done it all. Maguss disappeared, couldn't testify against him...

But still Lanyard was in jail. Prosecutor didn't want to let it go. How long now, in this concrete and steel pen? Six months?

He kept busy. The books had come—with the ritual signs he needed. It took some time to make the invocations work. But he had his Gift.

The prosecutor had secrets. The Voices told Lanyard about them, and Lanyard got a message to the proscecutor—who was suddenly interested in dropping the case...

But still he was in jail.

It didn't matter that he was. He had no cell mates. It was routine to block out the door with a blanket—no one questioned that. He had the freedom to make the necessary marks on the floor at night.

They didn't see him perform the rituals.

Lanyard knew that if you could invoke a demon, you could invoke the other side too.

It stood to reason. And one night, Reason stood before him.

You will soon be released, said the figure of light, hovering over the penta-gram. *Your blackmail and our influence have done their work. But you know the song. You have sung it yourself: You must serve somebody.*

"I will serve the Good," Lanyard said.

Will you serve us, indeed? It must be completely and without reservation—as An-thony did in the desert, though demons tore at his flesh. As Paul did in the Coliseum, though they killed him for their sport.

"I will serve you," Lanyard told the angel.

You will not serve me. You will serve the Higher. There is the One, neither he nor she, whom we both serve. You will leave here soon and find Simon Maguss and destroy his works. You have lost much—but you have something greater. Once more I ask: will you serve, without reservation?

"I will serve," Lanyard said. And he added:"I have chosen sides."

THE END

CPSIA information can be obtained
at www.ICGtesting.com
Printed in the USA
LVOW07s1546151117
556396LV00002B/551/P